'The multiplicity of perspectives serves to broaden Ebershoff's depiction not only of polygamy, but also of the people whose lives it informs. And this gives his novel a rare sense of moral urgency'

NEW YORK TIMES BOOK REVIEW

'This exquisite tour de force explores the dark roots of polygamy and its modern-day fruit in a renegade cult . . . compelling . . . with the topic of plural marriage and its shattering impact on women and powerless children in today's headlines, this novel is essential reading'

PUBLISHERS WEEKLY

'Wonderful . . . like A. S. Byatt, whose brilliant novel *Possession* also split the narrative between time periods, Ebershoff uses a series of fictionalized documents to add depth and perspective to his tale . . . thought-provoking'

SACRAMENTO NEWS & REVIEW

'Rarely has a work of fiction seemed more timely . . . a page-turning epic set amid a polygamous Utah sect eerily similar to those recently dominating the headlines . . . this tour de force lays bare the spiritual crimes committed to this day in the name of religious conviction'

VOGUE

'*The 19th Wife* is a big book, in every sense of the word. It sweeps across time and delves deeply into a world long hidden from sight. It offers historical and contemporary perspective on one of the world's fastest-growing religions and one of its oldest practices and in the process it does that thing all good novels do: it entertains us'

LOS ANGEL

www.the19tl

Also by David Ebershoff

PASADENA
THE ROSE CITY
THE DANISH GIRL

For more information on David Ebershoff and his books, see his website at www.ebershoff.com

The 19th Wife

David Ebershoff

BLACK SWAN

TRANSWORLD PUBLISHERS
61–63 Uxbridge Road, London W5 5SA
A Random House Group Company
www.rbooks.co.uk

THE 19TH WIFE
A BLACK SWAN BOOK: 9780552774987

First published in Great Britain
in 2008 by Doubleday
an imprint of Transworld Publishers
Black Swan edition published 2009

Grateful acknowledgement is made to Catherine Hamilton for her permission to
reprint her illustration on page 263.

A CIP catalogue record for this book
is available from the British Library.

Addresses for Random House Group Ltd companies outside the UK
can be found at: www.randomhouse.co.uk
The Random House Group Ltd Reg. No. 954009

The Random House Group Ltd supports The Forest Stewardship Council (FSC),
the leading international forest certification organization. All our titles that are printed
on Greenpeace-approved FSC-certified paper carry the FSC logo. Our paper
procurement policy can be found at
www.rbooks.co.uk/environment

Typeset in Giovanni Book 10/12.5pt
by Falcon Oast Graphic Art Ltd.

Printed in the UK by CPI Cox & Wyman, Reading, RG1 8EX.

2 4 6 8 10 9 7 5 3

for my parents
DAVE *and* BECKY EBERSHOFF

and for
DAVID BROWNSTEIN

Faith is to believe what you do not see; the reward of this faith is to see what you believe.

—SAINT AUGUSTINE

Like all the other arts, the Science of Deduction and Analysis is one which can only be acquired by long and patient study, nor is life long enough to allow any mortal to attain the highest possible perfection in it.

—ARTHUR CONAN DOYLE

And now, if there are faults they are the mistakes of men.

—THE BOOK OF MORMON,
TRANSLATED BY JOSEPH SMITH, JR.

CONTENTS

———

I

TWO WIVES

THE 19TH WIFE

FEATURING,

ONE LADY'S ACCOUNT OF

Plural Marriage and Its Woes

BEING

THE CHRONICLE OF PERSONAL EXPERIENCE

OF

ANN ELIZA YOUNG—

19TH AND REBEL WIFE OF THE

LEADER OF THE UTAH SAINTS AND

PROPHET OF THE MORMON CHURCH,

BRIGHAM YOUNG

WRITTEN BY HERSELF

WITH AN INTRODUCTION BY

MRS. HARRIET BEECHER STOWE

AND INCLUDING STEEL-PLATE ILLUSTRATIONS

EASTON & CO.

NEW YORK

1875

THE 19TH WIFE

———

In the one year since I renounced my Mormon faith, and set out to tell the nation the truth about American polygamy, many people have wondered why I ever agreed to become a plural wife. Everyone I meet, whether farmer, miner, railman, professor, cleric, or the long-faced Senator, and most especially the wives of these—everyone wants to know why I would submit to a marital practice so filled with subjugation and sorrow. When I tell them my father has five wives, and I was raised to believe plural marriage is the will of God, these sincere people often ask, *But Mrs. Young—how could you believe such a claim?*

Faith, I tell them, is a mystery, elusive to many, and never easy to explain.

Now, with the publication of this autobiography, my enemies will no doubt suspect my motives. Having survived attempts on both my life and character, however, I stand unconcerned by their assaults. I have chosen to commit my memories to the page neither for fame, the trough from which I have drunk and would be happy never to return to, nor fortune, although it is true I am without home and have two small boys to care for. Simply, I wish to expose the tragic state of polygamy's women, who must live in a bondage not seen in this country since the abolishment of slavery a decade ago; and to reveal the lamentable situation of its children, lonely as they are.

I promise my Dear Reader I shall recount my story

truthfully, even when it distresses me to do so. In these pages you will come to know my mother, who by religious duty welcomed four wives into her husband's bed. You will encounter the old woman forced to share her husband with a girl one-fifth her age. And you shall meet the gentleman with so many wives that when one approaches him on the street, he answers, "Madame, do I know you?"

I can, and will, go on.

Under what circumstances does such outrage thrive? The Territory of Utah, glorious as it may be, spiked by granite peaks and red jasper rocks, cut by echoing canyons and ravines, spread upon a wide basin of gamma grass and wandering streams, this land of blowing snow and sand, of iron, copper, and the great salten sea—Utah, whose scarlet-golden beauty marks the best of God's handiwork—the Territory of Utah stands defiant as a Theocracy within the borders of our beloved Democracy, *imperium in imperio*.

I write not for sensation, but for Truth. I leave judgment to the hearts of my good Readers everywhere. I am but one, yet to this day countless others lead lives even more destitute and enslaved than mine ever was. Perhaps my story is the exception because I escaped, at great risk, polygamy's conjugal chains; and that my husband is the Mormon Church's Prophet and Leader, Brigham Young, and I am his 19th, and final, wife.

Sincerely Yours,
ANN ELIZA YOUNG
Summer 1874

16

WIFE #19:

A DESERT MYSTERY

By Jordan Scott

PROLOGUE
Her Big Boy

According to the *St. George Register*, on a clear night last June, at some time between eleven and half-past, my mom—who isn't anything like this—tiptoed down to the basement of the house I grew up in with a Big Boy .44 Magnum in her hands. At the foot of the stairs she knocked on the door to my dad's den. From inside he called, "Who is it?" She answered, "Me, BeckyLyn." He said—or must've said—"Come in." What happened next? Nearly everyone in southwest Utah can tell you. She nailed an ace shot and blew his heart clean from his chest. The paper says he was in his computer chair, and from the way the blood splattered the drywall they're pretty sure the blast spun him three times around.

At the time of his death my dad was online playing Texas hold em and chatting with three people, including someone named DesertMissy. He spent the final seconds of his life in this exchange:

Manofthehouse2004: hang on
DesertMissy: phone?
Manofthehouse2004: no my wife
DesertMissy: which one?
Manofthehouse2004: #19

17

Sometime later—a few seconds? minutes?—DesertMissy wrote: u there??

Later she tried again: u there???? Eventually she gave up. They always do.

When my mom pulled the trigger my dad had a full house, three fives and a pair of ducks. He was all in. The paper says although dead, he ended up winning seven grand.

I once heard someone on tv say we die as we lived. That sounds about right. After my dad was shot the blood seeped across his gunsandammo.com t-shirt in a heavy stain. He was sixty-seven, his face pre-cancerously red. Everything about him was thick and worn from a life boiled by the sun. When I was a kid I used to dream he was a cowboy. I would imagine him out in the barn saddling his roan with the white socks, readying himself for a ride of justice. But my dad never rode anywhere for justice. He was a religious con man, a higher-up in a church of lies, the kind of schemer who goes around saying God meant for man to have many women and children and they shall be judged on how they obey. I know people don't really talk like that, but he did and so do a lot of the men where I come from, which is—let's just say—way the fuck out in the desert. You might've heard of us. The First Latter-day Saints, but everyone knows us as the Firsts. I should tell you right off we weren't Mormons. We were something else—a cult, a cowboy theocracy, a little slice of Saudi America. We've been called everything. I know all that because I left six years ago. That was the last time I saw my dad. My mom too. I know you know this but just in case: she was wife #19.

His first wife was more than willing to put the rap on my mom. For someone who wasn't supposed to talk to non-believers, Sister Rita had no trouble telling the *Register* everything. "I was up in the keeping room with the girls' hose," she blabbed to the paper. "That's when I saw her come upstairs. She had one of those faces—it looked funny, all squished up and *red*, like she'd seen something. I thought about asking but I didn't, I don't know why. I found him about twenty minutes after that when I went down myself. I should've gone down the minute I saw that face of hers, but how was I supposed to know? When I saw him in his chair like that, with his head, you know, just hanging in his chest like that, and all that blood—it was everywhere, I mean all over him, everything so, so *wet*, and *red*—well I started calling, just calling out to anyone for help. That's when they came running down, all of them, the women I mean, one after the next, the kids too, they kept coming. The house shook, there were so many running down the stairs. The first to get there was Sister Sherry, I think. When I told her what happened, and then she saw for herself, she started crying, screaming really, and the next one, she started crying too, and then the next after her, and so on. I never heard anything like it. The shrieks spread up the line, like fire, catching and spreading, one after the next and pretty soon it seemed the whole house was on fire with screams, if you know what I mean. You see, we all loved him just the same."

The next morning the Lincoln County sheriff handcuffed my mom: "You'll have to come with me, Sister." I don't know who called him in, he usually didn't get out to Mesadale. There's a picture of her being guided into the backseat of the cruiser—the rope of her braid flat against her back as she ducks in. The paper says she didn't resist. Tell me about it. She didn't resist when her husband married her fifteen-year-old niece. She didn't resist when the Prophet told her to throw me out. "No point in making a fuss"—she used to say that all the time. For years she was obedient, believing it part of her salvation. Then one day I guess she went *pop!* That's how these things go, you hear about it all the time. Except because of the suppressor it was probably more like a *phump!* than a *pop!*

Did Sister Rita do her in? Actually, it was the chat session. The *Register* loved the irony: VICTIM NAMES HIS MURDERER BEFORE SHE PULLS THE TRIGGER. Technically he didn't name her, he numbered her. But really, Rita's statement didn't help either.

It gave the sheriff enough. The next day my mom was booked and that picture was up on the *Register*'s home page, my mom sliding into the cruiser, her hair a heavy chain.

That's how I found out. I was at the library with my friend Roland. We were tooling around the web, checking out nothing in particular, then all of a sudden there it was, the story about my mom:

WIFE #19 KILLS HUSBAND

SIGN OF STRIFE IN RENEGADE SECT?

In the picture she's shackled at the wrists. Her forehead is white and glossy, reflecting a camera's flash in the dawn, and she has a look in her eyes. How to describe it? Should I say her eyes were dark and damp, the eyes of a small snouted animal? Or will you know what I mean if I say she had the scared-shitless look of a woman busted for murder and about to spend the rest of her life in the can?

II

WIFE #19:

THE RED IN THE DESERT

WELCOME TO FLIPPIN' UTAH

Before I go any further there are a few things you should know. I'm twenty years old but a lot of people say I look younger. In the last six years I've lived almost everywhere between southern Utah and LA, five of them with Elektra. For two years we lived in and around Vegas out of a beat-up florist's van with a bunch of hydrangeas stenciled on the side. I still have the van but now Elektra and I live in Pasadena, in a studio apartment above a garage.

I probably should tell you a little something about Elektra, because she's the only reason I made it, given the circumstances. She's got rich brown hair that turns red in the sun, yellow-gold nearly electric eyes— you'd swear there were bulbs behind them—and the kind of long long legs that make people turn around and whistle. Roland likes to say she's got the legs of a supermodel, but that's just him. I found her in a parking lot off Industrial about a year after I was kicked out. Her snout was in a Taco Bell bag, which is pretty much what I was doing too. I don't know what she is exactly—some sort of hound/bird-dog mix with a few drops of pit. That gives her cred with some people but I'm not into things like that. All I care is she's my girl. For the record she came with that name tattooed to the underside of her left ear. It looks like this:

Elektra
Bite Me!

If you want to know what I look like I should tell you what a customer once said: *You got a face like a fucking doll.* That old

23

guy, as he was paying me fifty bucks, he said, *Kid, you got some fucking roses in your cheeks. I like that.* In addition to the roses, I've got a high kinda girlish voice I used to wish was lower but I don't bother worrying about anymore. A priest I once went to (mistake) said my eyes reminded him of the blue sea glass he found on the Jersey shore when he was a boy. I left before he could look into them any deeper. Someone else, a loser with a wife and twins, said they were like two little sapphires, little gemstones he said, then paid me to put my arm somewhere it should never go. But I don't do that anymore. Those were my lean & teen years. Now I make a living in construc-tion, which I'm actually pretty good at. It's the only thing I can thank the Prophet for. I'm especially good at framing and roofing, which means I work outside a lot. Roland likes to say, "Another year in the sun, Jo-Jo, and you'll be old like the rest of us." He's the only person who calls me Jo-Jo. I don't know why he does it. My name's Jordan. Jordan Scott.

I'm telling you all this because people always get me wrong. I know what they see—hustler, twink, whatever. But I'm not some precious stone or some fucking doll. I'm just a guy who got totally screwed when he was fourteen and by all odds should be in jail or dead or both but actually is manag-ing just fine. That's it. That's all you need to know.

Oh, and this: once I was at the library in line checking out a book on the history of God and this finger tapped me on the shoulder: "What is someone like *you* doing with a book like *that*?" That's how Roland and I met. We don't have much in common except we hang out at the library a lot. It's a nice library, the Pasadena Public. I've never seen them bother anyone who doesn't have a place to go. Once the librarian, Sue, once she even let Elektra into the children's room to meet the kids. She liked that—Elektra, I mean. But this story isn't about Sue and it's not about Roland or Elektra and it isn't even really about me. It's about my mom, and I guess my dad, and about this bullshit Prophet who I used to believe could speak to God. I know, can you believe it? Unfortunately it's all true.

I was at the library when I saw that picture on the *Register*'s home page. "Oh my God, Roland," I said. "That's my mom." He was too busy studying last month's *Vogue* to hear me. "Roland, look." I had to kick him to get his attention. "My mom."

"Who? What?" Then he looked up. "Oh my God. Your *mom*? Really? How'd she get on the home page?"

"It says she killed my dad."

"She *what*?" He leaned into the screen for a closer look and his eyebrows shot up. "Oh honey, you told me it was bad out there, but you didn't mention that awful braid." He said something about my mom's Little House on the Prairie dress, but I stopped listening. That picture—

I can't explain it. I couldn't look away.

"Jo-Jo . . . Jordan? You all right?"

"Where do you think they're taking her?"

"Well, let's find out." Roland scooted over and began googling. "What's the name of the county out there in Utah?"

"Lincoln. Why?"

"Lincoln County . . . Utah . . . corrections . . ." He typed gently, as if protecting a manicure. "Uh-huh, this looks right. . . . OK, Jo-Jo, I think we're going to find her. Give it a sec." He clicked the mouse. "Yep, this is it: inmate inquiry. Her name?"

"BeckyLyn, capital B, capital L, no space."

He pursed his lips, like he'd heard something tacky. "All righty, let's see what we can find. Capital B"—click click click—"capital L. Scott, like the tissue. OK, just give it a second: there she is!"

And there she was, not her picture, but her name on a list of inmates:

BOOKING NO.	INMATE ID	LAST NAME	FIRST NAME
066001825	207334	Scott	BeckyLyn

He clicked her booking number and an hourglass turned on the screen. Then it came up: Inmate Information for BeckyLyn Scott. "Remember, Jordan, no one looks good in a mug shot. I'm speaking only from experience."

He was right. She was in a mustard jumpsuit, standing before a board that measured her height in inches (62) and centimeters (157). Her complexion was gray and cloudy. Her eyes pleaded from their sockets. "It's her," I said.

"Let's see her profile." Roland clicked the screen. Her right profile showed the hard tendons in her throat, her left revealed an ear as small as a shell. But it was the first shot that did me. That's how she looked the last time I saw her. Like she was in a trance.

"I don't want you to take this the wrong way," said Roland, "but I see a resemblance."

I hope you know what I'm talking about when I say every once in a while, not very often, I know exactly what I'm supposed to do with my life, even if I can't explain why. The trick is to tune in for it, like scanning the radio for a favorite song.

"I'm going to Utah," I said.

You should've seen Roland's face: "You're going to Utah? *Now*?"

"She's my mom."

"I thought you said you'd never go back there."

"I need to see her."

"After what she did to you?"

Right before we looked at the *Register*'s home page, Roland had been checking out this diet website with a banner that kept flashing LATER IS NOW! So cheesy, I know, but I couldn't get it out of my head. It was Sunday afternoon, I just got paid, I had a lame job installing a vanity on Monday I could get out of, and Elektra was always up for a road trip. "Later is now," I said.

"Oh please, later is later. Besides, I thought we were going to celebrate your birthday."

"Next year."

26

"Jo-Jo, what's gotten into you?"

"Look at her—her eyes, I mean. I need to see her. I'll be gone a day, two max."

"Sweetie, before you get in that van of yours and drive all the way to Utah, can I remind you of two small but highly relevant facts? One—and I'm sorry to put it like this—your mom dumped you on the highway in the middle of the night when you were—what?—fourteen. Not a nice thing. And two, she just popped off your dad. Are you really sure a family reunion's such a good idea?"

"I don't know, but I'm going." And then, "Want to come?"

"Oh, no thanks, honey, I'm going to hell in my next life. I see no point in dropping in early."

Outside of Barstow I called the jail. Turns out there's a twenty-four-hour rule, so I couldn't see my mom until the next afternoon. I tried to talk the officer into a morning visit, but she cut me off: "It's not going to happen, all right?" She went over the visiting rules, no interaction with other inmates, that sort of stuff, and how I couldn't bring anything into the jail except my clothes. "That means no jewelry, earrings, or body rings of *any* kind. If you weren't born with it, don't bring it."

"What about my dog?"

I don't know why I said that but it's a good thing I did, because by chance she was a dog person. She asked me what I had and I told her about Elektra. "Sounds like a beauty," she said, then went on to describe her own pair of corgis. "If you have any questions, you can call me back, I'll give you my direct. But I have to warn you: your mom has the right to refuse your visit and she doesn't have to give a reason. If that happens, I'll give you a ring."

I kept driving east on 15, looking at my phone to see if Officer Cunningham had called while I was out of signal. Somewhere past Vegas, Elektra became anxious, trembling and whimpering in my ear. I let her out to pee but that wasn't it. She's really good at picking up how I feel even before I know how I feel. She climbed into my lap and draped her head over my shoulder. I stroked her with one hand while steering with the other and I realized I was a little bit scared.

When I reached the Utah Welcome Center there was a message on my phone. I feared it might be Officer Cunningham telling me my mom didn't want to see me, but it was Roland checking in. "Honey, if it gets bad out there, promise me you'll come home, all right?"

The next day at the county jail I handed over my ID to Officer Cunningham. "Where's Elektra?"

Quick version of a long story: I met this goth girl at an internet café who agreed to watch her, and right about now she was probably eating cookies on a couch. I could tell the officer thought less of me for leaving my dog with a stranger, but it was 115 outside and around here you need to look hard for a scrap of shade.

Officer Cunningham passed me through the metal detector, punched something into her terminal, frowned, punched something else. "OK, here's the drill," she said. "Your mom's still on secure visits, which is never any fun. Go on through the door to the left, you're in the cubicle at the end. Officer Kane will bring her out in a few."

The cubicles looked like a row of phone booths, the kind you sit in. A small stool with a round red plastic seat. A yellow phone receiver mounted to the left partition. The room was pretty crowded, several women waving pacifiers and squeaky toys in a vain effort to keep their babies from exploding into tears. Visits were limited to two people but babies under one didn't count. It seemed everyone had brought as many infants as they could carry. A sign on the wall said, MOTHERS: KEEP YOUR CHILDREN UNDER CONTROL!

As if.

I waited on my stool, staring through the thick glass screen. In my reflection I saw the red patches in my cheeks. My eyes looked small and dark—they were my mom's eyes, anyone could see that.

After I was kicked out (they call it excommunicated, but whatever), I honestly thought I'd never see her again, and I have to say I didn't really care. I was mad, starting with God, then the Prophet, but my mom was next up on the list. I'm still mad at him—God, I mean—because my mom tossed me on the highway at two a.m. in his name. Trust me: that can mess you up. Instead of bawling about it, I vowed never to think about any of them again. You have to remember I was fourteen. I'd never left Mesadale. I knew jack about the world. In my backpack I had a sweatshirt, some sacred underwear (don't ask), and seventeen bucks. In my pockets: nada. In all fairness my mom took a risk slipping me the money, but it didn't feel like much at the time. I was real lucky that trucker hauling bedding picked me up after about an hour. He could've wanted a blow job or something, but really all he wanted was to talk about his wife. She had recently died in a fire and he couldn't keep the memories to himself. I rode with him to St. George. Together we watched the sunrise behind us in the sideviews. You ever see the sun come up over the Utah desert? Imagine the coals of hell burning in the clouds. "Man, check that out," the driver said at one point. "It's like God took a torch to the whole fucking sky."

On the other side of the glass, a corrections officer escorted my mom to the stool. Our eyes met, and it was like following your gaze in a mirror. Wherever I looked she looked. At the stool, at the wall clock, at the phone.

She looked more or less the same—the tough jaw, the small snout of a nose—but they'd cut her hair into a dense ugly shrub. I'd never seen her with a haircut. She could tell I was staring at it because she touched it, as if she were wearing a wig about to slip off. What else can I tell you about her? She was fourteen when she married my dad, which means she's

29

now thirty-five. Her voice is small and girlish, kinda like mine. She has those same roses in her cheeks. What else? For the record, she's my dad's niece *and* his first cousin. Which makes me . . . oh, you figure it out.

"Jordan? Can you hear me?"

"Yes."

"My goodness, look at you: you're all grown up."

"I heard about Dad."

"It's a tragedy."

"It sounds like a mess."

"I knew you'd come to see me. I've been praying for it."

I stopped, holding down a little rage. "Mom. Don't take this the wrong way, but that's not why I'm here."

"Yes, Jordan. Yes, it is." She was leaning in very close to the glass, her face done up in the pink and blue of irrational excitement.

"Look, Mom, can you tell me what happened?"

She sat back, the color wiped from her face. "I have no idea."

In the next cubicle a baby was gagging on sobs and tears. The baby's mom or aunt or whoever kept saying it's all right, everything's going to be all right—which in this case was a total lie.

"Was it how Sister Rita described it?"

"Why, what'd she say?"

As I recapped Rita's statement, my mom's eyes filled with tears. "It wasn't like that," she said. "That's just not the way it was."

"Then what happened?"

She hesitated, as if gathering up the memory. "You've never seen so much blood. I saw them take him out on the stretcher. That's when I knew—" But a sob got the better of her, and she couldn't finish. "Jordan, I know everything's been hard on you. Us saying good-bye like that. And now you seeing me like this. I never thought it would be like this. I always thought, well, I just thought—" Her voice cut off and she pressed her eyes with the heels of her hands.

When she calmed herself down she said, "Tell me what you've been doing all this time, where you've been, where you live. Are you married? Maybe you're a father yourself? I want to know if your life's at all like I imagined."

Call me crazy, but it seems to me if you throw out your only son because some con man Prophet told you to, well, it just seems to me you really don't have a right to know what comes after. "It's a long story," I said. "I live in California and everything's fine."

"Are you on your own?"

I told her about Elektra, and that seemed to brighten her up. "But, Mom, that's not why I'm here. Can you tell me what's going on?"

"All I know is there was some sort of hearing this morning. It only lasted a few minutes. I told Mr. Heber—"

"Who's Mr. Heber?"

"The lawyer they gave me. I told him I wanted to speak to the judge, but he said it wasn't the right time, just tell him your name. They were talking about bail, the judge didn't want to set any and Mr. Heber said that wasn't fair and he won, but it doesn't matter. Where am I going to come up with a million dollars? Then they brought me back here."

"At least you're out of Mesadale."

She switched the receiver from her left ear to her right. "It was your birthday yesterday. I kept thinking of you all day. Isn't it amazing how God works? I was thinking of you and you were thinking of me."

You know what, maybe Roland was right: I shouldn't be here. Maybe later was later. Maybe later was never. If I left now, I could be back in Pasadena before midnight. He and I could meet for a late-night coffee and a doughnut at Winchell's.

"Remember how you used to love the birthday parties?" she went on. "I can picture you when you were just a little guy, waiting in line with a paper plate for a slice of cake.

31

You were always such a good boy, Jordan, always so patient and good."

"To be perfectly honest, those are some of the worst memories of my life."

"What? Why?"

"Those parties were for the Prophet."

"I know, but that's what made it so much fun."

"Fun? Mom, they made us celebrate our birthdays on his. You realize how screwed up that is?"

"I don't know, I think it's nice, everyone celebrating together like that."

I caught myself. "OK, Mom, let's not do this."

"Do what?"

"Go over the past."

She paused. "I'm sorry, I didn't mean to upset you."

"Look, Mom, before I go, is there anything I can get you?"

"You're going?"

"It's a long drive home."

"Jordan, you can't go now. I need your help."

"What kind of help?"

"I need you to talk to Mr. Heber."

"About what?"

"About when I can get out of here."

"You should probably do that yourself."

"I did. And he said he couldn't say, which is unacceptable as far as I'm concerned."

You know how when you're away from your mom you miss her, and the minute you see her she starts driving you crazy? Multiply that feeling by a million.

"Mom, let me ask you this: why now?"

"Why now what?"

"I mean after all this time? Something must've happened. You always seemed so sure of everything. When you said good-bye to me that night, you told me you had to do whatever God said."

"That's right. Of course I didn't want to leave you like

32

that, I told you that. But I knew it was God testing me. That's what the Prophet said: BeckyLyn, this is your test, your test from God. It's not that I didn't love you, it's just what God wanted for you, and for me. I thought you'd understand that."

"You know what I understand: it's all bullshit. Everything about that place, starting with God, then the Prophet, then Dad. So when I read what happened with Dad, what you did, I was like thank God, she's finally woken up."

"What I *did*? Wait a minute . . . Do you honestly think—do you really believe I killed your father? Oh Jordan, no. No no no no no. How could you believe such a thing?"

"How could I believe such a thing? Mom, you're in jail."

"I can understand the authorities getting it wrong, but *you*?"

"Sister Rita spelled it out pretty clearly."

"Sister Rita?" She balled up her fist. "Just so you know: I did not kill your father. He was my husband. I was his wife. Why in heaven's name would I kill him?"

I could think of a million reasons. To tell the truth, it hadn't crossed my mind that she was innocent.

"On the Prophet's life, I did not kill your father."

It's a little weird to admit but I was disappointed by her denial.

And I didn't believe her, not for a second. "Then who did?"

"I don't know. One of the wives. But it wasn't me."

"What'd your lawyer say?"

"I don't think he believes me. He said he had to review a lot of evidence before he could come up with a strategy. I told him, I didn't do it, that's your strategy. I keep telling myself this isn't happening." She said that again: "This isn't happening." She dropped her forehead into her hand to bolster herself, then looked up. "Oh Jordan, isn't it wonderful, you being here, coming here like this."

"I guess."

"It's a miracle."

"Mom."

"I prayed to our Heavenly Father to bring you to me and he did."

Here we go again. "I seriously doubt that."

"Jordan, don't you see? There was a reason he made me send you away. So you could come back to help me when I needed you. We couldn't know it at the time, but now I understand. Look: there you were in California leading I'm sure a real busy life, and you happen to read about me on the, on the, is it the web or is it the net, because I've heard people call it both?"

"The web. The net. It doesn't matter."

"OK, the web. And something *told* you to come help me. Don't you see: if you were still in Mesadale you wouldn't be able to help me. It was God's plan all along. If that isn't proof, then I don't know what is."

"I'm not even going to respond to that."

"Then tell me: why were you looking up the local paper on that day of all days?"

"I don't know, every once in a while I read it online, just to see what's going on out here, but every time I do I get depressed."

"See!" She pressed her fingers against the glass, the tips going flat and white. "God told you to read the web yesterday. If it hadn't been for God—"

"Jesus, Mom, cut the God crap. That's not why I was online, I spend like half my life online. When are you going to be free of all of this shit?"

"Jordan, don't speak to me like that."

"Mom, I'm sorry, I just don't believe any of that." My throat was clamping up. "Not anymore." I set down the receiver and wiped my eyes. Goddammit, I wasn't supposed to crack up. That night, years ago, when the trucker dropped me off, I promised myself I would never cry again over any of it. And I didn't, not once, until now. Now my eyes were wet and there weren't any tissues in here, there wasn't anything in this place, just a red plastic stool and a yellow plastic phone and a wall of glass and a dozen crying babies. Fuck me.

"I should be going."

"Jordan, no. I need your help."

I took a second to think about what that might mean. "I'll see if I can make an appointment with your lawyer." Then I hung up. Through the glass I saw her mouth, *One more thing*. I picked up the receiver. "Yeah?"

"I'm very sorry for doing that. I didn't have a choice. I only hope you can understand that now."

"You don't need to say anything else."

"You need to know it's the only reason I would've done that to you."

"Mom, look, fine. It was a long time ago."

"I like to think you could hear my prayers. I guess you don't like talking about things like that anymore, but it's true. The only way I could sleep at night was knowing you could hear me pray for you." Her mouth darkened and puckered and she set down the receiver to cry. The officer behind her offered a packet of tissues. I could see my mom say thanks and Officer Kane say no problem, you take your time. She was on the heavy side, her uniform tight on her thighs, and was about as threatening as the senior citizen who greets you at Wal-Mart.

My mom picked up the phone again. "You'll help me, right? I know you'll help me."

I told her I'd see what I could do. She nodded. Then we hung up. For a while I didn't move and she didn't move, except for her hands, they trembled on the counter. Then they settled down, lying there small and white behind the glass, like a tiny pair of unclaimed gloves.

THE 19TH WIFE

MRS. HARRIET BEECHER STOWE

When I first heard of the enslaved state of the women of Utah, I, like many Americans, questioned the veracity of these tales. Surely the profane stories, the recollections of abuse and neglect, and the rage of the apostates speaking out against their Church and its leaders were exaggerations; or at least aberrations from the norm. In my years, I have met and corresponded with several members of the Church of Jesus Christ of Latter-day Saints, or Mormons—for many have stood forthright and firm in their opposition to slavery. My Mormon friends have impressed me as straightforward and sincere, rational and informed, a people who value education and industry as much as religious duty. Their greatest passion, it seemed, was their desire to pursue their religion in liberty. In my mind, the tales of conjugal debasement could not be reconciled with the Saints I knew, both by face and in the letter. The enmity the Mormons have engendered among so many, it seemed to me, came from a general ignorance of their customs, and a public fear of their private rites. I, for one, have long felt that we, as Americans, should let the Mormons practice their faith in peace.

Yet for some time now the stories have continued to blow forth from that desert region, like the livid Sirocco, from one plural wife after the next, and many gentlemen too, each reinforcing a prevailing impression of marital bondage for

36

so many women of Deseret. Was it possible these stories were true?

I first encountered Mrs. Brigham Young in February of this year, 1874, when she lectured at Boston's Tremont Temple. Her simple presentation, and her natural appeal, convinced me that she had little to gain, and much to suffer, by speaking of polygamy so frankly. It became clear that she would have much preferred a private life with her sons to the one she was leading as crusader, informer, and, now with this volume, author. Her life as a daughter of polygamy, and a wife of polygamy, had exposed her to many variations of this cruel institution, and she felt compelled to reveal it for what it was. It was also clear to me that she had no choice in the matter. Her opposition to polygamy had become her new faith, its abolition her salvation.

By the conclusion of our first meeting, and now upon reading her memoirs, I have become convinced that polygamy must meet the same final defeat slavery met a decade ago. Both are relics of Barbarism. We were right to conquer slavery first, but now with its eradication, we must set our sights on its twin. Many people call this the Mormon Question, just as, for many years, slavery was called the Southern Question. In fact it is a question concerning all of us, as a nation and a people. Our response to the moral and spiritual enslavement of Utah's women and children will define us in the years to come. Should you possess any doubts about the true debasement of the plural wife, or her child, I recommend the story that follows herein.

—Hartford, September 1874

THE CHURCH, YOUR DAD, THE HOUSE, HIS WIVES

I found Mr. Heber's name on a door between a dermatologist and a podiatrist. Inside I met a blue blur bustling around watering the ferns. "You must be Jordan. I'm Maureen. Mr. Heber's a little backlogged this afternoon—you have no idea what our afternoons are like when he's been in court—but I know he's really glad you called." Then she stopped. "Wait a minute! Who. Is. This?"

"Elektra. I hope you don't mind. It's too hot to leave her in the van."

"Of course it is!" She squatted with the agility of a gymnast to kiss Elektra on the snout.

My first impression of Maureen was Mormon Grandma. This was not an especially fond thought. It's not that I actively dislike Mormons, it's just that they actively dislike me. Maureen was tall and sturdy, definitely some pioneer stock in her big-boneness. She wore her hair up in an airy mass of curls, the effect of a once-a-week beauty parlor visit. Her outfit was all royal blue, slacks, matching blouse, and a cape of a sweater buttoned at the throat.

"Mr. Heber shouldn't be long, he's just finishing a call, I'll let you know the minute he gets off." She hurried back to her desk while I flipped through a copy of *Ensign*. It took about a second to find the article on, and I'm quoting here, defeating same-gender attraction. Eye roll, please. I swapped the magazine for *Us Weekly*. While I read about Hollywood bumps, Maureen typed up five letters, took seven messages, and worked her way to the bottom of a to-file basket. "Oh me," she said a bit wearily. Then a light on the phone console went out and she started back up again. "Ooops, he's off. Come on, let's get in there before he gets back on."

As she led me down a corridor, I said her hair looked nice. "Thank you! Just got it set this morning." From her smile I could tell it'd been a while since anyone had paid her a compliment. Roland says every woman needs a gay guy in her life: "Honey, we're the only ones who bother to notice a perm."

At the end of the hall Maureen hipped open an office door. "Here we are."

I know it's not fair, but my first impression of Mr. Heber was Mormon Asshole. His first impression of me probably was Beyond Redemption, so we were even. He was about seventy-five, a drift of snowy hair, and watery, untrustable eyes. On the wall several pictures showed him teeing off on golf courses around the world.

"Jordan Scott, it's a pleasure. I can't tell you how pleased I was when you called. Surprised, yes, but pleased even so." I apologized for bringing Elektra into his office. "Too hot to leave her in the car. Believe me, I understand. My wife won't leave our Yorkie in the wagon for five minutes. Now, Jordan, first I want to tell you how sorry I am about your mom. And your dad. And all of this. If there's ever anything I can do— for you, I mean—I hope you'll let me know." I'm going to spare you my mental commentary that was sidebarring this conversation, but you can probably guess I was liking this guy less and less.

"Can you tell me what's going to happen to my mom?" I said.

"My goodness, straight to business, a man after my own heart. All righty, have a seat. Now I understand you were just out at the jail. Tell me, how'd you find her?"

"Pretty upset. And confused. She doesn't seem to understand what's going on."

"I'm doing my best to figure that out myself."

"Did the paper get the story right?"

"As far as I can tell. Here, look at this, it just came in." He waved a file folder. "It's the ballistics report. Her latent prints showed up on the Big Boy. They found others, but they found a lot of hers."

"In other words, she's in deep shit."

"Your words, not mine. But yes." He came around from behind the desk to sit on the corner near me. "It's pretty screwed up out there in Mesadale, isn't it?"

"Look, Mr. Heber, I don't really feel like going into all that. Just tell me what's going to happen to her. And you don't need to sugarcoat it. She and I—we're not very close."

"I got that impression. I understand you left a while back. A lost boy, is that right?"

I hate that name, but that's what they call us, the boys the Prophet kicks out. "Yeah, something like that."

"I'm sure these past few years haven't been easy."

"Yeah, they pretty much sucked, but you know what, things are fine now."

"Do you mind telling me what happened? When you were excommunicated?"

"I don't really know what that has to do with my mom being in jail."

"I understand if it's hard to talk about."

"It's not hard, it's just it doesn't seem relevant to why I'm here."

Mr. Heber squeezed my knee. "Jordan, we're on the same team here, OK? We're going to have to trust each other. Eventually this will come up. A prosecutor's going to ask, if your mom could leave you like that, when you were just a boy, then perhaps she's also capable of killing your dad."

"It's a lot more complicated than that."

"I'm sure it is."

And that's how Mr. Heber got me to tell him the story of my mom dragging me out of bed and driving me down the highway and telling me to get out. "The Prophet made her do it."

"Your dad didn't try to stop her?"

"My dad. He was probably in the basement getting high."

"What prompted this?"

"It was pretty lame." I couldn't believe I was telling Heber all this—I almost never talk about it—but there I went. "I was holding hands with one of my stepsisters, this girl named Queenie. That wasn't her real name, but that's what I called her. We weren't doing anything, but out there boys and girls aren't supposed to hang out like that. We were just talking one day and I don't know why, I just took her hand. My dad saw us and he reported it to the Prophet. And that was it. I mean it's true, yeah, my mom left me there and everything, but in Mesadale they tell you all this stuff, like you'll go to hell if you don't do what the Prophet wants. And they believe it, *she* believes it. Fuck—excuse me—frick, I used to believe it. So one night, boom, she dumps me on the road, fast-forward six years, and here I am."

Mr. Heber and Maureen were silent. It's hard to know what to say after you hear a story like that. Then they figured it out. They both said how sorry they were. That's what people always say, *Gee, I'm awfully sorry.* I hate that. Look at Heber and Maureen: their eyes were full of the one thing I didn't want. How did this turn into a pity party?

"Just your regular run-of-the-mill polygamist boo-hoo tragedy," I said. Most people assume I was kicked out because I was gay. But I was fourteen, a late bloomer. I didn't know what gay was. Roland likes to read the columns in the women's magazines. He says I was holding Queenie's hand for reverse psychology reasons. I don't think so. I took her hand because she was my friend and I felt alone.

"Listen, the only reason I'm here is to find out what's going to happen to my mom. She's on her own and she needs someone to explain to her the truth. So go ahead and tell me what she's looking at. It's life, isn't it? Maybe a little less with parole?"

Mr. Heber said nothing.

"OK, no parole."

Still silent.

"If that's it, tell me. I can handle it. I'm really not surprised. I don't know, maybe it's what she deserves."

"I like you, Jordan. You're honest and you know a fact is a fact. I can tell you really want the truth—not all people do, you know. They say they do, but when it comes down to it, they don't. That's why I'm going to tell you everything I know. I'm afraid things don't look good for your mother. I'm very concerned she'll be found guilty." He hesitated, but only for a second. "And face execution."

"Execution?"

"I wish I could be more optimistic. But my job is to be realistic."

"You're sure?"

"I'm rarely sure." Mr. Heber returned to the other side of his desk. "I'm hoping to get her trial pushed out a bit. Give us some time to figure out what's really going on out there. She didn't kill him in a vacuum—that's the only thing I do know for sure. This wasn't a simple domestic dispute. I want to put the crime into some context. And meanwhile maybe the feds will finally get off their rear ends and do something about that so-called Prophet. As far as I'm concerned, it's that cult that should be put on trial, not your mom. And that's why I'm really glad you called. I could use your help."

"Me?"

"I'd like you to tell me everything you know about Mesadale, walk me through what it's like out there, what life was like for you, and the Prophet, what's he like, the church, your dad, the house, his wives, everything about the Firsts you can tell me."

"I haven't been there in six years."

"You know a lot more than I do."

I guess I could do that. It might help tweezer out the splinter of guilt I'd been feeling since I left my mom behind that slab of glass. "OK, so what do you want to know?"

"Whatever you think is most important. But I'm afraid not right now."

42

"Not right now?"

"I want to do this carefully, sit down, go over everything, make sure we cover all the bases. Maureen's going to take you back to her desk and find a few hours when we can really talk." He fished a gold-plated golf tee out of a tray and began rolling it around his palm.

"Are you kidding me?" Elektra stood up and shook out her ears. She needed to pee.

"I wish I had more time today, but I didn't know you were in town until a half hour ago. Maureen, take him up front and arrange something, all right? Squeeze him in as soon as possible."

In a flash she was on her feet. "Come on, let's have a look at the old calendar."

"Wait a minute," I said. "I can't just hang in St. George forever. I've got a job in California. A good job"—lie—"and an apartment. We're living out of the back of my van."

Elektra yawned, as if she'd heard it before. Maureen stood in the open door. Mr. Heber flipped some pages on a legal pad. This meeting was so over. "Jordan, we both want the same thing. You're going to have to trust me."

Just one problem: I've never been too good in the trust department.

HELL HATH NO FURY

The news out of Salt Lake's seraglio has caught even our attention. At last Mrs. Young—or should we say, a Mrs. Young—has told her husband enough is enough. This one—Number 19, if the numbers can be believed—has filed suit against the Prophet, Supreme Leader, etc. etc. of the Saints. All we can say is: It's about time. While husband and wife ensnare one another in accusation and counter-accusation, we would like to add two observations to the fracas. One, Brigham Young is a Confidence Man in the grand tradition of the hoodwinkers of the West. A message from Heaven has told him he should possess 19 wives? A message from Heaven has told us we should possess a finer house, a larger income, and at least one day each year free from this esteemed publication, but those minor miracles have yet to transpire. As for Mrs. Young, Number 19, we most respectfully inquire: What did she expect? At the gate of the slaughterhouse, even the squealing pig understands his fate. Could she not smell the blood in the air? Under some Divine plan, it seems Destiny intended these two noble creatures to be united in either matrimony or warfare, if there is a difference. As the battle begins, we shall mount our hill with somber hearts to watch out over the carnage.

THE BIG HOUSE

That night I couldn't sleep. Same with Elektra. She kept shifting on the futon and growling at every sound at the Welcome Center—car doors, motorcycles, eighteen-wheelers gasping in their sleep. At one point a t-ball team dashed from a minivan for the men's room, a gang of eight-year-olds calling one another pussy and dick. It was one of those nights when I never really shut my eyes.

Around four I started driving. Elektra sat alert in the passenger seat, the fur buckled on her brow. It was like she understood where we were going and didn't think it was a good idea.

Outside St. George, past the crystal meth dens of Hurricane, there's a long county highway to nowhere. It rises up, crossing an empty desert plateau with red mesas and stony mountains and stands of piñon in the distance. On the road there's nothing for fifty miles except a gas station, a lunch counter, and a wire cross marking the site of a fatal crash. If you keep going, eventually you'll hit the turnoff for Mesadale. Theoretically this highway leads to Kanab, then the Grand Canyon, but there are better routes to both, and there really isn't any reason to drive down this highway unless you're headed to Mesadale, or you're lost. It's got to be the loneliest road in America. Somewhere along here my mom dumped me that night. I remember there was a dead cottonwood beside the road. I remember wishing it would come to life and hold me in its limbs.

Ten miles before Mesadale I pulled over. With the engine off, everything was quiet, just a few early birds rustling in the sagebrush. After fifteen minutes a semi came along. I could hear it before I saw it, its thunder mounting, consuming the desert. When it passed, the van shook and Elektra barked once. The roar subsided and after a long time everything was silent again and the truck's taillights were lost to the night.

Finally there was pink in the eastern sky and I let Elektra out to pee. She ran twenty feet into the desert and started barking at a bitterbrush. Probably a jackrabbit or Gila monster. I called her back to the van but she ignored me and I had to drag her in.

I was parked by the sign telling you how far to Mesadale, but buckshot had chewed it up so bad you couldn't read it. Every time the sign went up the Prophet sent out an apostle to shoot it up. My dad did that once. I remember him boasting about it at breakfast. "Took out Satan's marker," he said, stuffing his mouth with fried ham.

I should probably make it clear why the Firsts aren't Mormon. Not like the Mormons you see on tv singing in the Tabernacle or cheering at a BYU game or the hottie missionaries chatting up strangers on the street. The guys who run the Mormon Church—those old dudes in out-of-date eyeglasses up in Salt Lake—they hate the Prophet almost as much as I do. They call him a heretic, a blasphemer, and a whole bunch of other things like rapist, pedophile, and tax cheat. The point of contention between the Firsts and the Mormons—you probably figured this out—is polygamy. The Prophet says when the Mormon Church gave it up in 1890, they sold out. That's when the Firsts broke away. It's why the Prophet—our Prophet, I mean—used to always say on Sundays, Brothers and Sisters, *you* are the first and true Saints. You are the descendants of Joseph and Brigham. You will be first in line at the Restoration when man hopes to be saved.

As you can imagine, the Mormons have another opinion on that. Can you spell *rift*? That book I was reading, the one about the history of God, it says this sort of split happens all the time. The Jews and the Christians. The Catholics and the Protestants. The Mormons and the Firsts. It's been going on forever and the only thing I know for sure is it messes up a lot of shit for the rest of us.

Over in the foothills I could see Mesadale waking up to the dawn. From here it was a cluster of white and yellow lights beneath the mountain. I knew exactly what was going on at each of those lights. I knew it the way you know a dvd you've watched a hundred times. A sister wife was flicking on a lamp to brush out her hair. Another was striking a match to light the stove. A third wife was pulling the string on the pantry bulb, hauling out a large box of corn mush. Ten, fifteen, twenty more lights in a house—each was a sister wife rising to perform her chores.

And the kids. About now the kids would be climbing out of bed, rubbing the sand from their eyes. They'd be forming a line at the sink to wash. The boys would be searching the boxes for a shirt. The girls would be helping one another pin up their hair. You don't talk much at that hour. You just dress fast so you can get to the kitchen in time for your plop of mush. Sometimes there was toast and canned peaches, but not always. Whatever there was, there was never enough. Only a fool would waste time taking a piss before getting something to eat.

As I drove closer I could see Mesadale had grown. There were a few hundred houses now, warehouses for families of seventy-five. No one knows how many people live out there but I'm going to guess twelve thousand, maybe fifteen. Counting is complicated. The numbers are part of the mystery. The less you know, the less you know.

The turnoff is hidden behind a stand of cottonwoods. It looks like a dry river wash, and even if you're looking for it, it's hard to spot. No one stumbles across Mesadale and that's the point. Roland likes to call the Firsts the Greta Garbo of cults. "Oh honey, that Prophet of yours, he just wants to be left alone."

As I left the asphalt, the van began to rattle. Elektra sat up and growled. No matter how slowly you drive, the road kicks up a cloud of red dust that can be seen from almost anywhere in town. The journalists who sometimes snoop around don't realize it alerts the Prophet's militia. I'm totally serious. You'll see.

About halfway up the road I passed a pickup headed out. Five wives squeezed into the cab, four across and one perched awkwardly in a lap. They were older, probably barren, which was why the Prophet would let them leave town like this. He never lets the girls out, but women like these, he didn't care. They stared ahead, their eyes vacant. They looked familiar. It was perfectly possible they were my aunts, cousins, or half-sisters, or all three. Elektra shoved her head out the window to bark at them. The women remained expressionless. It was as if they didn't see me and we were passing in two parallel worlds.

A couple of miles up the road you see the first houses. Eight, ten, twelve thousand square feet. Often two or three side by side in a compound. They're not mansions, more like barracks or barns, built cheaply from plywood, plastic sheeting, tar paper, aluminum, and sheetrock. Many are unfinished—an exposed side wall, a wing with a plastic roof, a front door made from pressed wood. When I was a kid my dad told me he couldn't afford proper siding for our house. That made me feel sad for him—I sensed the shame in his voice. But that wasn't the reason. It was to avoid property taxes. Some loophole I never understood.

One thing was different since I left: a lot of houses were now surrounded by walls. Or instead of a wall, a ring of trailers, circled like pioneer wagons. I guess the Prophet was getting paranoid. Of what, exactly? It's not like the government hasn't had a hundred years to shut this place down.

I turned on Field Avenue and halfway down there it was, our place— three houses and a couple of outbuildings on five acres of useless scrubby land. From the street it looked like nothing had changed. The dozen picnic tables where the kids ate except on the coldest days. The laundry lines with fifty little shirts flapping in the wind. The vegetable garden, the barnyard, the cornfield—all of it parched and pathetic. The property backed up to scrub and when I was little that's where I'd hide when I was afraid of my dad—of what he might do. The main house was a large rectangle of plywood stained dark green. Twenty bedrooms, a vast kitchen with pots the size of oil drums, and my dad's basement. The kids weren't allowed down there, just the wives, one after the next, each getting her piece. You know what's weird? A week earlier and he would've been down there right now, doing who knows what nasty shit online.

Here's something: I have no idea how many brothers and sisters I have. There isn't a good way to count. There's full, half, step, and foster. Who goes into the tally and who doesn't? I'd like to tell you I loved each of my siblings, but that's pretty much impossible. And what about the ones you've never met—the children a sister wife left behind somewhere to marry your dad? Do you count them? Oh, and your sister who's now married and no longer allowed to talk to you because you're a guy and she's a girl and around here brothers and sisters do it all the time? Do you count her? And what about me—I've been gone six years, the Prophet told everyone I was banished to the bleak pits of damnation. Do they count me? I wouldn't. I'm going to guess I have a hundred siblings, maybe one-ten. That's about as accurate as I can be. My dad used to say he never went to bed at night without thanking God for his children. And the crazy part is: I believed him. Every word.

Mind if I tell you some more? We slept in triple-decker bunks; or five to a bed, head to foot; or on the couch, four boys elbowing over three cushions; or on the living room floor, on blankets and pillows, twenty kids laid down like tiles. Shirts and sweaters in plastic garbage bins labeled by size. Shoes handed down. Tennis balls and kickballs stolen from one kid to the next. The only thing in that house that was all my own, that I never had to share with anyone, was a drawer in a dresser, twelve inches wide by fifteen inches deep. I measured it a million times. If you're bad at math, that's 1.25 square feet, which was really more than I needed because I didn't have anything to keep inside.

Saturdays were washing days: a pair of sister wives would fill a zinc tub with cold water, throw two boys in at a time, scrub their backsides with a brush on a stick, then fling them out. They changed the water every tenth boy. It would take all morning. But at least I wasn't a girl. The girls used the bathroom according to a schedule that kept the plumbing on this side of chaos. On Saturdays they washed their hair in special sinks. The Prophet didn't let them cut it, he said they'd need it when they got to heaven to wash their husbands' feet. Some of the girls got nosebleeds from the weight of all that hair. A few complained about it hurting their backs or getting headaches, but most said nothing, at least not to me. When the girls washed their hair it sounded like a mop in a bucket. You can imagine the clogs in the drain. It took hours to dry—they'd lie on the picnic tables and spread their hair out around them. I loved to watch them from the window in my mom's room. The girls looked beautiful like that, their clean hair fanned out like angels' wings.

Roland once asked if there was anything good about growing up in Mesadale, if I had one fond memory among all the bad. "One thing's for sure," I said. "You're never alone."

I stood outside the house, looking up at my mom's window. A roller shade was drawn halfway but I could see the aloe plant she grew on the sill. She used to break open its leaves and massage the clear liquid into her hands and throat. Sometimes I'd sit on her bed and watch her while I told her about school. Sometimes she'd squeeze a drop from the broken leaf into my palm and I'd stay with her until it had dried.

I saw someone in my mom's window, a dark shape pulling down the shade. They were all in the house, everyone, my brothers and sisters and all the wives, but I guess no one was coming out to say hello. Then Virginia shot out from the barn, running right for me and rolling over at my feet. She was thin and hot under her thick coat. A belly rub was all it took to make her love me.

That's when someone said, "What do you want?"

I looked up. It was Sister Rita. "I don't know if you remember me."

"I remember you. You shouldn't be here."

To be perfectly honest, Rita was never one of my favorites. She used her position as first wife to boss everyone around. You can't marry a new wife without the first wife's permission. So every time my dad wanted a fresh bride he went groveling back to Rita. I don't even want to think about what he had to do to get her to say yes.

"I'd like to see my mom's room."

"No."

"Please. Just for a few minutes."

"No. God sent you away. The Prophet revealed it. I can't go against his will."

I know it's hard to believe people really talk like that, but consider this: if you didn't know anything else, if your only source of information was the Prophet, if you spent seven hours in church on Sunday listening to a man who claimed to have a direct line to God, who your father and mother swore was a Prophet, and your brothers and sisters, and your teachers, and your friends, and everyone else assured you, promised you, his word was the word of God, and those that he damned were damned for all of eternity, you'd probably believe it too. You wouldn't know how to form a doubt. The Prophet told us all sorts of shit and we believed it, all of it, just ate it up.

Like once he told us that Europe had been destroyed in a battle of good and evil. He said it didn't exist anymore. France—no longer on the map. He described the fires of Paris, the bodies in the Seine, the cathedrals reduced to rubble, the wolves that had returned to the Champs-Élysées. I had no reason—no ability—to doubt any of it. Everyone around me said it was true. We didn't have tv, there was no internet when I was a kid, everything we knew came from the Prophet. The first time I met a Frenchman in Vegas, I was shocked. I actually said, "How did you survive?" That's the level of brainwashing I'm talking about. When I first told Roland all this, he said, "Oh honey, you've *got* to be kidding? You should go on *Oprah* or something." But I'm not kidding.

"I'm sorry about my dad," I said. "I'm sure this is really difficult for you."

"Go on, the Prophet doesn't want you here. You're scaring the kids. Turn around and go." The windows had started to fill with faces, eight or ten coming to look down at the stranger in the yard. Did any recognize me? Did any wonder how I fit into all the lies? I imagined one child, at least one, whispering, *Take me with you.* I imagined a tiny finger tapping on the glass.

Rita was now standing before me. I could smell the summer peaches on her breath. I'll try to be nice, but let's just say she was the complete opposite of sexy in her prairie dress and drooping hair bun. The sun had puckered her skin into a gray hide and the grim line of her mouth suggested she hadn't had a good laugh, or fuck, in fifty years.

"Jordan, my duty is to protect them. You know that. Now please go."

"Protect them from what?"

"Please. Before I have to call the police." And then, "I'm sorry."

The Mesadale police. You don't want to run into them. I said good-bye to Rita and Virginia and walked back to the van. Before I got in I looked back to the house. There were two kids in every window now, noses fogging the glass. As I drove down Field Avenue I thought about them. Who were they? Did even Rita know their names? I started thinking about the fate of my siblings: Jamie would be eighteen now, so probably kicked out. Charlotte would be seventeen, most likely married. And Queenie—she'd be twenty. No chance she still lived in the house. It was just a matter of how many sister wives she had by now. And the younger kids? I never got close to them. They were mostly anonymous to me— dozens of girls and boys I passed in the hall, all of them blond and freckled and thin. When you're one of a hundred, you look up to the older kids because they might offer a bit of love, and you hate the younger kids for taking up room.

I got so lost thinking through the parade of nameless children I didn't notice the police cruiser tailing me. Suddenly he was in my rearview mirror, dark glasses on top of an eat-you-alive grin. His left palm was flat on the steering wheel, his right arm draped across the seat back. I turned down a side street and he followed. I turned again and he turned too. We passed three women working in a small barnyard. They looked up, hoes in hand, their faces washed in sunshine.

I wanted to visit the post office but it no longer seemed like a good idea. Out here the police are the bad guys. Every member of the Mesadale Police Department is a polygamist. Once one of my stepsisters walked into the police station and said my dad was cuddling her. (Out here, if your dad says he wants to cuddle, get ready to be raped.) The cop at the front desk took some notes, then called my dad. "I'd watch out for this one," he said. "She came in here hot as a nymph." He drove her home and my dad took her down to his basement for an hour. I remember waiting for her to come back upstairs. When she did she had a hollow look to her, like her eyes had been replaced with glass.

People say, *Oh come on, it can't be that bad.*

Actually, it's worse.

People say, *Why don't the authorities step in and do something?*

I don't know, ask them. But there are a few theories floating around. Some people say the Mormons, who more or less own Utah, are embarrassed by the Firsts because of our connected past. They prefer us tucked away in the desert, where no one can see us. I guess they're still touchy when it comes to polygamy. Others say the Mormons secretly want to return to polygamy one day, so they let it slide. I don't know about that one. Another theory: some say it's a case of religious freedom—you know, people have a right to believe what they want and the authorities need to be careful about trampling on that. Maybe. Then I've heard a really good one: it's actually hard to prove polygamy in court. Think about it: it's not illegal for a man and a bunch of women to live together. And if the state doesn't recognize the marriages, how can they be breaking the law?

I have my own theory about why all this has gone down in Mesadale for so long: no one cares. They don't give a fuck about a bunch of interbreeders fifty miles from the nearest cell tower. It's funny, they call us the lost boys when we get kicked out, but really, we were lost the day we were born. When I lived out there I often wondered if anyone other than my mom knew I was alive.

I turned back to the highway. The cruiser stayed behind me just enough to avoid my wake of dust. He escorted me all the way, descending the gradual hill, kicking up his own red cloud. At one point he picked up his radio to call something in. If this were a cop movie, the camera'd cut to the interior of his cruiser. But this wasn't a cop movie, and I can't tell you what he was radioing. *All clear? He's gone? It's him?*

I reached the highway and the van stopped rattling. Behind me, the cruiser idled at the asphalt's bank as if it were a river too deep to enter.

The cop watched me drive off, making sure I was gone. In my rearview he grew smaller and smaller, then made a three-point turn and drove back up the long road into town. At the end of the day he'd file a report, lock up his firearm, and head home to a macaroni supper with his dozen lonesome wives.

III

EARLY HISTORY

THE 19TH WIFE

CHAPTER ONE
The Convert

Among the many questions I have encountered since my apostasy from the Mormon Church, none arises with more confusion, or mystification, than as to why I ever joined the Latter-day Saints. The American public recognizes the Mormon Missionary devoutly traveling the road, the young man knocking upon well-locked doors, toiling through sun and snow to spread his word. Many people, I now understand, mistake me for the Missionary's recent convert and wonder why a woman of reason would succumb to such persuasions. Once, at a lecture in Denver, a minister's wife scolded me, "That's where you went wrong, Mrs. Young! You should never have let those Missionaries through your door!"

In fact, I was born a Mormon, the daughter of early converts, two devout Saints who reared me on the Book of Mormon and the epic story of the birth of that faith—just as another pair might raise their daughter on the grand stories of the Old Testament. I knew of the angel Moroni before Gabriel; the first and second Books of Nephi before the Gospel of John. As a small child I joined the Saints' exodus from Nauvoo into Zion, and always understood it to be as miraculous as the Israelites' brave flight from Egypt.

Even so, the curious public, long wary of the roaming Missionary, often doubts the origins of my parents' faith, and thus my own. This bewilderment, and a general skepticism over sudden religious conversion, makes it necessary for me to describe my mother's entry into the Church, and that of my father, too, and how together they first encountered the doctrine of celestial marriage, or polygamy.

My mother was born Elizabeth Churchill in 1817 in Cayuga County, New York; and for the sake of this narrative I shall call her by her given name. When she was four, her mother, a Methodist of wavering conviction, died of cholera. At the time they lived in a one-room cottage of no distinction, the only decoration being a St. Louis fiddle pegged to the wall. The seizures came around midnight. Elizabeth's mother sat up in bed, cried out once, "My Lord!" and twenty hours later she was dead. Although only four, Elizabeth understood that when her mother had asked for God's mercy, it failed to come.

Her father, a penniless son of the Enlightenment, a musician by training, and a Doubting Thomas by temperament, found himself incapable of caring for his daughter. Two days after her mother's death, he deposited Elizabeth behind the iron gate of a house belonging to Mr. and Mrs. Brown, a childless, indifferent couple who took her in as their barn girl. Elizabeth's father promised he would return for her as soon as he could. She clung to that promise until she was sixteen.

Twelve years later Elizabeth left the Browns with a firm but inexplicable desire to travel to St. Louis. She could not articulate the impulse. True, it was the only city she recalled her father speaking of. Yet she was not so naïve to believe she would find him there. I will venture to say her desire was like that of the pilgrim—he does not expect to find Jesus in the orchards of Gethsemane, but even so he longs to visit Jerusalem.

Having made it as far as Pittsburgh by the grace of a family traveling west, Elizabeth resorted to the sole possession of a young woman with an empty purse. A passenger agent wrote her a ticket for voyage down the Ohio in exchange for an interlude in his booth, the shade drawn. The agent was a gentle man with a chin dimpled like the bottom of a pear. Afterward, he drew up a ticket to St. Louis just as he had promised. The two parted, as clerk and customer part at the end of an exchange.

The following winter in St. Louis, Elizabeth gave birth in the Catholic women's home to a baby with a chin imprinted like the bottom of an unripe piece of fruit. "The Sisters and I will bring him into the arms of God," declared the nurse-maid. This had been Elizabeth's intention as well, but once she held tiny, red Gilbert she could not bear to leave him. The next day she tied her bonnet's pearl ribbon beneath her chin and stepped into the streets of St. Louis with her baby babbling in her arms. She was all of seventeen.

I will not be the first to report there is little work for a girl in such a situation. Elizabeth was quick to recognize her only option. She accepted a position with Mrs. Harmony in her mansarded mansion with an ebony piano in the parlor. Her role could best be described as Girl No. 8.

This is how Elizabeth came to meet Captain Zucker, a trim Slav who wore his ginger mustache waxed to a point. Quickly he adopted her as his favorite among Mrs. Harmony's harem, visiting her *salle* each time his paddle-wheel, the *Lucy*, called in St. Louis. Eventually he proposed, "Elizabeth, my beauty, why don't you quit this by-the-dozen work and come live with me?" She moved out of Mrs. Harmony's house that day. Captain Zucker established Elizabeth and Gilbert in a cabin aboard the *Lucy* with walls flocked in velvet and a palm standing alert in a Cantonese urn. She had never known such luxury.

On the ship Elizabeth encountered a new kind of dignity. The sailors removed their caps when she passed, as if she were the mistress of the vessel, and the musicians liked to show Gilbert their shiny horns. For his part, every day Captain Zucker gave Gilbert a new toy—cloth balls, jack-straws, and a quoits set with a bright red hob. Captain Zucker spoiled Elizabeth with expensive gifts, including a pair of half-boots of Turkish satin and a parasol trimmed in peony, which she has since bequeathed to me.

The lone exception to this kindness emanated from the Reverend Rice, the *Lucy*'s man of cloth. He was a Baptist of a variety I am not familiar with and cannot say for certain still exists. The only greeting he could muster was a curt "Madame." He refused to acknowledge Gilbert, declining Captain Zucker's invitation to baptize him. "That damn Reverend wouldn't know God from a flea," the Captain would say. He often talked about expelling the Reverend from his ship but never summoned the courage. It left Elizabeth discouraged in many ways, but most especially in God—a distressing feeling for a young woman inclined to believe.

Eventually Captain Zucker paid Reverend Rice a large enough tithing that he agreed to baptize Gilbert. The Sunday before the rite—this was July 1834—they were upriver in Hannibal, Missouri. Captain Zucker sent Elizabeth into town to purchase embroidering cotton for Gilbert's gown and four buttons at a store with a sheepdog guarding its door. With her purchases and Gilbert in her arms, Elizabeth stepped over the dog into the sunlight, touched by an unfamiliar, open joy.

The *Lucy* was not sailing until nightfall. Curious about this stretch of the Mississippi, Elizabeth followed a path to the flatland between the cliffs and the river. The summer grass was damp and warm, and the sun was hot on the baby's brow. She walked about a quarter of a mile when she came across a crowd of twenty or twenty-five gathered in the shade of a buttonwood tree. A man of about thirty was speaking from atop a shipping crate, projecting as if two hundred were in his audience, or two thousand. Before this, many times Elizabeth had encountered a man calling out from atop a box, for at this time in our national history, prophet-preachers roamed the backwoods like bears. But this man, she has said a thousand times since, was unlike any of them. "All of you," he said. "Please come closer. I have a story to tell."

What first struck Elizabeth was the quality of the man's

voice—the hand-bell clarity and the force it achieved without the spectacle of bulging eyes and throbbing throat. "You won't believe what I tell you, not because you lack wits, or knowledge, but because it is not easy to believe. But if you can believe this tale, you will know the truth of all things, and your presence in the life after this one will be secure."

In those days few had heard of Joseph Smith or his Church of Latter-day Saints, which was four years old at the time. To Elizabeth, and the others gathered, he was a stranger without reputation or institution. His only tools for persuasion were his person and his fantastical tale of God's plan for man. Yet I must note the manner in which Joseph appeared atop the shipping crate that afternoon. He was a good head taller than most men and carried himself like a general or other such commander of a large force. I sometimes wonder if he shared the same physique as General George Washington—they were both taller than six feet, I understand, and strongly built. I often think he had the face a sculptor would use when cutting statues of the Great Men.

"I'm a farmer's son," Joseph began. "Originally from Vermont, but we settled in Palmyra—Palmyra, New York. If any of you have been there you'll know it as a bustling town of four thousand, surrounded by peaceful country, with many farms and brooks, and in the distance the gentle rolling drumlins and other hills. Yet in my youth, and even today, there was little peace in our village. There, at the crossroads, where almost every day I passed, four churches stood off in competition, each claiming to offer the true interpretation of God's will. I was an average boy in many ways, certainly of no higher intelligence than most, and my physical appearance, well, I'll leave it to you to judge my form. There was no reason to think that I, Joseph Smith, Junior—heir to a hundred acres and a stand of sugar-maples, and a cake-shop where my mother sold gingerbread and beer—that such a common lad would one day become a Prophet of God.

"But I was a curious boy, doubtful with many questions,

most especially—which Church, among the many competing voices, was best for me? Should I become a Catholic, a Baptist, a Methodist, a Shaker, an Episcopal? Was there another sect I was yet to know? Although only fourteen, I had enough of a logical mind to understand that when ten preachers claim to be the rightful interpreter of God, at least nine may be in the wrong.

"Torn by this question, and eager for an answer as only a young man can be, one fine day—it was early spring—I walked into the woodland and fell to my knees. I asked the Heavenly Father to lead me to the door of His preferred Church, for I wanted to worship rightly. The day was clear, and the sun had flooded the woods in its light, and the new, feathery leaves atop the trees were burnished like flakes of gold. For some time I prayed, searching for my answer, when to my great astonishment—and fear! for above all I was afraid—a glorious light, unlike anything I had ever seen, appeared before me. At first I thought it must be the light of the day coming through the trees. But it was not a beam of light but a shell, and inside this shell of light were two people, I saw, two men, Father and Son.

"Now, Friends, I know what you're thinking—I can see it in your eyes! You're saying to yourself, Pshaw! This is where the man's tale becomes fantasy. I can see such thoughts flickering—there!—across your brows. You don't believe me, but that's fine, you're experiencing the same questions I did on that day. For surely what was before me was not before me. Surely I was imagining it, or the sunlight was playing a trick! I was prepared to believe any explanation but the most plain—which was, as it always is, the Truth. Father and Son, God and Christ, had descended from Heaven to bring a message. They said, Do not join any Church, for none is the true Church of God. Since the time of Christ, the men who claim to be His rightful interpreters—the Apostles, the priests, the Popes, the ministers, the reverends, the fathers, all of them, and each—these men have led the world away from the true words and deeds of Jesus Christ. Joseph, they said, you are living in an era of Great Apostasy. Man on Earth has wandered from the Truth. But the time has come for its Restoration, and you will be its messenger.

"With this news, the Heavenly Father and His Son departed, leaving me prone in the mud. Now, what does a boy do with such news? How did I react upon learning I was to be a Prophet? Friends, I assure you I did my best to ignore all that I had heard and seen. You see, I was like yourself here today—my inclination was to disbelieve all that I could not understand. Yet ponder that, will you? If you cannot understand something, does that mean it is not true? Who here speaks French? Or Russian? None of you. Yet, were a man to say the sky is blue and the sun is hot in Russian or French, would that mean his words are not true?

"Three years passed. I was now seventeen. I still pondered the question that had originally taken me into the woods, but I had acted not at all on the knowledge God had provided me. Then one night—it was eleven years ago this September—a second miracle occurred. In my room an angel by the name of Moroni appeared at my bedside. He told me, as I'm here telling you now, that buried in a hill outside Palmyra was a set of golden plates. Yes, plates, and on them was a book written in an ancient language. This angel told me one day I would go to this hill and find the plates in a stone box. It was my duty, the angel said, to deliver this book to Man.

"What did I do? What would you have done? Yes, I think I know. Again, I did not believe it; or I did not want to believe it. Although I knew I had seen this angel, and talked with him, and knew the angel as something real, I did not want to believe the Truth: that I was a Prophet, here to communicate to all of Man. I waited. And a year later the angel returned with the same message. And so it passed each year for four years, until my time had come to dig up the golden plates. With my beloved wife Emma, I journeyed to the Hill

Cumorah and dug in the spot as the angel had described it. There, in a stone box, were the golden plates, along with a tool for translating, which looked much like a large pair of spectacles. If any doubt remained in my heart, it was now driven off by the fact of these items. I held them. I knew they existed, as I know now that you exist, and as you know, or at least I hope, that I exist. Carefully I brought the plates home and began the task of translating them, transcribing this miraculous book so all could read it. And here it is, the Book of Mormon, named such because it was brought to you and me by Mormon's son, the angel Moroni. Here it is. Here it is." Joseph lifted his personal copy to his heart and closed his eyes.

Now might be a good time to point out a singular truth of all Prophets, from Jesus through Muhammid to Joseph Smith. They do not come in unappealing form. A Prophet usually possesses beauty, in his heart, of course, but in his physical being as well. His refined features and powerful stature are among his most potent natural gifts. To deny this is to deny the truth of the Human and how We, both man and woman, function. I intend not to belittle the Prophet's achievements nor the import of his message. Yet ask yourself, Dear Reader—Would you stand in a hot field for hours with flies buzzing about your head to listen to a man with a disagreeable presence? Although this fact hints at Man's animal nature, it is the truth and therefore worth recording. There, I have said enough on this particular subject.

"When I go forth," Joseph continued before the crowd beneath the buttonwood tree, "and spread the news of this new Gospel, often I am asked, Brother Joseph, what is your message? Indeed, what is my message? What is the message of our new Church? What have the other men forgotten, and what am I here to restore? Friends, my message is clear, for it came to me from our God. We are here, all of us, we are here on Earth for but one reason, and that is to love. What was Christ's message? To love. The Truth is simple, as it always is.

I am here to restore that message to all of Man while we live through these last days.

"Now if you do not believe my story, nor have any interest in reading this Book, then peace to you, my Friend, for I wish you no ill. But take one thing from our meeting today. Take my love and share it with all that you meet for the rest of your time."

Joseph jumped down to greet the assembled, and there was much fuss made over him, people reaching to touch his coat. Enraptured, Elizabeth asked one of his companions for a copy of the miraculous book. She spent Captain Zucker's money on it. When at last Joseph made his way to her he said, "Tell me, Sister, where are you going?"

"Up the river and down."

"No final destination?"

"I live on a paddle-wheel."

"Then why not come with us? We've been to Independence defending our brothers. Now it's time to go home to Kirtland. It's a long walk to Ohio, but I promise you'll find a kind people there."

"And my son?"

"If you join us, I promise you both will be loved."

At the time, of course, Elizabeth could not know she had met Joseph and his Zion's Camp in retreat from their failed attempt to establish a new Zion in Missouri. Joseph, Brigham, Heber Kimball, and the other Apostles had been recently tested by a growing enemy. They lost fourteen men along the way to cholera, but their faith had strengthened in their long march home. On that damp day in July Elizabeth had followed a path through the summer grass and come upon a moment in History. Dear Reader, consider it! A stranger beneath a buttonwood tree promising love! Imagine the power this has over the lonely heart!

Elizabeth never returned to the *Lucy*. Joseph introduced her to Brigham Young, my future husband, who at the time was a humble carpenter from Vermont and only thirty-three. "This woman is joining us," Joseph said. "Look after her and her child." Brother Brigham followed these orders, never letting Elizabeth and Gilbert out of sight for the six-hundred-mile walk to Kirtland. We know Brigham now as Joseph's successor, a man of wealth and power, but then he was a woodworker, a glazier, a furniture maker. One could see his trade in his scuffed hands.

Brigham carried Gilbert for much of the journey and revealed himself to be a friend to my mother. The next day they stopped at a creek. He set Gilbert upon a bed of leaves, then guided Elizabeth into the water, across the mossy stones, until the current reached her breast. He gently pushed her head beneath the surface and blessed her. When she emerged she was a Latter-day Saint, and would always be.

After many weeks of walking they passed through a dark wood that opened onto a hilly clearing beside a river. Here the Saints' new city of Kirtland, Ohio, gleamed. Brigham gave Elizabeth a room in the small house he shared with his new bride, Mary Ann Angell, a recent convert from New York. "Gather yourself and rest," he said. "You are tired and your boy needs sleep. My wife will give you land where you can grow some cabbage. She'll invite you into her kitchen to bake bread. Her barn is your barn, and you may feed our pig, and when the time comes part of that pig will be yours. These are your duties now. Only when you are settled should you turn your mind to spiritual devotion. Now you must simply live."

On her first morning in Kirtland, Elizabeth set out to see the busy milling town. With Gilbert in her arms she went down to the bank of the Chagrin. While watching the river's quick current, and pondering the movement of her life, and seeing an imprint of her fate in the rippled water, a faraway voice cawed in her ear: "Must be the whore."

"I heard they picked her up in a Missouri brothel," a second voice hissed.

"Makes you wonder what they were doing there."

"And to think she brought her bastard here."

Elizabeth looked upriver. Far off two young women stood upon a fishing dock. Their voices had traveled down with the current, farther than they would have ever thought possible. Elizabeth pulled the bonnet over Gilbert's head and returned to Brigham's house. She never said a thing.

The next day at Sunday Services, following Joseph's sermon, Brigham rose to bear testimony. He paused, his throat darkening. "Before word of the Restoration came to Brother Joseph," he began, "and we knew of its Glory, we were destitute and depraved. Now, through His love and wisdom, we know we live in these latter days, these days leading up to Judgment and Redemption. We await them with our hearts full." Brigham looked to the collected souls cramped in a neighbor's parlor, some on the floor, many along the wall, others standing outside leaning through the open windows. "But if anyone here, or anywhere, believes himself, or herself, to be no less destitute or depraved than we were before our knowledge, if anyone here, or anywhere, believes he has already achieved Salvation, I ask him, or I ask her, to come forth now, and show yourself. If any of you think yourself purer, fairer, or closer to the foot of God than the rest of us, show yourself now, for I should like to know you. If any of you, because you come from a proud family, or your husband earns a fine income, or you possess a fine complexion and a multitude of bonnets, believes you are of a better kind than any of the rest of us, then step forward now and show yourself, for we all should like to know you. But beware, for although you may think yourself as such, He shall be the judge of all things and will not withhold His judgment. Who here thinks himself better than the rest? . . . Anyone? . . . No one at all? . . . I did not think so. Now go forth and prove to Him you are His Latter-day Saints."

After the services, the women of Kirtland overwhelmed my mother with gifts, clothing, cooking pans, jars of preserves. A widow named Graeve offered a permanent room. A drive was called for cotton, toys, seeds, and a vegetable plot. New friends invited Elizabeth for supper, others for singing. Sisters brought their babies to see Gilbert and everyone kissed his head when they met him on the street. Never again did someone speak cruelly of her past. The Saints knew of it, and understood it. They never pitied her, never shamed her, never again questioned her place.

So it was, through love and kindness, Brigham joined Joseph Smith in welcoming Elizabeth Churchill as his newest Saint; and so she was when soon thereafter she met another fresh convert, a blacksmith from New York, the man who would become my father, Chauncey Webb.

IV

THE ORIGINS
OF LOVE

LDS CHURCH ARCHIVES
SPECIAL COLLECTIONS
Pioneer Biographies & Autobiographies
Salt Lake City

Access to the Special Collections is restricted to Latter-day Saints in possession of a current temple recommend. Those unable to visit the Collections themselves may send a relative or friend on their behalf, provided he or she has a temple recommend. You may also engage an ancestral researcher or scholar, provided that he or she also has a temple recommend.

Updated by Deb Savidhoffer, Church Archivist, 9/3/2004

THE AUTOBIOGRAPHY
OF CHAUNCEY G. WEBB

———

PART I

Since the publication of *The 19th Wife* last year, I have been left with many questions about the nature of my life. In my daughter's book, she recounts a version of our family history in which I do not—in fact cannot—recognize myself. According to Ann Eliza, I have become a ghost of a man, my corporeal presence consumed by my many wives. In those pages, now read by hundreds of thousands across this land, she calls me "a man who wanders about the desert without soul"—a charge I find painful to read even now. With her words cold upon my heart, I have come to believe it would serve some purpose—whether personal or historical I cannot say—if I were to set down in my own words the story of how I came to be a Saint and marry five wives. In her Preface Ann Eliza writes, "I leave judgment to the hearts of my good Readers everywhere." Yet in truth, only two can judge a man: himself and God.

My mother first heard Brigham preach in 1833, while he proselytized in our village of Hanover, N.Y. She attended a meeting on a September afternoon and returned home agitated by religious fervor. "I'll be departing with Brother Brigham in the morning," she announced. "I have but a few years left on this Earth. I want to spend them with one who loves me." Underestimating the power of the new Gospel, at first I scoffed at her sudden conversion, yet the next day she left with Brigham to join Joseph in Kirtland,

O.H. I was twenty-one and for the first time in my life I found myself alone.

I was an apprentice in a blacksmith's shop then, with a bright future as a wheelwright, and I spent those lonely days, and often my nights, toiling before my forge. Often I think back on this time—more than forty years ago—and I ponder my future wife, Elizabeth, and her ordeals. About the same time my mother left me, Elizabeth was making her way through the streets of St. Louis, expecting a child. Of course I could not know this at the time; I could not even imagine such a woman. Yet in my musings about the past, I like to think each of us had set down on a path to find one another. Now I shall describe the road I chose.

Although I was still an apprentice to Mr. Fletcher, men came to me by name to repair their carriage wheels, for the reputation of my work had traveled as far as Buffalo. Although I had very little money, it was clear to me, especially now with my mother departed, that with hard work and good fortune, and the blessing of that mysterious being known as God, I might one day become a wealthy man.

I must admit—for my hope in recounting my long journey into polygamy is to reveal the truth, if only to myself—that I was not altogether sad when my mother left for Kirtland. Since the tragic and early death of my father, her great effort in life had been to preserve the dignity and grandeur of her widowhood. She wore her voluminous mourning gown the day she met Brigham; for Kirtland, she packed a small trunk containing blackcloth and somber lace. Tending to her had become a burden of minor proportions, for I was a young man in pursuit of those items which young men are known to pursue. There were many evenings I would have preferred to stay at the forge, with my apron heavy around my neck and the fire warm in my face, than return home for a silent supper of winter stew, followed by the long hours providing her wordless company while she worked her sewing hoop.

This, therefore, is why no one found greater surprise than I

in the depths of my loneliness after my mother's departure—
or the heights of my elation when her first letter arrived two
months later. "My good son—I have settled in Kirtland," she
wrote. "The Prophet Joseph Smith baptized me in our river,
the Chagrin. Do not scorn your mother. I am an old woman.
I was afraid of death until I met the Latter-day Saints. They
have promised me Glory in the Afterlife. I still hope to meet
you there."

I responded to her letter, declaring the emptiness of my
evenings and my general longing to see her again. She replied
that if I were to accept Joseph Smith as a Prophet, I should
come to Kirtland and be near her.

I was not yet prepared to do so. I knew very little about this
new Church except what my mother had relayed and the
gossip already surrounding it. Even then there were rumors of
unusual marriage customs. I wrote my mother, asking her to
explain why I should devote myself to a man who was no
more than any other man. "You do not know him," she
replied. "Although he is a man, he is the man on Earth chosen
by God." With each letter my mother's fanaticism expanded
until she wrote freely describing angels and divine revelations
and the miraculous golden plates. The letters confirmed that
I could not abandon my future in Hanover for a small city in
the Ohio swampland run by a man who promised that which
only the Lord Himself can deliver.

Then my mother wrote with a different sort of news:
"Kirtland is growing by the day. Newly converted Saints from
New York and Pennsylvania and even Vermont, New
Hampshire, and Maine, add to our census weekly. With each
passing month, the City expands into the forest. Any man
with an axe can make a fine living clearing the woods. Here,
in this growing Metropolis, one must think of Rome at her
birth to imagine it properly. There is an urgent need for a
second blacksmith and wheelwright. I told the Prophet my
son is the best in Chautauqua County. He has invited you,
my dear son Chauncey. The Prophet has invited you."

Not long after this, Mr. Fletcher came to see me at my station. He explained that his business was suffering—which I knew it was not—and told me he would have to cut my take on each wheel I repaired. I complained, knowing my work brought him his most profits, but he dismissed my outrage. "Your wheels are no better than the rest," he said.

With that, I hung my apron on its peg and left Mr. Fletcher's service for good. He expected me back in the morning, I am sure, but by then I was on my way to Kirtland, tying my fortune forever to the Latter-day Saints. The coincidence between the arrival of my mother's letter and Mr. Fletcher's duplicity has consumed many of my pondering hours over the years. Was it the hand of my beloved mother? Or the hand of God? Or is it possible one event can ensnare itself upon another, as a trip wire entraps the ankle, without reason, plan, or meaning? I cannot say.

The journey from New York to Ohio was relatively easy even back then. Wagons and carriages filled the road with travelers and journeymen— settlers and trappers and wandering preachers—yet none of these gave me as lasting an impression as the girl I met twenty miles beyond Erie while resting at a roadside inn. I supped in a small room lit by the hearth and, as I completed my meal, the innkeeper, a durable woman with full-blown gray-blue cheeks, asked if I needed anything more. "A bit of sweet? A hot-tot before bed? No? Then how about a nice girl?"

At once I understood the meaning of her offer. Rather than claim I resisted and voiced my offense, I must describe my reaction in honest terms. I was twenty-one years of age. I was eager to know a woman in such a manner. For most of my life I had assumed this would be my wife, but recently I came to realize that I might not have to wait until matrimony. In Hanover fear for my reputation kept me from visiting the brothel I knew existed above the printing shop. But on the road, in this dark forested limbo between my old home and my new, where nearly everyone I met seemed to be testing the pliability of Christian morals, I felt suddenly free of past and future restraint. "Mrs. Mack," I said, "who do you know?"

"I know a handful of right pretty ladies. How do you like 'em? Fat or thin? Dark or fair? The older ones know the best tricks, but the younger ones ain't got much in the way of fur. What will it be, Mr. Webb?"

I asked Mrs. Mack if she knew of a woman who was old enough to know her way through the activities she was proposing and yet not too old. "Right, you ain't looking for your mother, are you? Wait right here. Have yourself another whiskey. If you take the girl, the cup's on me." She scurried out the front door; her movement was low on the ground and slow but with enough agility that she reminded me, as the door closed behind her wide, hobbling rearside, of a gopher disappearing down its hole.

A quarter of an hour later she returned with a young woman. "This here's Jenetta. Pretty, isn't she? Originally from New York, ain't that right, dear? Came up this way to be near her gramps."

I bowed and the young woman said, with surprising boldness, "Which way's your room? I'll go up first to fix myself up."

This comment was so exotic—the notion of a woman working on herself, whatever that might mean, for me—that I could not speak and merely pointed to the stairs. Mrs. Mack said, "Second room at the top. Be fast, deary. God made you beautiful enough."

I sat for a bit, stunned, I believe, not only by Jenetta's beauty but by Mrs. Mack's frankness; I had never seen femininity in such full and assertive relief. Other than my mother, I realized, I knew few women except to nod hello on the streets of Hanover. Up until this point I believed that women came in but few varieties: the delicate virgin, the industrious wife, the declining widow, and of course the black-hearted whore. Certainly I had met others who fit into none of these categories, but the world presented them to me, or

76

perhaps more accurately, I saw them, in rather simple terms. In short, I was fast becoming overwhelmed by woman's great complexity.

When I entered my room, Jenetta stood at the mirror regarding herself. She wore a sort of sleeping gown that looked neither comfortable nor practical to sleep in. I asked if she wasn't cold. She wrapped her long, lovely arms around my neck and said, "I won't be." What ensued was of the usual sort for this kind of encounter, but I must note for these efforts that Jenetta led the way, initiating me to more pleasure than I had ever imagined possible on Earth. She stayed with me for the night, a cost that left my limited traveling funds worrisomely depleted, but I had decided everything in my earthly possession was worth making these joys last until the dawn. By sunrise I could not face saying goodbye, and proposed that she join me on my journey.

"To Ohio?" she laughed. "Oh critters, no. I got my husband right here with me."

"But Mrs. Mack said you lived with your gramps?"

"That's what I call my husband, he's so old. He'll be wanting his breakfast about now." She sprang from the bed, dressed, and departed as efficiently as she had arrived; and I buried my face into the pillow to inhale her sweet odor; and, I am afraid, to weep.

"Mrs. Mack," I wailed, "the most horrible and wonderful thing has happened. I have fallen in love. I must see Jenetta again."

"That's real nice, but I've heard it a thousand times before. Afraid you'll never find it again, but you will, I promise, you will. Now shouldn't you be on your way, Mr. Webb? Didn't you say your mother's waiting in Ohio? Thank you very much, dear, but get on, there you go, right now, good-bye!"

She swept me over her threshold into her garden and shut the door. I stood in the sunlight, desperate and confused.

Because I am an engineer and possess a mostly logical mind, and I like to believe I solve problems mostly through

77

analysis and rigor, eventually I talked myself into passing through Mrs. Mack's garden gate without once looking over my shoulder. Yet the head does not need to turn and the eyes need not gaze back for the heart to remain behind.

It was with such longing that I arrived in Kirtland. On that first night my mother served a feast of ham hocks followed by angel pie. "In the morning, I'll take you down to meet the Prophet and he'll get you work in one of the manufactories. Why didn't you eat all your pie? Go on, finish up. I baked it for you."

There is comfort in knowing that people remain the same.

As it turns out, my mother had overstated the case. Indeed there was opportunity for a wheelwright, but Joseph had invited dozens of men to meet the demand. I took a job in one of his wagon manufactories as a junior apprentice, earning less than I had in Hanover. "At least you're near me," my mother sighed in a great show of maternal care.

On Sundays, with little else to do, I accompanied her to services led by the Prophet, although I was still not a member of the Latter-day Saints. I remained skeptical, but Joseph had a presence unlike most men, with eyes wide and blue, and the stature of a man who knows his place in history. I did not have to attend more than one Sunday meeting to know the command he possessed over his followers. If he were not a Christian, he might very well have been a sorcerer—so capable of casting a spell he was.

"Look around!" he said one Sunday. "Look around and tell me what you see. Do you see gambling, drinking, swindling, the whoring that goes on throughout our country? Do you see the sin that walks down the street dressed as proud gentleman in top hat and dear sweet lady in her flimsy dress? Do you? Because that is not what I see. No, I see on those dirty streets those things that are missing—compassion, caring, love. When I look around I see neighbor ignoring neighbor, man snubbing wife, child abandoning parent. This is the Great Apostasy. For Christ taught us to love and so it has come to pass that He has returned in Revelation to restore love to our Earth. Such is the truth as I know it, as He has revealed it to me."

I had lived in Kirtland about four months when I came to accept that my future lay with Joseph and his Church. Despite my mother's high standing among the ladies who organized Kirtland society and its circles, I was merely a Gentile laborer. They would employ me as long as there was work that would otherwise go undone, but I could see a time in the future when there would be enough Saints to meet their wagonry needs. Joseph ruled Kirtland like a theocracy, and there was a firm strata of citizenship based on faith. The very best of the Gentiles were owed less than the very worst of the Saints. Thus my resistance to Joseph Smith's teachings began to erode. I respected his call to love; I responded more urgently to his call for able men.

It was about this time, on a late summer afternoon in 1834, at a picnic on the bank of the Chagrin, that I met Elizabeth. She was running in a woman's relay race with her leg tied to another girl's. The prize was a plaque engraved with the winner's name, the metalwork to be done by me. I stood at the end of the course, waiting for the winner to lean her breast triumphantly across the finishing ribbon, when I saw her for the first time. What struck me most was the difference between her and the women beside her. She appeared neither fair nor delicate, nor modest, nor full of wiles. The sun had tinged her complexion to the dark, delicious hue of an August peach. Her eyes were slow, cautious, and full of thought. I could see she was a young woman, yet she carried herself sturdily—her frame was forthright, solid, and full of honesty, and she seemed innocent of the many affectations and airs young women are known to produce and flaunt before a gathering of unmarried men. Elizabeth's simple blue dress opened at the collar, giving me a memorable glimpse of warm, red-pink flesh. My first opinion of her was such that I recognized her as a woman who knows her own heart. Then, and now, nothing could appeal to me more in a friend.

While I stared at her from across the field, Elizabeth was adjusting the rope that bound her leg to her partner—a plump, powdered girl sweating in the heat.

At the crack of the pistol Elizabeth and Martha began to run like a strange, hobbled animal, their eyes shining through the summer haze. When Elizabeth looked ahead to the finish line our eyes met—and it was then that I knew. Everyone was jumping up and down in excitement, but not I. I stood very still, observing her. Just then, the two young women ran ahead of the others, breaking through the finishing ribbon with such propulsion they fell into my arms. After unmooring the girls, I found myself alone at Elizabeth's side, unable to find any words. It was she who suggested we walk.

We strolled into a field beyond the picnic. Along the way I found the courage to squeeze her arm. I led her to a felled tree carved with initials, brushing away the dirt. I wished I had a large house to welcome her into, a drawing-room with a winged chair and extra bedrooms waiting to be filled; in time I knew I would—perhaps with her help. I told her so. As afternoon gave way to dusk, and the mosquitoes rose from the grass, I held her. As the blue evening fluttered down upon the field, I kissed her. I did not intend to kiss her a second time, but I lost my way. I would like to say it was the force of Christ and Joseph Smith that brought us together, or some other mysterious, celestial reason, but, to follow my established rule of honesty, nothing more noble than desire, and the early, vibrant shoots of love, pushed us into the grass. Lying atop her, my heart pounding in motion with hers, I knew we would marry; I knew this one would not abandon me in the morn.

We lay in the grass for some time. For a brief moment her

expression became unknowable; it was as if she had left me, her mind off and away. "Tell me your thoughts," I said.

"You know nothing of me."

I said to her, "You know nothing of me."

Then we talked about the future, as if what had preceded us need not matter; as if, through the compounding force of our union, we could determine all that lay ahead. We shared our dreams—a loving marriage, children, lots of children, a large framed house, and a family name that only rose in the community of Saints.

Elizabeth spoke of eternal salvation. She declared her love for Joseph Smith. As she spoke, the lantern of her face illuminated. "I've never loved anyone like Joseph. But there's something you must know." She recounted her life before conversion, her voice clear of shame. When she finished her tale she asked if it troubled me. "Really," I said, "your past is no different than mine."

"That's not true. For you the past is past. For me, my past is with me, in my son, Gilbert."

"I want to meet him." She set her cheek upon my breast, and I promised her I would love her child. "When can we marry?" I said.

"I'm afraid we can't."

I felt crushed, in the way Jenetta had crushed me. Desperately I asked why.

"You're not a Saint." For Elizabeth, it was a simple matter. Yet I would do anything to possess her. I wanted her for myself, every night, for the rest of my days. Forgive my effusion—if a man is honest, he will understand.

The next day Joseph baptized me at a bend in the Chagrin. As he held me beneath the current I cannot tell you that I felt something pass from him to me, as others have described it. They compare it to a bolt of lightning traveling through their frames—it is that sudden and powerful, a fury that can come only from God. For me, I felt nothing but the cold water and fingers of river grass upon my neck. That is all. The sensation was entirely of the Earth. In name, I was now a Saint. My motivations too were of the Earth—I wanted to marry; and I wanted to succeed. I believed in God and Christian goodness; of everything else I was less than sure. I am even less certain now, when I think back to all that has passed and the mistakes I have made. When I read again and again the outcome of my life, as my daughter has described it in *The 19th Wife*, I become unsure of almost everything—most especially of myself and my faith.

Joseph and I returned to the river bank wet and shivering. Awaiting me were my mother, whose life, I could not know then, was about to end, and Elizabeth, golden in the sunlight. We would marry the next day, and she would be my sole wife for a dozen years. Had I been told that day I would take another wife in the future, and others still, I would have sworn it not true. I would have insisted it was an impossible fate. Like most men, I believed my heart lay beyond corrosion and decay.

NOTA BENE

The Autobiography of Chauncey G. Webb, Part II, has been archived under restricted access in the Special Collections. For further information, please see a Church Archivist.

—Church Archives, January 16, 1940

V

═══

WIFE #19:

AN EYE IN THE DARK

IT ALL SOUNDS SO CHEESY NOW

———

"Officer Cunningham? It's me, Jordan Scott. Listen, I know the rules." I was driving back from Mesadale with Elektra in my lap. "But this is urgent. Any chance of seeing my mom? Like today?" The line went silent. Then, "You know the rules." I tried again and she turned me down. I went a different way, going on about not having a place to leave Elektra tomorrow. Officer Cunningham sighed, "Please don't do this to me." I apologized. Then I begged. Soon we both knew she was about to cave. "This is a onetime event, you understand?"

After leaving Elektra with the goth girl at the internet café, I passed through the jail's metal detector. Officer Cunningham didn't look pleased. "Let's not talk about this, all right?"

Ten minutes later Officer Kane was settling my mom onto the stool on the opposite side of the glass. We stared at each other for some time and it was like we were playing a game of who's going to go first. She picked up the receiver and said, "I feel like we ended on a bad note last time. I didn't know if you'd be back."

"Me neither."

"I was hoping we'd come to some sort of understanding."

"I went to see Mr. Heber." She stopped and through the glass she had the faded, frozen look of an old portrait in a frame.

I started to describe my meeting with Mr. Heber, but I hesitated when I got to the meat. "He said some pretty difficult things. About what might happen. You sure you want to hear this?" She nodded, and I asked again, just in case. "In a nutshell, it's not looking good. How should I put this? He thinks . . . you might . . . well, there's a chance—" But I chickened out. How do you tell your mom she will be executed?

"Jordan, you can tell me."

"You know what, he really should tell you all this." She urged me on. I resisted, but she kept asking, and no matter what, moms are pretty good at wearing down their kids. "It's just that there's a lot of evidence," I said. "I mean, a lot of facts, that, well, kinda indicate you did it."

She was looking into my eyes as only a mom can. "I see. You don't believe me."

"Mom, it's hard to know what's true. I mean, everything out there is so messed up."

"You have to believe me." This wasn't a plea, it was a statement.

I told her about my trip to Mesadale. "I went to the house," I said. "I saw Sister Rita."

"So you believe her over me?"

"She wouldn't really talk to me. I wanted to go up to your room, but she wouldn't let me in."

My mom set the receiver on the counter to say something to Officer Kane. She seemed agitated, her finger moving through the air to make some point. She picked up the receiver again. "Jordan, I only get three visits a week. You can't come back until Friday. We don't have a lot of time."

"I know," I said. "That's why I came today: to say good-bye. I'm going to have another meeting with Mr. Heber, help him with some basic info about Mesadale, then I'm headed back to California."

She stared at me calmly, her nostrils flickering. "Please don't go until I'm out of here."

"That could be a long time." I balled up my courage. "That might not happen. Ever."

For a long time she didn't say anything. Finally, "He thinks I'll be put to death, doesn't he?" The amazing thing was she seemed settled and certain, her eyes sharp and clear.

"Yes."

"And you're giving up."

"It's not like that."

"I guess you're right. You don't owe me anything."

"Mom, I just don't think I can help you."

"You should probably go."

"Mom, if there's something I can do, tell me."

"Please go."

"Is there anything else I can—"

She hung up. Officer Kane helped her from the stool. She looked at me once—Officer Kane, I mean. A face that said, She's your mother. They left, and I was on my own.

"Look who's back." Maureen was at her desk, typing. "We weren't expecting you till tomorrow."

"I need to see Mr. Heber."

"I'm afraid he's all booked this afternoon."

I wasn't going to wait. Elektra and I walked down the hall, right into Mr. Heber's office. He was on the phone, working on a legal document. "Uh, Jim, I'm going to have to call you back."

"I'm sorry, Mr. Heber," said Maureen. "I tried to stop him."

"I need to see you."

"Apparently. But first, calm down."

"I am calm, but this can't wait."

"All right, all right. Maureen, take some notes."

I unleashed Elektra and after a lot of coaxing got her to lie down. "I know this is going to sound crazy," I said, "but she didn't do it." Saying it out loud made it seem even more true.

"Tell me why you think that."

"It doesn't add up."

"How do you mean?"

"She still believes in all that stuff. The Prophet, the

church, polygamy as salvation, the whole thing. She wants to go back."

Mr. Heber removed his glasses to rub his eyes. "Is it possible she says she still believes in all that even though she doesn't?"

"Nope, absolutely not. It would give her an excuse. She didn't kill my dad."

"I'm still not with you."

"She had no reason to kill him. This is the crazy part: she actually liked her life."

"All right, let's go back to the basic evidence that led to her arrest. There's a chat session in which your dad says your mom just entered the room, which happens to be right before he was shot. We've got an eye-witness saying your mom came up from the basement around the time of his death. And we've got your mom's prints on the murder weapon. Right now I have no good explanations for any of those."

"Let's find them."

"I'm trying."

"Try harder."

"I need you to see this from my point of view. The way things stand it won't take a prosecutor much imagination to come up with a dozen hypothetical reasons why your mom would want to kill your dad."

"Hypotheticals don't matter. She didn't do it."

"We're a long way from proving that."

You know all that business about being on the same team? Suddenly it didn't feel that way. I had to ask myself why was this Mormon lawyer working for someone like my mom? His religion and my ex-religion have been at a standoff for more than a hundred years. "Why are you helping her?" I said. "Why'd you take this case?"

"I take lots of pro bono cases."

"But why hers?"

"Jordan, you want to tell me what's going on? You were here yesterday, and you and I were pretty much on the same page. Now you're doubting everything. Did something happen?"

"I went back to Mesadale—that's what happened. When you're there and see how screwed up it is, you realize nothing is what it seems."

"Jordan, settle down. I understand."

"You don't understand."

Mr. Heber snapped open a bottle of water. "Look, I don't blame you for being upset. I know you want something to happen right away, but that's really not the best thing for your mom."

"Then what is?"

"I don't like what's going on out there any more than you do. That guy, that phony Prophet, he's ruined a lot of lives, and along the way he's distorted my religion. And it's been going on for way too long. Jordan, things are changing. Almost every week there's another call to the FBI or the attorney general or the media about this. We need to let it play itself out. I don't want your mom to go on trial. I want the Prophet and his church to go on trial. So let's give it a little time, all right?"

"How much?"

"I'd like to stall this for several months, maybe a year."

"A year?"

"I know that sounds like a long time, but it isn't, not really. There's a lot of stuff going on that you and I don't know about. Rival factions, people running away, some challenges to the Prophet's authority. The Prophet's under a lot of pressure right now, both from the outside and within. Your mom's going to be a whole lot better off if she's part of that bigger story."

"I don't know who you're talking to, but I'm sorry, I was just in Mesadale and nothing's changed, it never has and it never will. Before the Prophet there was his father. And before him, his uncle. Con man after con man, for more than a hundred years, all the way back to 1890 and Aaron

89

fucking Webb." I stood up, tugged Elektra's leash, and we left.

Maureen followed us down the hall, quick on high-heel sandals.

"How do I get a new lawyer?" I said.

"Your mother has to request one."

"Fine, I'll tell her to."

"She'll end up with someone worse."

"Why doesn't he want to save her?"

"He wants to save her."

"Why isn't he outraged?"

"He wouldn't be a very good lawyer if he was always outraged."

I was so pissed I was about to start yelling, but then Maureen touched me, her fingers soft on my arm, and I lost it, just like a baby. Oh crap. The tears fell and they kept falling. "I don't know what to do."

She sat me down in the chair with a box of tissues. "Take your time." I kept saying I was sorry and she kept saying it was all right. She wrote her cell number on a sticky and folded it into my palm, just in case. Sensing a group hug, Elektra worked her way between us, shoving her nose into Maureen's crotch.

"Do you want to talk about it?" Maureen said.

I did, but I didn't.

"Was it strange going back?"

"Yes and no. No, because everything was the same. But yes, because I felt like a kid again and I kept expecting to see my mom."

"Can I ask you something? Something I just don't understand?" She scooted closer. "Why do all those people believe in him like that?"

"They don't know anything else."

"I know, but in this day and age."

"I know it sounds crazy, but our whole world began and ended in Mesadale. That was it. And you know what, for most of them—for most of us—it was enough."

She shook her head, as if she'd been told the most preposterous thing in the world. "Do you mind if I ask what he's like?" she said. "The Prophet?"

"He's . . . I don't know—I mean, I never really knew him. He was just always there, but I never really spoke to him or anything. I actually only saw him in church on Sundays. He'd stand very still as he gave his sermon, he wasn't a pacer or anything like that, just his feet planted in one place, and it was like he was part of the altar. The more I think about it, the harder it is to describe him. It's like trying to describe the wind."

"Is he old or young? Fat or thin?"

"He's old, but I don't even really know how old. You know how you know God's old, but you don't know how old. It's like that. I guess more than anything, I remember his voice. He wasn't a yeller, his voice was actually kinda soft and high, with the slightest lisp. I remember it being very gentle, very lulling, just pulling you in. When I was little I would sit in my mom's lap in church and she'd kiss my head and whisper, Listen, it's the voice of God."

"It's just not fair to tell children things like that."

"That's nothing. At school the teacher would pop in a cassette and we'd listen to the Prophet for hours. For the boys he often talked about priesthood history. Queenie told me for the girls he talked about home economics, the role of being a good wife, obedience, that kind of stuff. But most of the time, for everyone, he talked about the end of time, which was always coming soon. He told us how one day we'd have to slit the throats of our enemies, just like Nephi." I looked at Maureen. "You sure you want to hear all this?"

"If you want to tell me."

"They taught us how to do that in school, cutting throats, I mean. We had to practice on rabbits and chickens in the schoolyard. You must pray for the spirit while doing it—that's what the Prophet would say on his tape, and then he went on to describe how a human throat will look when the head's

91

pulled back and how to slice it from ear to ear and how the blood will look when it pours out thick and how not to be afraid. When we got older, we had to slaughter dogs and sheep. But I refused to do it, I could never kill a dog. I think those were my first inklings of doubt because I knew—I don't know how, but I just knew—those animals didn't have to die. It was all in preparation for the day when our enemies would come to slaughter us—that's what he told us. And we'd sit there for hours and listen to his voice coming out of the cassette player, and then there'd be a test. It seemed like the most natural thing in the world—to go to school and learn stuff like that from a voice on a cassette." I stopped and laughed. "I mean, it all sounds so cheesy now, but when I was a kid it really felt like God was in the room."

HAUN'S MILL MASSACRE
From Wikipedia, the free encyclopedia

MORMONS IN MISSOURI

In the mid-1830s, the **Latter-day Saints** (also known as the **Mormons**), facing religious persecution in their home of **Kirtland, Ohio**, began moving to western **Missouri**. The majority settled in a community known as Far West, but some 75 families settled beside Shoal Creek in Caldwell County, establishing a milling town known as **Haun's Mill**. By 1838, **Joseph Smith, Brigham Young,** and other Church leaders, as well as most of the Mormons, had relocated to Missouri.

Their hope of finding a peaceful home faded quickly. By the summer of 1838 tensions were high between the Mormons and the surrounding non-Mormon communities. The non-Mormons feared the Mormons for three reasons:

1) The Mormons voted in block and thus had quickly become a powerful political force in their new land.
2) The Mormons had swiftly, and some say surreptitiously, bought up large tracts of land.
3) Most controversially, rumors of polygamy had followed the Mormons from Ohio. Joseph and Brigham repeatedly denied the accusations, but many Missourians were suspicious of their new neighbors' marital customs.

On October 27, 1838, Missouri governor **Lilburn W. Boggs** signed an Extermination Order, which told the Mormons to leave the state or face extermination. The Mormons took the order seriously, but rather than fleeing they chose to fight, making plans for a military defense. Three days later, around four o'clock in the afternoon of October 30, between 200 and 250 members of the Missouri Militia rode into Haun's Mill. The women and children escaped across the shallow creek into the forest, fleeing with naked babies and frying pans. The men and a number of boys who refused to leave their fathers took up a defensive position in the blacksmith shop. The militia surrounded the building and shot at the huddled Mormons at close range through the loose chinking. Before nightfall, seventeen Mormons were murdered, along with one sympathetic non-Mormon, who had been there on business. Among those in the blacksmith shop, only one survived, the wainwright **Chauncey G. Webb**. Chauncey's wife, Elizabeth, and stepson, Gilbert, heard the nearly one hundred rifle shots from behind the mill's waterwheel, where they were hiding in shoulder-high water. During the battle, Elizabeth prayed for her husband's survival. When he was found alive, she, and many others, deemed it a miracle and long after spoke of it as one.

The close-range murders were particularly gruesome. Simon Cox was shot in the side, bits of his kidney splattering his fellow Mormons. Using a corn knife, one member of the militia chopped Thomas McBride, who was nearly eighty, into pieces. Another shot the top off the head of ten-year-old **Sardius Smith**, who was discovered beneath the bellows. But most offensive to the Mormons, and many non-Mormons, too, when word of the massacre got out, was that the governor had sanctioned the murders and thus they were legitimate in the eyes of the state's law.

After the Haun's Mill massacre, the Mormons began to flee Missouri, eventually settling on the Illinois side of the Mississippi at a swampy outpost then known as Commerce. Here they built the proud city of **Nauvoo,** which in five years would become the second largest in Illinois. Chauncey Webb, the massacre's lone survivor, moved his family to Nauvoo around 1840 or 1841, becoming the city's leading wagon builder. In Nauvoo, also known as Beautiful City, Joseph Smith and the Saints would experience their golden age.

The murders were never officially investigated, and no one was ever brought to justice. The massacre remains an important turning point in LDS history and is remembered annually through memorials, reenactments, and special prayers. The mill's original red millstone has been erected as a memorial to the victims. For many Mormons in the 19th century, Chauncey Webb's survival came to symbolize their resolve. Records show, however, that Chauncey Webb was a reluctant hero and disagreed with his wife's assessment that he had survived because of divine intervention.

REFERENCES

1. *History of the Church*, Vol. III
2. *Mormon Polygamy: A Historical Perspective* by Charles Green
3. "The Women of Haun's Mill" by Mary P. Sprague
4. *The 19th Wife* by Ann Eliza Young

I'M NOT AN EXPERT OR ANYTHING

The next morning I drove out to the Mesadale Post Office. Mailing labels, a poster of wildflower stamps, the FBI's Most Wanted—you might forget you were in an outlaw town until you met the postmistress, Sister Karen, in her Utah burka (think Laura Ingalls) and forty years of hair.

"I know I know you. Give me a second and I'll figure it out. I never forget a face." Sister Karen tapped her temple with a pencil. "Jordan Scott! My goodness, what brings you back here?"

"I'm looking for someone."

"You came to the right place."

"One of my sisters. Stepsister, really. Her name's Elizabeth the Second. Blond hair, blue-gray eyes. You know her?"

"You'll have to be more specific than that." Sister Karen wasn't being flip. In Mesadale the limited gene pool produced a common look— white-gold hair and fair, almost translucent skin that doesn't do well in the sun.

"She's pretty tall," I said. "Originally from Idaho."

"Originally from Idaho," Sister Karen said to herself while sorting the welfare checks. The Prophet used to preach about welfare, claiming it was our religious duty to cheat the government. "The Devil's people are meant to support God's people," he'd say. The sister wives passed around a cassette of him teaching how to lie on a single-mother form. The checks arrived so frequently you had to wonder who in Salt Lake and Washington had been paid off.

"I don't know if this will help," I said, "but I used to call her Queenie."

"Queenie! Why didn't you say so? Brother Hiram's wife."

"So she's married?"

"Of course. To Brother Caleb's son, Hiram. Real nice man. A police officer. They live up Red Creek, across from the canyon."

In a flash I imagined my old friend's life: the big barn of a house, the chicken-scratched yard, the softball team of wives. I saw Queenie mending her husband's night-blue uniform, letting out the waist. I heard the stampede of children on the stairs. "How many wives?" I said.

"Actually, it's just Queenie. Brother Hiram really loves that girl. The Prophet keeps pressing him to take another and he keeps telling the Prophet he doesn't want anyone else."

I thanked Sister Karen for her help. "I know you're not supposed to talk to me."

"I love the Prophet, but honest to goodness you can't go around in life not *talking* to people. You going up to Queenie's now? Do me a favor and tell her she's got a package down here."

I drove up the road next to Red Creek. It was midmorning and the streets were quiet. You might think, well, that's normal: the kids at school, the men at work, the women either at home or out at a job. Except that's not exactly how it was. Any kid older than eight was in school. The younger kids, I'm talking like five to seven, were looking after the babies or doing housework. Most of the wives were working, on the farms or in the few shops. Many worked in the church's sewing plant, making eyeglass cords. Some upholstered chairs and sofas in a furniture shop. A lot worked as secretaries over in church headquarters—doing who knows what, but I guess there's a ton of paperwork when you're planning for the end of time. Some women were nurses or midwives in St. George or Cedar City, usually the ones who couldn't have children. My mom used to work part-time at the co-op as a cashier. When I was little sometimes I'd go to work with her, standing at her side as she rung up the groceries. The only customers were other Firsts, usually three or four sister wives out doing the marketing. They'd fill five or six baskets with cartons of cereal and sides of bacon and cases of fruit cocktail. Sometimes they'd fight over apple or grape juice, and sometimes they never even spoke. I remember once a guy came in who obviously wasn't a First. He was in a pair of jeans and a t-shirt with a pack of cigarettes rolled up into the sleeve. He walked up and down the aisles like he didn't know what he was looking for. When he passed a cluster of sister wives, they stepped aside and looked the other way. The guy chose my mom's aisle to buy a chocolate bar. He was staring at us, and my mom drew me close to her side. "Is there a restaurant or a café around here?" the guy said. My mom shook her head. She rang up his candy and handed him his change. I watched the guy walk back to his car. I watched the car back out of the lot. I watched my mom reassure herself that she'd done nothing wrong in taking the guy's money and touching his flesh when she gave him his two dimes.

And the men? What do they do in Mesadale? Some worked construction out on jobs in Kanab and St. George, where the wages were good. The boys did a lot of the construction in town, putting up more houses for wives and kids and more and more church admin buildings. During my last year in Mesadale I helped reroof the church. I spent like half a year nailing down shingles. You know what Roland said when I told him that? "Oh honey, talk about an angel on the roof!"

But a lot of the men in the church don't work at all. Especially the Apostles, the band of loyalists who keep an eye on everything for the Prophet. My dad was an Apostle, and in exchange he got to marry as many women as he wanted. At this hour in the morning a lot of these guys were passed out, sleeping off a hangover or a high. I'll guesstimate half the men had a whiskey and/or meth problem, and maybe half of those played with vicodin and oxy cotton, which is easy to score in Hurricane and St. George. There's no point in telling you the Prophet officially bans alcohol and drugs, or that I'm pretty sure he deals.

Queenie's house was easy to spot: a small stucco ranch, probably two bedrooms and a bath. The other thing that gave it away: her husband's patrol car parked at an angle in the drive.

Across the street I turned up a dry gulley and drove into the canyon. The van picked its way up the wash, the tires grinding in the sand, until we were behind a bend where no one could see us. The canyon walls cast a long shadow that would keep Elektra cool. I poured a bowl of water and cracked the windows. I told her she was a good girl, but she knew what was coming: her tail fell limp off her ass. When I got out she started barking, howling like I'd eaten her young. It echoed up the canyon. When I shhhhhed her, that echoed too. This wasn't going to work.

"Oh, come on," I said, leashing her up. "You big baby." Her tail flicked back to life.

The canyon walls were cold and gritty and almost blue from the shadow. At the mouth of the canyon we stepped into a world of white sunlight. The difference in temperatures must have been thirty degrees. We ran across the road to Queenie's door and it opened before I could knock.

"Jordan, what are you doing here?"

"Good to see you too."

"Shhh, Hiram's sleeping. Come on, let's talk in the garage." She led Elektra and me across a dark living room, down a path worn in the carpet. In the garage she turned on a painter's lamp. A thick beery light illuminated a workbench and a gun rack mounted with rifles and shotguns. "What are you up to?" she said.

"I guess you heard about my mom."

"Of course I did."

"Well, I'm looking into a few things."

"Like what?"

"Like what really happened."

In this light Queenie's face looked yellow and cold. She hadn't changed much, still beautiful, still a rebel gleam in her eyes. Her mother married my father not long before I was kicked out. She was his 23rd or 24th wife, I think, a bucktoothed woman who ate her nails. They met through this polygamy personals website (www.2wives.com; check it out). She showed up at the house with her thirteen-year-old daughter, Elizabeth. My father started calling the girl Elizabeth the Second to avoid confusion with another girl. I remember how shocked she looked those first few weeks in the house: the livid brow, the sense of betrayal in her eyes whenever her mother called her Elizabeth the Second. She knew she had landed in a very strange place. As for me, I took to her because she seemed, well, kinda fabulous, although this was of course before I had ever used that word. One night she told me she hated everyone calling her Elizabeth the Second. "It makes me feel like the fucking queen," she said. The what? She gave me a brief tutorial on British royalty. At first I didn't believe her. The Prophet had said on one of his tapes that although England had managed to avoid total destruction in the last war, there was nothing there now other than a ruined people living in huts and sheds. "He's lying," she said. I told her she was the one who was lying, but this wasn't long after I had refused to slaughter the dogs and the sheep. These two events rubbed together, shaping a baby pearl of doubt. Six weeks later my dad caught us holding hands. You know the rest.

In the garage I asked Queenie what had happened after I left. "It was no big deal," she said. "Your punishment was excommunication. Mine was marriage. The Prophet chose Hiram for me. Or I guess I should say he chose me for

100

Hiram. Hiram was twenty at the time, so not really that old. We were sealed the next day. You know how it goes, you've heard the story a million times. But you know what— and this is the insane part— we fell in love. He's a good man. He loves me. He loves our little girl. Jordan—stop making that face."

"What face?"

"You think I'm out of my mind."

"No, no, it's great," I lied. "He sounds great."

Was she kidding? Love? In Mesadale? "I'm just surprised," I said. "Monogamy is sort of a no-no out here."

"I know. Lately the Prophet's been putting pressure on Hiram. But so far we've resisted."

I asked how her mom was. She looked down to Elektra, then back up. A gray storm had moved across her eyes. "She's dead."

"What? How?"

"She got sick a few years ago. Her kidneys."

"I'm sorry."

"But that wasn't it," she said. "About six months ago she started having doubts about everything. She wanted to leave your dad. She wanted out of here. So they murdered her."

"Excuse me?"

"They put salt in her dialysis machine. It crystallized her heart. She went into the clinic for a treatment and never came home."

OK, let me stop for a second. I know what you're thinking. And I'd be thinking it too. But in Mesadale it's not as unlikely as it sounds.

"Who do you think it was?"

"The Prophet. Well, not him himself, but a couple of his men. He wanted to show everyone what happens if you try to leave."

"You know this for a fact?"

"No, but I know it's true."

101

I think one of the reasons Mesadale's been ignored for so long are the stories like these. When they seep out, when people hear them, they think, Oh please. Salt in the dialysis machine? A crystallized heart? It sounds like a bad movie. And so the stories are dismissed, and the Prophet and his disciples have been left alone. Mr. Heber was totally wrong to think anything out here had changed.

"Anyway," said Queenie. "So you're like, what, snooping around?"

"Yeah, something like that."

"You don't think your mom did it?"

"I don't know."

"That doesn't surprise me. There isn't anyone more devout than your mom."

"I know, that's why I want to find out a little more."

"Did you talk to his latest wives? If I were you, I'd start with them."

"Why?"

"I don't know, it's just a feeling I have. Everything started to change with the last couple of wives."

"What are their names?"

"Let's see, Sister Kimberly is the newest. She lives behind the big house in a log cabin your dad built. Maybe start with her."

Then a little girl started crying on the other side of the house. "That's Angela, I need to go. You really have to get out of here before anyone sees you."

"Queenie, can I come back?"

"I don't think that's such a good idea." Then she softened up. "If you have to, yes, of course. Jordan, I don't want to turn all mushy on you, but after you were gone I never stopped thinking about you. I prayed a lot that you were OK."

"Me too. But I guess we're both doing fine, given the circumstances."

"I guess," she said. "You should go. And be careful." She

pressed a button and the garage door opened to a wall of blinding light.

"I almost forgot. Sister Karen has a package for you."

"Oh really? I wonder what."

But the sunlight made it impossible to read her eyes.

From there I drove out to Kanab, a high-desert town that's one part granola-hiker-ecotourist, two parts LDS. It's about forty miles beyond Mesadale, and arriving there is like time travel, *whoosh*ing in from the nineteenth century and landing in the twenty-first. I stopped at a sandwich shop called the Mega Bite and ordered a tuna fish from a girl whose name tag said 5.

"This is so weird," she said when she brought me my order. "I know you."

"You do?"

"You're only like my brother."

I was less astonished by this statement than you might think. The only remarkable part of this encounter was that she was a pretty teenage girl who had managed to escape Mesadale. The pretty ones never got out.

"My mom married your dad after you left. He used to talk about you. He said you fucked your sister. That chick, what's her name."

"I didn't fuck her."

"I figured that much, but that's what he said. He was just trying to scare us into never messing around with the boys. By the way, my name's 5."

"5?"

"Well it's Sarah 5, but fuck the Sarah part."

"Got it. And for the record, I was holding Queenie's hand. That's all."

"Oh, was that it? I used to wonder." She shrugged. "Anyway, I recognize you from your picture."

"What picture?"

"The one your mom kept in her room beside her bed. You were probably eleven or twelve in it, I don't know. It was at one of those birthday parties and you're standing in line with a paper plate, waiting for a piece of cake. Your mom showed it to me once."

"I don't even remember that picture being taken."

"You know what she said when she showed it to me? She said she was going to see you again in heaven. I don't mean to pick on your mom, but give me a fucking break."

"So who's your mom?"

"Kimberly."

"His last wife?"

"Yeah. I think she had something on your dad, because he'd do whatever she wanted. Like she said she wasn't going to live in that house with all those wives. The next day he started building her a log cabin. He made all the boys work on it, which pissed them off because they knew their moms were getting it worse. Anyway, that's where we lived, my mom and me. But they booby-trapped the place. It was always falling apart on us, a floor plank caving in, stuff like that. Once a window popped out on my mom. Nearly shredded her alive."

"So, 5. When'd you leave?"

"About eight months ago. My mom has no clue I'm living so nearby. I told her I was leaving Utah and never coming back. Guess that didn't happen. So anyway, what's going on with your mom?"

"I don't know. That's why I'm here."

"She's like in jail, right? It was all over the papers. Man, when I heard she shot him I was like, Lady, you beat me to it."

"That's what I thought until I got here."

"What was she, number fifteen or something?"

"Nineteen."

"The numbers are so screwed up. I doubt he really knew how many he had. It was all about pussy anyway. He was just counting cunts."

"Isn't it a little dangerous for you to be hanging out here?"

"I know," she said. "I probably shoulda gone to Vegas or Phoenix or something."

"They come into town pretty often, don't they?"

"Some of them, yeah. But you know what, those old guys have no idea who's who. No one but my mom remembers me. Here's the thing, I want to get my mom outta there."

"How you going to do that?"

"Same way I got out. There's this agency in Salt Lake that helps women like her."

"Really?"

"It's how I escaped. No one knows this, but there's a system to get messages in and out, you know, to people who want to leave. For a while they used the dairy fridge at the co-op to pass notes. Bet you didn't know that. Anyway, I heard about it and started communicating with them, and then they sent me a message telling me to meet them on the highway. So one night around three I sneak out of the house and run like crazy down to the highway. I had no idea if they'd actually be there, or even who they were. It all could've been a setup. It could've been the Prophet himself looking to screw me over. Literally. But I get there and this van pulls up with a man and a woman inside. I climb in and pray they're on my side. I know, can you believe it, me praying?

"Anyway, they drove me here to Kanab that first night and the next morning they were going to take me to Salt Lake, to this house for kids like me, but I was like, Thanks, I'll stop right here. They tried to talk me out of it, but when I make up my mind, forget it. I've been hanging around here trying to figure out how to get my mom out. When I heard your dad was dead, I went back to see her. I was like, Mom, let's get the fuck out of here. You know what she said? She tells me she doesn't want to go. She wants to hang around and play widow. She said she loved the old bastard. Is that fucked up or what?"

"It's pretty fucked up."

Elektra was growing impatient in the sun. 5 poured some water into her palm and Elektra licked it out. "You know what happens next, don't you? The Prophet's going to get some guy to marry all of them in one fell swoop. You know, keep the family together. And they'll all end up belonging to another man. Probably some young asshole who'll live another sixty years. No one would believe this goes on today. They're still looking for the Taliban, right? Well, hello? They're right here."

"Want to hear something crazy?" I said. "My mom says she didn't kill him."

"No shit."

"That's why I'm looking around."

"For what?"

"That's the problem. I don't really know."

"Well, let me know if you find anything out."

A customer came in with a large order of veggie wraps. 5 took her place behind the counter. She pulled on a pair of plastic gloves and began laying out a row of tortillas. By the time she was done another large order came in, then another. But she kept her eye on me the whole time. When I stood to leave she waved from behind the counter, a plastic baggie on her hand.

I called Roland. "Kanab? Sounds Kanasty. Oh honey, where on earth?" Then I called the contractor who gives me most of my work. He wasn't pissed about my skipping out on the bathroom vanity job. I was still on for next Monday, a job in San Marino redoing a nursery. "This lady's about to have triplets," he said. "Expect madness." Then I called my mom. Excluding calls from Mr. Heber, she's allowed only two calls a week. It took a while to get her on the phone. When I heard her voice, I told her I was going to see Kimberly.

"Is there anything I should know?" I said. The line crackled the way it does in a creepy old movie.

106

"I don't think she knew who I was before all this happened," she said. "The new wives pretty much ignore the old ones."

"Mom, I want to go up and look around your old room. Do you think I'll find anything there?"

"I doubt it. I wouldn't be surprised if one of the wives has already dumped my things and moved in."

After that I drove to a park and lay down on the futon in the back of the van. Elektra curled up next to me. I started reading that book about God. I was at the part about religion and war. I've been trying to get through it for a while now, but after a few pages I always fall asleep.

When I woke the sun was balling up and getting ready to set. It was time to go back to Mesadale. The closer I got, the redder the desert burned. Not red and orange and pink and yellow. Just red. Everything. Red and red and red. By the time I reached the turnoff, it was dark. I drove up the road with my headlights out.

Kimberly's cottage looked like one of those houses that comes as a kit in the mail. The windows were full of soft pinkish light. I heard water running in a sink. The front door was open and I could look through the screen door into the living room. A shotgun hung on two brackets above the mantel. I know my guns: it was a Big Boy .44 Magnum. But around here they weren't all that rare.

I called hello.

The water stopped. "Who's that?"

"Sister Kimberly?"

A youngish woman appeared on the other side of the screen, her hair up in an airy roll. She looked like one of those actors, if that's the right word, who works in a frontier-town theme park. "Can I come in?"

She knew who I was. "I don't think that's a good idea."

"It won't take long." I put my hand on the door.

"Please, stay out there." She locked the latch from inside. A shove would've yanked the door off its frame, but it seemed far-fetched. Me? Breaking down a (screen) door?

107

"Can you tell me what happened?"

"I don't know any more than you do. Besides, I can't talk to you. You know that."

"You can if you want to."

"Jordan, please."

"Five minutes. Give me five minutes."

I asked where she was when my dad was killed, and she said, "I was right here, of course."

I asked what she heard. "Nothing. Not until all the sister wives started screaming."

"Who was here that night?"

"I don't know, everyone, I suppose, but I never go in the main house."

"Did anyone leave right before he was killed? Anything suspicious like that?"

Through the screen, with the pinkish light behind her, she looked like a saint in an old painting, everything glowing around her beautiful oval face. "No, nothing like that. Jordan, what are you up to? You really shouldn't be here."

"Are you all alone?"

"Yes, of course."

"Don't you have a daughter?"

"Had."

"Had?"

"They took her."

"Who took her?"

Her eyes narrowed. "I don't know why I'm even talking to you."

"Because your husband was my dad. Where do you think your daughter is?"

"They've been coming for our young girls lately. Telling them all sorts of lies."

"Who?"

"The casinos."

"The casinos?" If it weren't so sad, I would've laughed.

"From Mesquite, and some from Las Vegas. They come over and take our girls."

"You're saying a casino kidnapped your daughter?"

"Yes, it just happened, right after he was killed. And I know what they do: they brainwash them, the pretty ones at least. The Prophet warned us to be on the lookout for people claiming to help our girls. They're the casinos." Tears came to her golden eyes.

"Here," I said. "Take this."

She hesitated, then unlatched the screen, opening it enough to take my bandanna. Quickly she set the hook back in its eye and dabbed her eyes. "The Prophet says I've got to forget all about her. She's gone into the world of sin and I can no longer love her, that's what he says." She let out a small cry. "But it's hard."

Those tears were real, that much I knew. We were standing close together, separated only by the screen. She said, "You should probably leave."

"Can I come another time?"

"What for?"

"To talk. To tell you if I find anything."

"I don't know." She shivered, and I left her, a silhouette in the screen.

I walked quickly around the side of the big house. I could hear the chatter of girls getting ready for bed. How many were still inside? No one knew: that was the thing. I felt sorry for them, everyone in my dad's house, even if one of them had put the rap on my mom.

A PROPHET ON THE MISSISSIPPI
AN INTERVIEW WITH JOSEPH SMITH

Special to the *New York Herald*
July 28, 1843

NAUVOO, ILLINOIS—Yesterday, in this beautiful city situated on a horseshoe bend in the Mississippi River, Howard Greenly of the *Herald* interviewed Joseph Smith, Jr., Prophet to the Latter-day Saints. Our correspondent met with Smith in the second-story offices above his Red Brick Store, sitting at the wood table where Smith regularly confers with the Quorum of the Twelve Apostles, his council of religious and political advisors. In the interview Smith would speak to the thus-called Gentile press more openly than he ever had before.

Smith is thirty-nine, equipped with a tall, lithely powerful frame, vivid in everything he does. Up and down the Mississippi he is famous for the flash in his blue gemstone eyes. His tenor voice carries far, with a natural clarity to it that attracts the ear. Since establishing his Church in 1830, this son of Vermont farmers has led his followers through a number of arduous relocations in search of a home where they could worship undisturbed, including colonies in Kirtland, Ohio, and Far West, Missouri, before settling in Nauvoo. Over the years Smith has been denounced as a charlatan, a plagiarist, and a speculator in fraud. He has been tarred-and-feathered, arrested for treason, chased across state lines, thrown in a Missouri jail cell, and faced orders of execution. He has seen his most faithful adherents slaughtered in pitiless battles such as the one at Haun's Mill. Yet each blow of adversity has only increased his position in the eyes of his devout. The Mormons, or Saints as they call themselves, revere him in a fervid manner unfamiliar to modern times. Nearly everyone in this bustling city of 12,000 speaks of him with the same reverence others reserve elsewhere for Jesus Christ, Son of God.

Smith's counselor and friend, Brigham Young, attended the interview. He is a quiet, thoughtful carpenter and glazier, with a stolid presence and fast, flinty eyes. This silent giant spoke but once, as the reader shall see.

H.G.—Can you tell us, are you a Christian?

J.S.—Yes. We believe in the Lord Jesus Christ fully. He is our Savior. We pray to him. We know he suffered on our behalf. He is at the center of all we believe.

H.G.—Then who are you?

J.S.—I am Joseph Smith Junior, son of Joseph Smith Senior and Lucy Mack Smith, and husband to Emma Hale Smith.

H.G.—Theologically speaking, who are you to this religion?

J.S.—I am the Prophet. The Lord has revealed many truths for man through me.

H.G.—What truths?

J.S.—He has restored the Gospel.

H.G.—The Book of Mormon?

J.S.—That's correct.

H.G.—Many people say it's a feeble imitation of the Bible.

J.S.—Have you read it?

H.G.—I must confess, I've given it a go a few times and couldn't make heads or tails.

J.S.—You didn't finish it, then?

H.G.—I did not.

J.S.—You strike me as a just man, so may I ask that you refrain from dismissing it before you've read it all the way through?

H.G.—Fair enough. What do you say to people who don't

believe we live in a time of Prophets and revelations? That the days of mystical events belonged to the ancients?

J.S.—I say, Look around. Tell me why the Lord should stop communicating with man now? Aren't we in need of His word more so than ever? Why would He reserve His right to speak to man solely in ancient times?

H.G.—For some it's difficult, even impossible, to believe the stories of an angel in the woods, and the golden plates buried in the hills, and the other myths of your creed's origins.

J.S.—If they can believe Christ rose from His grave, I do not understand why they can't believe the fact of plates of gold.

H.G.—Very well. You are also the political leader of Nauvoo. Is this perhaps an instance of Church and State being one?

J.S.—It is.

H.G.—And yet we have a tradition of separating the two. Christ himself called upon separating that which was Caesar's from all things spiritual. Why should Americans accept your arrangement here?

J.S.—If the people of Nauvoo can accept it, the American people should do so as well. Show me the harm it is to them.

H.G.—What is your position on slavery?

J.S.—We believe slavery even more morally corrosive to the owner than to the enslaved.

H.G.—There is a group called the Danites, also called Destroying Angels, which is known as a militia, violent in its mission, and commanded by you, similar to Rome's Praetorian Guard. Can you tell the American people who they are and what they do?

J.S.—You astound me with your vivid tales. I have never heard of this group, nor do I lead any private bands. Tell me, where do these stories come from?

H.G.—Your enemies have depicted the Danites as a secret police authorized to destroy those who speak out against you.

J.S.—Think of your source: My enemies can be expected to depict such things.

H.G.—Not only your enemies, independent observers, too.

J.S.—Show me an independent observer. I would like to meet such a rare creature.

H.G.—You're denying such a group exists?

J.S.—I ask you this: Nearly five years ago, a group of Saints was massacred at Haun's Mill by government sanction. A ten-year-old boy lost the top of his head to the Governor's militia. What was our response? Fury? Destruction? Revenge? No, we responded with grief and mercy, as Christ has taught us. If I employed a secret militia, shouldn't I have called them out to avenge that boy's death? [At this point, the interview was interrupted by Chauncey Webb, a leading wainwright in Nauvoo. His business pulled Smith away for some ten minutes. Upon his return, Smith apologized and explained the interruption.]

J.S.—Brother Chauncey, my good friend who was just here, has brought news of the arrival of a caravan of Saints. Their wagons have pulled in from the coast of Maine.

H.G.—Fresh converts?

J.S.—Yes, and new friends.

H.G.—Your Church is expanding rather rapidly.

J.S.—If it does so, it is thanks to the power of God and the Truth of His word.

H.G.—Yet isn't there another reason? For nearly as long as your Church has existed, rumors of polygamy have surrounded it. Can you tell us once and for all, do you practice polygamy?

J.S.—We do not.

H.G.—Are there exceptions?

J.S.—Our enemies create the exceptions in the mind of the public. That does not make them true.

H.G.—Do you have any idea why these rumors persist?

J.S.—We seek to practice our religion freely. In the history of man, those who have sought religious freedom have been

113

persecuted, maligned, and, if they are not careful, destroyed. We are no different than the early Christians in the Emperors' Rome. And yet, this country was founded on religious tolerance. And so it should be.

H.G.—I have been told you have at least twenty wives.

J.S.—Sir, my house is just up the street. You are free to search it. Let's go there now! If you find these twenty wives, please inform me.

H.G.—Sir, can you assure the general public that the Latter-day Saints do not practice plural marriage, never have practiced it, and never will practice it?

J.S.—I can assure you.

B.Y.—If I may interrupt.

J.S.—Of course.

B.Y.—Sir, why not ask our wives? Mrs. Smith, or my Mrs. Young, will gladly tell you about their households.

H.G.—Thank you, I wouldn't want to disturb them.

J.S.—I would think my Emma would have something to say if I came home with twenty women.

H.G.—Yes, I should say. So let's leave it at that, shall we? One last question: What is in your future?

J.S.—Peace, I should hope, to pursue our beliefs. In my heart I believe our countrymen deem this our right—for all Americans must be free.

AN EYE IN THE DARK

When I got back to St. George I bought a ticket for whatever was playing in the cineplex's Theater 8. I walked down the aisle to the front of the theater, folding a piece of paper into a little wedge. I opened the fire door and propped the lock with the wedge of paper. After fetching Elektra from the van, we slipped back into the theater. She seemed to know something was up because she came along silently, staying close to my side. I sat in the second row against the wall, and Elektra curled up at my feet. The movie was about a pair of detectives, one black and one white. They're not supposed to get along, but they actually like each other and they go on to catch a jewelry thief who has some connection to international terrorism, and then it turns out the black guy's Muslim and the white guy's a Jew. I know: what? Then I fell asleep.

I woke up, slowly remembering where I was. Elektra was asleep on my feet. The movie was ending, the credits rolling up the screen. But the theater looked emptier than before.

"Wow," a voice said from behind. "You must've been wiped."

When I turned around I couldn't see anything but an eye gleaming in the dark.

"You slept through the movie twice."

"What time is it?" And then, "Who are you?"

"Johnny Drury." He said it like we knew each other.

"How long've you been here?"

"A lot longer than you." The house lights were coming up, and now I could see the guy. He looked like every kid in Utah:

115

blondish, blue, a splash of freckles. "This place is closing," he said.

"Closing?"

"Dude, it's almost one in the morning."

I turned on my phone. The kid was right.

"Do you have a dog with you?"

"Look, I have to go."

"Me too!"

The kid followed me up the aisle. Now that we were standing, I could see he really was a kid, twelve or thirteen, a late bloomer, just this side of puberty. His turquoise muscle T showed wiry but strong kid-arms. The lobby was empty except for a heavy girl in a black-and-buff cineplex uniform vacuuming popcorn from the carpet. "Can't have a dog in here," she said, but you could tell she didn't care.

Outside it was still hot in the parking lot, the asphalt throwing back the heat. "Look, I'm leaving," I said.

"Yeah, same here." He had one of those kid voices that goes high and low and back again in one sentence. "How about a lift?"

"Where do you live?"

"Well, you see, right now I'm sort of in between places." He said it so smoothly, I figured he'd picked up that line from someone else. He followed me to the van, staying real close. He came up to about my chest, and I bet he didn't weigh more than a hundred pounds. "Nice van," he said, touching the pom-pom on the side. The truth is, it's a piece of shit and no one ever says anything about it except, that thing really run?

"I can drop you on St. George Avenue, but that's it."

"Awesome." He didn't wait for me: he crawled across the driver's seat to the passenger side and started bouncing in the seat. "This is the phattest van I've ever seen."

"Put your seat belt on."

"Where'd you say you were going?"

"Just tell me where on St. George you want me to drop you."

"Here's the thing." He forced his voice down an octave. "I wouldn't mind staying with you for the night. Just one night. That's all." He was talking in a voice he must've picked up from the movie. "But no funny business, you know what I'm saying?" He thought this was especially funny, slapping his thigh and throwing his head back in laughter, like a little kid watching a cartoon.

But this was my van and I wasn't going to be insulted by a kid. "No, I don't know what you're saying."

"You know. I'm no fag." More of the cartoon laugh.

"I am."

The kid stopped. He looked at me with big, no-shit eyes. Then he smiled. "I get it. Very funny. You had me for a second. Ha-ha." He stopped. "Wait a minute, you telling me you're a homo?"

"Only because you brought it up."

He whipped a three-inch kitchen knife out of his pants and pointed it at my chest. "You touch me and I kill you."

I knew he wasn't serious. In one slow gesture I took the knife from the kid. "What're you doing with this?"

"Protecting myself from pervos like you."

"Get out of my van."

"Fucking faggot." He unclicked his seat belt and pushed open the door and slid a leg out. He was so small his foot dangled several feet above the asphalt. But he didn't jump.

"Get out."

"Fuck you." The thing is, he said this almost tenderly. He stayed in the seat, his face all broken up. "I thought you were cool."

"You're the one who's not being cool."

He moved a little closer to the edge of the seat but still didn't jump. "Look, I'll stay with you tonight, but you got to promise you won't touch me."

"Kid, get out of my van."

"But why?"

"Because you asked for a ride and now you're calling me all

sorts of names. I don't put up with stuff like that anymore. That's why I blew off this place a long time ago."

The kid slid his leg back into the van. "Wait a minute, you don't live around here?"

"Nope."

"What're you doing here, then?"

"Long story."

"You run away or something like that?" He closed the door and the overhead light went out.

Then I figured it out. "Are you from where I think you're from?" I said.

"Yup." He pulled his knees into his chest. "Was it hard making it on your own? I mean, look at you. You got a phone and a van. You're rich."

"I'm not rich."

"To me you are."

"You said your name's Johnny."

He nodded eagerly.

"Want to get something to eat?"

"Totally. But first, can I have my knife back?"

Twenty minutes later we were outside the Chevron, eating a sack of microwaved burritos. "Now I know who you are," said Johnny. "But remind me: why'd you get kicked out?"

"I was caught alone with one of my stepsisters. What about you?"

"I was listening to the Killers. It wasn't even my disc, it was my brother's. But they caught me. I don't even like the Killers."

That wasn't the real reason. They get rid of the boys to take away the competition. With no boys around, the old men have the girls to themselves. I handed Johnny the last burrito. "How'd you end up here?"

"Two of the Apostles drove me in. Worst night of my life. I was crying my eyes out and they just sat up front and pretended like I wasn't there. I kept asking why're you doing this? I'm just a kid. How'm I going to live? But they wouldn't even

118

talk to me. I had to stare at their necks the whole way. I wanted to cut off their heads. If I had a better knife, I would've. You saw my blade, it's pretty lame. Then they left me in the parking lot of the Pioneer Lodge."

"When was that?"

"Six months ago."

"What've you been up to since?"

"Hanging out. I stayed in one of the Butt Huts for a while, and then I went down to Vegas, but I didn't really like it so I came back here."

"And the knife?"

"It's my mom's. I took it from the kitchen. It's the only thing of hers I got. See, she wrote her name on a piece of paper and taped it to the handle." He showed it to me proudly. *Tina*, in a bad blue cursive. His mom probably wasn't yet thirty.

"Do me a favor and be careful with that."

After that we watched the cars pull in for gas and the people running inside for cigarettes and visine. "Isn't your mom like in jail?"

"How do you know about that?"

"Everyone knows about that."

"She didn't do it. Everyone thinks she did, but she didn't."

Johnny was eating a bag of potato chips, tipping the remnants down his throat. "When I heard about what happened," he said, "I wasn't all that surprised. Things are weird out there right now. Something's happening. There were all these rumors going around before I left."

"What kind of rumors?"

"Like we were all moving to Texas or Mexico or something. And there was this stuff about your dad."

"What stuff?"

"I don't know. Just stuff like he was trying to take over from the Prophet. I don't really know everything, but I just heard stuff like that. Other stuff too. That's why I wasn't surprised when I heard he was killed."

I said nothing. Was the kid full of shit or did he know something? We hung around the Chevron for about a half hour until the manager told us we couldn't loiter. He was nice about it, just said the cops watch the parking lot and we had to leave.

I turned to Johnny. "Where to?"

"You tell me."

"Let's go out to Snow Canyon. I know this place we can park overnight. It should be cool there."

"OK, but no funny business."

"Get out."

"Kidding! I thought you gay guys were supposed to have a sense of humor."

We drove out on Highway 18. The road was dark, the only light from the moon and the stars. Johnny fell asleep, his head against the window and his mouth open. When I parked the van he rolled his head around, murmured, then went back to sleep. Like this, he really looked like a kid. It was hard to imagine anyone with a thump in his heart abandoning Johnny. I picked him up and laid him on the futon. I pulled a sheet over him and rolled up my sweatshirt for a pillow. I lay down behind him on my back with my arm behind my head. Elektra was curled up between us. I wasn't tired, and for a long time I looked at the ceiling of the van. Johnny was snoring. Nothing loud, just a soft little chug. Kids don't really make a racket when they sleep. I thought about what I would do in the morning. What did he know? I pondered it for a long time, then fell off into a shallow sleep.

CELESTIAL MARRIAGE

THE 19TH WIFE

CHAPTER THREE

The Doctrine of Celestial Marriage and the Death of Joseph Smith

Now, having described the religious conversions of my mother, Elizabeth, and my father, Chauncey, and their unyielding allegiance to Joseph Smith; having depicted the horror of the massacre at Haun's Mill and the long migration out of Missouri; having spilled perhaps too much ink describing the rise of Nauvoo, Illinois, and the peace the Saints found therein; having established all this for you, my Patient Reader, I shall move forward to the subject that no doubt first drew you to these pages: the doctrine of celestial marriage, otherwise known as polygamy.

On the evening of June 6, 1844, Joseph visited my parents' home in Nauvoo. He came bearing news. The Prophet stood before them in the keeping room, clearing his throat several times, making the Ah-hem sound familiar to anyone who knew him. (The skeptical Reader will ask, How does Mrs. Young know all this? To him I say, My mother has spoken of the Prophet's visit to her home at least once a month for the past thirty years.)

"I have received a new Revelation," Joseph began.

Elizabeth could not contain the excitement in her heart. For her, hearing a Revelation was all but the same as hearing the words of God.

"The Lord has commanded us to expand the Kingdom," Joseph explained.

Chauncey asked, "Do you mean we're leaving Nauvoo?"

Ever practical, he did not want to abandon his wagonry yet again. He had done so twice before, in Ohio and Missouri; often he said he would not move a third time.

"We're here to stay," said Joseph. "Nauvoo is our Zion. The Kingdom is to grow here."

It occurred to Elizabeth that Joseph had not heard her news. Hence she told him in September there would be a child. "If it's a girl I'll name her Ann Eliza," she announced.

"It's a blessing," said Joseph. "And now I must tell you the words of our Heavenly Father. He has commanded us to fill the Earth with Saints, to replenish the lands with the devout." As Joseph spoke, a high whistling sound mingled with his words. The source was a missing tooth, an injury from a mob attack in Ohio many years before. The whistling rang out like a tiny, tiny bell.

"What more can we do?" said Chauncey. He reminded Joseph of their two newborns lost in infancy and Elizabeth's poor health thereafter. Chauncey knew this child should be Elizabeth's last.

"I asked our Heavenly Father the same question," said Joseph. "What more can I do? Tell me, Dear Lord, what must I do to expand the Kingdom? Over time, the Revelation has made itself clear. Now I must share it with the most faithful, Saints like you."

"I'll have my child," said Elizabeth. "And if the Lord wants another I'll have another. And yet another, until He decides I can't bear more."

"You're a good woman, among the best of the Saints. That's why I've come to tell you what I know."

Joseph looked to the ceiling in a moment that suggested he was peering up at the feet of God.

"Do you recall my words about Abraham and Sarah?" he began. "God ordered Abraham to take another wife. This was not Abraham's wish, it was not Sarah's wish, but it was God's command. And so Sarah told Abraham to take Hagar as his wife, although she was his wife. Was Abraham wrong to do it? Did he commit adultery? No, because it had been commanded of him by God." Joseph stopped, then turned to Elizabeth. "Sister, do you understand me?"

Many times before this night, Elizabeth had heard the rumors of Joseph's marital relations. Faithless people permitted their tongues to flap, going on about a bounty of wives—a dozen, two dozen, some said more. Elizabeth never listened to such talk. It is true, once she witnessed the Prophet driving intimately with a woman who was not Mrs. Smith. Another time she spotted him calling at the door of the widow Mrs. Martin. Yet Elizabeth never permitted such evidence to indent her belief. Now Joseph had come to reveal the rumors were true. The incidents she had witnessed were indeed indiscretions—and she had defended the Prophet when he was indefensible. Even more startling, Joseph was telling her these acts of passion were divined by God! Imagine, Reader, this good woman's shock and dismay!

For a long time the room was silent, the evening sun burning low outside. Elizabeth looked up to find her young boys, Gilbert and Aaron, outside peering through the window, eager to catch a glimpse of the beloved Prophet. Their noses were pink and had the look of two fresh buds beneath a glass. Elizabeth shooed them away.

"As you know," said Joseph, "we must accept God's will."

The idea of sharing her husband, in the manner of lustful animals sharing a lair, was abhorrent to Elizabeth. She could not accept it as true. She turned in her chair, for she could no longer look at Joseph Smith.

"Sister Elizabeth, tell me, what do you say?"

"My husband has a wife," she said. "Me."

The hour was dusk. The room had filled with the silver of the gloaming. Joseph's face was now obscure, except the blue stones of his eyes. "I'll tell you, I first resisted this Revelation as well. My dear sweet Emma, she turned against it. She wanted nothing of it. For a long time we denied it. Many nights we prayed over it. Now the time has come to embrace

125

it, for it is the Truth. Consider why the Lord would want us to accept it. Think of what He has planned for the Latter-day Saints. He has chosen us to populate the Earth in preparation for Judgment. To fill the lands with the faithful. To ready His people for—"

"Stop!" cried Chauncey. "For God's sake, stop. We don't want any part of it."

For some time thereafter all three were silent, staring at the fire dying on the stone. After many minutes, Joseph said it was time to leave. Before he departed, he made a final attempt.

"I said the same thing. I begged the Lord to change this Truth. This was the one Revelation I pleaded to be not so. Do you think this is what I wanted? He has commanded it, as with all else. Your regret does not surprise me. I expected no other response. Before I leave I must ask one thing."

"My wife has said no," said Chauncey. "Even if she were to say yes, I would never agree."

The quality of his resolve placed him even closer to Elizabeth's heart. At this moment she felt a love for her husband that surpassed any emotion she had known before.

"I understand," said Joseph. "And I ask you to pray over the meaning of God's love."

When Joseph was gone, Elizabeth and Chauncey fell to their knees. They prayed for knowledge, but it did not come, for their hatred of the Revelation would not relent. Chauncey took Elizabeth's hand. In his fingers she felt his fury. It nearly crushed her bones.

"Tomorrow I'll go see him," he said. "Even if I have to wait all day I'll tell him we can't follow this order. The other Revelations guide us to lead a good life, but this one?"

"He says it's the Lord's will."

"No, this time Joseph is wrong. He's using his authority to cover his own personal sins."

"If Joseph is wrong about this . . ." said Elizabeth. Yet she could not finish. The meaning was too heavy to bear.

"I'll go tomorrow," said Chauncey. "And tell him you refuse."

"What if he says I'm unfaithful?"

"Do you believe you are?"

Yet the next day the events of history preceded Chauncey's defiance. On June 7 the *Nauvoo Expositor* published its maiden issue, every inch of its newsprint determined to reveal the truth about Joseph Smith. The newspaper accused him of "abominations and whoredoms." Most damning of all was the fact that former Saints were printing these stories, men who had once believed in Joseph and yet had come to recognize him as a liar and scoundrel. Each of the newspaper's two principal editors, William Law and Robert D. Foster, had a particularly damning story to tell. Law, a leading economic advisor to Smith, had learned that Smith had asked his wife—and by this I mean William Law's wife!—to become a spiritual wife. That is, quite simply, a theologically cloaked manner of inviting a woman to commit adultery. Robert Foster, a contractor, returned home one evening to discover his wife dining alone with the Prophet. She admitted the Prophet was trying to convince her to become a wife. The Prophet was, as they say, seducing women all over town.

There is no fiercer wrath than that of the cornered animal's. Joseph was wounded by the *Expositor*'s revelations. For years his loyal Saints had ignored the rumors of adultery, polygamy, and a Prophet who too often succumbed to lust, but now it was impossible, for the accusations came from friends. Law and Foster were among Nauvoo's most prominent, known for their honesty and devotion. On that day in June 1844, in the beautiful city of Nauvoo, beneath the high summer sky, there was not a Saint who did not have a cloud of doubt in his heart about Joseph Smith.

Joseph responded by denouncing the *Expositor* and the men behind it. This time, however, his denials were not enough. It seems he never considered telling the truth. Instead he gathered his city council, declared the *Expositor* a civic nuisance, and sent his men to destroy it. A squadron from Joseph's private militia, the Nauvoo Legion, cousins of the infamous Danites, marched over to the newspaper's offices, tore apart the press, and burned every copy of the *Expositor*.

It must be noted at this time Joseph's enemies beyond Nauvoo were taking aim. His theocratic rule in Nauvoo had long piqued the political elite throughout the country, stirring up profound animosity and suspicion. Clerical leaders all over Illinois were denouncing the Mormons and their leader as impure. With the *Expositor*'s unconstitutional destruction, Joseph's outside enemies had reason to pounce. Threatened by Joseph's accumulation of power, the Governor of Illinois could no longer tolerate a Prophet of God as a rival. The Governor charged Joseph with riot and treason, ordering his arrest.

The news of these events came as great confusion to Elizabeth. She prayed for understanding—is it a whoredom and abomination if it is commanded by God? *Heavenly Father, tell me.*

Before his arrest Joseph addressed his followers outside the new Temple. Chauncey and Elizabeth stood in the crowd, listening to the Prophet defend himself. "The newspaper lies," he cried. "The legislature lies. The Governor lies. Next, I tell you, the President of the United States will lie to you. Show me where in all Nauvoo are these supposed abominations and whoredoms? Where, I ask you? Where? If they are here, I should like to see them for myself and judge them for myself, as should you!"

These were the last words Elizabeth was to hear from her Prophet. She struggled to perceive their meaning. In her struggle she reached a pitiful conclusion—she was no longer faithful, for now, during Joseph's time of need, she had abandoned him to doubt.

The order came for Joseph to submit to the jailhouse at Carthage. At midday on June 24 Joseph and his loyal brother, Hyrum, and several others departed Nauvoo, riding through the Flats. They knew the dangers awaiting them. The hatred for the Saints, and Joseph especially, had grown in recent days. At night, packs of invisible men slit the throats of the Saints' oxen and burned their crops. They pulled Mormon men from their horses and threatened their wives. They poisoned their dogs. That bright June, the mood in Nauvoo turned dark and perilous.

Joseph rode to Carthage without force. Emma has since reported he said to her, "I am going like a lamb to slaughter." At Carthage he spent two nights. The jailer, Mr. Stigall, moved him and the others from the suffocating dungeon to the debtor's cell on the first floor, which exposed them to assassins, and finally to his own bedroom atop the stairs.

It was evident to all that the prisoners' lives were in danger. I do not believe we will ever know if Mr. Stigall, who lived in the jailhouse with his wife and daughters, played a role in the murder, although it is unlikely, for his daughters were present at the time of the attack. He was away from his post when the mob arrived on June 27 in the afternoon. There were between 150 and 200 men, many with faces blackened by coal soot. They stormed the jailhouse, mounted the stairs, and fired through the door into the bedroom. A ball hit Hyrum beside the nose. Joseph lunged to aid his brother, but he was already dead. Soon the attackers broke through the door. Joseph ran to the window—his only escape. It was twenty feet to the ground. He hesitated at the sill. Shots rang out and he took two balls to the back. A rifleman stationed at the water well below shot him through the heart. Joseph plunged out the window to the ground. Willard Richards, a witness and friend, claims the Prophet's final words were, "Oh Lord, my God!"

The agony of martyrdom is almost too much to bear. In the early hours, when the loss is fresh, there is no comfort in knowing Glory will live on. We speak of the martyrs of History but we cannot know the actual pain they suffered in their final living hours. They enter the realm of the mythic, but we must never forget these were men like ourselves. When their flesh is torn, they cry out. They suffer as you and I would suffer, although more bravely. Remember Christ. Although I am now an enemy to Joseph's legacy, I shudder when recalling his pain.

After Joseph's murder, his enemies across the county and the state believed the Saints would rise up in revenge. They fled or hid their families and livestock, fearful of Mormon wrath. Yet the Saints did not return violence with violence. Instead they withstood their grief in noble peace. Joseph's body was set out in the dining room of the Mansion House. Elizabeth, along with her two sons, waited hours to pass by his open coffin to see his historic face one last time. When she saw him, and the depth of his sleep, and truly understood she would not see him again until the Last Day, she wept.

Three years later, upon departing Nauvoo for the Utah Territory, my mother wrote a Testimony of Faith. She sealed it in a granite box that was buried at the Temple's foundation, there to be found by a new generation of Saints. Yet before she did so, she crosshatched a draft of her Testimony into a Book of Mormon, which she has since given me. I will quote from it here to describe, in her words, her reaction to the Prophet's death.

"I could not summon, neither then nor now, the words to depict the complexities of my grief. My Prophet was gone; but his death had freed me from his loathsome request. Had he spoke the truth throughout his life, erring only in his final days? Was this why he had succumbed to the enemy's ball? Or were his final words also true and devout? Upon seeing his body laid out, I prayed to God, frightened I had caused Joseph's fall. Was his murder, I asked, punishment for my doubt? Was I to blame? I feared the truth."

Thereafter, throughout the summer, the Apostles fought

over who would lead the Church of Latter-day Saints. At the time of Joseph's death, several, including Brigham, were away on mission, and the matter was not settled until the 8th of August of that year. On that day, at ten in the morning, Brother Sidney Rigdon gathered the community of Saints in a hollow east of the Temple. The day was warm and damp, the flies buzzing in the boughs. The grove could not provide enough shade, and many stood in the shadow of their horses. Brother Rigdon hoped to lead the Saints and asked for their support. At length he preached with honest remorse in his voice. Yet his performance had not convinced the Saints he was their leader. Brigham followed Rigdon, and to describe his appearance I must quote my mother's Testimony again, for it is in this passage she is at her most eloquent on the mysteries of belief.

"When Brigham took the stand to describe his grief and his hope for our Church, he inspired our hearts. He began to speak as Joseph had once spoken, adopting his voice and mannerisms, often clearing his throat with the familiar Ahhem and creating his peculiar whistle. As time passed, Brigham began to appear even more like Joseph, until it no longer seemed he was adopting the voice and expressions of our beloved Prophet—the familiar gestures of his right hand, the movement of body—but in fact the mantle of Joseph had passed to Brigham, and Brigham was now Joseph! In the limp summer haze, there before me, a miracle occurred. I saw Brigham transform into Joseph himself. Upon the stand, where Brigham had stood, stood now our beloved Joseph! As clear as the page before me now, and the lines of ink, our Prophet appeared.

"Some say it was a trick of the sunlight, or the ghostly way Brigham's voice traveled through the hollow. Others claim the heat had tampered with our minds; or fresh grief had overcome our reasoning. I understand why they might say such things, yet I write this now to say—I know what I saw. Before me, and the community of Saints, in the dappled light, for one brief moment in Time, Joseph returned, entering Brigham's powerful body, the two united by the force of God. Chauncey did not see this. My Husband becomes discouraged when I speak of it. Yet I know the fact of it as well as I know anything, for I understand why. Joseph had returned to clear the dark doubt from my heart. And so it came to pass."*

By the end of the day the succession was settled. Brigham Young was proclaimed the new leader of the Latter-day Saints. He was forty-three years old, and about to become one of the most influential men in the United States. Elizabeth rejoiced, for her experience told her it was meant to be. A month later, on September 13, 1844, she bore a tiny daughter who came into this world with the voice of a howling angel, I am told. That child, of course, was me.

*The authoress would like to assert that many eyewitnesses have left similar accounts of an inexplicable vision and that Elizabeth Webb was not unique in seeing that which could not be seen. Even some thirty years later, my mother still claims she experienced the supernatural on that summer day in Nauvoo.

VII

WOMEN'S STUDIES

Women's Research Institute
Brigham Young University
WS 492—Women's Studies Senior Research Seminar
Professor Mary P. Sprague
April 23, 2005

THE FIRST WIFE

By Kelly Dee

1.

The subject of this paper, Elizabeth Churchill Webb (1817–1884), is not familiar to many. She was an early convert to the Church and the first wife of wainwright Chauncey Webb (1812–1903), whose Nauvoo wagonry played a crucial role in the Exodus (1846–1847). Brigham Young personally chose Chauncey to lead the wagon manufacturing for the Pioneers in their trek to Zion.

My interest in Elizabeth Webb, however, has less to do with her role in supporting her husband during this historic period. Instead, I am more curious about her relationship to her daughter, Ann Eliza, who would go on to become Brigham Young's infamous 19th wife. In the 1870s and 1880s, Ann Eliza (1844–date unknown) became a leading crusader in the fight to end polygamy in the United States. In her battle against plural marriage she became a vocal enemy of both the Church and Brigham, writing a best-selling memoir of her experiences, *The 19th Wife* (1875). Her book, and especially her attacks against Brigham, continue to divide people today. Given that she was born into the Church, and her parents were faithful members, her deep hatred of Mormonism has surprised and confused many. It is therefore worth investigating her early family life, especially her mother's attitude to plural marriage. This is why I have chosen Elizabeth Churchill Webb as the subject of my seminar paper.

Specifically, I will use two key texts to depict this historic period in her life: 1) Elizabeth's recently discovered Testimony of Faith[1] to narrate the period in her life when she first accepted the doctrine of celestial marriage; and 2) her Exodus diary, written on her journey to Zion in 1848, an insightful document that has sat ignored in the Church archives for more than one hundred years.

2.

One day in the fall of 1845, Brigham Young walked to Elizabeth and Chauncey Webb's small but prominent brick house on the corner of Parley and Granger streets in the central district of Nauvoo known as the Flats.[2] The spiritual and political leader of the Latter-day Saints, and successor to Joseph Smith's title of Prophet, came alone. Such a private visit by Brigham Young, unannounced and unattended by aide, was an unusual event. No doubt Chauncey and Elizabeth were surprised to see him at their door.

The mood in Nauvoo at this time was anxious. Since

---

[1] In 1999, not long after the rebuilding of the Nauvoo Temple began, Church historians were excited to discover a time capsule buried in the original Temple's foundation. The capsule itself is a granite box, measuring three feet long and two feet wide and one and a half feet tall. An inscription on its stone lid describes the contents to be the Testimonies of Faith, or personal statements of belief, written by a number of Saints departing Nauvoo for Salt Lake in 1846. When Church historians and leaders opened the time capsule at the rededication of the Nauvoo Temple on June 27, 2002, they were disappointed to discover that water had destroyed, or partially damaged, a number of Testimonies, including an estimated twelve pages of the Testimony written by Elizabeth Churchill Webb. While frustratingly truncated, the surviving fragments of Elizabeth's Testimony provide many insightful glimpses into her outlook during this historic period (1844–1846). Today the document is held in the Family History Center in Nauvoo.

[2] Unless otherwise stated, my source is Elizabeth Churchill Webb's Testimony. General information about early Mormon history and Nauvoo comes from personal research conducted during my recent spring break trip there.

Joseph's martyrdom in June 1844, the Saints had been fearful of a massacre similar to the one at Haun's Mill. There were signs that a major raid was about to come. At night haystacks were burned in open fields. Dogs were beheaded and livestock poisoned. Carriages on the road to Quincy were ambushed. Illinois governor Thomas Ford warned Brigham to lead his followers out of the state; if he did not, the governor could not promise their safety. The Saints' future was altogether uncertain to everyone except Brigham, who was busy making secret plans for the Exodus that would lead his followers to what was still an unknown destination.

Brigham and Chauncey met in the keeping room at the front of the house. Elizabeth remained in the kitchen at the back of the house while her sons, Gilbert, age eleven, and Aaron, age seven, played outside in the orchard. Ann Eliza, now one year old, lay restless in her cradle beside the fire. The Webbs' house girl, Lydia Taft,[3] came and went through the back door, minding the boys in the orchard. They had invented a game of looking for the faces of Jesus, Mary, and Joseph Smith in the rotten apples littering the orchard yard this time of year. Lydia and the boys fed the apples to the billy goat, a spotted animal christened (ironically, it must be assumed) Mr. Pope.[4]

After half an hour Brigham asked Elizabeth to join them in the keeping room. With baby Ann Eliza in her arms, she went to see her husband and her Prophet. Elizabeth thought she knew the topic of the conversation: "I was certain he had come to remind me of the Revelation I feared most," Elizabeth writes in one fragment, referring to celestial marriage, or polygamy. "I know now I feared it because it was true."

First, Brigham had other business, however. He told her about the wagon order he had just placed with Chauncey.

---

[3] Her real name was Elizabeth Taft, but they called her Lydia to avoid confusion.

[4] See Taft, Lydia, Letters (Family History Library).

Soon he would announce an Exodus from Nauvoo, he said, commencing the following spring. "Our destination is Zion," Brigham explained. "Soon God will reveal its location to me."

Chauncey would lead the crucial effort to build the necessary wagons for the journey. Elizabeth took understandable pride in her husband's selection as chief wainwright. "He is a necessary man," she writes.

They discussed in detail the requirements.[5] Each wagon would need to haul two thousand pounds of supplies. Every fifth wagon would carry a spare front wheel, every tenth wagon a spare rear wheel. Every twentieth required a slot for a beehive. Brigham's meticulous orders displayed his considerable skills at planning and organizing. Before he was to lead nearly twenty thousand people across the plains and the Rockies, he was to think through every possible requirement and contingency. Between 1847 and 1869, some seventy thousand Pioneers would owe their lives to Brigham's painstaking planning, staging, and organization. This is why George Bernard Shaw called him an American Moses. This is why his statue stands in the Capitol in Washington, D.C., today, alongside other national heroes such as George Washington and Dwight D. Eisenhower.[6]

It is important to remember that at this time Brigham was still a relatively young man. Our image of him today is based on the later portraits made long after the establishment of the Utah Territory, when he had entered late middle age. In 1845, however, he was a vigorous man of forty-four. One immigrant described his face as "that of a sea captain"—firm, a bit square, with iron-colored eyes. He had wide cheeks, a small mouth, and an altogether determined look.[7]

_____

[5] Chauncey would end up building between 1,000 and 1,500 wagons used at various stages of the Exodus.

[6] Much of my general information about Brigham comes from *Brigham Young: American Moses* by Leonard J. Arrington (Knopf, 1985).

[7] To me, this younger Brigham looks a lot like Russell Crowe.

"It was no relief to know that he had come with a request for wagons, and not another," Elizabeth writes in her Testimony. "For I knew one day he would ask what I dreaded most." Understandably, she was frightened. Section 132 of the Doctrine & Covenants—the Revelation Joseph Smith had personally revealed to Elizabeth and Chauncey the day before his arrest—says that those who fail to meet the requirements of plural marriage cannot achieve Salvation. It is a point worth emphasizing: The Church—that is, the men Elizabeth believed and trusted most—was telling her that she would be condemned eternally if she did not submit fully to this hated custom.

"And yet, there is another matter," said Brigham. With those few words, the mood in the room had changed. The baby began to simper. Even as she minded her daughter, Elizabeth knew her fear had been warranted: Brigham had in fact come to discuss plural marriage.

"I know Brother Joseph discussed the covenant of celestial marriage with you shortly before his martyrdom. I know he shared the Revelation of plural marriage."

"Is it really the will of the Lord?" Elizabeth asked.

"It is."

As much as she loathed the idea, she then knew that this time she could not deny her Lord or her Prophet. She thought back to the meeting with Joseph. We cannot know how many times she blamed herself for his fate by refusing to comply, but such a sentiment appears forcefully in her Testimony.

"Tell me, Sister," said Brigham, "what do you say?"

"I will do as He asks."

It was done. Brigham blessed her. Elizabeth wept softly in her husband's arms.

A decade later, in a letter to one of his sons, Brigham describes how he had to "console the astonished hearers of this news. I told them that I too heard of it and hated it immediately. Yet if we are to listen to our God, and follow His command, we cannot choose those orders which most please us, and ignore those that cause us pain. For verily, it has been revealed, this is our way to Heaven, and to ignore the path is to ignore Salvation altogether. I remember telling a Brother and a Sister of the Revelation in Nauvoo. Together we fell to our knees and prayed. It was all I could offer, for the truth comes as such."[8]

Next Brigham explained to Elizabeth and Chauncey that the approval of the second wife belonged to the first. "Brother Chauncey must come to you for your consent. The choice of wife, who she shall be, lies with you."

A "small fury" burned within Elizabeth as Brigham explained the process. If she must submit to plural marriage, she wanted nothing to do with the selection of the wife. Although it is doubtful she thought of it in such terms, Elizabeth resented the complicity the institution was forcing upon her.

When Brigham was gone, Chauncey and Elizabeth discussed the matter. Chauncey probably hated the idea even more than his wife did. Unlike Elizabeth, there seemed to be a bottom to his faith. He said he would tell Brigham they could not follow his orders. "He cannot force us."

Yet for Elizabeth, it was too late. She had searched her soul and reached a truth. "We must obey," she said. For her, apostasy was not an option. She remembered what had happened the last time she had defied her Prophet. Thus, in the end, it was Elizabeth who decided Chauncey would take a second wife.

3.

Lydia Taft was seventeen when she left her family in Saint Clair County, Michigan, in the summer of 1844. A few months before, a missionary had come to preach from the

---

[8] Brigham to Brigham Jr., November 3, 1855.

Book of Mormon in a neighbor's parlor, electrifying Lydia with his news of the Restoration and his depiction of Nauvoo, the shining city on the hill. She left the meeting with a copy of the Book of Mormon, determined to read it. By the time she turned the last page, her faith was secure. "I knew. Mother, I knew!" she would later write in one of her three surviving letters.

When news of Joseph Smith's martyrdom reached her, she decided to travel to Nauvoo to live among the Saints. "The time is now. That's what Joseph Smith in death has taught me. Now! Oh my dear Mother. Please read this Book! And then come be with me in Nauvoo! It's a city that gleams upon the river bank, and men can see the white Temple from all directions, and every day the faithful arrive from all over the world."

After landing in Nauvoo, Lydia found work in the Webb household. At the time, Elizabeth was pregnant with Ann Eliza. It was a difficult pregnancy and she needed the help. When she hired Lydia, Elizabeth could not have imagined that a little more than a year later the girl would become her rival wife.

The only known picture of Lydia was taken many years later in Salt Lake. It shows a thin, tired woman with buried eyes. But in 1845, when she was seventeen, she was "pale and lovely," according to Elizabeth, "with a slow soft mouth and flecks of gold in her eyes."

There is conflicting evidence over who first suggested Lydia to become Chauncey's second wife. In the surviving fragments of her Testimony, Elizabeth writes, "Lydia no doubt loved my children. I had grown accustomed to her presence and the sound of her feet." In *The 19th Wife* Ann Eliza says she recalls her father looking at Lydia "in a manner a husband reserves for his wife." Perhaps he did so, but Ann Eliza's memory of it is doubtful (she was one year old at the time). We may not know whose idea it was, but by late 1845 Chauncey and Elizabeth had decided to enter a

141

plural marriage with Lydia. Now they only needed her to agree.

At some point, Elizabeth writes, Lydia began to eat with the family at the supper table. "She ceased being our servant in many ways." We don't know if this was after the idea was broached or before. We have Lydia's account of the actual conversation preserved in a letter to her mother. It took place late on a blizzardy night, the children already in bed. The snow was blowing hard, and the drifts were mounting past the windowsills. To Lydia, it seemed like the type of storm that would trap them in the house for a week. Chauncey invited Lydia and Elizabeth into the keeping room to pray.

After fifteen minutes on their knees, Chauncey rose and began to throw more wood on the fire. His back was to the women as he poked the coals. Without turning around, he described the Revelation, as told first by Joseph then Brigham.

"I know," Lydia shrugged. "I've heard of it too. Girls can talk."

Chauncey asked her opinion of the Revelation.

"I see it only one way. I will do what the Lord asks to carry forth His Kingdom." This is what Lydia says she said. There is no way to confirm whether or not she truly showed such resolve at such a young age. In reading through a number of letters and diaries by the early Saints, I have noted a pattern of speech that sounds more like religious text than actual dialogue. It is difficult to know if the early Saints truly used such language and diction, or if they recorded their conversations in a way that exalted their words. Even so, there is little reason to doubt that Lydia embraced the idea swiftly.

In *The 19th Wife* Ann Eliza says her mother thanked Lydia but privately fumed. I have tried to confirm this particular detail, but there seems to be little record of exactly how Elizabeth felt that night. Given what we know, Elizabeth most likely felt a sense of deliverance, accomplishment, and submission mixed with regret, betrayal, confusion, and jealousy. She writes of comparing her own hands ("worn, raw,

142

scraped on the knuckle") to Lydia's ("white as a petal, and just as soft"). There's a hint that she was surprised—and perhaps appalled—by Lydia's quick consent. Most painfully, Lydia claims that Chauncey, as he finally turned from the mantel, looked as if he might devour the teenage girl. "I could see he was so overcome with desire for me," Lydia writes to her mother.

"He could not speak. Men, for the most part, reveal their true thoughts in their shallow faces. Concealment will always remain the female art. I thought, if he could he would wed me that night."

In the surviving scraps of Elizabeth's testimony there is one line that stands out. I cannot identify the event that caused it, but it very well could be her description of how she felt after this conversation. "I cried through the night," she writes. "Until the dawn, and beyond." There is no reason to think these were tears of joy.

4.

On the clear, frozen morning of January 21, 1846, the Webbs and their housegirl gathered at the Nauvoo Temple. Although still under construction, the Temple had been used by Brigham for several months for services and sealing and endowment ceremonies. At the time the Temple was one of the largest buildings in the western United States. Built of white limestone cubes, it was like a beacon to the river traffic going north and south.[9]

Much of what we know about the sealing and the wedding ceremony comes from *The 19th Wife*. Chauncey wore a high collar that irritated his beard. Elizabeth was in a plain dark dress with narrow silk cuffs. Lydia had draped a new lace

[9] Although the Saints were preparing to abandon Nauvoo, hundreds of laborers continued to erect the Temple until their last days in Illinois. This effort always strikes me as a profound symbol of their faith in both their Church and Brigham.

shawl across her shoulders. Her iron hairpins caught the winter sun. According to Ann Eliza, Chauncey and Elizabeth appeared solemn, while Lydia seemed giddy.[10]

Brigham began the ceremony by sealing Chauncey and Elizabeth. The sealing ceremony varies little from most Christian wedding ceremonies. The difference, of course, is that instead of "until death do us part" the couple is united through eternity. Although this is typically one of the happiest moments in the life of a member of the LDS Church, we cannot assume it was so for Elizabeth. "She believed she would be with her husband forever—no doubt a comforting thought—but at what price?" asks Ann Eliza. "My mother stood in the Temple and the sunlight came down upon her. I believe if my mother ever had a moment of doubt, it was now." Elizabeth's account of this day was all but destroyed. Yet among the fragments one curious line leaps out: "Oh my faith!"

With Chauncey and Elizabeth now sealed, Brigham instructed Elizabeth to step aside. He guided her to his left, replacing her with Lydia, who "was bouncing on her toes."[11] Quickly he united Chauncey and Lydia in marriage. Their vows were also similar to those used at most Christian weddings. Here, at death, their marriage would cease. In the afterlife, Chauncey would have one wife, the woman who had just been ushered aside. How did Elizabeth feel as she stood by and listened to her husband devote himself to a girl almost half her age? How did she feel, knowing they would all return home, share in a wedding feast, followed by her husband withdrawing to Lydia's bedroom to consummate the marriage?

---

[10] In *The 19th Wife*, Ann Eliza writes about many events in her parents' lives that took place either before she was born or when she was too young to remember them. According to her public lectures, she wrote about her parents by interviewing her mother and her half-brother, Gilbert, while preparing her manuscript.

[11] *The 19th Wife.*

We must rely on her children, and our imaginations, for the answer. Ann Eliza writes: "After supper, the newlyweds retired to Lydia's room off the kitchen. My father had purchased a new brass-post bed. The lamplight reflected off the brass exotically, casting the room in a golden glow. My mother saw Lydia go in first, sit upon the bed, and remove the pins from her hair. Her hair fell to her shoulders in a flaxen wave. She brushed it out and it shone around her head like a halo. When my father came to Lydia's door she held her hand out and said, 'Come.' He closed the door behind him, leaving my mother to the dirty dishes in the pan."

Gilbert, Elizabeth's illegitimate son, witnessed the same scene, recording it in his diary.[12] "Lydia seemed eager for the night to come to an end. Her foot tapped as we ate and she said she was too tired for singing. After supper she disappeared into her room. Soon my father followed. I helped my mother with the dishes and the pots. I went outside to fetch water from the well. I had to pass by Lydia's window. I would be a liar if I said I did not look in. I witnessed what I expected—a mound of flesh. I didn't like the idea that they were doing this because of God. It's terrible to see your own Pa in such a manner."

It is worth noting that we have diaries and letters from many women who praised the day a second (or third, fourth, or even fifth wife) entered her house. A sister wife meant a woman was fulfilling her religious obligations. It meant she was that much closer to Heaven. More practically, a sister wife also meant help with the household chores and, typically, some relief from conjugal relations. Many women found joy in the institution. But many did not. The evidence suggests Elizabeth was among those who mourned the night she passed her husband to another woman. As one Pioneer

---

[12] See Webb, Gilbert, Diary (Family History Center). Gilbert Webb, Ann Eliza's half-brother, was an eloquent but infrequent diarist. He is best remembered for his written deposition provided in Ann Eliza's divorce against Brigham Young in 1873.

woman described it a decade later, "A piece of my soul chipped off that night and fell away."[13]

A curious postscript to Chauncey's first plural marriage: Brigham himself may have entered into up to eleven plural marriages the same month. The numbers have been a source of debate for more than 150 years. I have little hope of settling the matter here. According to some accounts, on January 21, 1846, the same day he sealed Lydia to Chauncey, Brigham took two wives himself, Martha Bowker (1822–1890) and Ellen Rockwood (1829–1866). The evidence for these weddings is far from ideal: mostly secondhand testimonies or statements made long after the fact. Yet given the secretive and illegal nature of plural marriage in general, and especially those of the leader of the Latter-day Saints, it is understandable that there is little paper trail.[14]

5.

According to Ann Eliza, the wedding night was an extended affair. Like many homes in Nauvoo, the Webb house, although comfortable, was not large. It is easy to imagine noise traveling from one room to the next, across the floorboards or through the space where a door meets its jamb. "My father tried to quiet the girl," Ann Eliza writes in *The 19th Wife*. "But she did not care. Lydia squealed like a pig at the docking of its tail. Someone less forgiving might say she wanted my mother to hear." This is the kind of secondhand reporting and passive-aggressive tone that Ann Eliza uses throughout her memoir; it's why many have dismissed it as unreliable. No doubt Ann Eliza is taking sides here; her bias

[13] "The Other Wife in Pioneer Homes: Recollections of Joy & Sorrow," edited by the Daughters of the Utah Pioneers (1947).

[14] The most conservative estimate of Brigham's total number of wives at the time of his death (August 29, 1877) is nineteen. The most liberal estimates are about fifty-six. Many LDS historians have settled on the number twenty-seven.

is hardly veiled. But when compared with Gilbert's version of events, one can see that she was more or less reporting the truth, even if her tone is sharpened: "That first night," Gilbert writes in his diary, "Lydia made herself known to my father and the rest of us too. I went to the barn to sleep, knowing the horses to be more quiet and always preferring their company."

"People change." That's Ann Eliza's assessment of Lydia following her marriage to Chauncey. The former house girl now expected to be treated as the woman of the house. Almost at once she refused to participate in the household work, demanding that Chauncey hire a girl to take over her old chores. She wanted a replica of every finery in Elizabeth's wardrobe: hat, pin, and glove. There was a nasty spat over a piece of jewelry Chauncey had given his wife when Ann Eliza was born, a pearl on a gold stick. Ann Eliza reports a fight between the two women. "Lydia scratched my mother until there was blood," she writes in her memoir. Elizabeth responded with a slap and pulling Lydia's hair. Ann Eliza analyzes this particular episode astutely: "So often plural marriage reduces a thoughtful, generous, mature woman to a sniveling, selfish little girl. Perhaps it is the cruelest outcome: the removal, and destruction, of a woman's dignity. I have seen it too many times to count. I forgive the men who have done this to womankind, but I never forget."

"In conjugal matters," Ann Eliza writes frankly, "[Lydia's] demands were even greater." It was common in a plural marriage for the newest wife to resent sharing her husband's affections with the previous spouse or spouses. According to Ann Eliza, "In the first two weeks of marriage, my father spent each night with his new bride. He offered little attention to his original wife. When it was time to retire he would kiss my mother on the tip of the nose and slip into Lydia's room. I know my mother wondered if she would ever see her husband again."

Even so, Lydia complained to Chauncey that he was

spending too much time with the first Mrs. Webb. Gilbert recalls the young bride sighing, "And what am I supposed to do while you're with *her*?"

As monstrous as these recollections make Lydia out to be, we should remember that she was still a teenager, naive, and devout. She was cast into a situation that even the savviest courtesan might not know how to maneuver. She feared that the secretive nature of her marriage meant it could be quickly abandoned, annulled, or even denied. During the first month of marriage, Lydia wrote her mother: "You were right, Mother. The meaning of marriage can be unknowable. I try to keep him happy, but sometimes I do not know what will please him, and what will cause a wrinkled look of displeasure. I do not cry in front of him, or before the children, and certainly not Mrs. Webb. When I feel the need, I go outside with the animals. My faith comforts me more than ever, for I know that God and His Son will now welcome me, when the time comes, for I have fulfilled my duty. I am now Wife." We must bear this in mind before we condemn Lydia: Her spiritual leaders had told her this was her path to Salvation.

Elizabeth put up with Lydia's selfish behavior for only so long. One evening she spoke with her husband. "I have drawn up a chart," she said. "On Mondays, Wednesdays, and Fridays, you will spend the evening with her."

Chauncey relented immediately. "You're right. Tuesdays, Thursdays, and Saturdays will be yours. I'll spend Sunday night alone, here in the keeping room. That'll even it out."

"On Sundays," Elizabeth said firmly, "you'll be with me."

6.

Such disharmony in the Webb household took place while the Saints were preparing for their greatest test yet. The Exodus was scheduled to begin with the spring weather, but new threats of massacre compelled Brigham to declare

Nauvoo no longer safe. On February 4, 1846, in the dark heart of winter, the first Saints crossed the Mississippi to Sugar Creek, Iowa. Brigham did not make the treacherous crossing for another eleven days, staying behind in Nauvoo to perform several Endowment Ceremonies to Saints anxious to be blessed before abandoning their beloved Temple. By March 1, some two thousand Saints huddled in wagons and tents in Sugar Creek. Their journey had begun, yet their destination was still unknown. From here Brigham led the Saints roughly 350 miles, at a rate of approximately six miles per day, to what would become a yearlong way station on the Nebraska side of the Missouri River, Winter Quarters, an exposed encampment roughly six miles upriver from the site of present-day Omaha.

Chauncey and his family remained in Nauvoo until early April 1846. He was too busy building wagons to join the early emigrants. Eventually they too packed up, leaving behind nearly all their possessions and wealth. The Webbs— Chauncey, his two rival wives, and three children— joined the Exodus, crossing the Mississippi in two bonneted wagons pulled by three yoke of oxen. They carried a year's supply of provisions, their clothing, and their faith. The Webbs reached Winter Quarters by midsummer. By September, some twenty thousand Saints had gathered there, each having placed his or her life into the hands of Brigham Young. Once a city rivaling Chicago, Nauvoo was now a ghost town. The wondrous Temple—the pride and handiwork of thousands of Saints— was abandoned. In a few years it would be in ruins, resembling a pile of ancient rubble in Rome or Greece, with animals sleeping among its stones.[15] The Nauvoo Temple would not rise again until 2002.

For Elizabeth Churchill Webb, this event would prove momentous. This is the moment she buried her Testimony in

---

[15] At the end of *The 19th Wife*, Ann Eliza poignantly describes returning to Nauvoo to see the Temple ruins.

the time capsule, leaving for us an eloquent, if incomplete, record of her faith.

7.

As every LDS member knows, the Saints would end up staying in Winter Quarters for almost a year. Under Brigham's direction, they laid out blocks of flimsy tents, open-sided dugouts, and simple log sheds, building a temporary city to survive the winter of 1846–1847. Brigham called it the Camp of Israel. The settlement included community facilities such as a gristmill, a school, and several workshops to produce basic goods. Among these was Chauncey's wainwright shop. Here, with help from his stepson, Gilbert, he built and repaired the wagons that would carry the Saints on their upcoming journey.

In January 1847, in a Revelation, God instructed Brigham to lead the Saints to the Rocky Mountains. The Heavenly Father assured His Prophet he would know the exact place to build their new Zion when he saw it. Word spread through Winter Quarters that a long journey would begin soon; everyone busied themselves with final preparations. For the Webbs, however, this meant their own departure would have to be delayed. Once again Chauncey's wainwright shop was needed to support the departing Saints, the majority of whom left Winter Quarters in the spring and summer of 1847. By the time Chauncey's work was done, it was too late for the Webbs to depart for Zion; the autumn snows would catch them. The Webbs would have to wait through the winter of 1847–1848 before they could join the new settlement in Utah.

According to Ann Eliza, during this time Chauncey was under the misperception that his plural marriage remained a secret. "Sometimes a husband is wrong about very much," Ann Eliza observes. In every society—from the forums of ancient Rome to the dorms of BYU—the romantic life of others has always been subject to gossip. The early Saints were no exception. Everyone knew that Lydia was now the second Mrs. Webb. As Ann Eliza puts it, "The girl made sure of that."

Elizabeth's pain from sharing her husband with Lydia was renewed when, in November 1847, Lydia announced she would have a child. Gilbert's record of how Lydia told Elizabeth she was pregnant is worth quoting at length.

My mother set out a stew and didn't say much, minding her own business in the way that she had since Lydia became her rival. The wind was fierce, blowing through the chinks in the logs. My mother never sat to join us, she ran from the table to the hearth and back with the biscuits and the drippings and everything else. Anyone would see the difference now, what with my mother in her apron with the gravy stain above her heart while Lydia sat at the head of the table in a Summertime dress too thin for November. Her complexion was as white as the frost on the water in the well. "Children, your father and I have something important to tell you," Lydia said. "Soon you'll have a baby brother or sister." She took my father's fist and held it up like she had won a relay race.

My Ma is the most generous woman I know. She never thinks of herself if there is someone else to think of. That's why she didn't speak. When she heard the news she took a step backward. One step followed by another, and again another. It was like a moment in a fairy tale because she seemed to disappear. I know it doesn't make any sense and it isn't possible and all the rest, but that's what happened before my eyes—my mother was swallowed up by Lydia's news. If the Lord can send an angel to Joseph Smith, then a woman learning the news of her husband's baby with his other wife can disappear. And that's what happened. She was gone. For a moment we didn't know where she was. I had to go out into the cold night to bring her in. She was shivering. Several times she said—not loud but soft in a whisper—"Please. No." I led her to her bedroll beside the hearth and removed her shoes,

151

and by now my mother stopped talking altogether. I set her under the blankets. "Lay quiet," I said. It's a hard feeling for a boy to put his mother to bed like she were the child.

8.

Thankfully, Elizabeth's impulse to document her life did not end with the Testimony of Faith. In *The 19th Wife*, Ann Eliza describes her mother writing a travel diary during the Exodus. Many Saints, especially the women, kept detailed records of their journeys. These documents, many now archived by the Church, have been central to our understanding of the arduous trek from Nauvoo to Winter Quarters and ultimately to Zion. I have relied on Elizabeth's Pioneer diary, written between May 1848 and September 1848, to narrate her story during this transformative period.

The Webbs left for Zion on May 4, 1848, in a company of 1,229 Saints. The column of 397 wagons driving westward carried every imaginable provision: stoves, bureaus, rockers, farm tools, a piano. The livestock roped to the rear of the wagons included dairy cattle, horses, mules, and spotted pigs. Elizabeth notes in her diary the sounds of the other animals: "dogs barking, cats mewing, thousands of bees buzzing in their hives, and a brown squirrel flitting about its cage."

The Webbs and their fellow travelers were following in the footsteps of the Saints who had traveled a year earlier along the old Oregon Trail. Brigham had established an ingenious system of roadside mailboxes at ten-mile markers—typically the sun-bleached skull of a pronghorn antelope or an American bison—to leave information about the trail, crossings, conditions, and so forth. In 1847, the journey for Brigham and his Saints had been treacherous and uncertain. By 1848, the trip, while arduous, was no longer a mystery. Ann Eliza was almost four years old at the time. Some of her earliest memories, she tells us in *The 19th Wife*, come from this trip. For her, the journey was a period of great adventure and joy. As the wagons rolled through the prairie grass, she would skip along, picking flowers—probably milkweed, phlox, and meadow rose—and singing hymns. The sound of more than a thousand Saints singing "The Spirit of God Like a Fire Is Burning!" must have fortified them through their long days.

The itinerary was almost always the same: Every day for four and a half months the Saints rose at five, ate a hot breakfast in the dawn, and pushed forward until dusk. They rested only on the Sabbath. In her Exodus diary, Elizabeth writes of ending a day and "circling the wagons, lighting the supper fire, and watering the animals. By the time the chores were done and the children fed, the blue night sky had turned black and was lit by stars. Often I stay awake to watch the moonlight shine upon the hides of the sleeping oxen, on their moist noses, and on the white brow of Ann Eliza, who always sleeps like an angel, whether sun or storm."

The hopeful quality of their journey changed dramatically when in early June Lydia gave birth. The baby—to be named Diantha—was born with complications. Already on the journey Elizabeth had witnessed in her company three newborns die, two followed by their mothers to their prairie graves. What exactly happened to Lydia and her baby we will never know. That the situation was serious is, however, entirely clear.[16]

Elizabeth immediately recognized that the lives of both mother and child were in danger. "Lydia lay upon the tickings in the wagon-bed unable to open her eyes," Elizabeth writes. "When I called her name she did not respond. The child Diantha was even more lifeless, tiny and still at her mother's side. I did not know what to do."

[16] According to a University of Chicago study by Professor Kwang-Sun Lee, "Infant mortality rates in the nineteenth century were in the range of 130 to 230 for every 1,000 births. The main causes were diarrhea, respiratory illness, and infectious diseases such as scarlet fever, measles, whooping cough, smallpox, diphtheria, and croup." For the mid-nineteenth-century mother, parturition in any situation could be dangerous; on the wagon trail it was especially hazardous.

At this time it was common for Saints facing illness to resort to prayer and the healing powers of priests. Elizabeth describes an Elder (I cannot determine who) sitting with Lydia in the wagon-bed. "He came at night when we had stopped beside a creek. He was an old man, so worn by the journey I doubted whether he would ever see the Zion we sung about. I worried over what he was capable of."

The Elder gathered the family around Lydia in the wagon. He set his hands upon her head and prayed for her recovery. He did the same with the baby. "If the Lord so pleases, then He will save them. Now you must pray," he told the Webbs.

"What if they don't improve?"

"Then the Lord must have a reason to leave your prayers unanswered."

This struck Elizabeth in the heart. Since the wedding more than two years before, many times she had wished Lydia out of her house. She admits to having prayed for the Lord to take her away. "Many times, when I am alone at night, I must listen to my husband visiting my rival in the manner he no longer visits me. How many times have I begged the Lord to end this humiliation?" she admits in her diary. "Yet again and again I find myself alone."

Before the Elder departed he said to Elizabeth, "Look after this girl and her child. Do not let them suffer. Do what you can."

Did Elizabeth hesitate? Did she think: This is my chance to be free of my competition and return my husband to me? We do not know. If she did, the selfish impulse soon passed. For two weeks Elizabeth devoted herself to Lydia's and Diantha's recovery, refusing to leave their side. During the daily trek across the summer plains, Elizabeth applied compresses and spoonfed water and gruel. "Above all," she writes, "I prayed."

The following passage from her diary is a remarkable articulation of her faith. It provides important insight into how many early LDS women came to terms, both practical and spiritual, with plural marriage:

154

I came to see the test the Lord had set before me. Previously I had allowed myself to hate my Sister Wife. I resented each breath she pulled from the air. I resented each morsel she plucked from the plate. I resented the dent in the cushion she left when she stood from the chair. I resented the tendril of hair left on the brush. I resented her voice rising to greet me. I resented her lips on the brows of my children. I resented the very qualities that made her a fellow creature of God. My dark hatred, too, had spilled over to her unborn child. Verily I came to see that the Lord Jesus Christ had set before me a test. Do I love? He asked. Or do I hate? He had heard the cries from my wicked heart and He took pity on me. Had He answered my prayers, and removed Lydia from our family, and destroyed her child, He would not have truly loved me. No! He loved me by testing me. When I first met Brother Joseph all those years before he said to me and others, "Let us pour forth love— show forth our kindness unto all mankind, for love begets love." I await my Day of Judgment with a heart bursting open with love. Yet I had forgotten all that I believed. Kneeling beside Lydia in the wagon-bed, my faith returned. The love the Saints had shown me returned. When it did, Lydia rose and the baby howled and their health was restored. Their recovery coincided with the restoration of my faith. I can never forget this! Its meaning is clear and shall always be.

By September 1848, the Webbs and their party had reached the cool red mudstone canyon of the Weber River, only a few days out from the Salt Lake Valley. At some point, Brigham had driven from Salt Lake to meet them. At night, around the campfire, he described the Mormon Canaan they would soon find over the mountains. After only a year in the Valley, the Saints had already built up a small city of one-room log homes, neat roads on a grid, an imposing fort to defend against Native American attack, several gristmills and granaries, dozens of shops for tools and goods, and some five thousand acres of thriving crops irrigated by a sophisticated system of shallow channels, locks, and dams. "Brigham told us," Elizabeth writes in her final diary entry, "of our Promised Land. God had revealed it to Brigham, and now Brigham was revealing it to us. I held my sister wife's hand as we listened to Brigham describe the world that awaited over the pass."

On September 13, 1844, Ann Eliza celebrated her fourth birthday. "Brigham held me and touched me," she writes in *The 19th Wife*, "and smiled such that I knew I was his favorite child. On my birthday he kissed me and declared, 'This beautiful child is the future of the Saints of Deseret!'" We will never know whether or not Ann Eliza, at the age of four, could remember this scene with such clarity. Even so, when she writes of it years later in her memoir, she notes, "I was happy because I saw my mother and father happy, and my Prophet happy too. I remember his fingers on my arm and the wool of his beard on my cheek. In no way could I have known many years later this man would marry me and then try to destroy me. There were no clouds on the horizon that September in Utah. The vista was clear."

When Chauncey Webb, his two wives, and now four children arrived in Salt Lake on September 20, 1848, they were, by all accounts, a happy family. Plural marriage, once so loathsome to Elizabeth in concept, had become a part of her daily existence. Elizabeth recorded this thought in her diary: "Brigham used to say: We make room for what the Lord gives us. How true, how true." She had accommodated Lydia into her household; and the second Mrs. Webb had come to appreciate Elizabeth's companionship. Each woman felt for the other's children the way an aunt might feel for a niece or nephew. In the next few years, as the Webbs worked to establish themselves in Salt Lake, Elizabeth came to accept the second wife. "Lydia is of our family, no more or less. So says God," she often told Ann Eliza.

As Elizabeth set up a new household and participated in the settling of the Utah Territory and grew into middle age, she would have little time to linger over the insults of polygamy again until 1855—when in one feverish, indulgent month Chauncey, who must have been suffering from what we would now call a midlife crisis, married three women, each under the age of seventeen. But that, as they say, is another story.

9.

I wrote this paper for three reasons. One, to show the effects of plural marriage on one woman's life. Her story is neither representative nor unusual. It is simply that: one woman's story. There are many other narratives, written or waiting to be told, that shed further light on the practice of polygamy in early Church history. Anyone familiar with even a few of these will know that many women despised the institution, while others rejoiced in it for practical and/or spiritual reasons. Among the practical reasons were the sharing of housework, child care, and the relief from sexual obligations to one's husband. The spiritual reasons were of the highest order: The happiest plural wives believed their entrance into Heaven was secure.

The secondary purpose of this paper has been to raise up the subject of polygamy as a legitimate and unfinished topic of inquiry for LDS scholars and writers. The Church, of course, banned the practice in 1890. Since then our leaders have spoken out forcefully and consistently against it. Any honest observer would have to concede that there has been no official connection between the Church of Jesus Christ of Latter-day Saints and polygamy for more than one hundred years.

Even so, there is no denying plural marriage was an important part of early Church culture. As scholars we must look at it rigorously, understand it honestly, and place it correctly in our heritage. Some present-day Church leaders have dismissed polygamy as a "noncentral" issue, a peripheral "sideshow" to the larger issues of accepting the Restoration of

157

the Gospel, understanding the Revelations, knowing the Lord Christ, and preparing for Salvation. Yet for some nineteenth-century Saints, such as Elizabeth Churchill Webb, plural marriage was so very much a part of their daily lives, of their terrestrial existence, that to label it as "minor" or "noncentral" is to, in effect, cast aside their very earthly experiences as "minor" and "noncentral." The fact of the matter is many of the men who laid the foundations of today's Church, including our beloved Prophets Joseph and Brigham, participated in polygamy with astonishing vigor. They sanctioned it, promoted it, spread it, and exalted it. They also lied about it. This is not a criticism, but a fact. Its sting can be lessened by facing it for what it is.

Just as a long and sustained critical inquiry into slavery has helped to fortify the national psyche and shore up our nation's moral standing, so too would an examination of our founders' role in this deplorable practice help clear, at last, the misperception that Mormonism and polygamy remain somehow entwined.

Make no mistake, our detractors continue to use the issue against us today. Best-selling books, influential newspapers and magazines, and popular television programs investigate present-day polygamy and inevitably connect it back to the LDS Church. We rightly protest such misrepresentation; we reasonably decry the unfairness of the coverage; over and over we try to correct the errors. Yet I believe that our strident denial of any connection has in fact hurt our image in the larger public rather than helped it. The LDS Church has been so intent on distancing itself from polygamy, on letting the world know that we stand adamantly and unequivocally opposed to the institution, that we have ignored its actual role in our own history. By repeating the message "That has nothing to do with us!" we inadvertently minimize the effects it played on our early members, especially its women. This strategy of putting a distance between the Church today and the polygamous acts of our forefathers—

while understandable—has been misconstrued by some as whitewashing or even denial. Hence the suspicion and the constant repetition of old stories and rumors. Hence the continuous and harmful misperception that polygamous sects such as the Firsts in Mesadale and the LDS Church are one and the same.

As scholars we can change this.

My last reason is more personal. I am the great-great-great-granddaughter of Ann Eliza Young. Although my family has always taken pride in having roots that go back to the Church's founding, we have also felt shame at being the offspring of such a hurtful apostate. When I was growing up, many in my family would refer to Ann Eliza as "that woman" or simply "her." They despised her as if they had known her personally. Few had actually read *The 19th Wife*. "Nothing but a pack of lies," my grandmother used to say.[17]

Despite this, Ann Eliza and her contradictions have long fascinated me. I decided to start my inquiry into her life with her mother, my great-great-great-great-grandmother Elizabeth Churchill Webb. This seemed the best place to begin an effort to unravel Ann Eliza's true history and legacy. I plan to continue my inquiry into Ann Eliza's life itself in my graduate studies next year. The research I conducted for this paper is an important foundation for that inquiry. This summer, when I'm in Salt Lake,[18] I hope to study a wide range

---

[17] For years LDS scholars have noted Ann Eliza's obvious bias and political agenda in *The 19th Wife*. Yet for this paper, whenever I could check her version of events against another source I found general agreement. To my surprise, I have come to the opinion that Ann Eliza's memoir, at least in the depiction of her mother's life and her family's years in Nauvoo and journey to Zion, is for the most part factually reliable, although her emphasis on certain matters, while skipping over others, can at times leave the reader with a distorted impression of early Church history. Whether or not the entire memoir is factually correct, especially the passages concerning her relationship with Brigham Young, will be part of my future research.

[18] I would like to thank the Department, especially Professor Sprague, for the generous work-study grant supporting my upcoming internship at the Ann Eliza Young House, which I'm really excited about.

of documents in the Church archives, some of which scholars have never had access to. I hope these texts will provide a fuller portrait of this complex woman and her complicated place in the history of the Church of Jesus Christ of Latter-day Saints.

Lastly, through my research, I hope to determine the fate of Ann Eliza Young. After a second edition of *The 19th Wife* was published in 1908, there is no further record of her. No one knows when she died, or where, or under what circumstances. There are no obituaries, no estate records, not even a death certificate. At some point after 1908 she simply disappeared. She was once one of the most famous women in America. She changed the lives of thousands of women by fighting to end polygamy, nearly bringing down the Mormon Church in doing so. And yet she has been lost from history without a trace. We simply have no idea what happened to her. Ann Eliza's death remains a mystery. But mysteries, by their very nature, are meant to be solved.

VIII

WIFE #19:

THE GUN ON THE SCREEN

I WAS LIKE WOW

"Johnny, wake up."

"What the—?"

"I need you to get up."

"Where are we?"

We were in Mr. Heber's parking lot. The bank sign across the street said it was eight in the morning and already ninety degrees. The kid sat up, his face creased from the futon. "You got anything for breakfast?"

I threw him a packet of powdered doughnuts and he ate them silently, cautiously, while I listened to the morning news. Ten minutes later Maureen arrived in a yellow Honda with a family of stuffed penguins in the back window. She sat for a minute, flicking a plastic comb through her hair. I got out of the van and knocked on her window.

"Jordan," she gasped. "Shoot, you scared me."

"Sorry, but I just realized you never gave me a copy of the police report."

"All right, just give me a second to land." Something caught her attention over my shoulder. "Who's that?"

Johnny and Elektra were coming straight for me, each panting like, well, like a dog. "This is Johnny. I'm looking after him for a friend." I sent Johnny and Elektra back to the van, but they didn't want to go. I had to give them each a little shove.

"Dick," he said.

Inside the office it was dark and warm. Maureen went around turning on the lights and the a/c and her computer while talking about how busy Mr. Heber was lately. Finally she went to the wall of file cabinets and started

163

riffling through the S drawer. "Here it is, let me make a copy. But first I want you to be honest—what's the story with Johnny?"

"He doesn't have a place to go right now."

"If he's a runaway, you should call the police."

"He's not a runaway."

"I see," she sighed. "Another lost boy. It just breaks my heart. Did you try Jim Hooke? He runs a shelter. The man's a saint. Let me give you his number." She pecked at her keyboard and brought up the guy's deets.

Maureen put the police report in a file folder for me. "It's pretty basic," she said, "but here you are."

It described the murder scene pretty much the same as the *Register* did. Whoever filled it out had been meticulous, measuring the distance between the door and the chair, the height of the blood splatters on the wall, that sort of thing. There was a diagram of a human body, which the investigator had marked where the bullet entered my dad, and a second diagram of the backside, showing the exit wound. At the bottom of the last page, the investigator signed his name: Hiram Alton. Queenie's husband. Well, there you go.

More interesting were two little questions next to his signature: *Were photographs taken?* A little yes box was checked. *Is the investigation complete?* No.

"Maureen? Do you have the photographs?"

"What photographs?" I showed her the report. "Let me check the file." But there weren't any photos in the file.

"Would you ask Mr. Heber?"

"Ask me what?" Mr. Heber stood in the front door, his wraparound sunglasses making it impossible to tell if he was pissed or what. "Maureen, what's going on?"

"Jordan wanted the police report."

"I see." He moved in the direction of his office, then turned around. "What did you want to ask me about?"

"The pictures. The report says they took pictures."

164

"I realize that. I made a request, but they haven't turned up yet."

"When will they be here?"

"Should be soon. We'll call you when they arrive. Maureen has your cell?" He might as well have been wearing a sign that said I don't have time for this.

"Before I go, I need to tell you something." I blurted out the whole business about Sister Kimberly and 5, about one of them lying about where 5 was the night my dad was killed.

Mr. Heber removed his sunglasses. He said, "Hmm." Just hmm. Nothing more.

"Isn't that fishy?"

"Yes, I'll agree those stories don't add up."

"What do you think it means?"

"I don't know."

"You don't know?" I'm not sure why I thought he would be able to take this info, drop it into some sort of thinking machine, and come up with the answer that would pop my mom free from jail, but I guess deep down that's what I expected.

"Unfortunately, there could be a hundred reasons why one of them or both are lying. But before you go any further, let me give you three bits of advice. One: most people lie. Two: the reason they lie usually has nothing to do with your case. And three: unless you're careful, their more or less innocent lies can really throw you off."

The thing about Heber was I never could quite tell what he wanted— my mom out of jail or me out of his office. "Come on," I said. "Not everyone goes around lying."

"No, not everyone, but you'd be amazed how many liars are always buzzing around a crime."

Maureen shrugged. "I'm afraid he's right."

About fifteen miles outside St. George, Johnny finished eating everything in the van. He wiped his sugary fingers on his thighs, burped, then thought to say, "Where we going?"

"Mesadale Police Department. I want to try to get those pictures myself."

"Are you out of your fucking mind?"

"Calm down."

"They'll kill me."

"They won't kill you."

"Dude, I know that place a whole lot better than you. Everyone's like freaking out." He punched the dash. "Stop this van!"

"Johnny, relax. When we get there, you can help me."

"If you don't stop right now, I'm going to jump out."

"Johnny, I know what I'm doing."

"So do I." He pulled his bag into his lap, opened the door, said, "You're so full of shit," and leaped out. It happened so quickly, I drove another fifty yards before I could stop. In my rearview Johnny rolled down the embankment with his bag tight to his chest. When he came to a stop he stood and slapped the sand out of his hair. Tough little kid. Stupid too. I backed up along the road until I was next to him.

"Get in."

"Fuck you."

"I'll make sure nothing happens to you."

"You know what they said when they kicked me out? They said if I ever came back, my mom would end up dead. So fuck you for taking me back there, and fuck your fucking van, and fuck your mom, I don't give a shit about her."

He started walking in the direction of St. George, hugging his little bag, but there was no way he could walk back to town. I backed up some more until I was next to him again, but he kept walking and I kept driving in reverse. "I didn't mean to scare you. Come on, get in."

"I'm not going anywhere with you."

"Fine. What do you want to do?"

"None of your fucking business."

166

"Look, all right, don't come. But let me take you back to St. George. I'll drop you wherever you want."

He kept walking but eventually said, "I'm not talking to you."

"Johnny, you're acting like a baby."

"What do you expect?" He wiped his nose with his shoulder. "I thought you were cool." We went backward like that another twenty yards.

"Hey, Maureen told me about this place, maybe we should go there."

He stopped. "What place?"

"Some guy named Jim Hooke. He has this house."

Johnny started walking again, and I threw the van into reverse.

"You know him?"

"You getting ready to dump me too?"

"No, not at all." Heber was right: people lie all the time. "Tell you what," I said. "I'll drop you at the movies and go to Mesadale myself. When I get back I'll pick you up."

He stopped. "Only if you promise to come back."

"I promise."

He pondered the promise, turning it over like a bit of treasure found in the sand. "Deal. But I'm going to need some cash for candy." I told him no problem. "And popcorn."

"I'll give you five bucks." I stopped the van and Johnny climbed in. Elektra welcomed him back with a lick. "Put your seat belt on."

"Whatever."

We didn't say anything for ten miles. As we approached St. George, my cell picked up reception again. There was a message. "Yeah, hi, Jordan, it's me, Maureen. Guess what. Those pictures came right after you left. You can pick them up anytime."

A PLURALITY OF WIVES:[1]
A DISCOURSE

———

DELIVERED BY BRIGHAM YOUNG IN THE TABERNACLE,
Great Salt Lake City, August 29, 1852

Now, following the words of Elder Pratt, I will tell you, in plain language, why we believe in the sanctity of plural marriage and shall always do so. Going forth you will meet those who question your right to this belief, and who shall tell you you are acting outside the law. Yet I shall tell you it is they who do not understand the law, and most certainly it is they who do not understand the will of God.

We believe in plural marriage because God has commanded it. He has spoken, first to Joseph and now to me. I cannot change the word of God to suit my needs, nor can I change His word to suit the politics of today. His word is the word of Eternity, and shall always be. A man who disagrees with our practice of plural wifery is disagreeing with God. His disagreement is not with us, but with his Maker.

We look to the authority of Scripture, for there, in the Old Testament, are many examples of man with many wives. If we accept Scripture as God's Truth, then we must accept it as unchanging and constant through Time. The Latter-day Saints are here to restore the Truth of God as He intended it for man. The entire Christian world, from Popedom to her many rebellious children, has run amok on the Truth of God. With

---

[1] This was Brigham Young's first public acknowledgment of polygamy. In laying out these arguments, he provided the Latter-day Saints with the spiritual/political armament to defend the practice for the next forty years.

Joseph as His Prophet, and myself after, God has set out to restore His Truths, and we are doing so.

Further, in taking many wives we are expanding the Kingdom. We are performing the works of Abraham. A man who marries many wives and a woman who joins a plural family—they are doing the work of God and will be exalted for doing so. They are closer to Glory than the man who refuses this doctrine, or the woman who refuses it. This is how it shall be.

Let it be known I am a son of Vermont's Green Mountains. I was raised with a deep awareness of the rights afforded to all by our nation's Constitution. The right to religious freedom is a right guaranteed to all. This includes the Saints of Deseret. If you encounter an antagonist who believes none of what I have just said to you, who believes neither in the Truth of God, or the Authority of the Scripture, or my position as His Prophet, then you should remind your enemy of our Constitution. There is no doubt it plainly protects our right to pursue our faith as we so believe. Brothers and Sisters, go forth and defend these rights, for they are ours to claim!

A WOMAN SCONED

———

"You stink," said Johnny.

"*I* stink?" But he was right: we both stunk. I turned in the direction of the pool. The envelope of pictures was in my lap but I didn't want to open it right away. I guess I was afraid of them. Not the gore, I could handle that. I just wasn't ready for what they might say.

The municipal pool attracts all sorts. Old ladies with achy knees, stoned teenagers, homeless guys avoiding the heat. I guess technically Johnny and I fell into that last lot.

"That's a dollar seventy-five for you," said the girl at the registration. "And a dollar twenty-five for your brother."

I didn't correct her, thinking it might hurt Johnny's feelings, but he piped up, "He's so not my brother." I gave him a don't-be-a-dick look. "What? You're not."

We threw down our towels on a quiet strip of concrete. Johnny took off, leaping feet first into the pool. He swam over to four boys hanging on to the lane dividers. It took him about ten seconds to become part of their group. They started a game of underwater tag and Johnny wiggled across the pool, looking happy. And clean. He was laughing with his new friends, karate-chopping water in their faces, oblivious of me.

There were twenty pictures in the envelope, xeroxes but clear enough. They documented the scene pretty much as I imagined it. There was the door to his basement den with the NO TRESPASSING decal. Inside, the painted concrete floor, the ripped corduroy sofa, the swamp cooler in the corner. His cot was unmade. Even in the low res of xerox the sheets looked filthy. Then his desk: a door over two filing cabinets, a computer, and a plastic margarine tub filled with rounds of ammo. The next photos were more graphic: his computer chair with a hole chewed through the mesh and wet with blood. The blood on the drywall, splattered like mud on a flap. A picture of the computer screen showed his poker hand and the chat session the bullet so rudely interrupted. Actually there were three chat sessions—so there's something the *Register* didn't report. The one that nailed my mother, between Manofthehouse2004 and Desert-Missy, and two others that looked pretty average, I mean given the circumstances.

Manofthehouse2004: where in st george?
ALBIL: u no the Malibu Inn?
Manofthehouse2004: yup
ALBIL: not far from there
Manofthehouse2004: live alone?

That's where the chat ended. You ever stop to imagine things differently? What if my father had been sitting there waiting in such overheated anticipation for the answer to his question—*all alone* or *my husband's gone till morning* or *with my girlfriend*—and his heart got so worked up with stupid male hope that it broke. Imagine it. His head lolling on his neck. His body going cold in the basement. Sister Rita would've found him like that, dead from a stupid old heart. Imagine if that's how it had ended for my dad. Everything would be so different now.

The second chat went like this:

SweetieNVAZUT: how old?
Manofthehouse2004: 47 but look 39-42.

(Please.)

SweetieNVAZUT: married?

171

Manofthehouse2004: yes
SweetieNVAZUT: go fuck your wife
Manofthehouse2004: rather watch u fuck her
SweetieNVAZUT: she got a hot pussy?
Manofthehouse2004: depends
SweetieNVAZUT: you nasty prick

They could've put it on his tombstone.

Johnny plopped down on my towel. "Let me see." But I turned the pictures over. "Hey, if I'm your sidekick, how'm I going to help you get your mom out of jail if you don't tell me everything?"

"You're not my sidekick."

"Love you too, bro." He flipped over on his back and turned his head. "Did I mention I knew your dad?"

"So?"

"I'm just saying he taught my Sunday school."

"Big deal."

"Yeah, you're probably right. I'm sure it was nothing."

"What was nothing?"

"Nope, it's not worth going into."

"What are you talking about?"

"You going in the pool or what?"

"First tell me what you're talking about."

"First go swimming. You reek."

I swam a few laps past a trio of teenage girls, each in a bikini smaller than the other. "You're such a slut!" one shouted to her friend. Clearly this was a good thing.

When I got back to my towel, Johnny was leafing through the photos. "What're you doing?"

"You see this one?" He was holding out the last picture in the pile.

"I've seen it. Now give them back to me."

"Man, look at him." It was the only picture of my dad. Manofthehouse2004 slumped in his computer chair, eyes rolled back in his head, mouth open, one hand turned at a funny angle like a claw. He looked ancient—the flesh hanging off his bones. Just a diabetic, arthritic, swollen-ankled, Viagra-popping old man. Why were we so afraid of him?

"Dude, that sucks. I know he was an ass and everything, but he was still your dad."

"What were you going to tell me?"

"Just that he used to teach us about the end of time. He kept saying it was coming soon. He used to bring his gun to church and show us how he'd fight the enemy until the end. It was kinda cheesy."

"That's it?"

"Yeah, like I said, it was nothing."

I lay on my back and threw my arm over my eyes. Do you ever wonder how you got where you are?

Then I sat back up.

"What kind of gun was it?"

"I think a Big Boy. Why? Is that important?"

"I don't know."

We went over to the internet café where I'd been leaving Elektra. The place was pretty sleepy, a couple of kids nursing lattes on a saggy couch. It was called A Woman Sconed, and the goth girl who worked there was in love with my dog. "Who's my girl?" she said the minute we walked in, and she wasn't talking about me.

I started drafting an IM. After a few rewrites I had a note that sounded friendly but serious. I sent it first to SweetieNVAZUT.

Hey, I know you once chatted with someone named Manofthehouse2004. Can I ask you a few questions? I'm his son and I'm just trying to find a few things out. He died the night you talked, actually he was murdered. There are a lot of things we don't know, and I'm trying to figure them out. I know this is weird, but it's true.

Johnny sat down, read my note on the screen, his lips moving, and about halfway through his brow squiggled up.

"What?" I said.

"Nothing. I'm not saying a word."

"You think it's too creepy? I was trying to make it sound sincere."

"This is your show, bro."

He was probably right. I wrote up an IM that didn't say much—just hey, want to chat?—and sent it off to ALBIL and DesertMissy.

The goth girl asked if she could give Elektra a cupcake. "On the house," she said. She reminded me of 5, which reminded me I needed to talk to her again.

"Holy shit!" said Johnny. "You've got mail!"

It was from ALBIL, and she went straight to the point: *You sound nice. Got a pic?*

"Score!"

"Johnny, sit down."

"Hey, wait a minute, let me see that pic you're sending her." He looked at the picture I pulled down from my myspace profile. "Not bad. But you look gay."

"I am gay."

"I guess just send it anyway. See what happens."

About thirty seconds later she wrote back: *Nice, wanna meet?*

"Dude, for a gay guy, you sure know how to work the ladies. Tell her to meet us here."

"Us?"

"Well, yeah. Besides, I'm just a kid. She'll take one look at me and know you're a decent guy."

He was right. About an hour later a woman walked through the door. She had that pale and plump look that made her seem both young and middle-aged. "You can have her," Johnny whispered.

174

"Be nice." I called out, "ALBIL?"

She looked a little startled when she saw Johnny. "You must be Jordan. Wow. You look just like your picture. Most guys don't, you know."

"I know. Sit down. You want something to drink?"

She was nibbling the stem of her sunglasses and looking at Johnny. "I didn't realize you were bringing your son."

"He's a friend. I'm just looking after him for a little while."

"Since moron's not going to introduce me, I'm Johnny." He offered his hand. It was at moments like this—when his hand hung out there, so small and clearly belonging to a boy—that I remembered how young he was.

"Johnny, you want to—"

"Yup, give me some quarters and I'll go play Ms. Pac-Man." I gave him the change in my pocket and he hopped across the café.

"I guess that means you like kids."

"I never really thought about it until he came around."

"How long're you looking after him?"

"Only a couple of days. Listen, ALBIL—"

"Alexandra."

"Alexandra?"

"ALBIL's my screen name. Alexandra Likes Being In Love. I'm a romantic. I probably shouldn't put that out there in the first five minutes, but there you are."

"That's all right." Now I really felt bad. "I have to tell you something. I asked you here because, well, I wanted to ask you some questions."

"Stop. I should say up front, you can ask me *any*thing. I'm just that kind of person. Nothing to hide. So just to get it out of the way, I'll start: I'm thirty-six, divorced, have two kids but they live with my wasband in Kingman, and you see these extra fifteen pounds, they're not going anywhere. I'm so glad you like kids. I mean, that's a relief because that would be a real problem."

"Um, that's not exactly what I meant."

"You know what? I like you."

"Here's the real reason I emailed you."

As I explained everything, her eyes opened to the size of poker chips. "Oh my God. Killed?" She pulled a napkin from the dispenser and held it to her mouth. "Wait a minute. You lied to me."

"I didn't want to. You gotta understand. She's my mom." Alexandra looked like she couldn't decide whether to stay or go. "Do you remember chatting with him?"

"I don't know, I'm still in shock." She fanned herself with the napkin. Johnny was absorbed in his video game, his little hands bonded to the joystick. "I don't know what's worse, you lying or your dad being murdered."

"The thing is, he was a real prick. I bet he didn't tell you he had more than twenty wives."

"Oh my God, it gets worse?"

"Yup. He lived in Mesadale. So, do you think you remember him?"

"There must be some mistake. I never chat with married men. I've been down that road. Twice."

"He probably lied to you about that. Do you remember anything?"

"I don't know. I mean, I do like to play some poker every now and then as practice. Two or three times a year the girls and I go to Vegas for the weekend, and I don't want to show up rusty. When did you say this was? Saturday? What time?"

"Around eleven."

"Yeah, that sounds right, I think I was online. But I don't know if I remember your dad specifically. I tend to strike up a chat with whoever's at the table. You know, to be friendly."

"He might have said he was pretty religious."

"Around here they all say that."

"Maybe he talked about trucks? He loved trucks."

"Ditto."

"He's a big hunter."

"Who isn't? Wait a minute! Was he the Gulf War vet with that strange disease?"

"No." We ended up doing this—the misfired question, the off-the-mark response—for another few minutes, but eventually we both realized their chat had been too insignificant to leave an impression. "I don't want you to think I spend a lot of time chatting online," she said, "but I guess I do."

"If you think of something, you have my email."

"Give me your number too, just in case." She wrote it down in a blank appointment book. Turns out Johnny had kept his eye on us the whole time because he raced away from the video game. "Could you help him?"

"Not really." She sounded like she had taken this personally. The bell on the door tinkled for a few long seconds after she said good-bye.

December 1, 1852
The Beehive House
Great Salt Lake

BROTHER GILBERT WEBB
Great Salt Lake

My Dear Brother Gilbert,

You ask a fair question, and I shall attempt to answer it fairly. Your facts are correct. Indeed there were instances when I publicly discussed our unique institution in a manner I knew to be not wholly forthright. If I am to be judged solely on this one indiscretion, without regard to other struggles and achievements, so be it.

Without seeming to evade your accusation, I should like to establish the context for my withholding. I need not remind you, I am sure, the persecution the Saints once faced. Lawless mobs, antagonistic governors and sheriffs, 100 foes to every friend—we were, and remain, a feared people. Shall we recall the dead from the Zion Brigade, Haun's Mill, and Far West? Is there a Saint anywhere who does not weep when he hears the name Carthage? We will forever hear the shot that took our beloved Joseph.

Above all, I see that here on Earth I have been charged with two duties. First I must do whatever I can to guide the faithful to Heavenly Glory. It is a humble task. Second I must protect the tens of thousands of Saints who risk their well-being because they believe in the Restoration. Had I openly acknowledged the institution before reaching the security of Zion, I would have risked the lives of all our Saints—yours too.

I appreciate very much your letter and invite you, Young Friend, to call on me at the Beehive House. I admire most among our youth he who can set forth with an open heart and a probing mind. Now go forth and share the Truth, for that is what it is.

Please send my greetings to your parents, your brother, Aaron, and your sister, Ann Eliza, angel that she is.

I am,
Most Sincerely,
Your Prophet

BRIGHAM YOUNG

THE HARDLY BOYS

———

"Where to, Nancy Drew?"

Johnny and I were on our way to Kanab. It was at that point late in the afternoon when it's so hot you think the car will spontaneously ignite. As we got closer to Mesadale we passed a truck with three old Firsts in the cab, guys with yellow white hair greased back and one eye squinted up. Between them they probably had forty or fifty wives and a hundred and fifty kids, maybe two hundred. The truck was worth fifty thousand bucks, pimped out with smoked windows and a roof rack. If you got twenty wives at home but the government recognizes only one as your legal spouse, the other nineteen can receive assistance. The more wives and kids, the more welfare checks. That's how a man with seventy mouths to feed and no job can afford a truck like that. And kickbacks from the church for pledging your life to defend the Prophet when the whole thing blows up.

We passed a billboard that said, ON YOUR OWN? NEED HELP? It showed a blond girl walking down a lonely road that didn't look like anywhere near here. An 800 number and an address in Salt Lake. I have a sister who got screwed by that sign. The number only works during the day. But no one can make a call during the day. My sister, she was the daughter of my dad's 12th wife (I think). One night she woke up at about three or four and slipped downstairs and called that number, believing they'd come rescue her. She even had a little bag packed. She was ready. But you know where her call was forwarded to? Straight to the Mesadale Police Department. Who called my dad. He drove her to his brother, who married her. I remember he told her, "You're sixteen, it's time."

We passed the turnoff to Mesadale and looked at the big houses in the distance. I thought of all the kids—the rashy infants, the scabby toddlers, the hungry boys and girls, the lonely teens, each desperate for love. I thought of my mom.

"Thank God we're out of there," said Johnny.

"I just wish I could help all the other kids."

"A lot more girls are escaping. At night, they just disappear."

"That must piss off the Prophet."

"There was this one girl, totally hot, maybe like fifteen, he was about to marry her but then she took off."

"Where are they going?"

"Anywhere but here."

In Kanab I parked about a block from the Mega Bite. Johnny was going to try to talk to 5. "Act like you recognize her from Mesadale. Tell her you ran away too. Then ask her when she left. I want to find out if she's lying. Here's two dollars."

"Two dollars?"

I gave him another three bucks and he rolled his eyes. "Give me a half hour." He hopped down from the van. He looked so sure of himself, so pleased to be able to help, that for the first time I worried how I'd get rid of him. While I waited I opened my map of California. In the folds I keep my cash. I had $192 and a credit card with something like $280 left on it. Gas was killing me. After four days in Utah, the only thing I knew for sure was I needed to get back to Pasadena in time for that nursery job. I called Roland but got voice mail. "I won't be here much longer," I said.

"Here's the deal," said Johnny, climbing back into the van. "She lied to you."

"How do you know?"

181

"I went in, ordered a ham and cheese—thanks for the money, by the way—and said, 'You look familiar.' She sort of looked at me like, *Do I know you?* So I said, 'You're from Mesadale.' See, the good thing about being a kid is I wasn't going to freak her out. She said, 'Yeah,' and I said, 'Me too.' So I go, 'Wait a minute, I recognize you. You're one of Brother Scott's daughters, right? I recognize you from church.' She just nodded and got a little uneasy, like maybe someone had sent me, which of course someone did send me, but she didn't know that, and so I go, 'Don't worry, I'm on the run too.' Then I go, 'So were you there when he was killed?' You know what she said? She goes, 'Yeah, I was trying to get my mom to leave, I knew something bad was about to happen, but she wouldn't come with me. Now I have no idea what's going to happen to her.'" Johnny stopped, obviously happy with himself. "So how about that for a lead!"

"You've seen too many bad cop movies."

"Just doing what you couldn't."

"Let's go."

"Where we headed now?"

"Put your seat belt on."

"What? Now you're my mom?"

We stopped at a taco stand and then drove out to an empty trailhead. While we ate the sun set, and the desert went from pink to red to blue to black. The moon wasn't up yet and it was very dark in the van, and the white taco bags were the only thing I could see. Elektra was asleep on the futon, and everything was very quiet except for the wind. I thought Johnny had fallen asleep when he said, "I've done it."

"Done what?"

"You know. With a guy."

"What?"

"In Vegas. A couple of times. I was down to my last buck." It was too dark to see his face. "I didn't like it."

"That's OK."

"I don't think I'm a homo."

"I don't think so either."

"But if I was, I think I'd like you."

"Thanks. I guess."

"Jordan?"

"Yeah?"

"I don't want to do that anymore."

"You won't have to."

"Promise?"

"I promise."

"Because I'd really rather be nailing a chick."

"You're the crudest person I know."

"Thank you."

Then we talked about all the stuff we had lived through. "Remember how the Prophet would say you could get a girl pregnant just by looking at her when you were horny?" Johnny threw back his head like it was the funniest thing he'd ever heard. "The best part is," he said, "I totally believed him. Man, I thought I'd knocked up every chick in town." We laughed and laughed about all the wacky crap we once believed. What else is there to do? Then we stopped laughing and were quiet for some time.

"Johnny?"

"Yeah?"

"We're going back tonight."

He said nothing.

"You up for it?"

He still said nothing. And then, "If you are."

IN OUR HOUSE
A Poem
By Lydia Taft Webb

In our house, Thou will find
Loving Sisters, true and kind.
Spouses living righteously
United by the words of Thee.
Numbers two, three, four, and five
The more souls gathered, the more alive!
We pray together, hand-in-hand,
Loving Thou and our husband,
For 'tis Thy will and Thy Command,
Together we shall enter Thy Holy Land!

—1853

Lydia Taft Webb, loyal second wife of Chauncey Webb, wrote this poem as an expression of her belief in celestial marriage. Two decades later, when the Saints began to face outside pressure to abandon polygamy, the verse was set to music and sung defiantly by plural wives throughout Deseret. The song remains a popular hymn among the Firsts and other twenty-first-century polygamists.

THE GUN ON THE SCREEN

As we drove into Mesadale, Johnny kept scanning the road. "So far so good. I don't think anyone's noticed us." On one of the side roads we passed a house roofed in plywood and tarp, with two horses hitched to a post out front. "That's my house," he said. "Such a shithole."

"Do you miss it?"

"What do you think?" And then, "It's weird, isn't it?"

"What?"

"Being this close to home."

"Except it's not home anymore," I said. "Not anymore."

Queenie's house was quiet, and the patrol car—just as I'd hoped—was gone. We were walking up the driveway when the garage door began to roll up, revealing a pair of feet. "Get in here!"

We ducked in, and the door started rolling back down.

Queenie's nightdress cut off at the knee, and she obviously wasn't wearing her sacred underwear. She could get publicly flogged for looking like that. Or raped. Or excommunicated. Or all three.

"I need your help," I said.

"Who's this?"

"He's a friend."

"A friend?" Then she figured it out. "Oh shit, Jordan, you're going to ruin everything."

"Calm down. Hiram's out, right?"

"Yes, but his new wife's in there."

"New wife?"

"They were sealed yesterday. The Prophet had had enough

185

of his monogamy. He said it sent the wrong signal. Hiram had no choice."

"Romantic. How old is she?"

"Old. Like nineteen."

"Barely legal," I said.

"Dude, you've seen those dvds?"

"Not now, Johnny."

"You're going to have to leave," said Queenie.

"I need you to find something out from your husband."

"Shhhh. Be quiet. She's a hawk. She already hates me."

I wished Queenie would just say fuck this and climb in the van with me and take off, but in real life people don't do that as often as you might think.

"Don't look at me like that," she said.

"Like what?"

"Like you think I'm crazy. I'm not like you, I can't just leave."

"I didn't just leave."

"You know what I mean. Besides, now's not a good time."

"Why not?"

Then it hit me: she was pregnant. How could I be so slow? "How far along?"

"Three months. I'm sure I'll be on bedrest soon. Last time I was on my back for like six months."

"Listen, that's real nice and everything," said Johnny, "but you got anything to eat?"

"You guys need to go."

"I know, but I'm starving over here."

"Wait right here," she said. "And don't make any noise."

While we waited Johnny checked out Alton's guns. Flintlock pistols, a couple of snipers, a pump-action shotgun, a boy's rifle, and an antique revolver with a gold cylinder. "If things get bad," said Johnny, "at least I've got my knife."

"You and your knife."

Queenie returned with a muffin and a glass of milk and Johnny downed them like he hadn't eaten in a week.

186

"Queenie, I need to ask you a question," I said. "Do you know anything about the police report?"

"Hiram doesn't talk to me about things like that."

"Can you ask him why the investigation isn't complete?"

"He'll wonder why I'm asking. And with her around, it's going to be even harder."

"Try."

"What should I tell him when he asks why I want to know?"

"Tell him a lot of people are talking about it, like the sister wives down at the co-op. They're wondering and they asked you."

She was thinking about it. "Even if he does tell me, how am I going to tell you?"

"Can you call my cell?"

"He'll know."

"Do you have email?" She and Johnny looked at me like, what a stupid question.

"Then leave a note at the post office with Sister Karen."

Queenie was very still. I knew she'd do it. "How much time do you need?" I said.

"Till tomorrow. Now you better go. She's going to wonder why I'm out here. And be careful. Do me a favor, Jordan, don't come back. I love you, but you're about to cause a lot of trouble."

The road back to the highway was deserted. The houses were lit up, but there was no one in sight. "I don't think anyone's seen us," I said.

Johnny turned to look back at the town retreating behind us. "I wonder why we came up with the bad, bad luck to be born here."

"I don't know."

"You know what my mom said when we said good-bye?"

"What?"

"See you in heaven." He snorted. "Heaven my ass."

"You know what my mom said? One day you'll understand."

That's when a jacked pickup pulled out from the brush and started following us. It sped in close, and a row of lights on the roof rack came on, filling the van with silver-blue light. "Shit," said Johnny. Elektra started barking at the window in the back door.

"Can you see who it is?" I said.

"Not with those lights."

The truck revved closer, then pulled back, then drove up on my rear again. Everything around us was black except for the hard lights on the roof rack. "I guess someone saw us," I said.

"Man, we are so screwed."

"Hang on." I swerved around on the road, throwing up a cloud of red dust. The truck slowed, giving me some space. "He's just playing with us," I said.

"You sure?"

"No."

"Who do you think it is?"

"Could be anyone."

"You think it's the Prophet?"

"No. I don't know." I slammed on the brakes. Elektra flew off the futon, and the truck swerved off the road into the sage-brush. His lights were on the desert now, and it was like the brightest moon had risen over the scrub and the sand. "Can you see anyone now?"

"Just one guy."

"What does he look like?"

"An asshole."

In my rearview I watched the truck back out of the sage-brush. Its monster wheels turned in the sand, spitting it out behind. The truck pushed itself over a ridge of sand at the side of the road and righted itself back into place. The lights were now pointing ahead on the road again, but we were out of their range. When we reached the highway I said, "We're OK."

"What if he follows us?"

"He won't. He can only pull that shit in Mesadale."

"I hope he doesn't take it out on my mom."

"He wasn't looking for you."

Driving back to St. George, I was trying to think things through, but Johnny kept yakking on about his mom and stepdad, how they'd screwed up his whole life.

"You want to know how my mom ended up with my stepdad?"

"Not really."

"We were living up near Brigham City, my mom and me, I mean. All of a sudden one day when I was five she just throws my crap in the car and drives us down here. I was like, 'Is this a vacation?' And she goes, 'You'll get used to it.' We moved right in with my stepdad. I'm not sure how they met, but I guess it was through the mail or the internet or something. I remember the first time I saw him I was thinking, Is that someone's grandpa? He was old even then. Skinny, with all that old-man skin and that old-man smell. He said, 'I think you'll like it here.' I just looked at him and said, 'I doubt it.' You know what he did? He smacked my ear. It was the first time anyone ever hit me, and I just looked over at my mom like, 'Are you going to let him do that?' I mean, I was so certain she'd drive us home that very minute, but she only said, 'Johnny, you got to listen to your dad.' That was when I knew she was a goner, except when you're five you don't really know what that means. All I knew was my mom wasn't my mom anymore, something had happened to her, and they told me if I did anything to piss the old guy off, God would take it out on her."

"It's the same story," I said. "Over and over."

"Man, I wish my mom would go and blow his fucking heart out too."

"My mom didn't kill my dad."

"Yeah, well, you know what I mean."

By the time we got back to St. George almost everything was closed, but the lights were still on at A Woman Sconed. The goth girl was leaning on the bagel bar, watching tv. She looked like she'd had the dullest night of her life. "Finally a

189

customer I actually like," she said. While Elektra and Johnny begged for cookies, I jumped on the computer to check email.

"Any word from the chicks?" said Johnny.

I clicked the mouse. "Looks like there's something from Alexandra."

"Dude, she wants you. Open it."

It was real nice to meet you Jordan. Im sorry about your dad. But guess what. I found his pic in my computer. We only chatted for a little bit so even if I did remember more of it Im sure it wouldn't be of much use. But here's the pic he sent me. I thought you might want it.

I opened the attached picture and slowly, from top to bottom, it appeared on the screen. There he was, with this message: *As you can see I like my guns!*

"Shit," said Johnny. "He used *that* to pick up chicks?"

My dad was standing in the basement in a cheap wine-colored tie, his arm around a woman whose face had been scratched out so lazily you could tell it was my mom. They were holding a rifle between them, the way a couple of fishermen would pose with their catch. There's one good thing about growing up off the grid: I know my guns. The gun on the screen was the Big Boy. And fitted to its muzzle was a suppressor as fat as a can of Mountain Dew.

IX

ZION

THE 19TH WIFE

Now, with your permission, I will tell the stories of my youth in the Utah Territory and how those years, the 1850s, led me to my fate as Brigham's wife. In the autumn of 1848, when I was four years old, we settled in Great Salt Lake City, a new settlement overlooking a silver saline sea. When my family arrived in this forsaken land, we were a wretched lot in possession of little more than our wagons and oxen, a milking cow, and the clothes encrusted to our backs. No doubt you have seen many daguerreotypes of the Westward-ho family: the bearded father in suspenders, the mother in an apron (she always thinner than her brood), the children with dark half-moons of exhaustion beneath their eyes. This is who we were, any American family waging everything on the West. Except, to this historic image, you must add Sister Lydia and her child, Diantha. To the untrained eye she would look like a widowed aunt, but by now my Dear Reader knows the secrets of the Mormon clan.

In our first year in Deseret, we were so busy digging, clearing, building, and sowing there was little time for misery. In order to represent the fullest form of honesty, I must confess that those early years in Zion were among the happiest my family has known. We, each newly arrived Saint, were set upon a purpose: to build a home while establishing a colony where we could be free in our beliefs. This is a noble cause, one that can inspire even the tiniest of hearts, such as mine was at the time, and return doubting minds to course. My father, ever industrious, set up a new wagonry and very soon his forges blazed. My mother, who never spent a day in school, was asked by the Prophet himself to teach one day a week in the Zion school house. (I won't expend ink by digressing into Brother Brigham's curious effort to establish the Deseret Alphabet, made up of thirty-eight mostly new characters which gave the Saints a secretive method of writing English. This alphabet was briefly forced upon the children of Zion, myself included. For a short time my mother, in obeying her spiritual leaders, had to teach it at the blackboard, all the while knowing it was useless backslang.)

Anyone who has embarked on a great adventure, started a new phase of his life, or begun life freshly in an unfamiliar land will understand the general excitement and sense of possibility of those early years in Utah. We were concerned less by what we lacked and more by what we one day might possess. This is a healthy vision of life, and for this we all owe Brigham Young. From his pulpit in the Tabernacle he set the tone of each day in the Territory. He demanded the laying out of orderly streets and set to building Temple Square on a scale so large he said it was not for any of us alive but for the Saints of the next century, and the century thereafter. He commanded the digging of artesian wells, which delivered fresh water along a pebbly flume to our door. He organized the city into wards and set up a bishop in each to lead the local population through times of duress and spiritual weakness. He tapped his most industrious men to open a tannery, a curriery, a crockery, warehouses for paint and whip, stores for shoes, cloth, soap, and candles, and quite nearly everything else. In no time there was a city where previously there had been a moonscape of sand, sagebrush, aloe, and the dusty cottonwood. All this sprang out of nothing—as the giddy wildflowers appear in the desert after the April downpour, each a tiny colored miracle aloft on the stalk; all evidence of God's might. Although Brigham Young would one day become my enemy, I must acknowledge all that which he created for his Saints. The "go-a-headitiveness" for which the Mormons have become known comes from, I believe, the leadership of Brigham at this time. In less than ten years he transformed a basin so arid and inhospitable that even the most intrepid and resourceful Indian nations had avoided it for thousands of years, into the City of the Saints, a metropolis of some twenty thousand souls and a thriving theocracy for him to rule with, he assured us, Divine legitimacy.

This, then, is what I called home.

In the late fall of 1854, not long after my tenth birthday, our idyll was interrupted by Brigham's selection of my father, Chauncey, and my half-brother, Gilbert, to journey to England to serve on a Mission. One might suspect that we would receive this news as an honor—an opportunity to carry forth the new Gospel to our distant cousins. Yet in those early days of the Territory, nothing was as it seemed.

Brigham Young, as President of the Church of Jesus Christ of Latter-day Saints, Lord's Prophet, Governor of the Utah Territory, and general owner of the largest businesses and industries in the land, had become a ruler of absolute authority. He controlled the Church, the civic government, the police, the press, the major economic institutions, including the busiest stores, mills, and warehouses, and owned much of the Territory's land, and other things, too. His holdings were so vast some claimed even he could not know all that he possessed.

By 1854 my father had become a wealthy man again in his own right. His wagonry was the most productive in the Territory. Because the railroad would not arrive for another fifteen years, Utah's isolation, and the great distances between its stakes, made wagon manufacturing one of the most valuable industries. With my father abroad, Brother Brigham would run the manufactory on his behalf. My father understood the arrangement immediately. "You'll have to cut back," he told his two wives. "The next two years will be long. Look out for each other." Saying goodbye to his family, my father kissed each wife, then his children. He told Aaron he was now the man of the house. The boy, all pimple and whisker, declared himself ready for the task. My father lifted Diantha in the air, twirling her around. She was of that age (six) and made of that peculiar demeanor that compels an otherwise modest girl to lift her hems upward anytime given the chance (I imagine the showgirl is made of the same fiber). When my father approached me, I bit down hard on a trembling lip. "How do I know you'll come back?" I said. He promised he would, but already I had my doubts.

The concept of a Mission is not easy for a ten-year-old to grasp. My father had always been a quietly religious man. I had a difficult time envisioning him—and tongue-tied Gilbert even less so!—standing before strangers and speaking of the Lord. The journey was long, the seas rough, and the climate in England, my mother said, damp and disagreeable. Floating through the schoolyards of Zion were stories of Missionaries who never returned: "A bloody Catholic put a ball through his head!" Speaking on behalf of Christ is a dangerous task, especially when the faith you carry forth is tainted by rumors of angels, miracles, and the harem.

"What if I don't recognize you after two years?" I worried as my father climbed into his wagon.

"In two years," my father laughed, "I might not recognize you."

Thus my father and Gilbert departed, their hearts dense with faith and fear. Of course I did not accompany them on their Mission, and therefore will leave his years abroad to my Dear Reader's imagination, which I trust is fertile and capable of filling in.

In his absence, the household of harmony and happiness crumbled. Very soon the payments from the manufactory upon which my mother and Lydia survived ceased. Distressed by her circumstances, my mother visited the wagonry to inquire after its affairs. Brother Brigham had appointed Mr. Morley to serve as general manager and foreman. He kept my mother and me waiting nearly three-quarters of an hour, despite this being our property. When at last he agreed to see my mother (he made no acknowledgment of me), the man said, "I have but a minute, Madame."

"My husband's been gone three weeks," my mother began, "and it's taken three weeks for our income to dry up. If you were me, wouldn't you come down here to ask? I have a household, Mr. Morley, and little ones. I need to know what I can expect for the next two years."

Mr. Morley was a thickly set pale man with a beard that grew in so darkly against his pallid skin, it appeared blue. "My first obligation is to the Prophet," he said.

"So is mine."

"Your husband and many others are over there in Europe converting Saints. Well, when these foreign Saints reach our shores they'll need wagons to cross the plains. Brother Brigham's placed an order for two hundred wagons. I need to cover the cost of the materials and pay the men and heat up the forge. That leaves very little at the end of the day. I can't go raising the prices on the Church, can I?"

"Of course not, but what about that little extra? When can I expect to see it?"

"Mrs. Webb, I'm very sorry if your husband didn't explain matters fully to you. This wagonry doesn't throw off much. Your husband hardly paid himself. The little bit of profit is now going to me. I can assure you it's hardly a fair fee. I'm sacrificing, too."

None of this sounded accurate to my mother, but she had no recourse, and she hesitated before articulating any doubt regarding Brigham and the Church.

"May I make a suggestion," said Mr. Morley. "You and the second Mrs. Webb might want to turn some of your house work into items you can sell. Are you any good with the butter churn? Making cakes of soap? I bet you make a fine hat. But really, Mrs. Webb, this isn't my realm. I know the women's organizations are good about helping women such as yourself."

Later that night, after we children had gone to bed, I overheard my mother and Lydia discuss the situation. Lydia, ever resourceful and bright, said, "I could bake batches of bishop squares and sell them to the hotel dining room."

"That's not enough."

"I'll knit socks and you can raise laying hens."

"Socks and eggs won't be enough."

"We could always rent out a room."

My mother reminded Lydia there wasn't a spare room to let out.

"I could move into your room," Lydia suggested, "or you could move into mine and we could fix up the empty one for a widow who needs a roof and if she's got little ones we can bring them in, too."

I imagine that the thought of another woman under her roof convinced my mother to find another path to financial stability. In the morning she applied to the Prophet's office for an appointment as teacher in one of the distant stakes. At this time Brigham was busy colonizing the vast Utah Territory, mapping it into a system of wards and stakes. (A stake is similar to a county, and each stake is made up of several wards; these are biblical terms.) Some wards were so remote and forsaken that few Saints wanted to move there. Teachers especially were in demand, for how could the Prophet encourage multiple wives and the voluminous offspring they produced if he did not provide schools for all those beautiful little heads? Within a week of her request, Brother Brigham dispatched my mother, Aaron, and me to Payson, sixty miles south of Great Salt Lake.

By January 1855 we had settled, as best we could, in a one-room adobe hut with a dirt floor and two beds flanking the hearth. Known for its high sun and desert climes, Deseret,

I should remind the Reader, is equally familiar with winter's bitterness. The wind whips, the snow blows, the temperature plummets, the ice collects. So it did this January in Payson, where wood was scarce, forcing us to fuel our fire by buffalo dung. Aaron, who at seventeen was of ample frame, took more than his share of the bedclothes. Each night was a difficult but eventually victorious battle of retaking the woolly territory my shivering body had lost to him, so that by dawn, after an exhaustive but committed effort, I finally had gained enough warmth to sleep an hour. I do not know which is worse: the rancid nighttime odors produced by a boy caught in the throes of early manhood or the stench of burning buffalo dirt. Needless to say, I had yet to become accustomed to our new lot.

Not long after our arrival, our new neighbor, Mrs. Myton, appeared in a flutter at our door. "Have you heard?" she gasped. "There's an Elder coming to speak in the Meeting House!" She was excited in a fluffed-up way, her arms flapping about. A Mormon Elder speaking to his people is a common event in every ward and so my mother inquired for further detail. Mrs. Myton handed over a broadside that appeared ripped from its post. "He's coming to Payson to discuss our sins!"

So it had been arranged that a Saint by the name of Elder Joseph Hovey would preach in the evening to the sinners of Payson. How or why Elder Hovey selected Payson I will never know, for I doubt it was any more, or less, sinful than the other communities of Zion.

Before his arrival, the town stirred with anticipation. Sister wives donned their finest scarves and swatted at their husbands until they had washed properly. Children scraped mud from their boots. Everyone wanted to appear clean at the meeting. My mother and I were no less susceptible. She hurried about our little hut in search of something to wear, while I rinsed out my stockings. Aaron, however, had recently acquired the dour, resentful air of his age. He had begun putting up a fuss on Sunday mornings, turning out for Church in an untidy manner that was all too deliberate and designed to provoke the sharpest of irritation in my mother.

"You cannot wear that," my mother advised when he put on a dirty shirt. Aaron shrugged that she could not tell him what to do. The women among my Dear Readers will recognize this confrontation between mother and son. After several repetitions of these seemingly irreconcilable positions, my mother relented, as every mother learns to do. "Go as you please," she sighed.

She turned to find me plaiting my hair. Since my apostasy from the Mormon Church I have been accused of many things, most of them wholly untrue. However, the accusations that I have always appreciated a pretty dress and other womanly finery, and have been known to spend a minute too long at the looking glass, is, I must confess, deserved and true. So be it: I am guilty!

The Meeting House was hot and unpleasant from all the people crowded into it. Many I had never seen before. Judging by the plainness of cloth and the dirt in their seams, they were settlers who had journeyed a day or more to hear the preacher. Such a setting, I will note, is a valuable scene to record the demographic peculiarities of plural marriage. Allow me to take one bench as an example: Near where my mother and I stood along the wall (while Aaron fidgeted with his pocket knife!) was a long bench that in most Christian congregations could hold two or three families. But here, on this portentous evening, I shall describe who sat there: First the father (always the father first!), a farmer in his patched shirt; then his lovely young wife, slender in her bodice; then the next wife, older than the first, yellowish hair with worrisome streaks of gray; in her lap was a boy of seven or eight in need of wiping his nose and his three little brothers and sisters squeezed in at her side; next to them, an older woman even still, her hair a dull drained buff, and a general emaciation that suggests the difficulty of her days; next to her were two lads about Aaron's age, their Adam's apples the size of rocks. And, because this is the way, next to her, an even older woman, hair too wiry to hold neatly in a bun; her head sat upright with dignity and grace upon a thick, tired neck. She had one daughter, full grown, portly, and unmarried; I can only presume they shared a bed in this man's house. I will make the presumptuous leap to state that the father at the opposite end of the bench had not visited his first wife's bed in a decade. So I present your average Payson family, in its full relief.

Finally, at a quarter past eight, Elder Hovey stood before the gathered lot. "Brothers and Sisters, I'm here to tell you that each of you, both man and woman, child and parent, is a sinner. Yet you have taken the first step toward redemption by being here tonight." The man carried on like this for nearly twenty minutes, accusing everyone gathered of sin. He assured us we were damned unless we cleansed our souls through confession. "Now who will be the first to confess his thievery, his deception, his lustful heart, his treachery and fraud, his perfidy, and—may the Heavenly Father forgive you—his lack of fervor in religion?"

The man was in possession of a fair, angelic complexion set off by dark, wavy hair. His touching, boyish appearance contrasted with his bullying sermon in a way that made his audience listen even more intently.

"Do you believe I am up here merely for the sake of rhetoric? Do you think I ask this question as a speaker's gesture? These are not the preacher's questions, left to be answered in the privacy of your heart. These are the questions of the reformer and savior of the soul. I ask you here and now: Who is prepared to repent? There is but one path to salvation: Repent, reveal your sins and allow yourself to be baptized anew! And so it has come to pass that now is the time for you to open your hearts and repent!"

He stared out at his audience, making each of us feel as if he were glaring into our individual souls and could see the lies and deceit. My heart was racing, so terrified was I of his power to know my most secret truths. I began to feel the urge to speak. I sensed that he wanted me, among the hundreds of people gathered, to confess as example. But what would I confess? True, I had coveted Missy Horman's velvet-trimmed cloak. I had prayed my father would return early from his Mission, even if it meant leaving souls unsaved. Once, I called Brother Brigham plump as a pig (not to his face, of course). Was this what Elder Hovey wanted to hear?

Upon the stage he paced back and forth repeating his calls until finally Mrs. Myton, our neighbor, shot up in her seat. "I can't stay quiet any longer."

"Sister, what have you done?"

"I have sinned." Gasps and clucks filled the hall.

"Tell us, what are your transgressions?"

"It's difficult to say."

"Yet you've already stood. We know for certain you're guilty. Now you must tell us your errors and we shall help you atone."

"I can't. They'll hate me for it."

"Who?"

Mrs. Myton wrung her handkerchief. She was a widow and had come to the Meeting House alone but for her spinster daughter, Connie, who had trouble seeing at night. Elder Hovey prodded Mrs. Myton: "Have you lied?"

"Well—"

"Have you stolen?"

"Well—"

"Speak, Sister. Hundreds are waiting for you."

"All right. I'll say it. I took her hen."

"Whose hen?"

"My neighbor's, Mrs. Webb's. When she moved in, her hen wandered into my yard and it was Connie's twentieth birthday and I just picked it up and before I'd known what I'd done it was boiling in my pot. I'll replace the bird, I promise."

The crowd twittered with shock. Many turned to look at my mother in order to offer pity and compassion, although a few, it seemed, appeared to suggest that she was somehow equally to blame. My mother had long wondered about that hen, which, truth be told, had never been much of a layer. Now, made aware of her status as victim of a larceny, she held me tight, uncertain of how to react. Was this a test of her as well?

"Was it one hen, Sister?" asked the Elder.

"Just one," said Mrs. Myton. "And I haven't slept well since." (This I would label a half truth, for just the day before I passed Mrs. Myton's window and heard a snoring equal to the clatter of picks in the quarry.)

"Mrs. Webb, tell us, can you forgive this wretched soul?"

"If the Lord can," said my mother, "then so can I."

"Very good," said the Elder. He stood contentedly before us, eyeing the gathered with an admixture of compassion and dignity. "Now who's next?"

Mrs. Myton had been the chink in the dam. What followed was a flood of confession. Brothers and Sisters raced each other to stand before their community and confess their sins: a stolen fence; a ladder borrowed but not returned; a handsaw pilfered from the mill. One dear woman, whose husband was up in Great Salt Lake with his second and third wives, pressed hard against her conscience to find a moral error in her past; all she could produce was this: "I once stole a rose from a bush that was not mine," she admitted in minor triumph. "To make matters worse, I pressed it in my Bible and have it to this day."

The admissions of thievery and deceit continued for three hours, reaching such fervor that it became almost a contest of who could admit to the greater sin. When one Brother stood and confessed mere doubt in his heart, he was nearly booed from the Meeting House. "What else have you done!" someone called. "Tell the truth!"

Then something unexpected occurred: Aaron stood up. "I've got something to say."

Elder Hovey stopped. "Tell me, Brother, what have you done?"

"I've been wrong to a girl."

"Go on." Clearly this was the type of confession Elder Hovey had been fishing for all night. Now that the topic had moved from larceny to true impropriety, the crowd of Saints was freshly enraptured.

"I promised I would marry her and I haven't."

"What will you do about it?"

"I'll marry her, if she'll have me."

Aaron had been such an undistinguished boy his entire life that many who knew my family did not know of his existence. He was average in every way: a plain appearance, a plain mind, a plain and guileless sense of purpose in life. I do not write this with judgment but simply as a matter of recording the truth—and in effort for the Reader to understand how exceptional his confession was.

"Is she here tonight?" asked Elder Hovey.

"She is."

"Will you make amends to her now? In front of your gathered Brothers and Sisters and before God?"

Every eye was on Aaron. He stepped forward, moving around the crowded pews. There was a great anticipation as he walked, everyone wondering at whose feet he would stop. When he had to step over a family seated on the floor, people stirred as if one of these girls—freckled like the leopard, all of them—had submitted to his will. But no, he was only passing. He paused before a black-laced widow whose husband had been lost in Missouri. Had she had her way with my brother? No, he was only hesitating before moving to, of all people, Connie, our dear, dull neighbor, who had celebrated her twentieth birthday unknowingly feasting on my mother's hen.

Imagine the stir when my brother took Connie's plump hand and asked her to become Mrs. Aaron Webb! His voice was so soft and timid that two older Sisters squawked, "What'd he say?" People began stomping their feet and a small section broke into a spontaneous hymn about atonement and the path to Heaven.

"And so this fine couple shall be sealed," announced Elder Hovey. "With their confessions, we can now forgive."

If Mrs. Myton had let loose a flood of stories of theft, my brother released a tidal wave of perversion too graphic to print. Suffice it to say: at least half the population of Saintly Brothers had a confession of the heart or, I should say, loins. The revelations continued for more than an hour, men rising to admit relations with women who were not their wives. The only resolution was marriage, even if the men were already wed. Elder Hovey asked several women on the spot, "Will you forgive your husband and permit him to marry the woman he has wronged in order to prevent his eternal damnation and hers?" Tell me, does a woman put to such a question have any option in her reply?

It will be noted that in this litany of intercoursal relations there were no confessions of liaisons between a man and a previously married woman. No man was stupid enough to admit to that. It is not for me to say whether such sins had been committed but not confessed, or if Payson was somehow spared from such unforgivable acts. In any event, after five hours of confession, we had heard enough. We left exhausted, my mother and Mrs. Myton forced to walk home amicably, newly united by crime.

THE 19TH WIFE

CHAPTER SIX
The Utah Reformation

The subsequent weeks brought great change and confusion to my depleted little family in Payson. The confessional meeting was followed by several more, some lasting all day, wherein every last sin imaginable and many never before deemed possible were confessed. There was never a more devout Saint than my mother, but she worried over the upheaval these meetings caused. "I don't understand it. People are lying about lying," she observed. "You can't impress the Lord with extra sins."

She was under a new duress, for Aaron had kept his promise and was sealed to Connie Myton in the Endowment House. It was a joyless ceremony, attended by but a few, myself excluded for I was too young to enter. Afterward, my mother served a custard cake to her new daughter and Mrs. Myton, who ate more than her share and left my mother with but a spoonful. (Why this sticks in my memory, I cannot say, but there it is once again: the truth!) After supper Aaron set about hanging a blanket along a wire run across the hut. Connie was to replace me in his bed, and I would sleep next to my mother. It was only that first night, as I tossed uncomfortably and plugged my ears against the strange noises from the other side of the blanket, that I learned that my mother's ticking was no more comfortable or soft than a dry river bed. She had given her children the finer mattress without once complaining of her sacrifice.

This is the sort of woman my mother has always been, I shall note plainly here.

Newly married, and awakened to the omnipresence of sin in our community, Aaron joined up with a gang of men who had taken it upon themselves to enforce atonement. These were frightening days in Payson. Although distracted by the vagaries of girlhood, I took full notice of the change of climate, and I am not referring to winter's end and the arrival of spring. During the first months of 1855, the confessions continued.

Those who refused to confess, or confessed they had nothing to confess, were dragged to meetings by young men, my brother included, and put before a hall of peers and shouted at to repent. "You're no better than the rest of us!" It did not occur to these mobs that a man or woman could in fact live righteously and therefore have no sins to offer up. The Church had been guiding all of us for years, long before Elder Hovey's arrival, to live sinlessly. I shall not bother to point out the broken logic herein.

In the evenings Aaron took down my father's rifle and went out to round up sinners. Connie, I am sorry to report, was a meek, twitching-nosed creature who squeaked from the corner of our hut. "When will you be back?" seemed to be her favorite phrase. When Aaron was out, I invited her to sit with my mother and me at the fire, but she preferred to stay on her side of the blanket, passing her time I do not know how, although every now and then a small sniffle would emerge from her and my mother and I would lift our eyes from our needlework.

Once I asked Aaron, when he came through the door flushed and excited, where he had gone off to. He hung up his gun like a hunter home from the kill and said, "Making sure all are saved." A noble endeavor, I am sure, but coming from a boy of seventeen who only a few months before feigned illness on Sunday mornings, it sounded, to my youthful and inexperienced ears, at least, insincere.

It does not take long, I do not need to tell you, for such an environment of confession to turn on itself. Soon not only were souls being cleansed, but neighbors were realizing they lived next to adulterers and thieves. Nearly everyone in Payson was told at some point he had been a victim by he who was previously deemed friend. This was enough to cast a long cloud of suspicion over the village. While the sinners were being re-baptized in the creek their minds were pre-occupied with their belongings left on the shore.

"It isn't right," my mother concluded in her admirably succinct way.

She wrote the Prophet, alerting Brigham to the hypocrisy Elder Hovey had unleashed in Payson. She was certain her old friend and counselor would not approve of such behavior, for where in the Book of Mormon were the tales of mass confession and repentance? (Well, maybe they are in there somewhere, because I might as well admit, as a child I read the book a dozen times but always its meaning escaped me. If you find hypocrisy in this confession, so be it, but I ask you, Dear Reader, pick up a copy yourself and tell me how long you last.)

Brother Brigham replied to my mother in a brief letter. "If they are sinful," he wrote, "then they should admit to their sins. If they are innocent, thus they are, and I pray, shall be." It would be incorrect to state this reply did not confuse my mother. She could have dismissed its ambiguity from any other Saint but Brigham, the man who had personally saved her with baptism in that cold creek all those years before. At the time she of course did not reveal the Prophet's response to me directly, yet in reconstructing these events for this publication more than one person has assured me he never clearly denounced Elder Hovey.

Had the events in Payson remained in Payson, this would be but a quaint story of provincial religious fervor. Yet, as History now knows, the mood of inquisition that struck our village was but a precursor for what would become known as the Utah Reformation. By the following winter of 1856, Brother Brigham and the other Church leaders instituted a like-minded reform throughout the Utah Territory. "All are guilty! None is clean until he has been cleansed!" So the charge went against Saints everywhere, even those who had never transgressed. The Utah Reformation showed far better organization than the little version originated in Payson. Brigham ran it like a General leading a War, commanding his Bishops, Elders, and others as if they were foot soldiers in a fierce battle for the soul. Among its many tactics in the campaign, the Church created a secret police disguised as local proselytizers called the Home Missionaries. Their function was to spy on Brigham's followers and carry out his will.

One afternoon my brother returned to the hut in such a somber mood, I feared he was bearing fateful news about our father. "I've been named a Home Missionary," he announced.

"What's that?" I asked in that way only an eleven-year-old can.

"We visit people in their homes, ensuring everyone's living righteously." Next he told my mother and me, and his wife in her corner, that he must put us each through a catechism. "That's how I'll know if your souls are pure."

"Child, sit down," my mother said. "You sound like a fool."

"Anyone who refuses the catechism must be reported to the Bishop." My mother told Aaron to stop his nonsense.

"I'll do it," squeaked Connie.

"You see," said Aaron. "My wife has nothing to hide."

He shooed my mother and me out the door into the garden. It was a fine spring day with a breeze rippling the grass. We waited upon a log beneath the cottonwood. Mrs. Myton spotted us from her window. "He promised he'd come over and do me when he's through with you!" she called.

"It didn't used to be like this," my mother said.

"Why is Brigham doing this?" I asked.

"It's the men around him. They tell him lies. There is no finer man on Earth than Brigham Young."

Imagine, if you will, the effect such a declaration can have on a young girl's heart. I was on the threshold of maturity, and acutely sensitive to how women responded to men. I loved no one more in this world than my mother. If she could love Brigham, even as his words and deeds created animosity in her own house, then my heart naturally followed course.

After nearly an hour, Aaron and Connie appeared in the kitchen yard. She had a confused, far-off expression, as if recovering from a sharp but temporary pain. "Is she all right?"

"She'll wait at her mother's while we continue. All right, Ann Eliza, you're next."

My mother told Aaron he could not interview me unless she was present. Aaron whined, an impetuous noise that reminded us he was not far from boyhood. "The Elders insist that each catechism be performed alone. Those are the rules."

"I won't let you talk to her without me." My mother folded her arms across her breasts—the universal maternal gesture that tells all children everywhere, This matter is settled.

Aaron relented with a huff and a stomp. We followed him into the hut. He had set two chairs opposite each other and he nervously indicated us to sit down while he perched on the bed. "Now I must ask you some very important questions. You must swear to the Lord you will answer honestly and truthfully."

I told him I would.

"All right, let's begin." He flipped through a pamphlet provided to him by our Bishop. "The first question is, Have you ever killed a man, woman, or child?"

"This is crazy," my mother snapped. "I've never thought about killing anyone until this very moment."

"Ma, I need to ask the questions in the order they're printed. Ann Eliza, yes or no?"

I could not help myself from laughing. "Who would I kill?"

"Answer the question straightforward and truthfully."

"No."

And so the inquisition continued. My brother, in earnest voice, asked the most ridiculous questions I have ever encountered, at least until my lawsuit against Brigham Young. He inquired if I had committed adultery. (This to an eleven-year-old!) He asked if I had drunk ale, whiskey, or wine.

"Are you finished?" said my mother.

"One more question. Do you accept plural marriage as true?"

"Are you asking me or Ann Eliza?"

"Both."

"My husband has a second wife. I think that clarifies my belief."

"Ann Eliza? What about you?"

"I think so." Oh, if I could take back that response!

The interview ended, as Aaron had been taught to do so, with instruction to observe the wishes of my mother and father (though absent) and to rightfully enter a plural marriage when I was of the age. "There," he said, reverting to his more accustomed role of son and brother. "How'd I do?"

"You'll be real good at this miserable task," my mother said.

Aaron, never exceedingly swift, took this as a compliment until he felt its underlying sting.

From thence Aaron, and many others like him, visited the houses of neighbor and friend, subjecting good men and women to a humiliating volley of questions. Most were afraid to turn the Home Missionaries away, for doing so would set off suspicion of being guilty of some great and yet unknown sin. During this time every Saint in the Territory underwent a re-baptismal, shivering in the fonts while their sins, no matter how trivial, were supposedly washed away. Within a few months, the people of Utah believed themselves the cleanest body of souls ever to grace the Earth. Despite my mother's denial, in truth all of this was done, we now know, at the behest of Brigham Young.

THE 19TH WIFE

CHAPTER SEVEN
Blood Atonement

Every now and then my mother and I journeyed to Great Salt
Lake City to shop in the well-stocked outlets of Main Street.
These were not frivolous trips—not as you, my young ladies
of the East, might think of a shopping journey—but, rather,
necessary excursions for survival. The stores in Payson, if you
were to call them such, carried such crude supplies that in
some ways it might have been more convenient were they not
in business at all.

On one such trip we—my mother and I, accompanied by
Aaron and Connie—stayed overnight to hear the Prophet
preach in the Tabernacle in the morning. For those who
have not visited the City of the Saints, the Tabernacle is an
enormous hall with a low, rounded roof that will remind you
of nothing so much as a giant tortoise. It is one of the Great
Buildings of the World, and, God willing, shall survive
centuries of man's folly to show itself to future ages.
Unfortunately, the world-famous turtle-roofed Tabernacle
would not be built for another ten years. No, on this particular trip in 1856, as the Utah Reformation was boiling over
into violence, the Tabernacle was a more modest affair
(although it was a vast improvement over the first Tabernacle
in the Territory, which was nothing more than a shady spot
beneath a bowery). Yet, no matter the edifice, the Saints
would always turn up by the thousands to hear their Prophet,
Brigham Young.

By now I was of the age to form a mature and reasoned

212

opinion of the great man. He loomed over my childhood as a beloved grandfather might: omnipresent and seemingly limitless in his influence over our lives; loving but also somewhat frightening; and as constant as the sun and moon combined. Before we moved to Payson, I would see him on Sundays or on occasion in Temple Square, and he would nod hello, for he was always friendly with children. Every child in the Territory knew where he lived, in the Beehive House behind a high stone wall. Many others have depicted him accurately, at least in visage, so there is little point in my expanding upon previous efforts. Except I shall note the appropriate metallic color of his eyes and the generally square and solid shape of his entire personage. In my youthful imagination I could not render a more apt representation of God.

On this particular Sunday the Old Tabernacle was full of expectancy. The Reformation had been sweeping the Territory for several weeks, fomenting a fervor of introspection, admission, and re-baptism. Twenty-five hundred Saints had come to hear their Prophet on how they could further atone. Surely some, though how many we can never be certain, were also looking for counsel on how to help their neighbors atone more effectively. Brother Brigham provided ample advice, for when he took the speaker's stand, his subject was atonement. I can assure you, nothing ignites an audience's heart like the discussion of someone else's penitence! Working himself into a magnificent outrage, Brigham Young announced, "There are sins that can be atoned for by an offering on an altar, as in ancient days; and there are sins that the blood of a lamb or calf, or of turtle-doves, cannot remit, but they must be atoned for by the blood of the man."

As if his point were not clear, the Prophet continued, "The time is coming when justice will be laid to the line and righteousness to the plummet; when we shall take the old broadsword, and ask, 'Are you for God?' and if you are not heartily on the Lord's side, you will be hewn down."

He continued, although I cannot be certain if it was on this particular day, "Will you love your brothers and sisters likewise, when they have a sin that cannot be atoned for without the shedding of their blood? Will you love that man or that woman well enough to shed their blood? That is what Jesus meant. This is loving our neighbor as our self; if he needs help, help him; if he wants salvation, and it is necessary to spill his blood upon the earth in order that he may be saved, spill it." (To my doubting Reader, I assure you these words are correct quotations and not mere paraphrasings. Brigham's words from the pulpit have always been dutifully recorded and distributed. You may search any archive in Deseret to learn that here I am transcribing his words verbatim without any enhancement or coloring.)

This was the doctrine of Blood Atonement—any man, woman, or child who did not believe in the doctrines of the Church, or the words of its leaders, could rightfully be destroyed by the sword. The Saints, already hot with religious fever, received the Prophet's words as Wisdom and Truth. Brigham had established his new doctrine and sent the Saints on their way to kill in the name of faith. Terrified, I broke into tears. Although I was young, Brigham's meaning was clear to me.

After the services we walked over to Main Street, where a restaurant sold ice-cream for twenty-five cents a glass, a high luxury well beyond my mother's crimped budget. Yet she knew I needed a distraction. As I probed the ball of ice-cream I asked, "Why does Brother Brigham want to kill?"

"He didn't mean it," my mother said. "Not like that."

"He meant it," said Aaron. He had finished his ice-cream and was digging into his wife's. "Brigham means what he says."

"Generally, yes," said my mother. "But this time he was speaking in metaphor."

214

Aaron looked confused, while Connie fidgeted with her curls. I thought, No doubt God had carefully selected them to be together.

Perhaps my mother's assessment was correct. Even so, the Prophet's tirade had a profound effect on me, and on many others. Here was the leader of our Church, the Governor of our land, a man in control of nearly every institution that made up our Saintly civilization, announcing from the pulpit that murder was justified in order to save souls. There, before my own eyes and ears, he asked men to murder! If he did not mean it, he should have said so.

Since then, I have heard the arguments against my interpretation of events: Brigham's words have been taken out of their original context (true, he often preached mercy and compassion); he was speaking in metaphor (perhaps, for it is true no one rushed out of the Tabernacle that day and lifted his sword like Laban); Blood Atonement was a product of its time, for the fiercely independent Saints were on the verge of war with the United States of America (could be, but does that justify it?). Excuses—that is all these are.

Those who disavow my testimony as merely (*merely!*) the tirade of a spurned wife, to them I say: You were not there! You did not hear the hatred in the Prophet's words. You did not see his fury.

I am neither theologian nor philosopher nor historian. I can only repeat that which I heard or which I know with near certainty others heard. The above quotes, as far as I know, are not in dispute. The dispute lies in their interpretation. Placing my full trust in my Dear Reader, I shall cease with interpretation now and leave that important task to you.

Yet I ask: Even if Brigham Young was calling for Blood Atonement merely for rhetorical effect, as some have argued, one cannot believe such vicious words would have no consequence. Make no mistake, there is no doubt that he dropped these appeals into this world. As poison enters a well, contamination must follow.

* * *

Word travels as swift as the horse. We returned to our hut in Payson to discover that Mrs. Myton had already heard of the Prophet's sermon.

"If Brigham declares this to be true, then it must be." Such was the analysis Aaron offered to his mother-in-law.

Connie, my dear sister-in-law, managed to peep, "Are we in danger?"

Aaron ignored her. "There's a lot of work in keeping souls clean."

"If Brigham's really so interested in cleanliness, he wouldn't have sent us to this dusty old town!" That was my contribution to the debate; you can imagine its reception.

There followed more general discussion of what the Prophet had meant. My mother genuinely believed that the Prophet, although susceptible to extremes, did not mean to incite murder. My brother, on the other hand, said there was little doubt about what should be done should we encounter an unrepentant sinner. This argument was repeated in households throughout the Territory in the subsequent days. It seemed wrong, even to my under-developed mind, for the Prophet, no matter his meaning, to have left his followers with such violent but unclear instructions of how to proceed.

Well, a minority of men found the instructions clear enough to act upon them. It was but a week later that rumors began to spread that a certain Mrs. Jones and her son, Jacob, had gone flabby in their faith. I did not know Mrs. Jones personally, although I could recognize her on the street, for she was tall for the female species and often wore elaborately feathered bonnets. (During the Reformation, some Sisters were known to condemn others for the mortal sin of overly fine millinery.) Mrs. Jones was a widow, her husband was lost at Winter Quarters, yet she had long resisted offers to enter a plural marriage. Enough men had felt the slap of her rejection that she was already, at the outset of the Reformation, a woman whom many suspected of disloyalty to the doctrine of spiritual wifery. Her son, Jacob, was Aaron's age but in many ways more of a man, and capable of growing a full brushy beard. Jacob held an unusual interest in the Indians, collecting headdresses and necklaces of beads. Outcast is too strong a word for Mrs. Jones and her son, yet this pair was never one with the provincial Payson.

They fought the onslaught of the Reformation as best they could. Although they attended Church meetings and paid their tithings, they resisted the public confessions and turned the Home Missionaries away from their door (Aaron happily supplied this bit of information). With Blood Atonement officially in the air, and the Prophet's words ringing in the ears of men inclined to violence, it took but seven days for the mob to settle on its prey.

Late one night, while sleeping in our hut, we awoke to an argument down the road, a scream, a plea, the sound of something heavy falling on something soft but thick, like a mallet to a sack of flour.

Connie flung the blanket along its wire, crying, "Aaron isn't here!" In the moonlight stood the most pitiful creature I've ever seen: She was trembling and tears dripped like wax down her face. "He told me to stay in bed no matter what."

My mother's face crumpled upon itself. "He's out there with them," she said. It is painful for me to recall, but my mother began to weep. Although my enemies have many times questioned my memory in accounting certain events, I will never let anyone accuse me of lying about my mother's tears that night.

Then two pistol shots cracked in the night, and each of us froze with genuine fear. Then came silence, and the long hours of uncertainty.

In the morning, word came that Mrs. Jones and her son were dead, their bodies disfigured and defaced. Officially, the stated cause was slaughter by the Indians. Aaron, who came

217

home before dawn, said "Jacob was always meeting up with the Indians for barter. Figures they'd go kill him one day. I heard he was stealing their feathers, or something like that."

"You can't lie to me," my mother said.

"Ma, I'm not lying. Go ask the Bishop. Go ask the chief of police."

Aaron made his point: He was only repeating the official account. Justice would not come, not here. In the afternoon, the grave-digger drove the bodies to the cemetery. The wagon passed by our hut, but my mother refused to let me look out, holding me to her breast. Connie was crying too and made Aaron hold her as she heaved.

The wagon made its way up the street. A few doors opened, the residents inside spitting at their fallen Sister and Brother. "Apostates!" they cried. "Go be with your Indians!" Others threw rotten fruit at the bodies; by the time the wagon reached the open graves, it rattled with old apples and wormy gourds. Yet the majority of residents, like my mother and me, stayed silent behind their doors, too frightened to peer out, or decry the violence, or doubt our Church. It is said that Mrs. Jones had been baking when the mob arrived at her door. There must have been a struggle, with her son coming to the hearth in her defense. We know this because the floury dough held to their fingers, and some in their hair, when the grave-digger drove them through Payson on their last ride before eternal sleep.

X

THE MISSION

LDS CHURCH ARCHIVES
SPECIAL COLLECTIONS
Biographies & Autobiographies
Salt Lake City

RESTRICTED ACCESS

RECORD OF PETITION FOR ACCESS

NAME: Professor Charles Green
DATE: Jan. 17,1940
DOCUMENT NAME: Autobiography of C. G. Webb
PURPOSE OF RESEARCH: Scholarly book on the end of plural marriage
PETITION OUTCOME: Declined, by C. Bock, Archivist

NAME: Kelly Dee
DATE: July 10,2005
DOCUMENT NAME: Autobiography of Chauncey G. Webb, The
PURPOSE OF RESEARCH: Master's Thesis on Ann Eliza Webb Young and the legacy of polygamy
PETITION OUTCOME: Approved by D. Savidhoffer, Archivist

THE AUTOBIOGRAPHY
OF CHAUNCEY G. WEBB

PART II

As Ann Eliza notes in *The 19th Wife*, our family's first years in Utah were marked by harmony and unified purpose. My two wives, once rivals, became companions—or at least it seemed so to me. If one of my wives nursed a deep wound in her heart, I never knew of it, for neither woman spoke of such injury during this time. In her book, Ann Eliza accuses me of "blithe unawareness" for failing to notice her mother's suffering. Yet when I look back on those first years in Deseret, I believe our family, even in its unique configuration, had achieved a happiness most can only pray for. At least I hope this was the case. This interlude of domestic contentment ended abruptly when Brother Brigham ordered Gilbert and me to England on a Mission. We departed in the winter of 1855, journeying via Saint Louis, reaching Liverpool's damp shores in the early days of a limp gray spring. There we rented a room from a young, talkative widow called Mrs. Cox, who shared a narrow house with her small daughter, Virginie, whose likeness to Ann Eliza made me miss my family even more.

That first day in Liverpool, and the early days thereafter, we were quick to learn what type of man will refuse to greet a plain stranger speaking of God on the refined streets of St. James and Great George. The gentleman strolling with his family and nurse; the nobleman nibbling toffees in his coach; the lady ornamented in satin and jewel; the sisters preoccupied with society and fashion—these busy people had no time, or disposition, to respond to our "Good day" or "Afternoon." Before them I felt like a ghost, for they had no awareness of me.

In Liverpool, God's most wretched souls congregated along the streets near Prince's Dock, for it was here they could rake through the piles of rubbish tossed over the shipyard's masonry walls. The one-armed sailor, the toothless hag, the skimpy orphan smeared with a lifetime of grime— here the saddest allotment of humankind sifted through the dirt with picking-irons in hopes of finding bread crusts, fruit rinds, and strips of filthy cotton that could be rinsed and sold for a penny. Every day at noon the sailors from the many ships from all over the world disembarked to dine at taverns such as the Baltimore Clipper and the Unicorn. This throng of salty men, with their odor of sea mist, and their ribald, foreign talk, poured past the beleaguered souls. Occasionally a sailor would toss a spare copper to a beggar, and a commotion would erupt in the chase for it. What pity it engendered in my heart and Gilbert's—a dozen hopeless men and women fighting one another for the smallest of coins.

On our first visit to the deprived neighborhood we passed a legless maiden perched on a wood platform with four small iron wheels. Her skirt was a cheap green calico, dirty and patched, yet she had fluffed it up and spread it about her with a touching amount of purpose and hope, so that she appeared, despite her missing limbs, almost as a lass sitting atop a picnic blanket. Propped before this stalwart girl was a panel on which a clear, strong hand had written out the brief narrative of her fate: *Sucked in by the harvesting machine*. At her side squatted a classically handsome young man, with silken black locks and Roman nose. His misery rested in his eyes, which had milked over with disease. Next to him crouched a skeletal woman with a starving babe latched to her shriveled blue breast. Beside her huddled a desperate young pair, brother and sister, I presume. They called out, "Please, we ain't eaten in four days."

"May we speak to you," I said, "about the Lord?"

"Please, do you have some bread?"

Gilbert broke off half of the butter sandwich Mrs. Cox had packed. He was offering it to the girl when the hag with the babe stole it, devouring it before our eyes.

"That was for the girl and her brother," I complained.

"It might as well've been for me and my child." The woman sat beatifically, as if she bore no remorse for her theft.

Gilbert offered the girl the second half, careful it landed in the intended hands. She shared it with her brother, while others all around shouted and cried for a morsel of their own.

"Now," I said to the pair of siblings. "May we have a word about Jesus Christ?"

"I'm sorry," replied the girl. "But I don't believe any of it. Not anymore."

I could not fault her. If I had been handed her fate, I cannot say for certain my faith would hold firm. Such misery is too profound to suppose we can know its meaning.

My son and I tried the young lass on the wooden cart. "May we have a word?"

"I don't want your pity, I want work."

"May we talk to you about Jesus Christ?"

"I don't need salvation, I need work."

We approached the young man with the clouded eyes. "Sir, do you have a moment to spare?"

"If you have a copper to spare."

"I don't."

"Then neither do I."

Thus our efforts passed, with no success for nearly a year.

Each night we would return to a coal fire lit by Mrs. Cox. In our room Gilbert and I would fall to our knees and pray for success and fortitude. By the glow of the candle I would write two letters, one to each Mrs. Webb. Often I struggled to offer each woman a unique account of my day, for I feared they might share the letters and find I had copied my sentiments from one to the next. If I signed my letters to Elizabeth *Your true husband*, then I carefully signed those to Lydia *Your husband most sincere*. As time passed, my longing for both women grew, and often I stayed up late, with Gilbert asleep beside me, writing out my desire to see each; and imagining the day I would. Any man who has endured a long separation from his wife will understand these yearnings.

One night, while on our knees, Gilbert said, "Father, I'm not sure how much longer I can do this."

It had been a difficult day at the end of a lonely week. The weather was damp, the city's mood foul, and a frivolous young woman done up in fox fur had passed us on the street, giggling to her companion, "What a waste of a good young man!"

"Father," said Gilbert, "I'm not sure we're achieving anything."

Startled by his quivering faith, there, before Mrs. Cox's glowing grate, I promised my son the next day would bring success. "I can't tell you how, or who, but you'll see your efforts rewarded." There is but one explanation for why I promised what I could not—desperation to tamp down my son's kindling doubt. He was an unknowable young man, distant in every way. Sometimes I suspected he privately accused me of vanity, hypocrisy, and the other sins of the wealthy and well-stationed. No doubt his questions about faith and the Church itself had deepened during our stay abroad; and I worried he might rashly choose to defy, or even depart, the creed that had saved his mother and brought them to me. I worried over his future, as all fathers do. It was this worry that kept me from sensing my own doubt unfolding within. In *The 19th Wife* my daughter accuses me of blind faith, "a blindfold woven from mammon and power tied across his eyes," she says. Her assault is cruel, I know, but I often wonder if her assassin's blade has been forged from an unalloyed truth.

The next day was bright with sun, as clear as the previous day had been gray. We spent nearly twelve hours in the quadrangle of the Merchant's Exchange near the statue of Lord Nelson. Everywhere windows were open to the breeze. Benign weather can add difficulty to the Missionary's work, for the general hopefulness of the climate helps Man forget his woes. Thus, the day was no different than all the previous, except one woman, done up in jelly-colored silk, wrongly accused us of stealing a bundle of lace which later turned up on a bench.

We returned to Mrs. Cox's little house dispossessed and weary. I carried a heavy shame for attempting prophecy. I could hardly muster a greeting to our landlady and her child.

"Right, 'ave a nice day, did you?" said Mrs. Cox. "Virginie, dear, leave the gentlemen alone, they've been out working for the Lord. Now I set your fire the way you like it, and I've just put the kettle on. Go and settle yourselves in and I'll fetch some biscuits, or if you like I can bring a plate of swipes."

Always loquacious, with very little to say but many words at her disposal, Mrs. Cox seemed particularly eager to hold us at the foot of her staircase longer than usual. "May I 'ave a word? If you're not too tired"— and when she saw we had failed to understand her intent she continued—"about your Church and your Book? I was born into the Anglican Church, of course. But ever since Mr. Cox's passing I 'ave to say I've 'ad me doubts."

It was then I understood. I moved to begin to speak, but Gilbert interrupted. "Father, may I try?"

His sudden eagerness to proselytize surprised me, and left me proud. We passed the evening in Mrs. Cox's parlor, Gilbert, for the most part, leading our discussion. Virginie lay upon the carpet, dressing and undressing her doll. Gilbert recounted the story of Joseph's Revelations, and the Latter-day Saints, a few times forgetting an important point which I added delicately, careful not to insult his capabilities. Mrs. Cox listened patiently, providing delightful commentary to the events of the Church's early history: "And 'e found the plates of gold in the earth, did 'e? Right lucky no one else came along. Most men would boil 'em down, they would."

"Would you like to read our Book?" said Gilbert. It was after midnight, and the street outside Mrs. Cox's window had fallen silent long ago. Virginie lay asleep in my lap.

She accepted it, holding it close to her breast. "Now then, I've got a lot of questions, but it's getting late so maybe I'll ask just the one that's been at me for some time."

I urged Mrs. Cox to ask whatever she needed to know.

"There's some who go round saying a Mormon man takes a dozen wives, maybe more. When I 'ear this, I say it can't be true. I got two Mormons living right 'ere in me 'ouse and I'd know, wouldn't I, if they kept a 'arem back 'ome."

Before our departure for England, Brigham had instructed us to evade the truth of plural marriage. "Far away, across the oceans," he said, "you will find the stranger cannot imagine the reds of Zion, nor the snowy heights of our peaks, nor the vastness of our great basin. Just as these ignorant men and women cannot see the beauty of our land, they cannot understand the uniqueness of our families. Speak not of the plural wife until our foreign brothers and sisters have arrived in Deseret and can see for themselves how red our sand blows."

For most men, myself included, the lie comes quickly and more naturally than we hope to admit. Thus I denied the truth of polygamy to Mrs. Cox, and forever after regretted doing so. I blame no one but myself for this misdeed.

"That's what I wanted to 'ear," she said. "Right, now I've kept you up late, 'aven't I?" She lifted her daughter while expressing such genuine gratitude and love that I knew for certain then and there we had converted our first soul.

Joseph Young, Brigham's son, was stationed in London on his own Mission. I wrote to him about our first convert, and he journeyed the eight hours to baptize Mrs. Cox. We met in a field dotted with sheep, beside a fast-running stream. He led Mrs. Cox into the water and submerged her. With that, we had brought forth our first Saint.

When Mrs. Cox emerged from the stream, her wet robe permitted the rosy color of her flesh to come through. To ignore her beauty would be to ignore God's mastery. To look at it would be to commit a sin. Yet I must confess I could not help but stare. Mrs. Cox stood in a sunbeam that gave her the look of a statue carved by the hand of an artist from classical Greece—a sheer marble gown draped over her form in such a manner that every curve was apparent to the day.

Later that night, after a celebration in the parlor, Gilbert and I lay upon our bed studying the Book. I sensed an agitation in my son—his foot was kicking the bedpost irritably. When I asked him to stop, for it was disturbing my concentration, he did so sullenly. I asked if there was a matter he wished to discuss, but he said he had nothing to share.

I have seen the gloomy air visit Gilbert many times. Aware of the stifled energies of the unmarried young man, I never pressed him on the matter. I decided the next day I would speak to him about marriage. There was a great possibility of meeting a young woman in Liverpool— a pretty soul eager for conversion and deliverance to Zion. My boy needed something to look forward to, I concluded, and having solved, or so I believed, my son's anxiety, I raked the coals for a final time, turned down the lamp, and settled beneath the bedclothes with a fine sense of accomplishment. It was still early, and the streets threw up the lamentable noise of urban sin—the singing drunk, the wench twirling on the sailor's arm, the gang of orphans scurrying across the cobblestones in broken shoes. It took some time for my mind to clear of the wretchedness below our warm, cloistered room and permit me to enter a peaceful sleep.

Late that night, after the clamor from the street had died out, a foreign noise woke me. I turned on my side and discov-

228

ered Gilbert missing from the bed. The moon shed a silver glow upon the room, illuminating the pink nosegays in the paper on the wall. I opened the door with such precision that its hinge brought no attention to my movements—a stealth which enabled me to witness, at the opposite end of the corridor, my son positioned near Mrs. Cox at her chamber's door. Their persons stood so close together a Bible would not pass between them. The window beside them was cracked and a night breeze wound its way into the hall, billowing their sleeping gowns in a way that unified them like a double cumulus cloud.

I cleared my throat. "Gilbert."

In unison they peered down the hallway in my direction. "Father—"

"Evening, Mr. Webb. Need some milk, do you? I'll fetch the pail."

"Father, I was on my way outside when I ran into Mrs. Cox. She asked me a question about the Afterlife."

"That's right. I was lying in me bed awake as the rooster, thinking about what will 'appen when it's time to go on. What I want to know is, will I meet Mr. Cox in 'eaven? It's what I was thinking when I 'eard 'is footsteps out 'ere, so I opened the door and asked. 'E was explaining 'ow things work when you came along."

"Mrs. Cox would like us to baptize by proxy her husband," Gilbert explained. "I'm willing to stand in his place."

I felt a great shame for my accusations and retreated to our room. Yet my ear remained pricked, taking in the click of Mrs. Cox's door and the fall of my boy's step as he made his way down the crickety stairs and outside. The privy door squealed with its recognizable glee. I was still awake when he entered the room. He climbed over me and turned to face the wall. In the moonlight I watched him pick at the seam in the paper until at last sleep transported me, for a few hours, to my two loving wives at home.

229

* * *

In March of 1856, almost a year before I had anticipated a departure from Liverpool, Brigham sent word that he needed me at home. He had selected me, above all men, to organize a new plan to increase the rate of immigration. Up until then it cost on average $55 in gold for one Saint to journey from Europe to Great Salt Lake, via New York and Iowa City, or Saint Louis—a reasonable sum for a voyage consisting of many thousands of miles on ship, train, and wagon. Yet Brigham had come to believe, for what reason I cannot be sure, that the Church needed a more economical method of importing its Saints. His advisors, to whom he sometimes overly deferred, had convinced him of a plan they called Divine. In *The 19th Wife* Ann Eliza regrettably but correctly labels it a scheme.

The largest expense of the voyage was the teams of oxen that pulled the wagons from Iowa City into Utah, more than one thousand miles, and therefore Brigham's advisors had concluded the oxen should be removed from the trip. The immigrant Saints, all of them, would pull their belongings across the plains and the mountains in hand-carts.

I complained to Brigham's son, Joseph, about the feasability of the plan but he dismissed my concerns. "The Prophet has chosen you. It's the will of the Lord. Now prepare to leave England."

A few days before departing, I came to a decision about my future. I wanted to take Mrs. Cox as my wife. If I were another man, with a different set of values, I suspect I might have had the opportunity to embrace her in her boardinghouse; and I suspect she might have accepted my kiss. But I am not such a man. I have made a vow to my wives never to stray, and I have not and never will.

"Will you and Virginie return to Zion with us?" I proposed one evening shortly before our farewell. I told her she could live in my household in Great Salt Lake and become a part of it.

For a long while Mrs. Cox did not speak. My meaning was not to deceive this woman by importing her to Utah and then, once she was an ocean and continent away from home, demand she become my wife. I have known Saints to do so to foreign women and even young girls of fourteen and fifteen. It is an abhorrence I was always sorry Brigham never spoke out against. This was not my intention with Mrs. Cox, but I could not outright discuss marriage with her until I had first discussed it with my beloved Elizabeth.

"'Ere's what I'll do. I'll give it a think tonight and tell you in the morning."

It is unsettling, even for me, to look back at myself and recount here the impetuous feelings early love can inspire in a full-grown man. Yet because I promised this to be a full and true account, I will commit to paper how my heart pounded in my chest! I wanted to run through the front door and shout in the street! I knew then she would come to Utah, and I knew she would marry me once Mrs. Webb had agreed, and I will admit my mind raced months ahead to our wedding night, when at last I could touch this lovely creature and she would be mine.

Our farewell was an awkward moment. A carriage came for our trunks. The horses idled in the mud while we managed to part Mrs. Cox's company. Gilbert, Mrs. Cox, and myself stood at her gate, each with a crooked smile that bore extended meaning. When Gilbert and I were in the carriage, Mrs. Cox pressed her face through the door. " 'Tisn't good-bye. We'll be right behind you in another month."

"The Saints will greet you when you arrive," I promised.

"I'll make sure of it," said Gilbert.

The carriage pulled away. We, father and son, turned to admire Mrs. Cox standing beside the ivy climbing her gate. In the wind the early red-green leaves trembled, brushing her throat and cheek.

When she was out of sight Gilbert declared, "Father, I'm going to marry her."

I was so startled by my son's announcement that I had to struggle to suppress my jealousy. "Marry Mrs. Cox? My boy, what are you talking about?"

"When she lands in Utah, I'll marry her."

"Have you discussed this with Mrs. Cox?"

"No, but I know she'll have me."

"Are you sure?"

"I've never been so sure of anything."

The leonine pride which resides in the cage of my heart had been stirred. I wanted to lash out and defend the woman who, in only a matter of time, would be mine. But I would not challenge my son in such a manner. I loved him too much. I had no doubt Mrs. Cox would become Mrs. Webb, my Mrs. Webb, that is, but to state the fact so baldly would leave him, I feared, irreparably harmed and, perhaps, weakened in the eyes of other women. The boy would need to marry soon, and I would help him, but he would not marry the woman I had already settled upon. Somewhere in *The 19th Wife* Ann Eliza asks, "Did my father not think himself selfish, claiming one woman when he already had two?"

Her question devastates me, even today.

Upon our arrival in Iowa City, we found, to great dismay, no materials for the construction of the hand-carts, no process of assembly, no leader with the temperament or skill to enact the Prophet's plan. Even worse, only a few days behind us was the first arrival of Saints—anxious souls from London, Glasgow, Copenhagen, and Stockholm about to spill from the train with their belongings strapped to their backs. They would need nothing more than shelter and food, and yet Brigham's agents had not prepared any. They had failed to establish a camp of any sort or stores of nourishment and water. The European souls—by early summer several thousand had gathered—were left to unroll their tickings in a field. When it rained, they propped coats and tarpaulins upon sticks. The kind people of Iowa City opened their larders to the emigrants, passing out bread, potatoes, and waxy wheels of cheese. There was no meat unless a pig was donated, or stolen. Water came from a single, questionable well.

Such conditions led to immediate squalor—the stench of the refugee camp is one that no man shall ever forget. Often I walked among these weary souls, looking for Mrs. Cox, grateful to never find her encamped in such suffering.

Always I saw the same question burning in the emigrants' dispossessed eyes: Why? Why had the Church that promised them Salvation and taken their money for the journey abandoned them in a prairie, a thousand miles from Zion? The Apostles sent from Salt Lake—men whose names I shall refrain from presenting here—told the hungry and disenchanted migrants that any impatience would be interpreted as distrust of God. "You have been given a Divine challenge. Only the faithful will pass." I cannot know whether the immigrants believed these men or were too broken to defy them.

By June, after much labor, the first carts were ready. They were a crude vehicle of poor craftsmanship and material in which I could take little pride. One cart could haul a family's personal belongings, no more than seventeen pounds of garments and bedclothes per person. The Divine plan conceived of a man pulling the cart, while his wife and children walked alongside. In reality, there were a large number of young girls traveling alone and widows with babes, or the elderly. These fair creatures were never meant to drag their earthly possessions across the plains and over the Rocky Mountains and yet that is what we asked them to do.

Given the disorganization of the mission, and the slowness of the building supplies, I advised Brigham's agents that the last party could leave no later than the end of June. The others would need to remain in Iowa City until the following spring. But these men, who were religious zealots, not organizational leaders, refused to adhere to my counsel. Against my orders, the last party of hand-carts left in the middle of August, walking toward their own death, I was quite sure. These foreign immigrants knew nothing of our climate or the mountains awaiting them. To make matters more precarious, the men who had promised to look over the immigrants like angels had sent them on their journey with criminally small rations—ten ounces of weak buckwheat flour and a little rice for each man and woman per day, an amount I understood to be approximately one-third of the average man's caloric needs; and five ounces of buckwheat flour, and no rice, for the child Saints. Many of the immigrants were from Northern Europe and the cold harbors of Sweden and Norway and thus spoke little English, certainly not enough to complain about these insufficient supplies. Along the trail, at infrequent posts, the weary Saints would find supplements of brown sugar, cured pork, and weak coffee dispersed by the fat, careless Elders assigned to the task. It takes little forethought to know this is not enough food to walk a thousand miles while pulling one's belongings. I advised the agents present that not only would the Saints freeze, they would also starve. One Apostle replied, "This is the will of Brigham himself. Take your complaints to him." Were he there and not one thousand miles away, I would have appealed directly to the Prophet. Instead, I was forced to argue in the ears of his men, who proved themselves wholly ordinary. There are many to blame for the tragedy that ensued. I include myself in that wretched lot.

With the last party departed, we prepared for the journey ourselves. We formed a party of two dozen men, mostly Missionaries on return voyage from their work in European lands. The party included Joseph Young, who I must admit had grown from boy to man during his years abroad. He too had seen the risk facing the emigrants and had complained about it. But not even the Prophet's son could affect the men who worked under the standard of Brigham Young. We left

234

Iowa City well-prepared, with teams of oxen and mules, our own wagons stocked with flour and rice, coffee and sugar, dried beef and pork, chickens, a pig for every five men, and a milking cow. This is how it should be done, and great pangs of regret overcame me, and Gilbert, too, as we overtook that last party of hand-carts on the trail. They saw us comfortable on the wagon seat, or nudging along the cow with a reed, and heard the chickens cluck from the cage, and certainly they must have wondered why they themselves were not so well-equipped.

On the Platte River's North Fork we joined an encampment of emigrants for one night. They were flung around several pits of fire, men and women and children alike, collapsed upon bundles of clothing and sacks of flour, too tired to set up camp properly. Many wore shoes held together by rawhide string. "What will they do when winter comes?" Gilbert asked, yet I could not answer him for the truth was too difficult to speak.

Gilbert and I, and the other men in our party, offered as much food as we could spare and handed over a pair of asses for the sick who were too enfeebled to walk. We promised we would send help once we reached the Salt Lake Valley. In the morning, with no more than a strip of sunlight in the east, we continued on our journey. Each man was determined to reach Zion as soon as possible. It was our only chance of saving these souls.

Upon reaching Great Salt Lake, our hearts broke open with relief. The city had grown in our absence, and had we not been arriving with urgent news, we would have stopped to marvel at Zion's progress. But there was no time for reflection and joy. At once Gilbert and I traveled home while Joseph Young went directly to speak to his father.

On the matter of the hand-cart expedition, this is where my account differs from that of my daughter in her published

235

memories. When Brigham heard of the danger awaiting these innocent emigrants, he shook with anger. He scolded the men, his apparent agents, who had misinterpreted his words. Certainly the Prophet wanted the expedition performed economically, but he had never meant to risk a life. Ann Eliza doubts the Prophet's sincerity, claiming Brigham had known all along the dangers and misery facing the emigrants. This is not true, for I witnessed the Prophet preach in the Tabernacle the next Sunday that every Saint in Zion must contribute to the rescue effort. He denounced the men who had made such reckless decisions in his name. He denied that the perils facing the emigrants were a test of God but said they were, rather, a sign of man's incompetence and indifference. As he orated, blood filled his throat. His voice reached across, or so it seemed, the entire Salt Lake Valley. It is impossible to deny the sincerity of his rage.

I should stop my account of the hand-cart emigrants to describe my return home. There were, of course, two homes to return to. Lydia lived in Great Salt Lake with Diantha; Elizabeth lived in Payson with Ann Eliza and Aaron, who had since wed the neighboring girl. Because I arrived in Great Salt Lake first, I stayed with my second wife on my first night back in Zion. Lydia welcomed me with caresses and boiled beef, a clean house, and a warm bed. Any man who has sustained himself through long intervals separated from his wife knows how welcome her initial touch is upon return.

I wanted to linger with her all day, all autumn and winter, in fact, but I knew I must ride to Payson. Word travels quickly in the territory. There was little doubt the first Mrs. Webb had news of my arrival. The separation is no easier on the man than it is on the woman, of course, and I knew Lydia felt it her right to keep her husband a few more hours. "Let me pretend a little longer you're all mine," she sighed. It was not a selfish statement, merely the honest expression of a lonely heart. It pained me to deny her. I kissed my wife good-bye and rode off to see my wife.

My homecoming in Payson was less joyous. Our separation had tried Mrs. Webb. I attempted to soothe her with an embrace, yet when I kissed her, I felt the subtle manifestation of suffering in her brittle lip. "How I missed you," I declared.

Gilbert and I explained the plight of the emigrants and our need to return at once to their rescue. Here my old affection for Mrs. Webb rose, for she became overwhelmed with concern for her fellow man. "The poor souls," she said. "Take them food and blankets and anything they need." She set to work preparing baskets of relief items. I found reassurance in her compassion. I slept well that night at her side.

In the morning I prepared to return to Great Salt Lake to assist in the relief effort. My good first wife said, "I'll be baking bread till the last of them arrive." Her selfless outlook perhaps explains my distress at Ann Eliza's sudden outburst.

"You promised you'd stay!"

I tried to hold the girl, but she shrugged herself away. By now Ann Eliza was twelve. The mysterious veil that falls upon a girl at the outset of maturity had descended. Her tears were those of a child. Her rage was that of a woman. I must admit, I was uncertain of what comfort I should offer.

"I have to help these people," I said. "They'll die if we don't. When I return, it'll be for good. I promise."

This was my mistake, one that I continue to rue. I was promising one type of return, while Ann Eliza was hoping for another.

When it was time to depart I asked Elizabeth to follow me to my wagon. Across the kitchen yard Ann Eliza stood in the door frame, carefully watching her parents. I did not believe she could hear us, but in her book she records the words of our conversation accurately.

"There's one thing I'd like to discuss before I go," I said.

"Tell me."

"On the subject of marriage."

Elizabeth winced—almost imperceptibly. "What is it?"

"There is a woman, from Liverpool, who might be among the emigrants."

"What is it about this woman I need to know?"

"If I find her, I would like—"

Are there any more difficult words for a husband to express than these?

"If she makes it to Zion, we might want to—"

"Yes?"

Then she understood. "Oh, Chauncey. You just got home."

"I know, but this woman will need a home. If I find her, I'd like to bring her here and you two can—"

Elizabeth lifted her hand to stop me. "You may have her."

"Elizabeth, please."

"You want her, and you'll have her. There's nothing more to say."

"I want you to know her, to approve of her."

"I don't want to know her."

"Then I can't marry her."

"You can, and you will."

"She might not even arrive. I might never see her again. I only wanted to raise the possibility. Elizabeth, are you all right?"

"I'm fine," she said. "I'll be fine." I tried to embrace her, but she waved me off.

I returned to Great Salt Lake with a miserable heart. I was there no more than half a day when the first hand-cart company arrived. These were the pioneering souls who had departed Iowa City in June, and now, at the end of September, they limped into Zion. Even outside Liverpool's docks I had never seen such a tragic lot. Men with the skin blistered off their palms. Women with hair falling out from lack of nourishment. Babes suckling air, their mouths dry and blue. Goblin-eyed children floating about. The emigrants had

238

walked more than one thousand miles, waded every river between the Mississippi and the Wasatch Range, pulled their belongings, and resorted to eating long grass and dirt when their flour ran out.

They stumbled through the city until they arrived at the gates of Temple Square. A crowd had gathered to witness their arrival. Thinking they had come to enjoy a triumphant parade, many people wore colorful clothing. They carried baskets of rose petals to shower upon the travelers. The shock on their faces said they could not understand how God—or Brigham—would let this happen to His chosen people.

Brigham emerged from his offices at the Beehive House. "Take them into your homes!" he instructed the Saints. "Bathe them! Feed them! Clothe them! Welcome them to Zion!"

At once the Saints descended upon the emigrants. Generosity to the stranger is one of our long traditions. Witnessing it still can cause a rise in my throat. I joined the effort, wading into the crowd, looking for a soul or two whom I could take back to Lydia's cottage for a meal.

"Excuse me, sir," a voice called out. "My sister's not well."

A hand petted on my sleeve. I turned to find a girl of fifteen standing beside a hand-cart. She pointed at another girl, perhaps a year older, lying in the cart at an angle that made her look all but dead.

"My sister was strong until a week back. She wanted to give up, but I told her I'd pull her along. We ate all our flour. There was nothing left. Then we ate our shoes."

Their feet were black as coal.

"Come with me." I pulled the hand-cart myself across the city to Lydia's cottage.

"My name is Margaret. My sister's Eleanor. Margaret and Eleanor Oakes."

"Where are you from?"

"London. We were house-girls for Lady Wellingham when

239

we heard the Prophet's son speak. I said to my sister, 'Let's go to America.' She didn't want to, not at first. Then our situation changed and we no longer worked for Lady Wellingham. We didn't have a home when we encountered Mr. Joseph Young a second time. I said to Eleanor, 'Lightning doesn't strike twice.' "

When my wife saw the anguished sisters, she set to work laying out dresses and preparing a meal of ham hocks and lima beans. She assured Margaret and Eleanor they could stay as long as they needed. "I'll help you plant your feet," Lydia said. I thanked my good wife for welcoming the girls. Lydia's cottage was small, her allowance almost nothing, yet she offered Margaret and Eleanor everything she could, and more. "Maybe you're too good for me," I later told Lydia in private.

"Probably," she replied.

I left the household to return to organizing the relief effort. When I returned that evening I found two sparkling young women, their complexions polished to the yellow-rosy hue for which the English are known. They sat on the rag-rug playing with Diantha, showing the child how to dress up her doll. I could see Diantha already loved Margaret and Eleanor like sisters. She kissed each on the peachy cheek.

With food and water, Eleanor had been restored to such vigor that when she saw me, she leapt to her feet to embrace me. "Thank you, Mr. Webb! You saved my life." Her form in my arms was both soft and firm.

Margaret followed, kissing my forehead. I was aware of the wet impression lingering on my brow for some time.

This was a great deal of female attention for any one man, and I struggled to maintain my composure. If I were not wearing a beard, no doubt the girls would have seen the deep blush in my cheek. "We should thank you for putting your trust in us," I managed.

Margaret and Eleanor returned to the rug, helping Diantha

assemble a puzzle. Lydia took up her sewing in her rocker, and I joined them in my chair with my mother's Bible. Yet I found, with such female splendor before me, I could not concentrate on the words. It was as if I were trying to read without my spectacles. My mind wandered elsewhere: to Mrs. Cox, wherever she may be. To my sweet Lydia in her rocker—how much she had transformed from girl to woman since she came into our house in Nauvoo. To Mrs. Webb in Payson. I loved her as no other, but that love, over the years, had evolved from romantic to respectful—an evolution that might be expected in long relations between man and woman.

I thought of all this, but foremost in my mind were the two girls on the carpet, their slim legs folded beneath them. Eleanor had a slightly longer throat, I noticed. Margaret, although younger, was fuller in the breast. I had divined, through careful questioning, that she had come into trouble in London. It was for this reason Lady Wellingham had dismissed them from her household. Pondering her fate, I became overwhelmed with desire. I wish I could write that I looked upon these girls as a father looks upon his children. That had been my intention when I led them to my wife's cottage. But my intention had exploded into a terrible passion, one that I immediately recognized.

"I think I shall go to bed," I announced.

"But Webby!" cried Eleanor. "So soon?"

The sisters unfolded their legs, like colts lifting themselves from a bed of straw, to kiss me, a pair of lips on each whiskery side. The sensation was so great that I felt bolted into my chair. Many minutes passed before I could unlatch myself. I was slow to see the anger in Lydia's narrowed eyes. "I thought you said you were retiring," she finally said.

Yet I could not sleep. My ears remained pricked to the sounds of the sisters—their cheering when the puzzle was complete; their feet upon the floorboards; the water of their ablutions; their whispers when they were in bed and believed

241

no one could hear. What were they discussing? Was it possible they were speaking of me?

In the morning, I rode to Payson. I burst into Mrs. Webb's house, my old heart thumping in my throat, prepared to make my speech—when she stopped me. My Elizabeth! Her face is always honest and good! She never masks her intentions! Disguises her heart! And yet I had descended upon her with a request that would require she deceive herself.

"Did the woman from England arrive?" she said.

"Yes! Or I should say no. No sight of Mrs. Cox. I'm frightened for her. Oh, Elizabeth, you should see the poor creatures who arrived yesterday. Barely alive. And behind them on the trail are the bodies of who knows how many dead. It was a terrible day."

Pity appeared in her eyes. "You shouldn't be here with me," she said. "You should go and help as many as you can."

"I will, shortly, but first, there's something I need to tell you. Ask you, that is."

She peered into my eyes, searched about, and located the lust and greed. As she recognized it, her face broke apart into shards of woe. "Another wife?"

"No, not another. Or I should say, instead. Instead of Mrs. Cox."

"Chauncey, listen to yourself."

"I know. I can hardly believe I'm saying these things. But something's happened. And I know that this is what I must do."

"Who is she?"

"You should have seen her. She was a waif! She has no one."

"Chauncey. How many is it going to be?" My wife turned away from me and began to weep into her own shoulder. "I never thought you were this kind of man."

242

"She needs me. She needs a home."

"Where will this end?"

"Elizabeth, we both know this is our duty to God."

I had probed Mrs. Webb's most tender spot. She could not deny that the Prophet had made this clear. Her faith was always pure, while I layered mine with expediency. I am ashamed of many things, but none so much as when I excused my passions in the name of God.

"What's her name?"

"Her name?"

"You don't know?"

"Miss Oakes."

"Miss Oakes? You might want to ask her given name before you marry her."

Elizabeth returned to her kitchen chores. Her restraint of tongue deepened my already profound respect for her. Were I not blinded by my desire, her noble actions would have caused me to reconsider my next step.

I should note that I was not aware that Ann Eliza was behind the curtain during this conversation. Later she told me she had overheard it, but I never believed her, for more than once she had resorted to fabrication in order to manipulate my feelings. Yet in *The 19th Wife* she repeats this encounter with a recollection that all but matches my own. She describes Elizabeth's pain as a spade of sorrow sharp enough to hollow out the soul.

The question remained: Which Miss Oakes would I marry? Would it be Eleanor, with her affectionate habit of calling me Webby? Or Margaret, with her calming voice that suggested, to me, at least, the sensibility of a young woman who knows much about the world? Each had her unique merits and appeal.

I invited the older girl, Eleanor, on a stroll through Temple Square. She appeared for our assignation in Lydia's finest walking dress, the scalloped neckline revealing a swath of flesh I found impossible to ignore. To think God had nearly permitted this creature to perish!

"Tell me, have you heard anything about celestial marriage?"

"Do you mean polygamy?"

I nodded.

"Same as in the Bible?"

"That's right. No different than the forefathers."

"Back in England, Brother Young was asked about it at one of his meetings. He denied it, he did. Told a hundred people nothing of the sort existed, not in his father's Church. Most people believed him. Not me. I said to Margaret, 'I know they go around marrying this girl and that, it's what they believe.' Margaret said, 'Is that right?' And I said, 'It is. I've heard some women speak of it. They say it's not so bad. In the kitchen four hands are better than two. That's what they said.' Margaret said, 'Ellie, don't be silly.' But I said, 'It's not silly if it's true.' "

"So you understand it?"

"I suppose I do. A man takes a wife, and then another. That's all there is to it, right?"

"Yes, and we call it celestial marriage."

"Do you? Quite a fancy name for buggering all over the place."

I was having trouble discerning her opinion on the matter and ventured forth with the necessary delicacy. "The Lord revealed this truth to Joseph Smith."

"Did He? Then it must be true. What about you? How many have you got?"

"I have two wives."

"Sister Lydia here, she's what? The first or the second?"

"She's my second wife."

"Where's the first?"

"South of here."

"Does she mind sharing you like that?"

"She knows it's part of her salvation. My first wife, Sister Elizabeth, is the most devout woman I know."

"She isn't jealous?"

"Not that I know of."

"Are there any others?"

"At the moment, no."

Eleanor chuckled and poked my breast. "Why, Webby! Do you plan on taking another? Is that what this is all about? You want me for your third wife? Is that why you asked me out for a stroll? Oh, Mr. Webb, you're quite the sneak, aren't you?"

I cannot think of a time when a woman had reduced me so swiftly to a quivering mass of nerves. If I were a young man, I would wax rhapsodic over the beauty before me—the eyes, the lips, the small upturned nose! Yet I am no Romeo and shall leave the wordplay to the poets.

"Is it?" she pressed. "Don't be shy. Tell me what's on your mind." She was teasing me, and I could not speak. "Why, Webby! You're as red as the rose."

A thought entered Eleanor's head, and her own countenance darkened. "Or is it Margaret? Have you led me all the way here to ask me about my sister?"

"I hardly know where to begin," I said.

Up until that point I had managed to hide my true feelings from myself. Now I understood I desired both.

Both! I cannot explain what had overcome me. Perhaps the long months of Missionary work had pent up an uncontrollable longing. Perhaps something within had been starved in Liverpool, and now I was inhaling a certain kind of nourishment just as the weary emigrants devoured loaf after loaf.

I tried my best to tamp down my yearnings. "I want to marry you," I said.

Eleanor took my arm, bringing it close to her breast. "I'll do it," she said. "I want to have my place in this Church."

I deposited Eleanor at Lydia's gate and went to speak with the Bishop. As with all government, there is a certain amount of bureaucratic lethargy encrusted around the Church's administrators, but not so when the issue is celestial marriage. It took only a few hours to arrange. Brigham himself conducted the ceremony that afternoon. To me he advised, "Treat her with equality."

Eleanor and I spent our wedding night at Brigham's hotel. She had been my wife no more than twelve hours before she summoned the dressmaker and the milliner. She wasted no time drawing up a list of items she would need in her future home: a stained-glass window, a visitor's settee, a crystal chandelier. The list lengthened by the hour. One day as Mrs. Webb, and she had nearly bankrupted me.

Yet I worried not about the expense of maintaining three houses or the envy Eleanor's demands would install in the hearts of Elizabeth and Lydia. Instead, my worries were those of the vain young man—did Eleanor find me appealing? Did she mind my odors? How did I appear to her when I stepped outside my clothes? I am not proud of this regression to boyish idleness. Yet here I am.

Thus my follies continued. If only they ceased that day.

The day after our nuptials Margaret visited us at the hotel. Eleanor showed her sister the embroidered ribbon that, when yanked, brought the butler to the door. She laid out on the sofa the swatches of material the dressmaker had left behind. The sisters turned to the list of household items. With Margaret's help it doubled in length.

"You'll live with us, won't you?" asked Eleanor.

"I don't want to intrude on Mr. Webb."

Eleanor leapt across the room, attaching herself to my arm. "Mind? Don't be silly! Webby doesn't mind a thing!"

It was now apparent I had married a frivolous girl who would drain my accounts and ignore my orders. My mistake was clear: I had chosen the wrong sister. I had only myself to blame. Soon Elizabeth and Lydia would learn of the promised crystal chandelier, and each would rightfully demand her own. I would spend the rest of my life devoted to the wagon manufactory to support my domestic situations. What had I done? For what cause? I left the sisters to unwrap a bundle of packages delivered from the shops. The packing paper crackled so loudly, they did not hear me depart.

In Payson, Elizabeth froze in shock. "Another wife?"

"It's not like that. They're sisters. They'll live together."

I had found her outside busy beating her rugs on the line, while Ann Eliza twirled on the swing hanging from a nearby tree. "I won't do it unless you consent."

"You don't care what I think."

"You're mistaken."

Elizabeth continued beating her rugs. "This isn't what the Lord had in mind. He didn't mean it to be like this."

"What do you want me to do? Tell me, and I'll follow your command. You're the first Mrs. Webb, you'll always be the first."

"I want you to leave my house."

"May I marry this girl?"

"I don't care what you do." Her beater came down hard on the rug, bursting a cloud of dust in my face. Ann Eliza laughed at her ridiculous father.

"Are you withholding your consent? Because if you are, then I'll drop this matter right now."

"Stop," she said. She leaned against the side of the house, exhausted. The dust had settled on her skin, and she appeared worn and gray. "It's your choice, we both know that."

"The Prophet says it's your decision."

"The Prophet."

It was the first time I had heard her speak of him bitterly.

"Elizabeth, what should I do?"

"Marry the girl, I don't care."

"Elizabeth."

"Go. Please go." I tried again, but she shoved me off.

When I left, Ann Eliza followed me to my wagon. "Do you want to replace Mother?"

"No, no, no, no, nothing like that at all."

"Then what are you doing?"

I tried to explain but failed. "One day you'll understand."

"I doubt it."

My daughter's rejection continues to sting. Perhaps that has been the most troubling aspect of reading Ann Eliza's book—learning of the hatred I had inspired in her young heart.

Margaret accepted my proposal. Only after I had her consent did I inform Eleanor. She absorbed the news sourly, claiming I had deceived her. "If you think this gets you out of buying me that chandelier, you should think again," she yipped. "And I mean the large one with the three tiers." I assured her she would get her chandelier.

That evening the Prophet married Margaret and myself. Our wedding night was spent in a room down the hall from Eleanor's suite. She was now mine, but at what cost? In the morning Margaret moved into Eleanor's rooms. They were now sister wives in all senses, and I was their fool.

What occurred next, and how this conjugal folly ended, might be taken as proof that the Lord punishes those who misinterpret His words. In less than a week I had gone from two wives to four. Almost any Saint will tell you this was not what the Lord intended in His Revelation. Even I was surprised by my conduct. As Ann Eliza reports in *The 19th Wife*, neighbors and acquaintances commented. Although four wives is a small number compared to the dozen or more among the Apostles and the most powerful Elders, and the countless Brigham himself has amassed in the Lion House, the swiftness of my third and fourth matrimonies caused more than a few tongues to flap.

During my week of matrimonial indulgence, other men more selfless than myself had continued to rescue the emigrants stranded on the trail. Day after day teams left Great

Salt Lake loaded with supplies. Brigham himself headed the organizational planning. I understand a large map was posted in his office, marked with red dots between Utah and Iowa where emigrant parties waited for assistance. He led the campaign like a commander in battle, and the swiftness of his decisions would go on to save many lives. At an encampment on the Sweetwater, near the Rocky Ridges, despair had already descended on dozens of emigrants. Food was gone, and death took one emigrant after the next. The survivors, weakened themselves, exerted their final energy to dig a mass grave. But with the arrival of nourishment, the survivors' ordeal had come to an end. Brigham's efforts were at last saving lives.

Such a scene repeated itself across the trail. Rescuers led the hand-cart expeditions over the mountains and into the Great Salt Lake Valley. Some arrived grateful for salvation. Others arrived angry for what they perceived as treachery. Some joined the community of Saints. Others, once restored to health, left for California, abandoning the leader who had brought them so far. Throughout the autumn the emigrant parties continued to arrive. Once or twice a week they appeared at the mouth of what became known as Emigration Canyon. They would descend from the mountains in a weary column, arriving at Temple Square, just as the party that brought Eleanor and Margaret to me had done a month before.

By November, the last party reached Zion. They were the most miserable of all. Noses, ears, and fingers blackened by frostbite. Mothers of dead children wandered with their arms cupped around the ghosts of their babes. Broken men wept. It was a terrible sight, but at least it was the last of the hand-cart fiasco.

Standing on Temple Street, I witnessed these final emigrants stagger into our beloved city. With me was my most recent wife, Margaret, who thankfully never showed as much interest in her tailor as her sister did. She cried for her fellow journeymen, her own ordeal still fresh, and showered them with white chrysanthemums. It was startling to see how starvation and deprivation had removed their individuality. Each now appeared similar—eyes sunk into their skulls, cheeks carved out, lips the color of ash. I held my new wife as we watched the last of the souls pass before us. All was silent, except for the creak of the cart-wheels—the crying iron will remain in my ear until my final day. As will the shout that rose up from the mass of starving souls: "Virginie, look! It's Mr. Webb!"

At once Mrs. Cox and Virginie ran from the parade of misery into my arms. She was as much an image of wretchedness as the other souls, but in truth even more so, for I had known her previous beauty. "Mrs. Cox, I didn't know," I said. "I didn't know."

Stunned and wordless, I led Mrs. Cox and the girl to Lydia's cottage. Once again my second wife welcomed strangers into her home. As Lydia worked through the evening, satisfying her visitors' needs, on occasion she shot me a glance that said all too clearly: Another wife-to-be? I took Lydia outside. "It's not what you think," I said.

"What do I think?"

"You think I've brought her here as a future wife. Well, I haven't."

"I hope four is enough."

I assured Lydia four women could meet my needs. "I have another plan for Mrs. Cox. You'll see."

Despite my previous affection for Mrs. Cox, I had come to realize that the feelings generated for her in Liverpool had been supplanted by my present conjugal duties. My plan was this: I would reunite Mrs. Cox with Gilbert in Payson. I would be more than happy to see my son take over as her betrothed. After all, this is what he wanted. Even Elizabeth would respect this arrangement. "You'll like Payson very much," I told Mrs. Cox on the journey south. "I know Gilbert will be glad to see you."

I deposited Mrs. Cox and Virginie at Elizabeth's house. If

Lydia had restrained her displeasure, Elizabeth did not hesitate to unload hers. She pulled me into the barn, where Ann Eliza was watering the horse. "Don't tell me she's another one of your brides."

"No, no, no—you don't understand. Gilbert's the one who wants to marry her. He's long had his heart set upon Mrs. Cox. True, she's a widow, but she isn't a year or two past thirty. And although she comes with a child, she also comes, I believe, with an income that should help our boy establish himself beyond our purse."

Elizabeth softened. "Does he know she's here?"

"I was just about to set out to find him."

I left my wife with the feeling one has after a narrow escape from danger and located my son at the manufactory. "She's arrived," I reported.

"Who?"

"Mrs. Cox."

Gilbert dropped his mallet. "Mrs. Cox? And she's well? Virginie, too?"

"Weary but well. The child, too. Very much the same indeed. She's waiting for you at your mother's house."

I was not privy to his first conversation with Mrs. Cox, but I know its outcome. Later that evening I found my son in a tavern, drunk on whiskey. I lifted him by the collar to carry him home when he said, "It's you."

"Of course it's me. I'm here to take you home."

The boy swatted me away, stumbling, trying to right himself by gripping the bar. "That's not what I mean," he said. "It's you she wants."

"You're drunk."

"Not drunk enough not to know that she came all this way to marry you."

Although intoxicated by the quart, he spoke the truth. Mrs. Cox had journeyed to be my wife. I had given her enough signal to ensure, in her mind, my intentions. I had a promise to keep.

"She will be the last," I begged of Elizabeth. "But I must go through with it."

"Three in one month," she said. "Three!"

"There'll be no more. You have my word."

"Your word."

"I promise."

"If you marry her, you'll never live with me again."

So it was. I married Mrs. Cox in Salt Lake and settled her in a cottage between Lydia's and the one shared by Margaret and Eleanor. I have spent the years since shuttling between their beds. I do not believe I have ever in my life behaved more like a beast than during this period, for this is how a dog acts, not man. Three wedding nights in three weeks—alas, all excessive pleasures must be repaid.

Yet to say I regret my marriages would imply I regret knowing these women. Only with Eleanor is this the case. Among the others, each is a kind-hearted woman who has been asked to bear more than she should. I have vowed to them all never to marry again. I shall keep this promise. Already I had more than my share. I tried to apologize to Elizabeth. She waved me off. "What's done is done," she said. I tried again, but she shut her door in my face. On the third attempt she said with quiet resignation, "I forgave you long ago."

The noteworthy sorrow had reached its climax and was now in retreat. My family, in its new form, would press on for many successful years. I only wish I could say the same for Ann Eliza. Often I wonder if it was I who set her on a path of antipathy to our faith. How else to explain the root of her rage?

Here beside my writing table lays open her book. How many people across the country hold *The 19th Wife* in their hands? How many are meeting me through its pages? And yet now that I have recounted my own memories, and peered into the well of my soul, I can see that my daughter has portrayed me with accuracy. Her words have destroyed me because they are true. She concludes her long assessment by writing, "In the end, I suppose my greatest disappointment has been in realizing my father, like Joseph and Brigham before him, tried to shroud his passions in the mantle of religion. He used God to defend his adultery. I have yet to hear him acknowledge his lies."

Yet some truths come too late.

I am, I realize, but a man.

WIFE #19:

THE CON OF THE WEST

BACK AT THE MOTEL GRAYBAR

"There it is," I told Mr. Heber. "Proof of how my mom's prints got on the Big Boy."

He leaned across his desk to look at the picture again. "Tell me where you got this."

I walked him through my meeting with Alexandra and her chat session with my dad.

"Oh, for crying out loud." He pressed a button on his phone. "Maureen, can you come in here? Listen, Jordan, these date stamps are thrown out of court all the time. Everyone knows they're usually wrong." The door cracked open. "Maureen, would you make a copy of this?"

She looked at the picture. "This your dad?"

"So what if the date stamp's wrong," I said. "We have someone who says she received this picture just before he was shot, and that's a big deal." He didn't say anything. "Isn't it?" Still didn't say anything. "Mr. Heber, am I totally clueless, or what?"

"I'm just thinking of all the ways a prosecutor could tear this apart. We're going to have do better."

"But right now it's all I've got."

All this, everything I've been telling you, it was happening too fast. I stared into Heber's face—the slick, Aqua Velva complexion, the eyes blue as dawn—but it was like seeing a set of meaningless colors and shapes. I couldn't pick up anything from this guy. You know when your mind's off, just wandering anywhere but where it should be, and you open a book and you see the letters but they don't make any sense? Might as well be Chinese? It was like that. I thought of my mom in her cell. Did she understand any of this better than me?

"Jordan, let me give you a little advice. When you find a lead, you've got to turn it over and over, again and again, look at it from every angle before you decide what it is. That's how things work around here. Think of every reason this photo might not help your mom. If it's still got some value after you've done that, then you're on to something. Ask Maureen, she's the best."

"Not the best," she said.

"Look, I've been back in Utah for—what?—five days, and at least I've figured one thing out: there's no such thing as perfect evidence, Mr. Heber. Or the complete truth, or whatever you want to call it."

Heber and Maureen stared at me, working hard not to roll their eyes. So much for my little speech.

"I went out to see your mom yesterday," Mr. Heber said.

"And?"

"And she's not telling me some things she really should be."

"Like what?"

"Her story about what she was doing that night is still a little fuzzy. That's not going to work. I keep getting the sense there's something she doesn't want me to know."

"Maybe she'll tell Maureen?"

"No, I think she'll tell you. Go back and see her, Jordan. Find out what you can."

"I thought you were leaving Utah." My mom was cradling the yellow receiver between her shoulder and her chin.

"I decided to stay." And then, "I believe you."

She looked up, the glass partition magnifying her eyes.

"I know there's all this evidence against you," I said. "But I believe you."

Everything was the same at the jail today: Officer Kane, the ammonia covering the smell of piss, the row of women weeping into yellow handsets, baby-talking to their children who were growing up without them. I used to tell Roland Mesadale was like living in jail. But it wasn't. Jail was like living in jail.

I held the picture up to the glass. "Do you remember taking this?"

"Of course. That was just last week. It was our anniversary."

"Your anniversary?"

"Yes, I wanted to take a picture with your father. I got dressed up and asked him to put on a tie, and we went down to his den and shot that picture."

"Who took it?"

"No one. We used the automatic button thingy." I told her how I got the picture. It upset her to hear her husband was sending it out to strange women, but she understood why this was a break.

"But we need more," I said. "I need to figure out why Rita said she saw you coming up from the basement."

"Because she did. Your father had asked me to see him, and we talked for some time and I was on my way upstairs when I passed Sister Rita."

"What'd you talk about?"

"It was a husband-and-wife conversation."

"Mom, the more I know, the more I can help you."

"Let's just say we had a conversation about the time he was spending with me. Or lack thereof." Some facts are less good than others. And this was one of those facts. It was a potential motive—jealous wife.

"Did you have an argument?"

"I wouldn't say an argument, your father and I never argued. But we discussed the matter, and I told him how I felt."

"Which was?"

"He's my husband, and I expected to see him from time to time. That's all. And that's when I went upstairs. And then—"

259

She looked down at nothing in particular, just away. "And then I never saw him again. That's the hardest part. I always thought I'd spend the rest of my life as his wife." She took her time to collect herself. "You know what Officer Kane said after you left the last time? She said you'd be back. I told her I didn't think so, but she said she could see it in your eyes." A few feet behind my mom, Officer Kane stared out into nothing. Clearly she wasn't supposed to get involved.

Isn't it interesting what a stranger can offer? A little wisdom, a little mercy, a little love. That's what I was thinking as I drove off from the jail. And this: unless I came up with better proof, twelve strangers in a box would decide my mom's fate. It's crazy to think it could come to that, but I guess it happens all the time.

My father brings home his fifth wife, Mrs. Cox, while I greet her warily from behind the door.

WOMEN AND CHILDREN FIRST

———

I called Maureen. "I have a big favor to ask."

"Shoot."

"No, a really big favor. I need you to drive Johnny and me to Mesadale. Right now. I wouldn't be asking if you hadn't—" That's all I had to say. She agreed to meet me at A Woman Sconed in half an hour.

When I got to the café, the goth girl and Johnny were playing Ms. Pac-Man and Elektra was sleeping on the couch. "How'd it go?" said Johnny.

"I need to get some info out of the house."

"Like what?"

"I'm not sure exactly."

"How you going to get in there?"

"I'm working on it."

"Sounds like an awesome plan you got going there." Johnny went behind the counter to get me a cupcake. You'd think he owned the place. "Here. Maybe this will help you think."

That's when I had an idea.

When Maureen pulled in, Johnny said, "What's she doing here?"

"Come on. It's all part of my plan."

As we drove out to Mesadale, I was still thinking things through. Johnny kept saying you sure you know what you're doing and I kept saying yeah. He was up front and I was in back with Elektra. Some dry cleaning was hanging back there and every time Johnny cracked the window, the plastic wrapper would blow in my face. Elektra thought Maureen's stuffed penguins were dog toys and she kept knocking them over with her snout. I'd tell her no and she'd do it again, which is pretty much how things go with her.

As we passed the shot-up sign on the highway, Johnny said, "Get ready to enter another universe."

"What do you want me to do when we get there?" asked Maureen.

"I'm still thinking."

"You better hurry up," said Johnny.

"These your husband's clothes?"

"No, Mr. Heber's. He likes me to fetch his laundry. I know I shouldn't, but some things just aren't worth fighting over." In the plastic wrapper was a pair of gray slacks and a couple of white dress shirts.

"You think he'd mind if I borrowed them?" I said.

"What for?"

"I need to dress a little less, I don't know, a little less—"

"A little less gay?" said Johnny.

"A little less LA was what I was thinking."

"Go ahead. I'll take them back to the cleaners. He'll never know the difference."

"Pardon me while I change." Tucked in the backseat, I took off my clothes and put on Mr. Heber's, which felt really weird. The shirt fit, but the pants were loose in the waist.

"Here," said Maureen. "I have some safety pins." She handed me a plastic box of gold safety pins and I quickly fixed the pants.

"How do I look?"

"Pretty blah," said Johnny.

"Good, that's exactly what I was going for. OK, we're getting close. Johnny, can you tell Maureen where the turnoff is?"

"Sure, why?"

I lay down on my side on the backseat. Elektra thought this meant it was cuddle time, and she curled up in the crook of my arm. "Because I want to drive into town without anyone seeing me. And you too. Once you spot the turnoff, Johnny, I want you to slide down in your seat."

263

"It's coming up."

"Maureen, you see it?"

"Yup."

"OK, turn there. Johnny, you get down. And Maureen, all you need to do is follow this road about four miles until you see the post office on the left. Tell me when you see it and I'll tell you what to do."

I heard Maureen's turn signal, and Johnny was crouching down in the well in front of the passenger seat. He kept giving me a thumbs-up sign and whispering, "This is so cool!" When the car left the asphalt everything started rattling hard. "Just keep going up this road," I told Maureen. I could see her profile. She looked very confident, her mouth set firm, and I could tell she was doing this not because she was a nice person or a good secretary, but because it was right.

"I see the post office."

"Turn into the lot. Park in the last spot on the right."

"It's full."

"Then park next to it."

The car slowed, turned, and came to a halt.

"Now everyone stay still while I tell you what's going to happen. Maureen, you're going to go inside. The postmistress's name is Sister Karen. I'm pretty sure we can trust her. Tell her you're waiting for me there. She'll let you hang out. Maybe she'll let you into the back so no one sees you. But even if someone sees you, it'll be fine, they'll have no idea why you're in town."

"What about us?"

"When she's been inside for five minutes, we're sneaking out and walking up to the house."

"What about Elektra?"

Dammit. I forgot to include her in the plan.

"We should've left her with the goth girl," said Johnny.

"Never mind. Maureen, you're going to have to take her."

"If we really can trust Sister Karen," she said, "then wait a second, I'll be right back."

A few minutes later, the driver's-side door opened. It was

Sister Karen. "I'm going to slip Elektra in through the loading door. No one will see her." Then they were gone, and Johnny and I were left alone.

"What now?"

"We're walking. Slip out of the car, stay low, run to the far side of the post office. I'll follow you." He did everything I said, and a minute later we were standing against the hot concrete bricks of the post office's western wall, hidden from the street. "Now we'll just walk up one of the side roads. If we play it cool, no one should notice us."

We started walking. It was probably 110 and I could feel the sun on the side of my face. Maybe that's another reason the Firsts have been left more or less alone for so long. It was hot as Mars out here. No one wanted this land.

"So far so good," I said. This side road was quiet, some big houses, some empty lots. Not a lot of traffic. Anyone who saw us would assume we were two kids walking back from the co-op.

"So what's the plan?" said Johnny.

"You're going to think I'm crazy."

"Too late."

"You got your knife?"

"Yeah, why?"

"Here, give it to me."

At the back of the lot, I began cutting branches from the scrub. "Start breaking off some twigs and make them small and very thin, like tooth-picks. We're going to start a fire."

"We are?"

"Actually, you are."

He screwed up his eyes. "Dude, you're a total nut job."

"Just break off some twigs, we need kindling. I never thought I'd say this, but thank God we're out in the middle of the desert. This wood is bone dry."

When we had a good pile I said, "Now we need tinder. Do you have any lint in your pockets?" He pulled out a few wads and set them delicately atop the pile of kindling.

I checked the pockets of Mr. Heber's pants. In one I found

a couple of wads of white lint, in the other two dry-cleaned bucks. "Here, shred these up."

"You're going to burn money?"

"Just do it." I found a stick about a foot long and hacked a notch in each end. I bent down to unlace one of my shoes.

"What are you doing?"

"I'm making a bow." I gave him a quick lesson on the bow-drill method of starting a fire.

"Where'd you learn this shit?"

"You forget, I was on my own for a long time." I got the pieces ready for him and told him he'd have to keep at it for a long time. "The trick is to catch the coals and get them onto the tinder. It's going to take a while, but if you keep doing it, it should work."

"Why am I doing this?"

"Because I'm going to sneak through the cornfield, then behind Sister Kimberly's cabin. That's where I'll wait. When you get the fire going, throw as much wood on it as you can, then go back to the post office. Don't run, just walk calmly like you belong here. That's the good thing about Mesadale: there are so many kids, no one will notice one more."

"What about you?"

"When the fire starts, hopefully everyone will come out of the houses, and I can slip inside."

"You really are out of your mind."

"I know. But it might work."

I waited behind Sister Kimberly's cottage for almost an hour before I saw the white smoke. The smoke darkened, first gray, then black, then I saw a flame. From the big house I heard a scream, then another, and another after that, and they spread until all the women were calling out. The commotion began, people spilling out of the houses, babies crying, women and children running to the back of the lot with pots of water. Pretty soon there were at least seventy-five people at the back of the lot, the women in their prairie dresses and the kids in their hand-me-downs.

I didn't run. I walked straight to the side door and went inside. No one was in the hall, but I heard two women talking in a panic at the top of the stairs. If they were to look down, they would've seen me, but they were distracted by the fire out the window. I made it to the door that led to the basement stairs but found a tiny padlock, like a luggage lock, on an eye and hook.

The wives at the top of the stairs were deciding whether they too should go outside. One was saying we should go out and the other was saying someone needs to stay with the babies. Just then a baby started wailing, and one of the wives said you go check on him, I'll look in on the others.

The lock was so delicate, it looked like it belonged to a doll. I jammed the lock with Johnny's knife. A couple of shoves and it broke apart. One of the wives upstairs said, "You hear that?" But the other said, "It was Timmy, he threw his paci across the room."

I tiptoed down the stairs. At the bottom was the door with the NO TRESPASSING decal. I slowly pushed it open. It was the first time I'd ever been down here. My dad called it his sanctuary. Ever since I left Mesadale, I thought of it as his grave.

It didn't look like a death scene or anything. The blood had been sponged up, and everything looked like he'd just left and would be back any minute. Even the hole in the chair seemed harmless. But the truth is, you can tell when you're where someone's died. I could feel it, like a bad vibe, like you don't even want to know what shit went down here. I stood there feeling that feeling for a while. That's when I figured out where to look: up on the shelf above the gun rack, where the Big Boy used to hang. I rolled the computer chair over and climbed up to get it. It was a Book of Mormon turned over on its side. But inside wasn't the Book of Mormon. The text looked like a log a foreman would use to keep track of times and outputs on an assembly line. There was a long column of initials—R, K, S, S1, P3, etc.—and a row that showed the days

267

of the week. I climbed back down and rolled the chair back to the desk. Outside I heard the fire brigade, men yelling, trucks idling, a diesel pump.

I rolled the chair over to the window well. I opened the window and climbed up into it. The well was one of those steel half tubes you put around a basement window to hold back the soil. That's when it happened, the thing I never thought would happen. I heard a couple of cars screech in, doors slamming, then that voice I'll never forget: "Sisters, be not afraid."

The well was big enough to crouch in. Its lip projected four inches above the ground, and if I was very careful, I could peer over it. I was on the side of the house and everyone was in the back, but I could see the Prophet's suburban with the smoked windows and bulletproof plating. One of his bodyguards circled the car, checking things out. He looked like a weird cross between a missionary and a mercenary— formal slacks, a short-sleeved dress shirt, a soldier's buzz cut, and a nine-millimeter semiautomatic tucked into his belt.

While the men worked to put out the fire, the Prophet gathered the women and children around. "There's nothing to worry about," he said. "The Brothers will have the fire out in no time. Sisters, come closer, and I will explain what's happened, for I want you to know what I know; and I can see from the fear in your eyes you want to know what I know. There are two explanations for this sudden fire here today. First, some will tell you it's a heat fire, nothing more. We are in the middle of the summer in the middle of a drought in the middle of a desert. And so that is what it is, a heat fire, and there is no mystery to it all. If that is what you believe, then so be it. Yet others will tell you, it's a message from God just as the burning bush was God's message to Moses. I will let you decide which it is. I won't even tell you which I believe it to be. Yet think wisely, Sisters, for you will be judged on what you believe, both now and ever after, when you meet our Heavenly Father at his gate."

A lot of the sister wives and the kids were crying and the Prophet said, "Why are you afraid? The Lord will protect you if you've been obedient. For it is obedience upon which you'll be judged. If you loved your husband and obeyed him, and you, children, if you loved your father and obeyed him, if all of you have loved God and obeyed him, then you will be taken care of, both in this world and beyond. Do not be afraid." He was as close to shouting as he ever got: "Do not be afraid."

There were a lot of other people around too, neighbors, Apostles, whoever, coming to see the fire and the Prophet, everyone in the back. Now was a good time to run for it. I started climbing out of the well when I heard the Prophet say, "I know many of you are wondering what will happen to you, and to this house, who will lead it, you ask, how can you now be a wife when you no longer have a husband? I know you fear living out your days without a husband, and you worry how you will be admitted to heaven having left earth without a husband. But I do not want you to worry, for tomorrow I will come to you and I will marry you myself, each of you, and this house will become my house, and you my wives, so that when you rise to heaven and are asked by God himself whether or not you are wife, you can tell him you are his Prophet's wife, and with this news I promise he shall let you in."

The women started cheering, and crying too, and dogs were barking and babies howling. The bodyguard made a sweep around the suburban again. When he was gone, I climbed out of the well. I moved slowly down the drive to the street and then away from the house. With all the other people around, I was just another kid carrying his Book of Mormon. I looked over my shoulder once. The fire was smoldering, the smoke dying. The men were hauling their equipment to their truck, the women and children were returning to the house, and the Prophet was nowhere to be found.

September 12, 2005

Prophet and President Gordon Hinckley
The Church of Jesus Christ of Latter-day Saints
50 East North Temple
Salt Lake City, UT 84111

Dear President Hinckley,

I want to introduce you to a promising young scholar from BYU named Kelly Dee.

Kelly is working on her master's thesis, a project I know will enhance our understanding of Church history. She is honest, hardworking, and devout. Yet despite these qualities, she has run into various roadblocks gaining access to certain documents in our Archives. Why? Because her subject is Ann Eliza Young, Brigham's infamous 19th wife. In the late 1930s an LDS scholar named Charles Green tried to write an authoritative account of Ann Eliza but was thwarted by the Church at nearly every turn. I sincerely hope Kelly does not meet the same fate.

I am writing to you personally because I believe in the importance of her scholarship. Although Ann Eliza Young is no hero of mine, and there is no doubt her faulty memoir has caused considerable harm to the Latter-day Saints in general, and Brigham's reputation in particular, nonetheless honest inquiry and critical scholarship should always be encouraged and valued. It's central to everything we do, as members and as God's children.

I hope you will encourage your colleagues throughout the Church to further assist Kelly with her scholarly requests. Her search for the truth can only benefit us, today and always.

Sincerely Yours,
DEB SAVIDHOFFER
Church Archivist

CONFIDENCE, MAN

―――――

I knocked on the post office delivery door. I knocked again. "Sister Karen, it's me."

Maureen and Johnny were playing a hand of Texas hold em. Elektra was curled up on an empty mail bag. They looked surprised to see me, like they hadn't expected me to ever return.

"What?" I said.

"A fire?" said Maureen. "Honestly."

"They put it out."

"How big was it?" said Johnny.

"It doesn't matter," said Maureen. "We need to get going." She stood up, swatting the dust from her ass. The back room was filled with bins of WIC checks—I could see the marbled pink paper through the envelopes' windows. It was always a big day in Mesadale when the WIC checks arrived.

Sister Karen asked if everything was all right up at the house. I told her the Prophet had come by and what he had said to the sister wives. She frowned. "He's not going to marry all of them."

"That's what he said."

"I know, but he's going to cherry-pick, so to speak. He'll take the pretty ones, the young girls, and he'll farm out the rest. It makes me sick."

"Boys," said Maureen, "I need to get on the road."

"What the Prophet doesn't seem to understand," said Sister Karen, "is the wives talk. And they've been talking a whole lot lately."

"Boys."

"Wait a minute, Maureen." To Sister Karen: "Talking about what?"

"Ever since your dad was killed, they've been splitting off into rival packs. Sister Rita's leading some of them, and a lot of the other women are following Sister Kimberly. I can guarantee you the Prophet's not going to marry Sister Rita. So she's got to have all these women on her side. If she forms a group of ten or twelve, that's ten or twelve welfare checks, and it's hard to ignore that. But there's no doubt the Prophet wants to marry Sister Kimberly, so a lot of the other wives are aligning themselves with her."

"You've got to be kidding me," said Maureen. "This is just crazy."

"No crazier than some of the stuff you believe."

Maureen flinched, like someone had touched her inappropriately.

"I'm sorry," I said. "That didn't come out right."

"Dude, your mouth and foot have to stop meeting like that."

Maureen threw her purse strap over her shoulder. "I'm going out to the car. Don't be long, I need to get home."

"Johnny, would you go after her? Tell her I'll be there in a sec. And stay down low in the car." He left, and I was feeling awfully alone on this mission. But I wasn't finished. I asked Sister Karen what she thought would happen at the house tomorrow.

"Oh, he'll definitely marry some of them, but the question is what will happen to the others. Already one's disappeared."

"Who?"

"Sister Sherry. You probably don't know her. She was recently reassigned to your dad. She was married to Brother Eric, but he was excommunicated for challenging the Prophet on some matters. He had four wives; the Prophet took the youngest and split up the others. That's how Sherry landed with your dad. But she's been missing for a few days now."

"What do you think happened to her?"

"I don't know. She could've run off, but I don't know." She looked at me, deciding something. "I shouldn't be doing

273

this." She opened a drawer, lifted out an organizing tray, and held it above her head. An envelope was taped to the bottom of the tray. "After Brother Eric was excommunicated, Sister Sherry came in here and gave me this. She said if anything ever happened to her, I should contact this address." She removed the envelope from the bottom of the tray and opened it. On a piece of paper was an address in Denver. No name, no phone, just 43 Atwood Street, Denver.

"You think Sherry went there?"

"She might have. I don't know, Jordan, but I just have a feeling she might know something about what's going on. Why don't I write her address down for you."

"Never mind, I got it memorized. I should be going."

Sister Karen stuck her head out the delivery door to scan for trouble.

"It's clear." Elektra and I ran to the car and lay down on the backseat. I told Maureen to drive out the way we came. "Just play it cool." Johnny wanted to chat but I told him to shut up until we were on the highway. Maureen drove down the red dirt road and I could see the dust rise behind us. The car shook and rocks shot up and clinked against the underside of the car.

When we got to the highway, the car stilled and the only sound was the lull of the wheels turning against the pavement. "Do you see any cars?" I said.

"No one."

"Ahead or behind you?"

"No one."

"Johnny, it's OK." And we both sat up.

"Man, that was awesome."

I changed out of Mr. Heber's clothes. "I'll get these cleaned," I said.

"I'll take care of it." We argued over that, but Maureen said, "Jordan, it's fine."

I told them about what Sister Karen had said, about Sister Sherry disappearing to Denver.

"Denver," said Johnny. "I was there a few months ago. Not bad."

"She thinks this wife might know something."

"Why would she think that?" said Johnny.

"That's just it: she doesn't think that. She wants me to drive all the way to Denver to talk to someone who isn't there."

"Dude, what're you talking about?"

"We can't trust her."

"Sister Karen? But she just helped us like big-time."

"I know, but she wants us out of town. Something's about to happen and she doesn't want me anywhere near Mesadale when it does."

"You're sounding paranoid."

"I don't care."

"Dude, have you been watching *24*?"

It was late afternoon and the sun was hitting the car at a low angle. Everything ahead of us was yellow and gold. Sometimes when you're driving down a back road in Utah, you think if there is a God, then he probably had something to do with all of this. It's just that fucking beautiful.

"Maureen," I said, "who's that?"

"Who?"

I pointed at the souvenir hanging from her rearview mirror. On one side it said ZION, 2006, and on the other was a picture of two young women standing in front of the famous lone tree, the pine bending atop a mesa of stacked red sandstone. I'm sure you've seen it. One of the most famous trees in the world.

"That's my granddaughter, Jess, and her best friend."

"They look nice," said Johnny. "How old are they?"

"Twenty-three?"

"They married?" said Johnny.

"Oh no, they're up in grad school. They take their educations very seriously." I asked what they were studying. "Jess is getting her master's in nutrition," she said. "And Kelly—Kelly, she's studying history, I think it is."

"History?"

"Snooze," said Johnny.

"So what'd you find up at the house?" said Maureen.

"My dad's fuck chart."

"His what?"

"Oh, my God," said Johnny. "You found his fuck chart? Let me see." He grabbed it and started flipping through it. "Yup, that's what this is."

"Jordan," said Maureen, "what is that?"

"I guess the more polite term is a marriage management notebook. He used it to keep track of the time he spent with each wife, when he ate with whom, how much time he spent talking with each, that sort of thing."

"Yeah, and who he fucked and when."

"Johnny."

"Dude, am I telling the truth or what?"

He was. That's why all the boys called them fuck charts. Almost every man kept one and there was nothing the boys of Mesadale liked to do more than find one and read it. On my dad's chart there were a lot of indecipherable notations, letters and numbers and squiggly marks.

"That's code, dude. Code for what the women like under the sheets. You can't expect a man to remember all that."

"Oh please," I said. "As if he cared."

"I'm telling you. My dad had one just like this, and we cracked the code."

"Jordan," said Maureen, "you realize it's stolen. We can't use stolen evidence."

"I know," I said. But actually I didn't know that. "Even if there's some important information in it?"

"It gets automatically thrown out."

"No exceptions? Because this has something really useful."

"No exceptions."

Well, that sucked, because on the last page my dad had made a note that on the night he was killed he spent an hour alone with Sister Rita in her room.

276

* * *

Maureen dropped us in the parking lot of A Woman Sconed. When I said good-bye, she simply held up her hand. I guess she was still hurt by that stupid thing I said about her faith back in the post office. That's the thing about religion: people believe what they believe. Never mind if it makes no sense to you. They say the best thing to do is not talk about it. But that's pretty hard around here. That's pretty hard when everyone's always talking about it—especially when they exclude you.

It was Friday evening, and by Monday morning I needed to be back in Pasadena. I didn't know when I'd see Maureen next. I tried to thank her for all her help, but she stopped me. "I'll tell Mr. Heber you'll be in touch with him about the notebook." She pulled out, the stuffed penguins swaying as she turned out of the lot.

"You really messed that up," said Johnny.

"Would you shut up for once?"

He climbed into the van. "Don't blame this one on me."
I sat on my rear bumper and called Roland. I listened to his line ring and ring. Voice mail. "Yeah, hey, it's me. Things have been a little intense lately. Anyway, I'll be home soon, maybe even tomorrow. Anyway, if you get—" But I lost the signal and left the rest of my message on a dead line.

I left Elektra with the goth girl, and Johnny and I drove over to the swimming pool. We both needed a bath, and I needed to think about where I was. After jumping in the water, Johnny sidled up to two teenage girls catching the last rays of sun on a patch of grass. "You let me know if you ladies need some help applying that suntan lotion, all right?"

"Fuck off."

"Asshole."

"Nice to meet you too, ladies."

"Loser." The girl who said this was lying on her back in a strawberry bikini. Her downy thighs glistened in oil. It was apparent why Johnny wasn't ready to give up.

277

"Let me start over. I'm Johnny, and despite my first impression, I'm actually a nice guy."

It was enough to get the second girl to smile. She set down her paperback mystery and said, "I'm Jen. And this is Laura."

Johnny seized the opening: he sat on a tiny corner of Jen's towel. Fifteen minutes later, he was sharing half of it. They were laughing, and once Johnny pointed in my direction and the girls looked over at me with profound curiosity. The wind had shifted and their voices were no longer clear, but I caught a few scraps of conversation, including, "He's pretty OK." And then, "But I love his dog."

And so that's where I was: sitting on the lip of a public pool, my legs hanging in the water. My mom was still in jail, Maureen was pissed, Johnny was ignoring me, Elektra was off getting a sugar high, and who knows what Roland was up to. And my dad was still dead. It was Friday evening. If I was going to make that nursery job on Monday, I needed to wrap things up.

"Yo, Jordan! Get over here!"

Johnny introduced me to the girls as "the dude I was telling you about." And then, his voice dropping: "Listen, dude. We're going to head back to Jen's house. I'll catch you later."

"What do you mean, *later*?"

"As in, later. As in, not now. Dude, chill."

"Where will I *catch* you?"

"Man, what's your problem today?"

The low sun speckled on the water. All around kids were running and divebombing into the pool. A gang of teenage boys was sharing a pack of Marlboros. Two old ladies were wading in the shallow end. "Nothing's my problem."

"So I'll give you a call." He rolled over, exposing his narrow back. He was thin and strong, and his shoulder blades sharpened as he reached for a sip from Jen's Coke. In another life, Johnny would've been a high school wrestler with a so-so GPA. Now he was just a sweet little con.

278

XII

THE ACTRESS

THE 19TH WIFE

CHAPTER NINE

Secrets of the Faith

Not long after I turned sixteen, I fell ill with a malady that remains unexplained to this day. I took to bed with a sodden chest and fever. After three days my mother sent word to my father about my condition. They had lived separately since my father's conjugal spree four years before, he in Salt Lake switching beds among his wives, and my mother and I alone on a small, productive farm in South Cottonwood, about ten miles outside the city.

When my father saw my true condition, he accused my mother of neglect for not having called a doctor. They argued for some time at the foot of my bed over how to improve my health. Finally she conceded her prayers were no longer adequate and sent for the one man she believed could restore my condition—Brigham Young. Brigham decided I should receive my Endowments—a sacred honor bestowed on few youths outside his immediate family. For the first time since I fell ill, my mother's face sparkled with joy. For a woman with a faith as deep as hers, this was as high an honor as one can hope for while on Earth.

The Endowment Ceremony is a ritual so secret that a Saint risks expulsion from the Church, and even death, should he reveal its contents; it is so esteemed that Saints speak of it as second in glory only to their promised ascent to Heaven. Up until this point, I had spent little time pondering theological truths. I accepted everything I was told about God, Christ,

281

and Joseph and his Revelations, and Brigham's Divine authority—for everyone I loved told me these were true. If you were to ask me at this age if I considered myself devout, I would have enthusiastically replied, Yes! I prayed, attended services, sang the hymns with full lungs, and tried to live by the Articles of Faith and all the other wisdom Brigham imparted in his sermons on Sundays. I never once wrestled over any metaphysical questions for myself, for Brigham's churchly system, all-inclusive as it was, left no open territory in the theological landscape to mull over. Thus, I believed my Endowment Ceremony would be the highlight of my young spiritual life. Yet now, so many years later, I understand I believed all this simply because I had been told it was so.

The next morning at seven o'clock, still under the spell of fever, I entered the Endowment House. In those days it was the most sacred site in all of Great Salt Lake, and the most secretive. Those who had been inside were forbidden to speak of it. Such secrecy encouraged every kind of rumor; some described the interior as a simulacrum of Heaven itself; while others suggested it was as dark and dank as a crypt. The Endowment House is said to share architectural traits with the Freemason's Temple. As a young man Joseph encountered Freemasonry, and perhaps joined a Lodge, and thus some of his detractors have declared the Endowment Ceremony a derivative of Freemasonry's ritualized meetings. Both utilize secret grips and passwords, a structured order of personal development based on degrees, and other symbolic gestures and signs. Yet having little personal knowledge of the Freemasons' organization, I cannot verify these claims. However, I can reveal to my Dear Reader that the only exoticism inside the Mormons' Endowment House is the unusual number of bathing tubs.

Once through the doors I was met by Sister Eliza R. Snow, one of Joseph's many widows whom Brigham had married shortly after his martyrdom. Sister Snow led me into a vast bathroom with a row of zinc tubs divided by a long green curtain. I was not the only one present—five other women, all unknown to me, had come for their Endowments as well. In addition to them a dozen women, most years past sixty, stood around, for what purpose I did not know. The old women, buttoned up in blackcloth, stared at me intently, and when it came time for me to strip my clothes, they chose not to avert their eyes.

"First we must cleanse you," Sister Snow explained, helping me out of my dress. In a matter of seconds she had me crouching in a steaming bath. Sister Snow had a heavy, downward appearance. The skin of her cheek looked as if it might slide off the bone. The old woman bathed me with great enthusiasm, scrubbing as if sudsing the flank of a horse. There is an indignity to such submission, especially with others looking on. Yet, given the circumstances, it was difficult not to hope—not to believe, I should say—that this ancient woman, with her raw red hands, could scrub away my mysterious malady.

Next Sister Snow raised a horn above me, declaring it to represent the horn of plenty. Olive oil filled the horn, and in a swift motion similar to how a butcher slaughters a pig, she pulled my head back, exposed my throat, and dribbled oil across my brow. "Sister, I ready thy head for glory." The oil ran into my eyes and ears, and yet I did not fidget or break the solemnity of the moment despite feeling like a slab of meat being dressed for the broiler. "Sister, I anoint your mouth." She poured the oil across my lips. "Sister, I anoint your breast." The oil was slimy upon my chest and flowed down the flesh in between.

Sister Snow continued: My stomach, my thighs, my loins! Soon I glistened in oil. I was miserable, and yet this was supposed to be the greatest day of my life. I wanted to ask: Did Jesus intend this? But I dared not. Sister Snow was so certain in everything she did, I knew my doubts had to be wrong. And so I stood naked, golden and slick, while the line of old women ogled and prayed. I glanced to my oiled companions in this ritual, but each woman, as naked as I, had shut her eyes.

I had deduced what was transpiring on the other side of the green curtain: several Brothers were receiving their anointments. I could hear them sloshing in their baths and the slurping oil trickling into their unthinkable regions. Reader, recall I was sixteen: Find me the girl of this age who does not giggle when imagining fat old men greased up like pigs!

Cleansed and anointed, I was ready to dress for my Endowment. Sister Snow handed me two undergarments, each made of plain muslin. The first was similar to a sleeping-set, the shirt and drawers of one piece. Sister Snow explained that I must always wear it until I entered my grave. "It will keep you safe," she said. "And protect you from the assassin's bullet and the enemy's sword. If only Joseph had been wearing his at Carthage."

The second garment was identical to the first and was its replacement. When I needed to wash one, I would remove half of the first and cover myself up again with the second before removing the rest of the first. This way I would never be naked again. If Mormondom's young men rebel against the Church's restrictions against alcohol and tobacco, the young women rebel against the sacred undergarment. I have known many girls to secretly trim theirs with lace, satin ribbons, and other frippery. Oh, were Brigham to discover this concealed truth, would he be angry or pleased?

Atop this unpleasant item, I was dressed in a white dress and a secondary skirt, bleached stockings that bunched at my ankles, and soft linen slippers. Over this I wore my Temple robe—a baggy item with a strip of linen belting it in place. For a hat, Sister Eliza tied a small flag of Swiss muslin to my head. I looked like nothing so much as how a schoolmistress would dress a child in a pageant of angels. I felt silly and very much like a little girl; and yet none of the women around me seemed to share my sentiments. They held out their arms, letting the Sisters pull on their clothing as if they were corpses being prepared for burial. (In fact, these were the garments we would be buried in, whenever that grim day came.) These women were older than I, certainly more knowledgeable, and I was ashamed of my own lightness of spirit in comparison to theirs. I told myself I must stop thinking the way I was. I prayed to God to reveal the magnitude of the moment.

Next the curtain dividing the bath-room was pulled back in a dramatic fashion, similar to how a theater's curtain swiftly reveals a new scene. Standing opposite were six men dressed in their own white robes and caps. Men are generally less capable of tolerating discomfort, and for the most part they fidgeted and looked to their feet. Anyone could see they were embarrassed to stand before their friends and neighbors in outfits suitable for a doll.

We were ushered into an empty interior room. Two male voices from above interrupted the silence. At first I could not understand what they were saying, but then, as if they had moved in closer, their words became clear. Elohim was talking to Jehovah, who was growing more elaborate and excited in his chronicle of the origins of the world. I thought I recognized Jehovah's voice as Brother Allan's. An Apostle, Allan is the barber Gilbert visits and possesses a grand baritone. I knew I should surrender to the fantasy, as the others were doing. I told myself to concentrate and to believe. And yet, as you no doubt know, no one can force belief. Even so, for the next two hours, I tried and tried, draining off the last of my energy in the effort.

Brother Allan, or, I should say, Jehovah, recounted how God created the Earth and the seas, the beasts and the trees. Behind us, a curtain opened to a stage. The scenes of Genesis appeared in cut-out and costume, as they might in an earnest but budget theatrical production. Adam, or a young man I did not quite recognize playing Adam, took center stage, followed by Eve, played by Mary Jane Cobb. Some said she had recently married Brigham. The Prophet never claimed her as one of his own, although many years later, she and I would become acquainted, and she shared with me a detail of Brigham's personage only a wife could know.

Before us, Adam and Eve acted out their own familiar drama. Somehow, the unsurprising and long-known denouement terrified the audience. Everyone was enraptured, and two women actually gasped with fear when the serpent—a man in black mask and tail, knee breeches, and hands dusted with coal—slithered onto the stage. Once again I felt alone in my suspicions and blamed myself. Only a weak soul could not share in the terror of Man's downfall. But the whole event left me numb. I have heard an esteemed medical doctor say that illness is the loneliest state. I would argue that doubt deserves that claim.

Next a second, recessed curtain drew back to reveal Satan. I do not know who played him, but he was a slim, athletic man in a tight black suit with strips of fuchsia and black stockings. He wore a mask meant to be frightening, with two soft little horns, like the fuzzy knobs atop the head of a lamb. I was disappointed that the Church, with its celestial insight, could not conceive the Devil with more originality. Satan danced around, tormenting Adam and Eve, neither of whom was gifted with the art of Tragedy, and then ran among the men and women in the audience. Everyone loves a devil, and this audience was no exception. They made noises like people watching a fireworks display. Meanwhile, I felt I might faint from exhaustion and looked for a bench to sit down.

"Up, up, up, up!" Sister Snow tooted, pulling me back to my feet. This hard little woman supported me in her arms. From whence does such might come?

Thereafter, we filed onto the stage, all the while Satan prancing about. Whoever was beneath that mask possessed a long pent-up desire to dance and flit about like the happiest of bumblebees. Next came a series of visitors, each representing Christianity's many sects—the Quaker, the Methodist, the Baptist, the Catholic. Each representative claimed his was the way of Christ. They surrounded us, shouting their positions, until a great cacophony overtook us and several members pressed their hands to their ears. For dramatic effect, I will admit, this was the pageant's highlight, for I came to understand, almost instantly, that for two thousand years men have been claiming there is but one way to God: Mine!

Satan chuckled over this war of opinion. "You see, Man has fallen into my trap!" Although I am not a writer, and this memoir is my only attempt to capture life in words, despite this lack of skill and experience, even I would suggest a revision to Satan's script.

Thereafter the Apostles instructed us on a number of passwords to be used as we graduated through the degrees of the Order of the Melchisedec Priesthood; and a set of tickling grips or handshakes that would reveal ourselves as true Saints in the hereafter. Next Sister Snow leaned into my ear, cupping her hand around her mouth, and whispered, "As you enter the Celestial Kingdom, call yourself Sarah, for this is your secret name and shall guarantee your entry. You must never reveal this name to anyone other than your husband on the day of your sealing. Otherwise, take it to your grave. Do you understand?" In my mind I turned over this new name—Sarah!—many times, taking pride in its Biblical symbolism. I promised myself I would protect it throughout my life, as if it were my child and its very life depended on my care.

The woman beside me was a shriveled, bent-over creature; it was clear to all that she would require her secret name sometime soon. Sister Snow leaned into her ear.

"Can't hear you, child," yawped the old woman.

Sister Snow attempted a second delivery in a slightly louder voice.

I thought I heard her say Sarah as well, but this would have been impossible. I told myself I had not understood Sister Snow correctly; and that I should not worry. Yet I have always wondered if Sister Snow named the old lady Sarah, and the other women, too; and if in the Endowment House each woman is given the same secret name, its celestial qualities tarnished by much abuse. Once, after my marriage to Brigham, I asked him about this. He reddened in the face and laughed, "You know what I love about you? Your fertile mind. My goodness, Ann Eliza—why are you always prone to the conspiracy?"

What followed was a nearly two-hour depiction of Joseph Smith's life, the angel Moroni's visit to his bedroom, the discovery of the golden plates, &etc. The final scene showed Smith's murder in the Carthage jailhouse and the Mormon people wandering without Prophet or leader. But just when all seemed lost, the Apostles appeared on the stage, banished Satan to his rightful fiery hole, and pronounced Brigham Young the new Prophet. Brigham Young would lead his Saints to Zion and redemption.

In the red deserts of America, Salvation would be achieved. The end.

Or so I thought. The Apostles, playing themselves, told us to kneel in a circle, led us in promises and declarations. We raised our arms into the air. The women vowed total submission to their husbands. The men vowed never to marry a wife without permission from the Church. Together we promised to obey the Church's authority fully. We swore to take retribution for Joseph Smith's murder and to defend the life of Brigham Young, even if it meant shedding blood. Finally we swore never to reveal the secrets of the Endowment Ceremony. Punishment for doing so would be disembowelment, followed by one's tongue and heart knifed out of the body and burned. The Apostles informed us of this penance with such menace and certainty that each of us shook with fear.

At last at three o'clock in the afternoon the ceremony was over. While the others wept, I simply sat on the bench, spent and empty, but not in the way I had anticipated. Of my illness, I was certain I had never been closer to the grave.

That night my mother and I slept at Lydia's cottage. I lay

awake upon the bed, unable to fall off, while she slumbered beside me. With each breath she emitted a small purr and her eyelids fluttered with dreams. I envied her peace of mind and the certainty of her faith. I longed to know what she knew; and to take comfort in it. I thought about my long day at the Endowment House. Why was I different from the other Saints—all good souls with open hearts. From where had my skepticism come? I tried to fall asleep, but my mind ran with the images from the ceremony. Each time I recalled a detail— Eve, with her beautiful hair; or Satan, hopping on one foot—something inside me provided commentary that was neither sincere nor serious. *Why is Eve wearing a horse-hair wig? I didn't realize Satan knew the Scottish jig.* I became convinced I possessed a wicked soul, and that I was alone in my wretchedness. I would die soon, I concluded, and I was to blame.

After a while I could hear my father and Lydia above in her bedroom. They were talking about Diantha's performance in school. "She can recite the Articles of Faith all the way through." Their voices softened, then went silent altogether, and I heard the familiar creak of the bed, the sigh of the feather mattress as it absorbed two people embraced as one. Then nothing—the effortful silence that was so familiar in a house of many wives.

I got up and went outside. It was a clear night and the smoke tree was in silhouette along the fence. The smoke from the chimney was thick in the crisp air. The mountains rose blackly over the Valley and the three-quarter moon cast a silver net over everything. I sat on the stump by the water pump, looking back at Lydia's little house. A candle burned in her room, and after some time my father appeared in her window. He looked out over his land and the houses beyond. I am sure he did not see me, even though the moonlight caused my robe to glow. He stood for a long time, as if something grave were on his mind. Then with his tongue he wetted his finger and his thumb and, in a gesture I could not see, snuffed out the candle. The window went black. The house was now dark and after a little while the smoke from the chimney thinned and died out. A poet might have thought the world had come to an end but for the wind turning the tree's early leaves.

In the morning I woke to find my illness in retreat. There was no way to explain it, although many people tried.

THE 19TH WIFE

CHAPTER TEN
The Prophet Enters My Life

Sometime after my recovery, I acquired my first beau. Finley Free was a sensitive, artistic young man who liked to sketch me in my mother's garden. By chance he was the younger brother of one of Brigham's favorite wives, Emmeline, who by most accounts was Number 10, although, in truth, I believe that number discounts the existence of a few wives Brigham married and quickly abandoned for reasons we shall never know.

Our friendship was still in its early days when Brigham summoned my mother to his office at the Beehive House. As President and Prophet of the Church, and leader of the Utah Territory, he was indeed a busy man. My mother could only presume that the matter to be discussed was of grave concern. Yet when she sat opposite his desk, Brigham, in a serious voice more suitable for lawyering than meddling, advised my mother to break off the relationship between myself and Finley.

My mother came to my defense. "All he does is sketch her sitting on the fence."

"Sister, trust me. The boy is weak in the soul."

Brigham's interference was so unusual, and delivered in such dire tone, that my mother had no reason but to believe it was based on informed opinion. When she relayed it to me, I was equally puzzled, for I knew Brigham to be many things, but one was not a liar.

The next day I met three friends at Goddard's Confectionery on Main Street. Although Katherine, Lucinda, and I had gathered for cake and conversation only three days prior, enough had passed in the interval to fill several hours with the important details of our lives. My news of course concerned the Prophet.

"I always liked Finley," said Katherine, a talented friend known for her skill in hair-art. Her interest in hair started with her own yellow locks, which she was always stroking and plaiting and otherwise playing with. "Why would Brigham want to protect you from him?"

"It's perfectly obvious," said Lucinda. "He's jealous."

"Jealous?" cried Katherine. "Of Ann Eliza?"

"Don't be daft. Of Finley." Lucinda was a quick girl with a perfect memory. She could recall every Sunday outfit I had worn since I was twelve.

"Why would the Prophet be jealous of Finley Free? Does he want to draw?"

"Katherine, you know I love you, but sometimes I wonder what goes on in that head of yours. Ann Eliza, explain it." Lucinda turned in my direction and flipped over her hand in a gesture that said—*Tell her*.

"The only thing I can think of is he somehow learned that the Endowment Ceremony has left me with quite a few questions."

"Ladies, when will you open your eyes?" Lucinda looked to me and Katherine and back. Her grayish eyes had the silver sheen of a looking glass, and I could see something of my own reflection in them. "He doesn't want some boy flipping around your yard."

"Why not?"

"Honestly, do I have to do all the thinking around here? He wants to marry you himself."

"*Marry* me?"

"I'm afraid so."

An extended clatter of female speculation followed—of

292

how Brigham would propose, what number wife I would become, of whether or not he would establish me in my own house, as he does with his favorite wives, or encamp me in the Lion House.

"This is silly. If he were to ask me, which he won't, but if he were, I would say thank you very much but no. I'm going to marry a man who wants one wife."

"Good luck," said Lucinda.

Katherine proved equally supportive. "No one says no to Brigham Young."

Only a few days thereafter, while I was walking home in the afternoon, the Presidential Carriage appeared out of nowhere, pulling up alongside me on the road. I was so surprised by its appearance, I almost did not recognize Brigham in the driver's seat. "Quite a walk for you, Sister. May I drive you home?"

It was unusual to find the President driving alone, for typically his revered coachman, Isaac, a former servant to Joseph Smith, drove him about the city. I wish I could report that I declined the invitation and continued on my way, but I accepted his extended hand and settled in next to him on the leather bench.

Once on the road he said, "Now I understand you've been going around telling people you would never marry me. I'm sure you don't know how much that wounds me."

If it surprises my Reader that a man as preoccupied as Brigham Young would have the time or the inclination to gather information on female gossip, then I have not skillfully portrayed the complete control with which he ruled the Territory. He employed a network of spies who wandered through public gatherings, listening in for opinions of heresy and apostasy. No doubt one had been nearby at Goddard's, dispatching an urgent report to the Beehive House.

"Tell me: is it true?"

In most tales, this would be the opportunity for the hero to act bravely. Yet I was not prepared to defy Brigham Young. "It's not true," I lied.

"Ann Eliza? Are you blushing?"

"Yes."

"Is that color because of me?"

Brigham smiled, believing the red in my cheek had exposed an affection for him. Why is it the most brilliant men can be the least perceptive? For the rest of the journey he was as pleasant as the most humble and sincere gentleman, calling upon the delights of the fair weather. He spoke of the flowers in the gardens we passed and his love of the rose. He never pressed himself upon me, showing such deference and delight at my company that it was as if I were riding with a man who was wholly different from he who had just attacked me with my own words. When we arrived at my gate, he leapt to the ground to help me down. "I'll see you Sunday." He tipped his hat and bowed.

"Sunday," I sputtered. "Yes, Sunday."

The carriage threw up a cloud of dust as it coursed down the street, and heads poked from windows to get a glimpse of the Prophet. When he was gone my mother and Connie descended upon me, asking if I had really come home with Brigham Young.

After the incident in the carriage, Brigham disappeared from my life. He made no attempt to call, send word, or greet me at the Tabernacle on Sundays. I became, once again, one of some fifty thousand Saints under his command. My mother accused me of having offended him. "You must've said something. Brigham doesn't turn up like that, then disappear."

During this interval, my interest in Finley Free diminished. I became tired of the afternoons perched on the fence rail. "You only want to sketch me," I complained. "Don't you like to talk?" He set down his stick of charcoal, took my hand, and together we discovered he had nothing to say. We struggled to make a connection of intimacy, but his eye was on his artistic pursuits, and mine was on—well, at that age, everything around me.

"I'll tell you why you lost interest," said Lucinda. "It's because you've got Brigham on your mind."

"Don't be cruel," I said. Yet I remained curious why Brigham had not called since our drive.

"Maybe he knows you're no longer close to Finley," suggested Katherine.

"Poor Katherine," said Lucinda. "How long have you lived in Utah?"

"As long as I can remember."

"And yet you still don't see. I pity you, I really do. At least Ann Eliza understands."

I pretended that I did, but in truth, I did not. I had no idea what would befall me.

Then one day an invitation arrived to visit Brigham in his office. My mother and I arrived at the Prophet's compound a half hour early and waited outside the wall. I turned my attention to the Lion House, which sits across a small court-yard from Brigham's home. Many of his wives lived there, and his children too, in small rooms and apartments similar to those one might find in a depot hotel. I saw some women coming and going from the front door above which the famous stone lion perches. Some of these were girls about my age, dressed gaily in plum and blueberry silks, as was the fashion that season. They chatted in hushed voices and giggled as I would giggle with Lucinda and Katherine. Were they Brigham's wives or daughters? Or both? (He was known to marry more than one step-daughter.) A severe woman walked up the street, passing those of us in line to see Brigham. Her collar appeared to strangle her and her mouth twitched violently, as if she were busy nibbling away on the inside of her cheek. She passed through the gate and entered the Lion House. No doubt she was one of Brigham's early wives. A plump, overheated woman in front of us said to her companion, "I'll bet you he hasn't visited her since Nauvoo."

"Nauvoo?" said the companion. "I'd say it's been since Kirtland. If he ever did."

My mother stood stalwart in their ribald breeze.

At exactly four o'clock Brigham greeted us at the door to his office. Although it was autumn, the weather had been especially hot, and Brigham was wearing his summer costume familiar to all in Deseret: the prunella suit, a vivid white shirt kept pristine by his laundress daughter, Claire, and a neck cloth. His Panama hat hung from the hat-tree beside the door. He was now around sixty and looked very much like a man who had accomplished much in his day. His wide brow was creased and thick, his jowls heavy and tufted with white whisker. His girth was large enough to fill the chair, and then some, behind his desk. Yet he was not altogether unappealing. His flinty eyes sparkled as they must have when he was a young man.

"I've got a proposal for you," he said.

My mother sat up and began a speech I had not known she had prepared. "Brigham, you know quite well I love you as much as anyone. But be kind to my daughter. She's now barely a woman and sometimes she doesn't know what she's after. Please consider her happiness as well, not merely yours."

"Sister Elizabeth, it's her happiness I have in mind. Now let me make my proposition, then you'll see for yourself. As you know, our theater had a successful opening this past March. Our second season begins on Christmas Day. I would like your daughter to join the company. As an actress."

His gaze lingered upon me in such a mysterious fashion that I was at a loss to interpret his meaning. "I'm not an actress," I said.

"I don't want my daughter on the stage."

"Of course not. You shouldn't. Not just any stage. But this is my stage. We would never put up anything wicked. I can't think of a more perfect setting for Ann Eliza's talents."

Since my apostasy, Brigham has publicly accused me of

always loving an audience. Many newspapers have reported him as saying I all but begged him to put me on his stage. This could not be further from the truth! I pondered his proposal for several days, coming close to turning him down. But I sensed my mother wanted me to follow Brigham's command; and I will admit I was at the age when any young woman has a mild curiosity about standing on the boards with the clamshell lamps upon her. Thus, I reluctantly accepted Brigham's proposal and joined his theatrical company.

I debuted on Christmas Day 1862 in the Irish lampoon *Paddy Miles' Boy* in the minor role of Jane Fidget. Because my talents were new and untrained, I refrained from complaining about my limited time on stage. Next I appeared as the comedic heroine in *The Two Polts*. Thereafter I played the ingénue in *Old Phil's Birthday*—a role more suitable for my physical attributes and instincts. In one week I had gone from novice to veteran. In one month I was a player the critics, some from as far as California, mentioned in their columns. If I am to believe them, my dramatic gifts were effortless and well-disposed. One wrote, "Miss Webb possesses the most natural beauty to be seen in Utah in recent memory." Why I remember that particular line of criticism I cannot say.

By January I had become such a part of the company, and so enfolded in the weekly repertory, that the long drive to and from my mother's house in South Cottonwood was no longer practical. It was decided the most practical thing would be for me to move into the Lion House.

At the time, the Lion House was one of the most infamous private homes in all of America. Many speculated about the activities taking place inside; and every Gentile visitor to Salt Lake, on his way to California, made certain to see it, standing before its wall, gazing up at its cream plaster and green shutters, hoping to witness a salacious endeavor within. Newspapers whose editors disliked Brigham ran cartoons of him, plumped up in bed in the Lion House, twenty wives about him, ten on each side. They called it by many names—Brigham's harem, his seraglio, the hen house. Brigham's supporters, on the other hand, often referred to it as "the Mount Vernon of the West." Even in the Territory, were you to ask the most loyal Saint how many wives lived inside, he would not know. The mysteries of its hallways, and what transpired beyond its notorious dormer windows, kept tongues busy with speculation. I know this for, since my apostasy, everyone, it seems, wants to hear about the inner workings of the Lion House.

I arrived one afternoon just before dinner, greeted in the glassed-in vestibule by Sister Snow, my old friend from the Endowment Ceremony. She led me up the stairs to a hallway bisecting the length of the top floor, ten doors on each side. Along the way we passed half a dozen children and several women I did not recognize. The children ran past me as if I did not exist—excited, straining creatures accustomed to many women and few men. The women were Brigham's wives, although they called one another "Aunt." Each took me in with a silent glare.

At the end of the hall Sister Snow opened a door to a small room with a sunflower paper that was dirty where pictures used to hang. There was a bed, dresser, and a tiny stove. "I hope I didn't drive someone out of her room."

"You didn't, so don't let it trouble you. Dinner's at four-thirty. See you downstairs." Sister Snow has always given me the impression of a woman who is ready to die but will outlive everyone she knows.

Dinner was an affair for fifty, overseen by childless Aunt Twiss. She had been a young widow in Nauvoo when Brigham discovered her notable domestic skills. So industrious was she that other women gossiped about her as if she had committed a crime against them personally. Once a week Aunt Twiss stayed up through the night to scour down her hearth, so that it might gleam in the morning light—an effort that caused some women to boil red with envy. Others chittered on about her method of sweeping: on her knees with a hand-broom, from one corner of a room to the opposite, and back. If her thoroughness in keeping house angered some women, it pleased Brigham, who had been employing her many useful skills since their marriage a few days before departing Nauvoo in 1846.

The large dining room was in the western part of the basement. When I entered for the first time, Aunt Twiss sat me at the end of a table with a group of girls called the Big Ten—Brigham's elder daughters, ten young women known all over the Valley for their interest in fine clothing and attachment to the curling iron. Aunt Twiss pointed out my chair and said, "I hope you like eggs." She was neither hostile nor friendly, merely overwhelmed by a compulsive desire for efficiency. She wore a heavy, burdened brow and a complexion over-heated from her work. I would soon learn, from four separate sources, that Brigham had never visited her conjugally and never would. "Yet every night, she props herself up in bed, in a fancy sleeping bonnet no less, as if he might come!" one of the Big Ten would go on to laugh in my ear.

The room was loud with women and children, but at precisely four-thirty Brigham arrived. Immediately everyone fell silent except for a few restless children, who were promptly pinched behind the ear. Brigham blessed our food, and afterward we ate a light supper of eggs and spinach, followed by composition tea. Brigham sat at the head of the table, with Sister Snow at his right and Aunt Twiss at his left. I quickly noticed that they dined on pigeon and gravy, with bread, butter, peach jam, and a bowl of strawberries and blackcaps.

Throughout the meal women approached Brigham to discuss their domestic business, and for some, I would later learn, this was their only chance to consult their husband on matters typically discussed between man and wife at the table. Brigham hardly had a chance to eat while advising his wives, although it would not take a sleuth to deduce he must have taken a second (or third?) meal elsewhere. The wives formed a line behind him. When her time came, which was limited to a minute or two, each wife had to leap into her topic while everyone, including her rivals, listened in.

"I need a new kettle."

"I found my hand-glass in Sister Clara's room."

"Susannah isn't reading properly."

"There'll be another next June."

No matter how serious, or petty, the situation, this was the only opportunity most wives had to discuss their affairs with their husband.

Often a child—one of fifty-seven—climbed his leg and swung from his arm while he conversed with his wives. He was always playful with them, singing "too-roo-loo-rool-lool-or-lool" or producing a raisin from his pocket. It must be said that Brigham loved his children, was interested in their well-being, and guided his wives on discipline and other matters to their proper rearing. Yet even his sincerity could not compensate for the fact that fifty-seven children shared his fatherly heart.

During this the Big Ten huddled in the corner to discuss the topics all girls of this age find most urgent. I felt alone in this foreign world and assumed I would be excluded from it.

My brooding was interrupted by a touch to the wrist. "Aren't you the actress?"

I turned to find a slender woman a few years older than myself extending a gentle hand in greeting. Pinned to her breast was a brooch of glass grapes as green as her eyes. "I'm Maeve Cooper."

"Are you one of his daughters?"

"Step-daughter. My mother is Amelia Cooper." She pointed across the room. "Number thirty-four."

"Thirty-four what?"

Maeve laughed brightly, throwing back her chin. "You are new here, aren't you?"

"Do you mean his thirty-fourth wife?"

300

"Don't worry, lately he's slowed down." She cocked her chin and thought about something for a moment. "I'd say about fifty."

"Fifty what?"

"Weren't you about to ask me how many he has in total?"

I liked Maeve immediately and embraced her as an ally in the Lion House. She told me she had been a small child when her mother married the Prophet. "But I might as well be a stranger to him," she said. "I'm convinced he doesn't know my name." And then, "Not that I care." She was a sly, dangerous girl and our bond was cemented that first evening.

"Here's what you need to know. Never be late for supper, never be the last one in at night, the ironing is done from dusk to dawn, and don't bother trying to speak with Brigham directly. Anything you need you can get from making friends with Aunt Twiss or Harriet Cook. Twiss is somewhere between number twenty-five and forty, I really don't know. And Harriet, I'm pretty sure she's down around number four or five, so I don't need to tell you how long she's been around. Anyway, they might look a bit grim, but they're really sweet old girls."

After supper we moved upstairs to the front parlor, also called the prayer room, where the women gathered in circles to knit, sing, and talk in the evenings. It was Sunday night and the theater was dark. There were some eight or ten wives present, plus daughters and friends. I felt as if each wife had a careful eye on me. "I won't let it bother me," I told my new friend. "At the end of the season, you and all these women will see me pack my trunk and move out. They have no reason to be jealous."

"That's what Elsa said."

"Elsa?"

"Never mind. Tell me about the theater. What's on tomorrow night?"

"No, Maeve, tell me. Who's Elsa?"

It took no more pleading for Maeve to recount the story of

what she called "wife number forty-seven or forty-eight, I think." A coloratura soprano imported from Wadowice, where the beautiful girls are dark and cold. According to Maeve, she was a shapely creature with a mane of red-black hair who sang with one arm draped across an alabaster pedestal. Brigham hired her to entertain at his private occasions, commanding her to sing his favorite bel canto roles from the Italian repertory. "She lived in the room across from yours," Maeve said. "Then he married her. She didn't want to, but what choice did she have? She was all alone. Her money came from him. She barely spoke English. How could she leave Utah? The wives made her life miserable."

"What happened?"

"She disappeared. Ran away, probably. But it's not an easy crossing to California. I should know. Some say Brigham's Danites went after her and murdered her in the desert. Forty miles out there's a pile of white bones by the road and the girls say that's Elsa. The way the wind whistles through the sockets in the skull, it sounds like her singing, practicing her scales."

"That's not true. I don't believe it."

"Neither did I. Not at first. But the truth is she was here one night, and gone the next. If you mention her to Brigham—and I'm warning you not to—he'll turn red as a pepper and huff out of the room. A few wives, when they knew she was really gone, they raided her room and fought over her silk."

"It can't be true."

"You're probably right. Even so, no one can explain what happened to her."

The next night at the theater my mind was preoccupied. I fear I gave one of my lesser performances, but the audience forgave me. Looking out into the theater, with thousands of eyes glowing in the dark, it was impossible not to wonder: What would become of me?

THE 19TH WIFE

CHAPTER ELEVEN
Marriage and Its Aftermath

For the next three months, I turned my attention to the theater. The more time I spent on stage, the more comfortable I became and, perhaps, the more my talent took root. I was cast as the little sister or ingénue in a number of slight plays no longer remembered, including *That Blessed Baby* and *The Good-for-Nothing*. The players, myself included, launched a movement to offer more serious fare, but Brigham re-enforced his ban on tragedy. "I won't have our women and children coming here to be frightened so they can't sleep at night." (He would later revise this policy, when he discovered he could not attract a certain beautiful Gentile actress to play in *Macbeth* rewritten with a happy ending.) There was also, for a time, a prohibition against sentimental romances that glorified monogamous love. I remember one evening when a Saint of about seventy stood up in his seat and hollered, "I ain't sitting through no play where a man makes such a cussed fuss over *one* woman." He turned to his twenty-four wives: "Git up!" They filed out of the theater, all twenty-five, in a noisy column. For any actor pursuing his art, Brigham's theater was not always a venue of ideals.

Despite these restrictions, the theater became my refuge from the Lion House. I spent most of my time there, arriving early in the morning and staying until long after the curtain fell. The Lion House served as nothing more than a waystation, and I had little time to consider the plight of the women stranded there. For several weeks, the only time I saw Brigham was when I was on stage and looked into the Presidential box. He was often with six or seven wives and a number of children, watching raptly from his velvet-padded rocker.

After each performance, I would sit at my dressing table, my heart anxious whenever a knock fell on my door. Yet always it would turn out to be one of my new company friends coming to share in the triumph of our evening, or my director, with notes to improve my technique. One night— it was during my run as Emily Wilton in *The Artful Dodger*—I sensed Brigham's gaze upon me with special intent as he leaned forward on his cane. The director had placed me upon the stage so close to Brigham's box I could nearly feel his eyes upon my flesh. In the final act, I stumbled on my lines. For a long moment—one of the longest in my life—I could not think of what to say. I looked about me, but my co-actor offered no assistance, for my stumble had thrown off his presence of mind as well. I turned and found myself looking into the Presidential box. Brigham mouthed the words *I shall be* . . . and it was as if an invisible hand had reached down and turned a crank to revive my memory and I carried on to the end with a particular intensity that brought the audience, Prophet included, to its feet.

Afterward, sitting at my table, I waited for the inevitable knock. I knew Brigham would come tonight, and I would have to thank him for his assistance. Up until then I had tried to deny the grasp he had about me, but this incident had made everything clear. I worked in his theater, I lived in his house, he was my spiritual leader, now he even told me what to say!

Then it came: the knock on my door. "Brother Brigham—"

Yet I opened the door to find a stranger greeting me with a box of sugar-stick jaw. "Will you permit an admirer to commend you on your performance?" The man spoke with an English accent, had a rugged complexion, and wore boots caked in plaster. His name, I soon learned, was James Dee. We spoke for what turned into an hour about the theater, his passion for Shakespeare, and Brigham's silly ban on tragedy. "What a lovely Ophelia you would make!" he said. Dee plastered log cabins for a living, a more lucrative practice than I might have realized, for he owned a fine six-room house not far from Temple Square. "I might be revealing too much in telling you I have been following your career."

"It's hardly a career, Mr. Dee. I've only been on the stage a few months."

"Yes, but already your talent outshines your peers."

I scolded him for his flattery and decided this was a good time to open the box of candy. We sampled the sweets, then, alas, parted company. "Farewell!" he cried. "Thou art too dear for my possessing."

There might be no greater cause for caution than a suitor who quotes the Bard on the threshold. Yet, Dear Reader, please recall at the time I was eighteen. I had been standing guard against Brigham's inscrutable affections for so long that Mr. Dee's slipped unnoticed under the gate. He promised he would return the following night, and he did. He said he would bring me a yellow rose and there it appeared, on my dressing table, a tight bud upon a long red-green stem. He said he would read *Twelfth Night* aloud to me, and he did so. In the first week of our acquaintance he kept each promise he made. He offered to help my mother with a crack in her ceiling, arriving at the promised hour. He balanced atop his ladder while my mother and her visiting sister wives looked on with interest. "Who's this one, then?" Eleanor asked. "Wish I had someone bringing me a box of sugar-stick jaw."

Mr. Dee made his presence felt so quickly and with such command that I could not help but grow feelings for him. By the seventh day of our friendship, we were in love and engaged.

"Engaged?" cried my mother. "You hardly know the man."
I reminded her she hardly knew my father when they
married. "Even so, I must tell you something: I don't
trust him."

"How can you say that? After he plastered your ceiling!"

"I used to know men like James Dee."

Like any young woman defying her mother, I stormed out
the door.

At the Lion House I sought an ally in Maeve. "Tell me
you're happy for me," I begged.

"I wish I could."

"You too? But why?"

"Because I know Mr. Dee. In reputation." We were in the
parlor, gathered for the evening in a corner where the other
women and girls could not overhear. Maeve whispered, "He's
known to know many women."

"Again, I don't believe you." We argued for as long as
we could before our voices disturbed the wives from
their knitting. They looked our way with desperate interest.
I knew at least one of them would not stop until she
had learned the subject of our debate. Polygamy inspires
this in otherwise thoughtful women—the relentless need
to know another's business. And yet what did I have to
hide? Soon Mr. Dee would move me out of the Lion
House and I would never have to suffer another night
with the eyes of a dozen lonely wives dismantling me with
their glares.

I could see that my new friend Maeve was not really as close
to my heart as I had believed. The root of her displeasure, I
assumed, was jealousy. I blamed this not so much on Maeve
herself but on the warping effects of polygamy. Even its
children can't escape its distortions of the heart.

For comfort, I turned to my old friends Lucinda and
Katherine.

"Tell me what he looks like again?" inquired Lucinda.

"Is he kind?" asked Katherine.

There is great comfort in knowing that old friends, even after a gap of time, remain the same. Neither knew anything of Mr. Dee. Neither had a reason to doubt my judgment, although Lucinda said, as we left Goddard's, "I wonder why your mother doesn't like him."

I could look back and examine why I ignored the counsel of those I loved most. A number of reasons might explain it, but none more so than my desire to escape the clutches of Brigham Young.

"Tell me," I said one evening to my betrothed. "What do you think of plural marriage?"

"Horrid institution."

"Even if it's the surest way into Heaven?"

"If you ask me, it's our Church's one great stain. I sometimes worry it'll be our undoing."

I nearly collapsed with relief. With this declaration locked in my heart, James Dee and I were married on April 4, 1863, in the Endowment House. Brigham sealed us before a small group, including my mother, whose rumpled face told me she could not enjoy the day. For a bridal dress I wore a bulky robe and ugly green apron. Beneath this, the sacred undergarments embroidered with cabalistic designs at the breast, navel, and knee. Brigham invited Maeve to attend the ceremony, and although she was no longer my closest friend, an old and gentle affection for her renewed itself on that special day.

I was scheduled to perform in *The Artful Dodger* on my wedding night. Brigham asked if I would prefer to hand the role over to my understudy. "Never!" I was a professional and I would meet my obligations. And so as a fresh bride, I took the stage. Word had spread that I had been wed earlier that day. When I made my entrance the audience erupted in congratulatory cheers. The applause repeated itself each time I entered from the wings and again at the end of the evening. By the time my husband and I returned to our rented room at Brigham's hotel, I was afloat on the triumph of the day.

It was the greatest moment of my marriage. Rare joy would follow that eve.

The first trouble came swiftly, when Dee suggested we move in with my mother. "What about your house?" I said.

"It's rented. I thought they'd be gone by now, but their plans changed. Lovely family of Saints. A wig-maker, he is. You should see what he can do with a horse's tail. Only one wife, a nice girl from Sweden. They asked for an extension. They've a child who's not been well. What could I possibly say?"

Reader, what could *I* say? Temporary financial trouble had recently forced my father to retreat from supporting four separate households. A few months before my marriage, Sister Lydia and Diantha had returned to my mother's house, as well as Mrs. Cox and Virginie. I told my husband her house was full and he would not be comfortable.

"It's only for a month or two."

"I don't want to live in a house full of wives."

"Darling, I don't know what to tell you. It's that, or a tent."

My mother accepted us without any complaint or I-told-you-so's. She was also grateful for Dee's plastering skills, for a number of chinks and hairline cracks in her walls had been preoccupying her. Dee, skillful in the art of pleasing a mother-in-law, fixed whatever she asked of him, whether of plaster or not. He even plugged the mouse hole behind the stove with a stopper he whittled down to size. "It's good of you to help her like that," I told him after we had been living with her for a month.

"Do I have a choice?"

"If that's how you feel, next time tell her no."

"Oh, Ann Eliza, aren't you sweet. Life isn't so simple. I can't say no to your mother."

"Of course you can, if there's a reason."

"You are a child, aren't you?"

"Don't speak to me like that."

"You really don't understand. Your mother, she's been

308

dying to have a man to boss around. What with your father living anywhere but here, she's had all her wifely energy bottled up."

"You don't know a thing about my mother."

"When I agreed to move in here, I thought you would side with your husband, but that was my mistake."

"Agreed to move in here!"

Oh, you can imagine the words that ensued. When our argument had worn itself out, I went to bed but found myself too agitated to sleep. I lay awake through the night, waiting for dawn when I could ask Dee his true feelings about our marriage. But I didn't have to. The next day I met an even clearer version of my husband, and I cared not for him in the least. We were strolling on Main Street when we happened upon Maeve. A delicate veil framed her lovely if overlong face. I introduced my friend to my husband. The exchange was brief and un-noteworthy until, after our departure, Dee said, "Who is she?"

To my Dear Female Readers, I ask—is there a question more devastating to the heart? Three simple words, when put together on a husband's lip, are constructed of nothing but betrayal and deceit. Or at least in Mormondom, where a man's whim can bring him another wife. "You met her at our wedding," I said.

"That's right, now I remember. She was in blue, with some sort of large broach—a bunch of grapes, wasn't it? Yes, it's all coming back. The blue, the grapes, the position on the breast. Indeed."

"She's one of my friends who warned me against you."

"Don't be coy, darling. Tell me exactly what you mean."

Repeating the rumors back to my husband would bring me no happiness. It would only make me look the fool. I therefore fibbed my way around the truth. "There have been a few words spoken that your faith is less than full." Oh, what a mistake to be dishonest!

"My faith! Is that it? She doesn't know me from Adam,

309

does she? She doesn't know anything about my good family I left behind in England for my faith. She doesn't know anything about the hardship of my journey here, it's a big ocean, the Atlantic is, and rather rough in December. I arrived with no friends, no contacts, nothing more than my plastering trowel and my faith. My good faith. Now why would this girl go on about the sincerity of my belief? Because I haven't fifteen wives, is that it? Does everyone around here think a man's got to have his own harem to be a true Mormon? If that's it, if that's the reason my good reputation's been tarnished, then I'm quite sure something can be done about it." If only that were the end of his speech, but I shall spare the Reader the second phase of his rant. My husband's monologue ended with: "I love my Church, and I'll prove it if I have to."

As you no doubt know, the best way to incite outrage is to attack false piety. When provoked, the insincere man must certify his earnestness. It is the animal in him—the scratching, the grunting, the marking of territory. This is how I account for Dee's subsequent actions. A few days later he announced, "I saw Sister Maeve. By chance we happened to be visiting the tinsmith at the same time. She asked after you."

"Please don't do this to me."

"Do what? By the way, you said Maeve lives in the Lion House?"

"That's right, upstairs, the seventh door on the left, tell her I say hello. And while you're there, why not call on Brigham's daughters? I'm sure the whole of the Big Ten will appeal to you."

"No need to get prickly, my love. Maeve's an attractive girl—what with those enchanting green eyes—but not a beauty in the classical sense, wouldn't you say? . . . Love, what's wrong? Where are you going?"

I abandoned my husband on the curb.

After only a few months of marriage, Dee and I were in

steady battle. He knew how to torture me and never once passed up the opportunity to turn the knife. "I was thinking of taking a second wife," he would say, igniting me with rage. No doubt he took pleasure in seeing me degrade myself in fury. Even the threat of a plural marriage reduced my composure and self-containment; its ugly promise reverted me to childish dismay. During these days, I was in rehearsals for the upcoming season at Brigham's theater, set to open in October. As my marriage collapsed, I became more and more disengaged. The disruptions of home-life consumed me. By the time we went into dress rehearsals for the season premiere, I withdrew from the company, never to return to the stage.

Reader, do you not see! *This* is polygamy! Not the family portraits of forty, bursting with clean, smiling children and simple, proud wives. Before I married Dee I was a reasonable and assured woman. A man's word could not destroy my self-regard. I was but eighteen and I had already defied Brigham Young! Now, in a few short months, I had become one of those pitiable creatures—the woman who begs for her husband's attention and weeps when she is alone. Those who know me today would not recognize me during this period. I take no pride in my former self, but my mission in writing this book would not be served were I to portray myself as always strong, always defiant, always certain of my path. Polygamy undermines even the most resolute.

Such was the pathetic state my husband had reduced me to when I discovered I was carrying my first child.

THE 19TH WIFE

CHAPTER TWELVE
Brigham Rescues Me

I shall refrain from detailing our marital discontent, which went on for the next two years. Our arguments were always of the same variety—Dee noting a young girl, speaking incessantly of her beauty, followed by reports of the two strolling downtown. If only the unfaithful heart could act with originality! Every so often he would mention spending time with Maeve, and my greatest fear was that she would become my sister wife. I endured this for two years, my sole comfort, aside from my mother, coming from my boys, first James Edward, whom I later took to calling Eddie in order to expunge any memory of his father, and, in 1865, Lorenzo Leonard.

During my recent travels, as I have discussed my personal history from the lectern, many times a woman in the audience has inquired, *Mrs. Young, why did you ever put up with that horrid Mr. Dee?*

Why, indeed? I can offer many reasons, although none is inspiring or that which we expect from our heroines. I was young. I had two small children. I knew no women who had divorced their husbands, and so this option was all but foreign to me. Lastly, I did not wish to admit I had been wrong. These "excuses" are not exceptional, but they reflect my truth, familiar as it may be. Honest Reader, if you peer into your own heart, I know you will understand.

I shall jump forward, then, to an evening in the autumn

of 1865, when Dee interrupted a quiet hour in my mother's sitting room by saying, "Ann Eliza, dear, did I mention I passed your old friend Maeve?"

The boys were playing with wooden blocks on the carpet at my feet. I watched their glossy heads bent over the house they were erecting. James, the elder, was showing his brother the different sizes. They were so pure and free of matrimonial agony!—and I became mournful that they would not remain so forever. They would grow up in Deseret, and suddenly I had a vision of my boys as young men, marrying women one after the next, consuming them with gluttonous speed, inflicting their own version of conjugal tyranny upon undeserving hearts. My boys would become their father.

"Ann Eliza? Did you hear me? I saw Maeve."

"I heard you."

"Now I don't want you to get upset, but I went ahead and asked her to marry me."

"What did she say?"

"To be perfectly honest, it wasn't the first time I asked. I've been in pursuit for many months. But I'm telling you now because this time, ah, yes, this time, she said, 'Let me speak with Brigham.'"

"I see. And if he grants her permission?"

"We'll marry as soon as possible."

"Where will she live? Because she won't be moving in here."

"Yes, you see. The timing could not be better. My tenants have decamped. Gone down to St. George, God bless them. My little house is free. It's not very big, and the stove is old and you have to duck when you climb the stairs, but Maeve doesn't strike me as the kind of girl who cares about those things."

"Not at all."

"Please don't be like that. Maeve has never said a bad word about you. She loves you like a sister."

"Why are you telling me all this?"

"Always in a rush, aren't you? All right, then. We both know I can't marry again without your approval. So I'm asking for it. There you are. After this, I won't ask for another thing."

The next day I called at the Lion House. More than two years had passed since I had lived there, but little appeared different. True, there was a new rotation of wives and visitors, along with the attendant children and widowed mothers &etc. Yet the mood was as I had left it: the dim halls, the constant patter of feet on the stairs, the girls whispering behind open books. On my way to Maeve's room I passed Aunt Twiss. "We've missed you," she said, weighed down with a basket of wash.

I confronted Maeve immediately. "You've seen Dee," I said.

"Yes, he's been plastering downstairs for a month. Did he tell you I sent my good word?"

But I would not be deceived by her innocent demeanor. "What did Brigham say?"

"About what?"

"About Dee's proposal?"

"Proposal for what?" Then she understood and her eyes widened into little pools. "Oh, Ann Eliza. You don't think—" She rose to close the door. "It's not what you think."

"Did my husband propose to you, or did he not?"

"I'm telling you, you don't understand. He's proposed to me six or seven times now, and each time I tell him I can't marry him. But he persists."

"Maybe he persists because you encourage him."

"He persists because that's the sort of man he is. His head's thick as his plaster."

"Why did you tell him you would discuss it with Brigham?"

"Because I was tired of his attentions and I knew Brigham would shoo him off. Ann Eliza, can you keep a secret?" It was a clear morning and the early light from the window framed her in a shimmer of white sun. "You mustn't tell anyone, but I'm Brigham's wife."

"What?"

"Number fifty-something or other. For the past six years."

"Why didn't you tell me?"

"Because Brigham wants to keep it a secret. He realizes that people are beginning to talk about his wives. He didn't want another wedding in the news."

"Why would you marry him?"

"Because he's Brigham! How could I say no?"

"But why not leave him now?"

"Oh, that's why I've missed you." Maeve stopped to kiss me. "Yes, why not leave? There are a thousand reasons. I have no money. I know no one outside Mormondom. Leaving would mean leaving my mother as well. Where would I go? How would I get there? What's between here and California? A desert white with bones."

"There must be a way."

"Maybe there is, but what then? And what about later, after I die?"

We both knew such defiance would mean exclusion from Glory. I'd be a reckless friend to advise her to risk her Salvation. "I can't take that chance," said Maeve.

"What did your mother say when he told her he had married her daughter?"

"It broke her heart three times. Together her husband, her Church, and her daughter had betrayed her."

I held Maeve, and our old friendship repaired itself with this intimacy. I stayed with her for an hour, then kissed her good-bye. That evening Dee and I were in the parlor of my mother's house. He was busy with the newspaper while I worked my needle. The boys were on the carpet with a yellow ball.

"James," said Dee, folding down his newspaper, "be a big boy and climb up and get your father the dictionary." I told my husband I would do it. "No, let the boy."

"It's too high."

"Let him stand on a chair."

"He'll fall."

"Not if he's careful."

James was so eager to please his father that he dragged a chair to the bookshelf and struggled to stand upon its seat. "James," I said, "get down." But the boy was determined. "Dee, he's going to fall."

"Let him try. You're bringing him up soft."

We argued some more until little James, not even two years old, was wobbling upon the chair, struggling to reach the dictionary that was higher than his head. It was absurd! I leapt to my feet and pulled the boy from the chair. Dee flew to grab the boy from me. "Let him be!" Our beautiful child was caught in a tug-of-war. Dee yanked on his legs so roughly that the boy began to cry.

My father happened to be visiting that night, discussing financial matters with my mother in the next room. "What's this?" he said, rushing in—my mother half a step behind. He shoved Dee in the shoulder, sending him reeling against the carpet. He landed so hard he popped the air out of the yellow ball, which caused little Lorenzo to burst into a fit of laughter. "You don't go around roughing up children," shouted my father. "Not in my house."

After two and a half years, I could no longer hide the true state of my marriage. I told my parents the full and miserable account, and within an hour they asked him to leave. Dee protested, claiming his various rights, but my father dragged him to the wagon and drove him to Salt Lake, depositing him in the street.

In the morning, my father and I went to see Brigham. I maintained my composure as I told the Prophet the intimate details of my marriage. Throughout my story, Brigham maintained a sympathetic gaze. His brow buckled at the most painful parts, and his lip ruffled with true and deep empathy. "You have been treated worse than an animal," he said. "You must divorce him."

"But how?"

"I shall tell you." Brigham proceeded to lay out a legal strategy for me to be rid of Dee. In his power as leader of the Church, he dissolved the marriage at once. But for purposes of custody, he advised me to file for a divorce in the Probate Court of Great Salt Lake County. "I will do whatever I can to facilitate this. I'll write the judge personally. I'll serve as witness. I promise you"—and here he touched me, or so it seemed, with his iron eyes—"that you will be free from this man before Christmas."

On December 23 I gave testimony before the court. Dee failed to appear, and in short order I was divorced from my husband with full custody of my boys. Brigham had honored his promise with such resolution that on Christmas Day I gave thanks to God for the birth of His son and the wise guidance of our Prophet. On that glorious day there was no Saint in all of Mormondom who owed more to Brigham than I.

XIII

CONTRACT
OF FAITH

WRITTEN DEPOSITION
IN THE CASE OF

ANN ELIZA WEBB DEE YOUNG
Versus
BRIGHAM YOUNG

No. 71189

*On this 3rd day of October, 1873, in Salt Lake, in
the Territory of Utah, Gilbert Webb personally
appeared before me, Judge Albert Hagan, counsel
to the plaintiff, Ann Eliza Webb Dee Young, to
enter into the record of this Special Examination a
written deposition consisting of his Testimony in the
matter between the plaintiff and Brigham Young.*

I am Gilbert Webb, thirty-nine years old, son of Elizabeth and
Chauncey Webb. I received my ordinances in the Nauvoo
Temple in January 1846, in the state of Illinois. I presently
live in South Cottonwood on my father's land. I work as a
shepherd, rancher, and wagon manufacturer. I have two
wives, Kate and Almira, and eighteen children. My statement,
as written here, is limited to my knowledge of, and direct
experience with, Brigham Young, President, between the periods
of May 1866 and March 1868, leading to my indebtedness to
him, and the engagement of my sister, Ann Eliza, to become
his 19th wife. With our Heavenly Father watching over, I
swear everything I write here is true as far as I know it and
I know no other version of these events.

It started on a Sunday in May 1866. My wives and I stopped on the Salt Lake Road under the nine o'clock sun. The Prophet wasn't due for another hour. By my count more than a thousand people had come out to greet him and a thousand more would come before ten. The valley was green from the grass and out to the East the mountains were blue with morning shade and white on the cap with old snow.

My wives had stitched a welcome banner saying "The Daughters of Zion—Virtue" and held it above our heads on two sticks. Under the locust we could feel the spring chill on our necks but when in the sun it was hot as June and my wives fanned themselves with the leaflets announcing the Prophet's visit.

Up the road I could see my ma and pa, along with his wives. Sisters Lydia and Eleanor held a banner that said "Mothers in Israel." Ann Eliza was with them, along with her boys, James and Lorenzo. It looked as if she was holding a banner that read "Hail to the Prophet," but the woman next to her was carrying it. There were so many people it was hard to tell.

After an hour a brass band led Brigham into town, followed by a brigade of children waving sticks with ribbons on the ends, then the hundred carriages in his party escorted by fifty horsemen. People stood three deep along the road and everyone cheered and waved. "Do you see him?" cried Kate, bouncing on her toes. "All I see is a hat in a window." Almira set her hand on my shoulder and jumped a foot off the ground. "That's him all right," she said. "I recognize the brim."

I picked up one child after the next, set him on my shoulders, gave him a glimpse of the Prophet, then set him back down and picked up the next. There were twelve then. The oldest was eleven. By the time I hoisted the baby, Brigham was down the road.

We followed Brigham over to the bowery. It was an open-air structure, with a roof of branches held up by columns of white pine. My wives and children filled two benches, leaving no room for me. I stood next to them in the aisle, leaning against one of the columns. Two of the boys were fidgeting, pinching each other on the knee. One of the boys belonged to Kate, the other to Almira, but both were mine—I could see my chin on them, dimpled underneath.

When Brigham took the pulpit everyone went silent, even the children. "Good Morning, good Brethren and Sisters," he began. "I've come to your fine village to greet you because I want to talk about families, yours and mine. As you know, I have a large clan, made up of many sorts, my sons and daughters each with his own mind, or her own mind, and my wives, each with her own way of looking upon the world. I cherish nothing more than hearing one of my wives tell me what she thinks about the news of the day, or the progress of her hat-making, or whatever preoccupies her mind—for each is unique in her outlook, and it is this that makes her a child of God. I cherish when my wives, or my children, respond to my words given to them as husband, or as father, or as Prophet. Indeed, they have much commentary about my words as your Prophet and Leader, sometimes telling me I have spoken well, other times telling me my meaning is unclear. Every now and then one of my daughters, or one of my wives—yes, always the women—asks why anger and choler—for that is what they believe it to be—colors my sermons and other public commentary. When I speak to my family in private, as opposed to you and the other Saints of Deseret, I speak no differently, for my role in guiding them as father and husband is no different than my role in guiding your spirits toward our Heavenly Father. And thus, if you think I am admonishing you unfairly for your habits and ways, know that I admonish my daughters and sons, and my wives, in the same way. I know sometimes they think I am old and not aware of today's fashions or tastes, but my wisdom comes not from the newspaper or the gossip buzzing about the counter at the store, but from our Book and the other words the Lord has shared, and from prayer, and thus I speak a truth which transcends the customs of this year, or of this decade, or even of this century—a truth that shall guide you through eternity. And so, it is with your good patience I have a few things to say about your habits and your ways. If you believe I am haranguing you, you are correct, for I harangue you with a heart heavy with love—"

Soon after Brigham started speaking I admit I began thinking about my lambs and how high the grass was already this year and how much they'd bring when they went to slaughter. I must've been day-dreaming for a long time because Brigham was deep in sermon before I heard much of what he had to say. On this morning two themes interested him above the rest—the fashion of the women and the drinking habits of the men. Sometimes when he gets going on sinning it's hard to know if he'll ever stop.

"My goodness, Sisters, if another one of you comes to me to discuss the fashions of the Gentiles, I shall tell you, Go, dress like the Gentile woman, appear as the whore, if that is what you want. You tell me about the hoops and the heart-shaped collars and the silks that cling and reveal the shapes of all of you; you ask why you cannot wear what the women of Paris wear, what the women of New York wear. By all means, you may wear the fashions of New York, the couture of Paris. If that is what you want. And if it is what you want, then you shall understand why I must assume you also want to be known as the whore. So be it. Sister-whores, order as you like from the Eastern catalogs! Dress as if you were walking up Broadway! But in doing so, know that you are not a Sister to me—You are not a Latter-day Saint! So ponder your choice in garment, Sisters. For the cloth on your back reveals much more than your lovely shape."

Hearing the Prophet talk of women's hoops got one of my boys snickering. The wives tried to settle him, but the boy was worked up. He laughed until Brigham called him out:

"Young man, why is this funny?" Brigham was sixty-six, fat and vigorous, with a large head that went red and dark when he condemned his people. His chins and mustaches quivered when he cried my boy's name. The boy didn't peep again all day.

"Brothers, you laugh when I talk about our Sisters' interest in frippery? You nod in agreement that our women are choosing silk over Saintliness? But what about you? You, Brothers, your sins are worse, far worse. For although our women debase their bodies when they don a dress that enhances their tother ends, you, Brothers, you debase your souls when you drown your days in whiskey and rye. If the Sisters worship at the altar of the catalog, you, Brothers, kneel before the bottle and the barrel. Each drink shall be remembered. Each sip shall be tallied. Each swallow shall swallow you!"

I looked to survey my brood. Kate's eyes had glazed over. I gathered she was pondering the rolls of Boston wallpaper Dalby's had put out for sale. Almira was upright and alert with envy for Mrs. Ball's quail-feathered bonnet bobbing across the aisle. I looked forward to hearing all about it at the supper table. My twelve children were asleep, propped against one another or slumped over in their mothers' laps. Little Gilbert lay like a pup on the ground. Sometimes I could not believe they were mine. Certainly twelve is not a record. In Deseret twelve children causes no comment. Sometime soon Almira or Kate would announce a thirteenth. The fourteenth could not be far behind.

For a while now I sensed Brigham was looking down in my direction. True I enjoyed whiskey as much as the next man, but no more so, not enough for Brigham to call me out. In the last year only once did Jamison have to dump me at the door too drunk to walk. I've never lifted my hand to either wife and by God never to my children. So why was Brigham gazing my way? His eyes shone the way the sun catches a scar on a plow's blade. Perhaps a false rumor had spread and reached his ear. I'd seen it happen—stories passing as if they were fact and men condemned because of it. I try not to ask too much of my wives but if I hear them sharing out tittle-tattle I tell them to stop and go back and clean up their debris. I once heard my pa say, Live by rumor, die by it too. And so it be. Now, with Brigham's stare on me, I figured someone I didn't know to count as my enemy had gone about twisting up my name.

Yet I came to see he wasn't looking at me but admiring my sister standing nearby. Ann Eliza was twenty-one now and more beautiful than ever. I am no poet and can't depict beauty and won't try. Since divorcing Dee she had turned down half a dozen marriage proposals. More than a few men had come to tell me of their desire to take my sister's hand.

After the services, we all walked home to my ma's house for supper. Along the way, the Presidential Carriage pulled up. Brigham stepped down and asked Ann Eliza if he might walk with her.

My brood and I were twenty paces behind this scene. We could see them plainly but the wind was wrong for us to hear. My wives galloped forward, dragging the children and me, stopping ten paces from their target, where we were close enough to pick up their words.

"You've never looked finer," Brigham remarked.

"You've never sounded angrier," said my sister. "When you return to Salt Lake, please send my best to Mrs. Young."

If Brigham grimaced or winced, I could not see it. "They ask after you. They remember you fondly from your stay."

"I remember some of them quite fondly as well." Each time my sister jabbed the Prophet with her words, my wives looked at each other with quick-moving eyes that spoke a language all their own.

"Do you think you'll ever remarry?" Brigham asked.

"I hope not."

"What if it were your duty?"

"Thankfully it isn't."

Brigham took Lorenzo in his arms. As he continued to walk with my sister, more and more people speculated on the nature of his interest. Kate whispered her theory: "I guess it's time for a new wife. It's been nearly a year."

"He's chasing the wrong hoop," said Almira. "He's the last man in Utah she'd ever marry."

"She *says* that. But look at her!"

Without my wives I would have been at a loss for interpretation. My ma's house was near and I could tell you exactly what was on my wives' minds: Would Ann Eliza invite the Prophet in for supper? Before a decision had to be made, my ma swooped in.

Following the meal Brigham asked my pa and me to meet him in my ma's house for a discussion. After some talk about the May grasses and the water levels, Brigham got into his purpose. "Chauncey, Friend, I've known your daughter since she was a babe. I've watched her grow from child to woman. When she met Dee I tried to warn her but she wouldn't listen. I would've married her myself, but I'd just only recently taken Amelia as my wife. Washington was after me just then, going on about my wives. It wasn't the right time for another marriage. I can't tell you how it strained me to watch that man abuse her. And those boys. I want to make those boys mine. I want Ann Eliza for my wife." Brigham implored my pa for half an hour. He didn't think to address me. It didn't matter, I didn't want to be a part of it. Brigham finished his appeal with a promise. "I'll treat her well."

"How will your wives treat her?" my pa asked.

"They will love her. When she stayed with them, they took her in."

"That's not what she says," I said. "She was lonely."

"Lonely?" said Brigham. "In the Lion House?"

"That's what she said."

"Did she?" asked my pa.

327

"She was very young," said Brigham. "It was her first time away from her mother. Of course she'd be lonely. But this time, no, she'll have me, and the boys, and Mrs. Webb, if she wants, she can come live with us. You know my great fondness for Sister Elizabeth."

My pa thought about all this. "Maybe you should ask her now."

"First I need you to agree. If she doesn't care for the Lion House, I'll set her up in a fine home of her own, furnished as she likes, and provide her with five hundred dollars a year. Each boy will have a room. I have a house in mind—it's not far from mine. There's a tree out back with an elbow where the boys can build a tree house. I'll help them. Think of it—your daughter will have a husband. Your grandsons will have a father."

"You should ask her," my pa said again.

"Yes, but how does it sound to you?"

"I can't talk about it anymore without consulting her."

"Let's say seven hundred and fifty dollars. Will that be enough?"

"I don't know."

"One thousand? How's that?"

"Brother Brigham, I can't speak for my daughter."

"Yes, but will you recommend it?"

"I can only present it," said my pa.

Our meeting lasted an hour. "Walk me to my carriage," Brigham said to me upon conclusion. At the road, the Prophet asked about my family. "How many children are there now? Ten, eleven?"

"Twelve."

"That's a lot of mouths. It can strain a man. I see you still live on your pa's land and tend his sheep."

"That's right."

"You need a little fortune to come your way."

"Doesn't everyone?"

"How much do I pay you for your sheep?" I told him my

328

deal with the Church's butchery. "Let's improve it, shall we? Another dollar?"

"I'd appreciate that."

The Prophet rested his hand on my arm. "Now I need your help. Will you tell your sister to take my offer?"

"It's a good offer," I said. "But that doesn't mean it's good for her."

When I returned to the house my pa was already telling Ann Eliza about the Prophet's proposal. "I'm afraid he loves you," he said.

"Did he say that?"

"In his own way."

"His own way is to love one woman, then the next, then the next again."

My ma entered the fray. "Ann Eliza, settle down. You act like he's come to lock you up."

"Hasn't he? Isn't that what he wants—for me to be one of a hundred wives?"

"He doesn't have a hundred wives," said my ma.

"No? Then how many?"

"That's enough," said my ma. "All Brigham's done is propose."

Ann Eliza cooled her fury. "Mother, I know you love him. And I love him too, but as my Prophet, not my husband."

"You think you're smarter than everyone," my ma said. "But you're not. I'm not blind. I know Brigham has his weaknesses, but do they erase everything good he's ever done?"

I went out into the kitchen yard. I had no more desire to be with my wives than I had to be back in that argument. My only place it seemed was outside in the night. The moon was up and lit the path to my cottage. The cattle were lowing and the sheep were bleating and the night was empty but noisy too. I could smell the rye in the paddock and last year's hay in the barn. It was cold, and the cold gathered in the stones of the path.

When my wives greeted me at the door, I stopped them before they could begin. "Not tonight," I said. "Not tonight."

They offered milk and cake but I was not hungry and asked the women to let me alone. They retreated to their bedrooms, one door latching, then the next. Upstairs the children slept, four boys across the Mormon sofa, two babes bundled in the cradle, the rest divided between two beds. I had a vision of myself in the future, five or six years along, gone silver in the beard, another six or eight children under my roof. And if I were foolish enough, maybe another wife. What was to stop it—this terrible vision of my future days? When I thought of happiness I thought of my horse bending to drink from a stream. I thought of a meadow where the only chatter came from the jays and the squirrels. I thought of a bedroll under the stars. I thought of stretching out beneath the night, falling asleep alone.

I drifted off in my chair but woke at midnight. Sunday was my night of rest from my women and typically I slept in the bed behind the kitchen, but I didn't want to lie down there tonight. I went outside. The wind had kicked up, throwing around the cold. There was a dew that'd go to frost by dawn. Inside the barn my sorrel greeted me with a sneeze. The barn smelled of hay and manure and cold water in the metal trough. I climbed up into the hay loft, disturbing a hen. I lay down and propped my head in a saddle and threw a striped saddle blanket over my chest. A barn cat with a bend in his tail tiptoed through the straw and climbed on top of me. His paws delicately dented my belly and his bent tail flapped my face. A stranger might think I had argued with my wives, sleeping in the loft like that, but I hadn't argued with anyone. I was very tired and the cat curled up and pulled his tail up alongside him. He was very small and in need of milk and he didn't weigh anything at all on my chest where he slept, going up and down, up and down.

* * *

Over the next year my wives gave me two more children. First Almira, then Kate. A boy and a girl. I loved them as much as a man can divide up his heart among fourteen. It's a queer feeling, slicing up affection like a wheel of cheese. I've heard them say the heart's bottomless but I don't agree. I love my boys and girls but when my mind is clear I have to admit I wish I could give out more love. There's another queer feeling to it too. A man isn't meant to greet a new baby at the rate of more than one a year. But the men of Deseret got to adjust. Sometimes you get two a year. If you've got three wives, that might mean three. It goes on from there. I felt myself moving on in years faster than I should. I was already hard in the bone and tired, like a man who's winding down.

The more children my wives gave me, the more I needed my pa to fish me out. I relied mostly on him for my land, my house, my wagons and teams, my sheep and the hands I hired, and my accounts at the store and the granary. Even my horse was his, a nice little sorrel with front socks and heavy feet. When money went tight, I borrowed from a neighbor or took credit at the hardware. I always meant to pay down my own debts but it never worked out. My pa would hear about my holes and fill them in.

That's how it went for a long time and that was how it was going to be. I knew this as a fact when the latest baby was born to Kate. She was a dense little thing with a carrot swirl of hair. Holding my fourteenth child for the first time I became sick with a feeling that I'd failed. When I was a young man on Mission with my pa, I'd lie awake in our bed and picture myself as a husband. As I pictured it, I owned a small board house in a meadow with a tin chimney. It was so clear in my mind I could even picture the white smoke puffing from the chimney in the cold spring air. I saw the mountains big and shiny above the house and my wife working the vegetable patch while I plowed the field. I saw a babe in a basket napping in the sunlight. I imagined a supper table set for two with the plates turned down. Those were my dreams.

Soon after the baby's arrival I went to see Almira in her room. It was her night. I found her waiting on the bed in her nightdress and the bonnet with the braided ribbon. "Shut the door," she said. "We need to talk."

Yet she had said enough—another baby was coming. All was clear.

I looked out the window. It was early spring and the final winter storm was coming. You could see it from the way the moon burned behind the clouds. My wife came to my side. Her fingers played with my sleeve. "You're supposed to be happy."

I don't know how much longer I stood at the window. Might've been an hour. I don't know. The mountains were black and hidden but even when you can't see them you know they're there. For a long time I was ashamed to look at my wife. When I turned around I couldn't see anything but the white bonnet crumpled in her hands.

It snowed nearly a foot that night, but by daybreak the sun was up and already melting the pack on the southern roof. When I went out the path to my pa's house was hidden, but from the way the wind was blowing soon it would clear. I waved to Ann Eliza out on her porch. She was in a green dress and the green was strong against the house's white boards and the snow. She had done it. I reminded myself of that. She had escaped a life she did not want.

I rode out to Lark's Meadow, my horse chopping through the snow. Lark's is a long narrow meadow with a timber of white pine on one side and the foothills on the other. The mountains stand tall over it, and half the meadow can go marshy in the spring. It was a good spot for sheep because of the grass and the water and the shade.

When I reached the meadow I pulled up for a look. The sun was just then clearing the mountains and the snow hadn't begun to melt. Everything looked hard and cold like in January and the white pines bent with the snow on the bough and the creek ran with ice. The log cabin at the far end was white with snow and it looked like no one had been to the meadow in some time and that wasn't right.

I rode down to the cabin and tied my horse. "Harkness?" I called.

"It's about time!" Harkness yelled from inside the cabin.

When I opened the door I found him roped to a chair. "What happened here?"

"First get me out of these damn ropes." They'd worked the rope around Harkness a dozen times. The knot was tight and the cold made it stiff and unworkable and I had to cut the rope. When Harkness was free he jumped around the room getting the blood back to his legs. "Thought I'd freeze to death in that damn chair."

"How many?" I said.

"Two."

"That's all?"

"The wind was picking up and I didn't hear them ride in. They were carrying, each with a Winchester and a pistol."

"What time was it?"

"About an hour before the snow."

"Local," I said.

"How do you know?"

"They were waiting for a storm to cover their tracks. They seem familiar?"

"Not really. But they knew what they were doing. They had them all rounded up and out the gate in a couple of minutes. Had a few dogs with them showing the way."

"Meanwhile you sat in that chair."

"Waiting for you, Sister."

"It's not funny. I just lost a hundred sheep."

"And I nearly lost my legs tied down in this cold."

"Here's my handkerchief. Go have a cry and come back when you can tell me who they were."

333

"They were two rustlers just like you imagine them. Quick in their dealings and good on a horse and real comfortable holding a gun."

I built a fire in the stove. I boiled some coffee and fried a pair of sausages and we ate without talking. Outside the sky was clear and the sun was strong. When I left the meadow was green again and springy under foot. You could smell the pine resin burning off the wet trees in the sun.

Eventually Harkness found my sheep out on Van Etten's land, up in a high pasture a mile off the road. Their brands had been burned over but if you looked you could see what had come first. Van Etten had been suspected of rustling a couple of times before. No one trusted him much, he was known for reporting false crimes to Brigham's office. When I went to see Van Etten he denied knowing anything. He puffed up his chest but I told him I knew my sheep. "If you don't stop accusing me," he said, "I'll go to the Prophet." He was wearing his rifle but I was madder than I could remember. "I'll go to him myself," I said, and that's what I did.

I rode up to Salt Lake and took my place on line outside the Beehive House. When it was my turn I told Brigham my business.

"If you're certain," he said, "then I'll speak to the man." A clerk in armbands interrupted Brigham to sign some papers. As he went about scratching off his name, he asked after my family. "I understand you've had more children. No one can accuse you of not doing your part. I hope you're managing." I told him I was. "Glad to know it. Now you'll send my regards to your sister?"

I told him I would and got up to leave.

"In a hurry?" He laughed, his flesh pressing against the buttons of his coat. "Sit down and tell me your plans. You've lost a hundred sheep. That must be difficult for a man in your position."

"It'd be difficult for any man."

He went quiet. Anyone could see his mind turning behind his eyes. "What do you know about telegraph poles?"

"They go in the ground."

"That's about all you need to know. How many teams do you have?"

"Ten wagons and sixty mules."

"That might not be enough."

"For what?"

"I need a man to deliver poles to the line my son's running out from Denver."

"I can do it."

"They're moving fast, making twenty-five miles a week."

"I can do it."

"How does two dollars and fifty cents a pole sound? Cut, shaped, and delivered."

This was the type of deal a man waits most of his life for. There was good timber at Lark's Meadow. If I hired enough men and bought a few more teams it would work out all right. Brigham and I went over the details but it was all pretty clear. I'd set up a mill in the meadow to debark them and plane them and dry them in the sun, then treat them with the creosote. The teams would deliver them to the line. I knew I could do as fine a job as any man in Utah. We shook on the deal.

Cutting and curing a telegraph pole is a simple process. Most any man with a good team and strong timber and quick saws can do it. The only special requirement is capital. For the men and the extra wagons and provisions I needed $11,000. I borrowed half the money from a Gentile banker named Walter Karr and the other half from a Mormon banker named Alfred Eagleton, at 5 percent a month. The job would be complete by mid-summer. After paying back the loan I'd have plenty to build out my house and keep my wives happy a few more years. I got ahead of myself and for one night thought about taking another wife. The truth is I'm as weak as the next man, maybe more.

My wives were happy with the news. "We'll help out by making your men their meals," said Kate.

Almira was showing under her apron, and for the first time the sight of her belly made me glad. "I'll fix up the food in the morning," she said, "giving each man one of my special peaches, and Kate will drive the food out to Lark's. That way the work won't have to stop."

It didn't take long for us to reach twenty-five miles a week. The men laying the poles weren't my men but we liked working together. With each delivery they said my poles were good, well-planed poles with a base as wide as it should be. They knew what was coming, which means they could dig their holes better and faster and stand the poles the right way. The job ran easy and smooth for everyone and I think everyone working on that line felt the way you do when you know well-earned money's coming your way.

By July we were nearing Denver. That's when Brigham called me to his office. I thought he was going to pay off the job in advance because my work was quality work and everyone said so. "You've done such a fine job," he said. "I want you to take over the line running to Montana. They're in real trouble and might not finish this year. I'll give you three dollars for every pole delivered, and a dollar for standing it in the ground."

A man who's recently made real money has but one inclination, and that's to make more. That same day I drove a load of poles north myself. I spent about two weeks straightening out the job and pulling up the bad poles and filling in old holes and digging new ones. On the Denver line the Prophet's office paid me twice a month. But once I started driving north the payments stopped. I needed those deposits to pay my men. After three weeks I was low and could barely pay them out. After four weeks I spent everything I had to keep the men on the roll and the line extending north.

When I went to see Brigham about the dried-up payments, his secretary kept me waiting for a long time and then told me to come back the next day. The next day it was the same. I couldn't wait another day in Salt Lake. I needed to ride back up to the job. Even though I wasn't being paid I knew I couldn't stop driving the line. In summer winter feels far away, but not if you've got a line of poles to get in the ground before frost. That's what I was thinking as I left Salt Lake, and that's all. I never thought I'd never see my money. I've seen swindling up close. I've heard all about it and always shook my head, wondering how a man could be so foolish to hand out his money to a crook, because a crook looks like a crook and talks like one too. And that's how I thought about swindling. I don't have the kind of mind to imagine the Prophet cheating, and I'm both sorry and glad I don't.

It took a month to see the Prophet. By then I couldn't hold down my anger. My men were chewing me up and some had walked off and the job was behind. They accused me of swindling and some talked of stealing my teams. When I finally got to see Brigham, I blew apart. "I've got thirty men laying your poles and I haven't seen a penny from you since I sent them north."

"From what I hear, your poles are rotting. On top of that you're behind schedule. Now why would you expect me to pay for that?"

That's when I lost my head. I leapt across his desk and fisted his lapels, shaking him hard. "Give me my money!"

"Get off me." He shoved at me but I held on.

"You're cheating me," I said, "and you know you're cheating me, and there's nothing worse than a cheat who knows he's doing it."

Brigham put together enough force to throw me down. I was on the carpet with my hat bent beneath me. He looked as fresh as he does on Sunday morning. "What about our deal?" I muttered.

"Produce a contract, and I'll honor it."

"You never offered one."

"That's because one isn't necessary among old friends. Brother Gilbert, I will pay you as soon as you've earned it."

Two clerks appeared to escort me from the Beehive House. They dumped me on the curb at the head of the line. Everyone on the street was looking at me. It's not every day a man gets thrown out of the Beehive House. "He's a liar!" I yelled, warning anyone who could hear. "He's a cheat and a liar!" The men on line pretended not to listen and I know for certain each of them couldn't wait to get home to repeat the story at the supper table. I'm sure the story moved up and down Deseret faster than if it had been sent on our telegraph.

The next day I rode up to the job to explain everything to my men. When I got there my foreman pulled me aside. "Thank God you're here." I asked him the trouble. "The poles, they're rotting off at the ends." We walked a line of poles. At each one he pointed up and it was true, indeed the top was black and soft. I asked my man what was wrong. "One of two things. Either the curing didn't take . . ."

"Or?"

"Or sabotage."

I didn't know what to think, not then or now, but the truth was Brigham had been right: my poles were no good. I gathered my men up and told them the job was done. I explained as best I could the circumstances, but I no longer understood them as well as I'd thought. The men didn't care about my troubles, whether my timber hadn't cured or Brigham wasn't paying or anything. "I'm a pole layer," said one, "and I've laid your damn poles." They spoke angrily, cursing my name and this damn job. They were rough men of the West, used to settling debts by any means. They surrounded me—maybe thirty at once—and they demanded to know what I was going to do. "Give me two days," I told them. One man, a con from Nevada, said he wouldn't wait a third.

To pay my men I sold my teams and my gear and the little bit of land my pa had given me. I sold everything I could to clear up with my men enough so they would never call me a cheat and a liar. I asked my bankers for a deal to pay off the debt. Karr agreed to forgive the remaining money if I paid half. But Eagleton wanted all his money and interest and penalties too. I can't blame him for it, but I didn't have it. When Brigham heard, he was angry I favored the Gentile banker over Eagleton. He spoke about it in a sermon. "There's a brother here who feels he owes more to a Gentile than a Saint. I ask you: Would you trust him?" I didn't favor anyone but that's how Brigham saw it and how most people saw it, too.

By the spring of '68 I was bankrupt and facing legal suits. Eagleton, with the Prophet's blessing, was coming after me. Debt's a cruel hole. The more you try to climb out of it, the more it caves in. That's what I learned. And don't go into business with the Church. There's no way to wind up on the right side.

So with all this behind me, was I surprised to see the Presidential Carriage in my ma's yard that day in March? I'd been expecting it for some time. I heard it from the barn—the wheels squealing, the leather reins twisting, the horses clopping to a stop. The door swung open and the Prophet eased himself out with one hand on the roof. The carriage swayed with him as he stepped down and the springs groaned and the horses flicked and twitched. My ma came out of her house and I came out of the barn and we met the Prophet on the path. "Sister Elizabeth, I've come to warn you about your son," he said. "He owes a good Saint money. He's wrongfully accused a close friend of rustling sheep. He's cheated me with a bad job. Something's got in him, Sister. I'll have to take steps."

"I'm paying out what I can," I said. "And those sheep were mine."

"Brother, you're not acting like a Saint."

"Brigham," my ma said, "neither are you." My ma says she's never been angrier in her life. You might wonder why she didn't quit the Church then, but she's not like that. She's always saying she lives in the middle, where everything has

339

two meanings, and the shades are gray. There are those who say my ma pushed Ann Eliza into her marriage with Brigham. There are those who say my ma hoped to see her own standing in the Church rise by marrying a daughter to the Prophet. But those who say these things about my ma don't know her. My ma never once cared what others think of her. She cares about one thing only, and that's her God.

"Brother Gilbert, consider yourself warned." Brigham climbed into his carriage and it tipped with his weight. He shouted to his driver and the team bucked and lunged forward and the carriage swung around and drove up the dirt road to Salt Lake.

"He's not the same," said my ma. She was white with anger. "He used to be another man." I told her not to worry, but we both knew there was plenty to worry over.

Two days later the letter arrived.

Sir—

Let it be known that in consideration of your recent actions, and your refusal to acknowledge outstanding debts and false claims of slander and libel, your challenges against fellow Saints and honest men stand, from this day forward, as challenges to the Church itself and therefore as apostasy. A board, chaired by myself, shall gather to determine your future participation in our beloved Church, both today and in the Everafter. Any appeal should be made to me directly; otherwise you shall receive notice of the date and time of your trial.

I am still most solemnly &c. your Prophet—
BRIGHAM YOUNG

I rode up to Salt Lake. By now the rains were mostly gone and on both sides of the road the grasses were high. Most of the time I go along, doing what comes up next, but this time I knew I had to go a particular way. At the Beehive House

I told the secretary my name. He was a thin old man with a long blue nose and old yellow hair. If you threw him on a scale I bet he didn't weigh a hundred pounds. There was a long list of men waiting to see the Prophet but the old man told me to wait in the hall, Brigham would see me right away.

The hall was decorated with a red and blue runner and a glass lamp hanging from the ceiling on three little chains. How many times had I been there in the last year? Six or eight or more. Most men don't have any business with the Prophet except listening to him on Sundays and reading the proclamations and every now and then making an appeal for a plural wife. I thought of that dream I once had: the house in the meadow, the smoke in the chimney, the wife, and the child. It all felt far away.

When I met Brigham he said, "I haven't yet set your trial date."

"What do I need to do?"

Brigham perched on the corner of his desk. He wasn't going to say any more until I broke down. He wanted me in a puddle on his carpet, and there I went: "I don't want to leave. I've got my family, my wives, my children. Where will I go?"

I'm ashamed to say I wept in his office. He stood by, letting me crack up like a woman. When my face was streaked and bent up, he passed me a handkerchief with his monogram in gold. "What do you want?" he said.

"I want to be a good man."

"I can help you."

A few minutes passed with Brigham pacing and going to his window and looking out at the front garden and returning to his desk to review the paper at the top of the pile. The whole time I sat in a heap in his visitor's chair, wiping up my face.

"Ever since your sister was a child," he began, "I've seen her as my own. I've protected her, watched out for her, made sure your family was tended to. I invited her to live next door to be near me. I asked her to join my theater so I could look at her every night. All of your troubles will be gone if you can convince her to marry me. I'm sure it's impossible for her brother to see her beauty as I do: but she's the most splendid woman who's ever set foot in Deseret. Her eyes, her throat, her skin."

There's something to see a grown man gushing like a boy. If I hadn't been in so much trouble myself, I'd have been disgusted by it and told him so.

"Go to your sister, tell her of my qualities, convince her that she will never want for anything. I'll give her a house, I'll care for her children, she'll have an allowance and freedom. Anything she wants will be hers, but she must be mine."

"She doesn't listen to anyone."

"Make her." He shook his mouth out like a twitching horse. "You know women: they can be brought home and tamed."

"I'm not sure that's true."

"No, not always, but with Ann Eliza I sense that this is what she wants."

"And my debts?"

"Forgiven. Your position in the Church: restored. Your name: exalted. Your financial situation: vastly improved. I'll pay you an allowance to help you meet your family needs. What do you need? A thousand a year? Two? I'll give it to you. You tell me what you need, but bring me your sister."

"I can't force her."

"That's not what I want. I want her to see for herself what I can give. I think she fears marriage will somehow restrict her. In fact, it will be just the opposite. Make her see this. That's all I ask."

He stood in his window. His beard appeared pink in the sunlight and his cheeks were full and red. "Gilbert, have you thought about taking another wife?"

"Not much."

"In this scenario, you can if you like. If you find a woman to join your household, you'll be able to invite her in." He was so overcome by anticipation, I thought he might kiss me. "You'll speak to her?"

"I'll try."

"Go now." He led me to the door. He didn't open it until he'd made his final plea. "Go now, and when you've succeeded come to me."

"And if I can't?"

"You will. I know you, and I know her."

He showed me into the waiting hall and thanked me. Outside I stood on the steps of Brigham's house for some time. I could see into the window of his office. He was behind his desk, conducting business and negotiating something or other with his next visitor. Might've been a railroad deal or a building contract or might've been a bargain concerning a man's soul. It was always from one to the next with Brigham Young.

I went to Ann Eliza's house. I found her in the kitchen, feeding the boys. They were fussing over the food and throwing peas about, and my sister looked harried. "What is it?" she said. I told her I'd come back later. I went to the barn and lay down in the hay loft and lay there for some time thinking. The barn cat came over and curled up on my chest and went to sleep.

In the evening I went back to Ann Eliza. "You look upset about something," she said. I told her I'd come from the Beehive House. I described my conversation with Brigham, and as she came to understand it she became very still and sad.

"I'm leaving tonight," I said.

"Leaving?"

"Before he can kick me out."

"What about Kate and Almira? What about the children?"

"They'll get on. Pa will look after them. I can't stay. Brigham's made that clear."

"What will happen to you after?"

343

"I don't know." My sister wasn't asking about after I left the Utah Territory and the Church. She meant after death in the beyond. We understood eternity to be a welcoming place only for the Saints. This is what we believed. It's all we knew to believe to be true.

"You can't," she said.

"I don't have a choice."

"I do," she said.

"I won't let you."

"I've made up my mind."

"Ann Eliza, please—" I pleaded with my sister for an hour or more but she had made her decision. I didn't want her to, I never wanted her to, but I'm an honest man and I will admit here down in the deepest crevice of my heart I felt a throb of relief. I dislike myself for feeling it, but it's true.

The next day Ann Eliza accepted Brigham's proposal and soon they married and that's how my sister became the 19th wife. If it weren't for me it would never have been so, and this is the truth as far as I know it and I swear by it, and for this I've never felt more ashamed.

XIV

WIFE #19:

OFF THE STRIP

AND I SHOULD HELP YOU BECAUSE—?

So Johnny was gone and Elektra and I were on our own. No big deal, we were used to it. In the morning we drove out to Kanab. It was nice enough—the hot wind and the am radio singing *redneck woman* and the quiet that comes when you're alone.

The Mega Bite wasn't open yet but 5 was behind the counter laying out the cold cuts. The ceiling light cast a sickly green on everything: she was pale and green and the slices of ham and turkey looked green too. Eventually she saw me in the window and came to unlock the door. I told her I wanted a turkey club but she said, "You didn't drive all the way out here for a fucking sandwich."

"Maybe not."

"How's the sleuthing going? Find your killer?"

I told her not yet but in a way that didn't reveal much.

"Got it," she said. "You don't want to share any clues with a girl who's got a fishy story."

"Maybe."

"Save yourself the time, I had nothing to do with it." She stopped. "You know what they say: follow the pussy."

"Isn't it follow the money?"

"Same thing." She finished making the sandwich and pulled a long knife to slice it in half. "You talk to my mom yet?"

"Yes," I said. "Did you talk to her?"

"Not in a while. How is she?"

"Shaken up."

"I know, it's crazy. I think she actually loved the guy." After a moment 5 set her elbow on the counter and planted her chin into the heel of her palm. "While you're out nosing around, I wish you could answer the real mystery."

"What's that?"

"Why?"

"Why what?"

"Why do they keep on believing all that crap? Where's the skepticism? Why don't they ask themselves—just once, that's all it would take—why none of it makes sense?"

"If it's the only thing you know—"

"No, that's not it. I mean, sure, yeah, if it's all you know it's hard to imagine anything else. But I'm talking about something different. I'm talking about why they never once have any suspicion that something's not right. You don't need to know anything to have a doubt. You just need to listen. To yourself. Why are so many people so lousy at listening to themselves?"

"Maybe they're scared."

"Of what?"

"Of death. Of what comes after."

"And I'm not?" The more we talked, the less certain I was of where 5 fit into all this. "That reminds me, there's this website you might want to check out: 19thwife.com. It's some antipolygamy group. I guess they help women escape and do legal work and stuff like that. Maybe they can help your mom. But for all I know it could be a trap. Anyway, check it out. Oops, time to open up. Morning rush." She unlocked the door to let in a man and his college-age son. The boy was all arm and leg, with an Adam's apple the size of a rock. He inhaled his muffin the way you or I would eat a nut. When they were gone, 5 said, "You liked him."

"He was cute, so what?"

"You need to get laid."

"Tell me about it. But first I need to get my mom out of jail."

"I wish I could help you."

348

"Then tell me what you know about that night."

"I already told you: nothing. I wasn't there." I know I blush bad, but 5 went as red as the peppers in the prep tray. "I can't help you," she said. "I don't know anything about what happened to your dad."

"He was your dad too."

"Stepdad. Look, I got to get to work. See you around." She shouldered her way through the swinging doors, into the kitchen with the canned tomatoes and a fresh delivery of presliced ham.

On my way back to St. George, a cop pulled me over. I was going eight, maybe ten miles above the limit, but that's not what this was about. We both knew it, each of us sitting behind our wheels at the side of the road. The cop stayed in his cruiser for a long time doing paperwork. His lightbars were spinning blue and red, and they got Elektra jumping around barking at the rear window and the fur on her back was up like a brush.

The brim of the cop's hat hid his face and the late morning sun made it hard to see anything. When he stepped out of the cruiser the sun was behind him and all I could see was a black cutout coming toward me. Elektra lost it, showing her teeth and howling like she was ready to sacrifice herself in my defense. I tried to calm her but she sensed I was scared. "It's all right," I said, but you can't lie to dogs.

"I'm sure you know why I'm pulling you over."

"Why don't you tell me."

Elektra shoved her snout out the window and began licking the cop's hand. "Hello, puppy." I handed him my license. He cupped it in his hand almost like it was something delicate that might blow away, then handed it back. "Here you go, Jordan."

"My registration's in here somewhere," I said.

"That's all right. Why don't you step out of the van."

"Why?"

"Just step out of the van."

"OK."

"Now let's go back to the station."

"Why? "

"C'mon, leash up the dog and let's go."

"I'm not going anywhere."

"Jordan." The guy touched my arm. He looked familiar, but almost everyone in Mesadale looks familiar. He was about thirty, a regular guy in decent shape, like a JCPenney underwear model. "I think it's time you and I had a talk."

When I got out of the van, I saw who I was dealing with. Shield number 714, Mesadale Police Department, Alton. Well, there you go.

"Is something wrong with Queenie?"

"She's fine. Everything's fine. You and I just need to have a little chat."

"Can't we talk right here?"

"C'mon, let's go." I got Elektra on her leash and we followed Alton back to the cruiser. The lightbars were still spinning and Elektra was tugging at the leash. She didn't like any of this and she didn't want to get in the car. The highway was empty and it was eleven in the morning and I'd bet a buck it was already 110 out on the asphalt. The poor girl, her paws must've been burning up.

Elektra and I rode in back, watching the road through the grill. This was my first time in the back of a police cruiser, and you know what—it sucks. There's something about looking out at the world through a steel grille. Even if you haven't done anything, you feel guilty. A voice came across the police radio and Alton spoke into his mike, saying something about home.

"Am I under arrest?" I asked.

Officer Alton laughed. "You're not under arrest."

"I know, silly mistake, crazy me. It's just that I'm in the back of a cruiser talking to you through a fucking cage."

350

He didn't say anything else until we pulled into the police station lot. "Just follow me."

"What about Elektra?"

"Bring her in."

I walked with her close at my side while Alton kept me close to his. His hand was at my elbow, but it was a weird proximity. It wasn't like I was being apprehended, but it wasn't like I was free.

"Do you want to tell me what's going on?" I said.

"In a minute."

In the station we passed a desk manned by a cop who looked like Alton, only redder in the face. "I'm going into three," Alton said.

"What do you got?"

"POI."

"I'll tell the captain."

Officer Alton shook his head. "Not yet. Let me figure out what he is."

"Want me to take the dog?"

Alton shook his head. "We'll keep her." He led me down a hall into a small room with a table and two plastic chairs. "Have a seat."

"I get it," I said. "Interrogation room number three."

"This isn't an interrogation."

"What's that—a two-way mirror?"

"It is."

"Who's on the other side? The whole police force?"

"No."

"Maybe the Prophet himself?"

Alton dragged a chair around so it was next to the other and sat down.

He set his hat on the table and his forehead was dented with a red band. "Fine, don't sit. But I thought it would be more comfortable for you. Jordan, would you stop looking at the mirror. No one's on the other side."

"I'm not quite ready to believe you."

"Maybe you should."

"Why don't you first tell me what this is all about."

"I know you've been to see my wife."

I once saw a movie about this guy accused of killing his girlfriend. When they hauled him in he kept saying to himself, Don't say anything, don't say anything. He thought it so hard that those words appeared on the two-way mirror and for the rest of the interrogation he kept looking at those words. In the end, the cops got nothing and they had to let him go. The thing was, the guy actually killed his girlfriend, strangled her with her sweater, and that's how it ended, the guy being released into the world.

"Jordan?"

"Yeah."

"Queenie told me you wanted to know why the investigation's still open."

"You checked the no box."

"Can I talk to you not as a member of law enforcement, but as a"—he searched for the word—"as a friend. The Prophet, he wanted me to talk to you."

"Me?"

"He thinks you're right."

"Right about what?"

"He thinks someone else killed your dad."

This was either going really well or I was totally fucked. "Why does he think that?"

"Because it doesn't make sense to him either. Your mom, she never liked making a fuss. Why would she start now? The Prophet knows you've been snooping around. Turns out he's got the same questions as you."

"So why'd you bring me here?"

"You look like you could use something to drink. I'll be right back."

When he left I looked at myself in the mirror. My eyes were what I saw—not my hair or my nose or my skinny arms. Just my eyes. They seemed to float on the smoked glass.

Alton came back with two waxed paper cups of apple juice. He set the cups on the table and I took mine. It was a small cup, like what you use at a water cooler. The juice was golden pink and clear. Alton gulped his down and swiped his mouth with the back of his hand. "Man, I love apple juice." And then, "You're not drinking yours?"

Now might be a good time to tell you about the vitamins. Sometimes at school they would pass out vitamins. Each kid got a waxed paper cup with a pink vitamin rolling around the bottom. Once I remember they passed out cups with a pink powder in it. The room monitor filled each cup with apple juice and made us drink it. He said it was fluoride for our teeth, but it tasted like baking soda. The vitamins made you feel groggy and you'd go kinda blank for a couple of hours. Not exactly passed out, but not really there either. I still don't know why they did that to us. Maybe they played more of the Prophet's tapes while we were drugged, with him talking about murder and stuff like that. Maybe they raped the girls. I really don't know. Once I saw a kid refuse to take his vitamin. They hauled him out into the school courtyard to lash him with a horsewhip. He still refused. That night he was kicked out. The chance of that kid still being alive is slim to none.

I pushed the cup away. "No thanks."

"You sure?"

"So the Prophet thinks I might be right about my mom?"

"That's right, and that leaves him concerned."

"I have a hard time believing he's concerned about my mom rotting in jail."

"Well, that too, but what I mean is, if she didn't do it, the killer's still out there."

"And he's scared he might be next on the list."

"In a nutshell, yes." Alton leaned forward, his face close to mine. I could smell his sweat and the white-bar soap he used to wash his hands. "He thought maybe you and he could help each other."

"Let me get this straight: the guy excommunicates me and now he wants my help?"

"You might want his as well."

"I doubt it."

"He knows everything about this town, where everyone is, who's doing what, everything."

"Everything except who killed my dad."

"Look, you both want the same thing. You want your mom out of jail and the Prophet wants the killer. It's a win-win."

"No such thing. Give me one good reason why I should make a deal with the guy who ruined my life."

"Because he could save your mom."

He handed me a slip of paper with a phone number on it. The handwriting was so bad you'd think a six-year-old had scrawled it out. I pushed it back to him. "Keep it," he said, but I already had it memorized.

"You'll take me back to my van?"

Elektra and I followed him down the hall and out the station door. Overhead the sun blazed, reflecting against the white concrete, and for a second everything flashed white and I couldn't see. I lost my way and had to reach for Alton.

"Here," he said. "Take this," and the cop offered his big stone of a hand.

Welcome to 19thwife.com! We're the only online community (as far as we know!) of explural wives (and their children) telling THE TRUTH about polygamy in America today! We take our name from Ann Eliza Young, who fought to end polygamy in the US in the 19th century. She was a totally bad-ass chick! To join, <u>click here</u>. To read, scroll down.

Posted by GirlNumber5 (July 2)

Can someone please explain to me how the LDS guys go around saying all the Doctrine & Covenants are the word of God and that Joseph Smith heard them through revelation but put an asterisk on that because it turns out Joseph was all wrong about the one that deals with polygamy. Huh? So if that one's a mistake, what's to say all the others are true? I mean, isn't that why the Firsts, as much as I hate them, in some ways don't they actually make more sense than the Mormons? They believe in all the D&Cs, they don't pick and choose. How can the Mormons go around *editing* God? If you ask me, it proves the whole thing, whether LDS or Firsts or whatever, is a piece of crap. But I'm open to persuasion (doubtful).

(<u>11 responses</u>)

Posted by KADeeBYU (July 6)

There's a big difference in what you're talking about. First of all you're taking everything out of context. Second the D&C

you're referring to, Section 132, was revised and repudiated by President Woodruff, when he released his Manifesto on October 6, 1890. What you're not understanding is that our theology is not static. It's an evolving, changing entity, which is wholly consistent with the way things work in life. Why should religious doctrine be static when nothing in the natural world, including Man, is static? Throughout time, in every culture, religions and theologies of all sects and creeds have always evolved. They have to. Those that don't inevitably die out. Please don't make the mistake of equating the Latter-day Saints of today with the Firsts. Although our faiths originate from the same doctrines, long ago we chose separate paths, which is why we now stand so far apart.

Posted by GirlNumber5 (July 7)

Huh? Either the D&Cs are the word of God or they aren't. You can't have it both ways, Baby.

A FRIEND IN THE NIGHT

As soon as my cell picked up a signal, I called Maureen. "Why would the Prophet want my help?"

No response.

"Maureen, what do you think?"

"I'm sorry, my granddaughter and her roommate are here visiting. We're out on the patio and it's hard to hear."

"I know I probably shouldn't call you on a Saturday. I just felt like telling someone about this."

"And I'm glad you did. I know Mr. Heber will want to hear all about it on Monday. Or will you be back in California by then?"

"I don't know."

"Either way, let him know." I heard a splash, like someone jumping in a pool. "I should go now."

"Maureen, is everything all right?" She said everything was fine, but I could tell it wasn't, not really.

When Elektra and I walked into A Woman Sconed, the goth girl barely looked up from her manga. "The computer's down," she said. "You can try the lobby of the Malibu Inn, they have a computer for guests. Just go in and pretend you're staying there. They won't say anything if you act cool. The day manager's chill. Hey, where's your brother?"

"He's not my brother."

"I know the feeling," and she flipped a page.

It was that time of day when few people are around a place like the Malibu Inn. Last night's guests had checked out and tonight's were still on the road. The guy behind the desk said, "Can I help you?"

"I'm just going to use the computer for a second."

"Are you staying with us?"

"Not really."

"The computer's for guests only."

"Since no one's around would you mind if I hopped on for a few minutes? I need to check my email."

He was a neat guy, his polo tucked snugly into ironed khakis. Maybe twenty-five, yellow hair flicked up into little gelled spikes—nothing too punk, but just a tiny bit cool. "Oh, all right," he said. "But if a guest needs to use it, you'll have to get off."

"Fair enough."

The way the computer was set up, my back was to him. It was an old machine and it took a while to get a connection. I could feel the guy's eyes on me, and just when I felt like I needed to turn around he said, "By the way, my name's Tom. In case you need anything."

"Thanks. Jordan here."

At last I got into my email box. A message from Alexandra with lots of chatter about her cats and kids and a guarantee: "I make a mean macaroni." Tons of spam, but my program filters most of it out. That's how I ended up deleting the email from DesertMissy. I only know about it now. Had I opened it, I would've saved myself a lot of trouble and close to five hundred credit card bucks in gas. But let's put that on hold.

"I thought you might want a Coke." I was so startled by the gesture, I didn't respond. "Or a Diet Coke?"

"If you have one, yeah."

"Sure, that's what I drink, too." The guy dropped two tokens into the Coke machine. "So where's home for you?"

"California."

"Nice. Me, I'm originally from Provo, but I've been down here a while."

He seemed to want to talk about his life and I didn't want to talk about mine, so I let him go. "I started out in room service at the property in Cedar City. That was five years ago.

358

Then I became a night clerk and eventually assistant manager, and then the owner transferred me down here. He set me up pretty well. You know what the crazy part is?" I couldn't imagine. "I was planning on leaving Utah. Probably for California. Like you."

"Maybe one day."

"I mean, St. George isn't exactly the dream location for a single gay guy."

Was I being hit on in the lobby of the Malibu Inn?

"LDS?" he said.

"Sort of," I said. "But not anymore."

"Yeah, me too. I was kicked out when I was twenty. What about you? Did they kick you out or did you quit before they could do it?"

"I was definitely kicked out."

"I know, I was so shocked because I wasn't even really out to myself." The guy stopped, as if all the thoughts about his past were pressing inside his head. Then his eyes returned to the present moment. "What're you doing later on? Want to get together or something? I'm off at six." I tried to make an excuse, but I came up blank. "Meet me here around seven. Room 112. We'll go out."

"You live here?"

"Yeah, they put me up. It's not as nice as it sounds." Tom appeared so cleanhearted and gentle that I felt something stir in my chest, and I was shocked by the sentiment. I'm definitely not a romantic kind of guy. The last time I had a date was never.

"Awesome. I'm really looking forward to it. Now I should get back to work. They start rolling in about now." On cue, a dusty motor home pulled into the Malibu's portico.

I was headed over to the pool when I saw Mr. Heber's Lexus in his office lot. I had to ring twice before he came to the door. He looked surprised to see me. Surprised to see anyone.

359

He was in a pair of golf shorts and bare feet, and his reading glasses up on his head. "I'm sorry to disturb you on Saturday," I said, "but I saw your car."

"That's all right. I try to sneak in here for a few hours on the weekend to get ahead."

While he led me back to his office, I told him about Alton and the Prophet. "What do you think?"

"I want you to be careful, Jordan."

"Do you think I should talk to him?"

"That might be hard to do."

"Why's that?"

"I was going to tell you this on Monday. The Prophet's now officially a wanted man. The feds finally got off their duffs and put out a warrant for his arrest. He's wanted on sexual assault on a minor, conspiracy to commit sexual assault on a minor, and racketeering. They went out to Mesadale last night."

"He's in jail?"

"They couldn't find him."

"Couldn't find him? He was right there yesterday afternoon."

"I'm sure he was, but no one's talking. Here, let me show you." Mr. Heber turned his monitor and got onto the FBI's site. On the Wanted by the FBI page, there was a grainy picture of the Prophet. He wasn't on the Most Wanted list, but he was a Featured Fugitive, and his picture was right beneath Osama bin Laden's.

"That's an old picture," I said.

"It's all they got." He clicked on it and brought up the Prophet's rap sheet.

DESCRIPTION

DATE OF BIRTH USED: August 19 1936 or December 25 1941 or December 25 1946
PLACE OF BIRTH: Unknown
HEIGHT: 5'7" or 5'9"

360

WEIGHT: 145–155 pounds
OCCUPATION: Unknown
SCARS OR MARKS: None known
HAIR: Brown/light brown or gray
EYES: Blue or gray
SEX: Male
RACE: White
REMARKS: Suspect may be residing in or around Mesadale, Utah; also has ties to Arizona, Nevada, Texas, Idaho, and northern Mexico

SHOULD BE CONSIDERED ARMED AND DANGEROUS

"Why now?"

"I told you, things've been heating up. Your dad's murder was probably the catalyst. I think they finally realized this is about a lot more than a man sleeping with a bunch of women. Anyway, Jordan, it could all be very good news for your mom."

This seemed like as good a time as any to tell Heber about my visit to the house. I didn't go into details like the fire. "But I managed to get down to his den, and I found this."

I handed him the fuck chart disguised as the Book of Mormon. Mr. Heber fanned through it, stopped to read something, fanned some more. "I already have it. They found it during the search on his hard drive." He dug around in a file and pulled a stack of papers to compare the two copies, flipping between the pages.

"You mean I went through all that to get something you already have?"

"You really should've talked to me first." He kept on flipping between the two charts, matching up the tables and the notations. Then something caught his attention. "Wait a minute, you might have the latest version. Let me make a copy."

We leaned against the copier, waiting for it to warm up.

"There's something that's been bugging me about all this," Mr. Heber said.

"What's that?"

"How many wives did your dad actually have?"

"I don't know, twenty-five-ish. But they never tell you that. I think it's a way to keep everything confused. You know, the more confused you are, the less likely you are to realize you're being screwed."

"What's interesting about this marriage management notebook is, if we can believe it—and I think we can—it looks like he had twenty-seven wives." The copier was ready, and he lifted the lid.

"I know this is going to sound screwy," I said, "but if the law doesn't recognize these marriages, then how can it be polygamy in the eyes of the law? It's sort of a chicken-egg situation."

"It's an old dilemma. Goes back to the nineteenth century and Brigham. It's probably why the feds left Mesadale alone for so long. You can see why they're going after the Prophet for racketeering and the stuff with the underage girls. They can get him on that."

"If they catch him."

"The thing about men like the Prophet is they need a stage. They need to tell people what to do. That kind of man can't stay in hiding forever. When he's all alone in a basement or an attic or wherever, he can't run from the truth about himself. He'll come out," said Mr. Heber. "They always do. And when he does, they'll catch him and then it's welcome to the clink."

"And my mom?"

"I'm working on it."

"Any luck?"

"To tell the truth, I'm afraid not."

* * *

362

Tom opened the door to Room 112 and a snowy-faced golden retriever lumbered off the bed. He was a gentle old guy with a white muzzle and a plumed tail. He lifted his paw to scratch my thigh. "That means he likes you," said Tom.

"What's his name?"

"Gosling's Joseph Manna from Heaven."

"What?"

"But everyone calls him Joey."

"He looks like a good boy."

"He is. When I got kicked out I took Joey with me. He's literally the only thing I have from home. I'm lucky Mr. Saluja lets me keep him here, I mean I've had him since I was eleven. Oh, my gosh, I just realized: I don't even know if you like dogs."

"If I like dogs? Hang on a sec." I went out to fetch Elektra from the van. She sensed something was up and switched into a higher gear of spaz, straining on her leash and barking, preparing for a big entrance. She dog-sledded me across the parking lot and exploded into Room 112 in a whirl of canine chaos. You know how dogs get so excited they can't decide what to do? Elektra jumped on the bed, off the bed, back on the bed, slurped out of Joey's water bowl, ran over to Tom with water running out of her jowls, leaped into the air to kiss him, then back to the bowl, back to the bed, and back to Tom's feet, back to the bed, and so on. "Sorry, she's a little nuts at first."

"I never met a dog I didn't love." Joey, on the other hand, wasn't so interested in Elektra. He scooted over to the far side of the bed and lay down with his snout on his paws.

"What do you feel like doing tonight?" said Tom. "Want to catch a movie?" He was still getting dressed, tucking his shirt into his pants and looping his belt. It was weird to think he lived in a motel room, but I guess no weirder than living out of a van. He started looking up the movie times on his laptop. He was sitting and I leaned over from behind. Turns out he's the kind of guy who wears cologne, which I usually hate, but on him it was sorta nice. Cinnamon and cedar. Maybe some lemon and smoke.

"Don't hate me if it's lame," he said, "but I kinda want to see that movie about the retarded kid and the missing dad."

We got ready to leave, filling the dog bowls with water and telling them to be good, and there was a tiny moment when we looked at each other. We were thinking the same thing, we could kiss and fuck right now and skip the movie. But I don't know, it didn't seem like the right thing to do, which totally isn't like me. Anyway, outside in the parking lot there was a little tussle over who should drive—he thought my van looked cool, but I didn't want him in my van because, well, I was living out of it and that's probably not the best information to reveal on a first date. In the end I won and we drove to the cineplex in his tidy Toyota.

"So what happened with you and the church?" he said.

"It's a little complicated."

"It always is." He was fiddling with the radio, stopping when he found a song by the Killers. "For me it happened my sophomore year. I was at BYU, and you know what that place can be like. I was up in Salt Lake with my soccer team and one night I just kind of gave in and went to a gay bar. It was my first time ever in a place like that. I mean, I hadn't even kissed a guy or anything, but I knew, and I wanted to go. And guess what: someone saw me. I'm still not sure who, but they sent an anonymous letter to my bishop outing me. The bishop sent a really scary letter to my parents and it was a total flippin' mess."

"That sucks."

"What about you? Did you have a trial?"

"Not exactly."

"I did. I mean, the works. I had to go before this committee who were all these guys I've known my whole life like my soccer coach and the guy who used to drive my carpool. And they were all sitting behind this table and I was sitting on this metal folding chair and they just came out and asked me—was I a homosexual? On my way into the trial I thought I was going to lie. It never occurred to me to confess, because I knew what that would mean. Good-bye life as you know it. But when they asked the question like that, and it really did feel like a trial and everything, it just hit me: I can't lie, not if it's true. So I said, Yes. My coach said, Do you know what this means? And again I said, Yes. Nothing more. And so he goes, Do you realize with this confession you'll lose many things, but none more important than the salvation of your soul? And so you know what I said? I said, What do you want me to do about it? And that was it. Excommunicated. My parents cut me off. And that's how I ended up at the Malibu Inn. The owner's from India, and he doesn't care about anything except how I do my job."

"That's messed up."

"Tell me about it. But it had to happen. There are a lot of things I don't know, but one thing I know for sure is those men weren't speaking for God. They say they were, but they weren't. God isn't like that, not my God, anyway." He turned into the cineplex parking lot. "Now what about you?"

"The thing is," I said, "I'm actually not LDS. I'm a First. Or was. I'm from Mesadale."

"A First? No kidding. That's crazy. You mean like a gazillion wives and everything?"

"Yep, a gazillion wives and everything."

Almost anyone will tell you if your mom's in jail for killing your dad, it's probably a bad idea to talk about it on the first date. Which is probably why I told Tom everything right there in the cineplex lot. When I finished he said, "Shoot, that's a lot to deal with." And then, "There's no way this movie's going to be more interesting than our own lives."

He was right, the movie wasn't any good—a retarded kid, an absent father, a bitter reunion, a reconciliation. None of it true. Halfway through I took Tom's hand. It felt like the hand of a gentle, capable man. I was pretty surprised that such a hand belonging to such a man was warming up in my clutch, but there it was and here we were and some things sour only if you think about them too much. During the credits, just before the lights came up, Tom leaned over to kiss me.

"I think I like you," he said.

And that's when I heard Johnny say, "No PDA, dude."

I turned around. Two rows back, Johnny's eyes shined in the dark. He was alone, his t-shirt filthy with popcorn. Slowly the house lights came up on his jackass smile and he said, "Aren't you going to introduce me to your man?"

Some of Brigham's wives developed a system of private communication within the Lion House. Two sister wives, or sometimes more, would circulate a copy of the Book of Mormon, into which they would crosshatch a private conversation about topics such as their children, the other wives, and domestic business like cooking, keeping house, and social gossip heard at Brigham's store. Most often, however, the subject was their mutual husband, Brigham. On file here is an approximate transcript of a private dialogue between two of Brigham's wives written in a kind of shorthand across the pages of the Book of Alma. From the events discussed we know it dates to the spring of 1868, shortly before Brigham's marriage to Ann Eliza Webb. Due to the cramped, unnatural style of handwriting, we cannot identify with any certainty which of Brigham's wives wrote these words.

—He's after another.
—It was only a matter of time. Does Amelia know?
—I doubt it. He'll tell her only when it's too late.
—I'd like to see her face when she finds out she has a new rival. So much for everlasting beauty.
—Guess who the new one is.
—I'm not familiar with the girls of Salt Lake.
—Remember the actress?
—Say it isn't so. She thinks she's the queen of something.
—I hope she enjoys her position at Number 19.

—I thought he tried to reel her in before, but the fish fought him on the line.

—I heard he set a trap for her.

—She'll make a fine counterpoint to Amelia.

—That's the only consolation. He was always longing for her, wasn't he? Even when she lived here, his eyes always followed her around the room.

—He never knows when his eyes are popping out of his head.

—If only it were his eyes sticking out from his person.

—I'd scold you if it wasn't true.

—Although I see a silver lining in the arrival of the 19th.

—What?

—He's less likely to come knocking on my door.

—He hasn't knocked on mine in eight years.

—See, Brigham is correct—God does indeed answer our prayers!

"Every Sunday?" I said.

"Every Sunday," said Tom. "Ten a.m."

It was eight in the morning and we were on our way to Vegas for—you're not going to believe this—church.

"What if you're tired?"

"I drag my rear out of bed and I go. That's what it means to make a commitment."

"But Vegas? For church?"

"What's a two-hour drive when it's something you believe in? Besides, what else am I going to do on a Sunday morning?"

"I don't know, lie in bed and fuck?"

"You know what I mean." He rocked my shoulder the way you do when someone's told a good joke. "Besides, I love this drive. Look at those mountains. You know God's been hard at work when you see those."

OK, so we weren't a perfect match. I didn't expect this to last long anyway. They never do. But we'd had a good time last night. I stayed over at the Malibu and Tom put Johnny up in a room next door and, well, we got up early for church.

"So this church," I said. "It's for gay Mormons?"

"It's actually for anyone, but that's generally who comes."

"Isn't a gay Mormon like an oxymoron?"

"Do I look like an oxymoron to you?"

"An oxymormon."

"I think you'll find it's a really nice place."

"I don't get it. If the Mormons don't want you in their church, why do you want to be in their church?"

"I don't want to be in their church. I want my faith. That's all. I don't need to go to their temples to have my faith."

Out on East Sahara Boulevard, two miles off the strip, we pulled into a strip mall. The church shared a parking lot with an insurance agent, a massage parlor, and a head shop. Tom turned off the engine and kissed me. "Happy fifteen-hour anniversary."

"This is by far the longest relationship I've ever had."

"Are you always this romantic?"

"Usually."

"Come on, let's go inside. And try to enjoy yourself."

"I'll try, but church and I have some bad blood."

"That wasn't a church, that was a cult. You can't let one con man with a thing for teenage girls go and ruin all the love Christ put in your life."

Should I go home now? I didn't say that, it'd be too cruel. Tom was too good for that sort of ridicule. Besides, he didn't talk about Jesus all the time. Just often enough to make me wonder if we'd last another fifteen hours.

"Look, I know you're always internally rolling your eyes when I talk about God—I can see it, Jordan—but I'm sorry, that's just who I am." He kissed me again. "Besides, I know that's what you like about me, deep down, I can see it behind your sneer."

Who was this guy? I could go over his physical inventory, his green eyes and how they changed to gray at night, his Matt Damon smile, a mouth literally crammed with teeth, his slim waist and grabable ass. Is that why I spent the night with him in Room 112? Or was it an even more basic need: he had a bed and a shower and a tv, and he liked kids and dogs, especially Elektra, who right now was curled up on a wide motel mattress in front of the a/c with the tv on and kibble in her bowl? Or was it something else?

Tom leaned into the backseat and shook Johnny's arm. "Time to get up, big boy, we're here."

Johnny yawned. "Where?"

"Church, chop-chop."

"You can't be serious?" Johnny sat up halfway and rubbed his eye with a fist. "I thought you were kidding."

"Why else would we drive to Vegas on a Sunday morning?"

"I don't know, hookers?"

"Not today. Now get up."

Johnny flopped back down onto the seat and pulled his Raiders ski cap over his eyes. "Dude, wake me when it's over."

"Tom," I said, "forget it. He'll be fine out here."

"No, no, no. I didn't drive all this way just so you could sleep in the car."

"What difference does it make?"

"Why don't you go in and find out."

"Dude," said Johnny. "You sure you're into this guy?"

"Tell him to get up," said Tom.

They were both looking at me as if I had some control over the situation. "He doesn't listen to me. Let him sleep."

"He's just putting on a show. He wants to go in, he just won't admit it."

Tom got out of the car and opened the back door. He plucked the cap off Johnny's head. The kid's hair shot up with static. "What the fuck?"

"Tom, this is crazy," I said. "We're not his parents. He can do what he wants."

Tom looked a little defeated. "Jordan, it's not going to hurt him to sit there for an hour."

"I don't want to be the only kid," said Johnny.

"You won't be."

"I thought this was a gay church."

"Gays can have kids."

"Tom, man, I hate to break it to you, but you and Jordan aren't having kids, I don't care how hard you try."

"Tom, let's just go inside. He's fine out here." I got out of the car and started walking.

"Then why'd he want to come with us, anyway?"

"Because he didn't want to be alone."

371

We walked through the door, and a man in a leather vest and a bushy mustache descended upon us. "Tom! Who is *this?*"

"This is Jordan. He's my—"

His what?

"My new best friend."

"Jordan, welcome to our church." The man hugged me, which wasn't so unusual because other people were greeting and hugging, but this guy whispered into my ear, "I hope you find the peace and love God wants you to have," while squeezing my ass.

When the guy was gone I said, "He felt me up."

"He did not."

"I'm telling you, he did."

The church looked like a bingo hall or a senior citizens' center. A blank space with a dropped ceiling, bad lighting, and coffee stains in the carpet. The color scheme reminded me of the lobby of the Malibu Inn, purple on beige with hunter green accents. Some queen had stenciled a garland of grapes around the walls. The whole thing depressed me. I know, how does a guy who's been living out of his van get off calling anything tacky? But it was.

Tom waved at a lot of people and they came over to hug him and shake my hand. "You have a lot of friends," I said.

"And what could possibly be wrong with that?"

It's pointless to argue with someone so logical. Still, he seemed to know everyone—the chatty dyke in Hello Kitty suspenders, the diabetic guy on the mobility cart, the kid with the safety pin in his eyebrow who wasn't much older than Johnny. His name was Lawrence; two weeks ago this little church helped him off the streets. "Thanks in part to Tom," he said shyly. Tom denied doing anything out of the ordinary. "All I did was make a phone call. You got the job yourself." Lawrence's patchy, anxious face was an assortment of pimples and whiskers and lingering hurt. He pressed together his courage to tell me, "You're real lucky, man."

When the service started the pastor asked if there were

any special visitors who needed an introduction. "Tom. Please don't."

But it was too late. Tom was on his feet saying he was here with me. The congregation—there were about seventy-five people—said "Hi Jordan" or "Welcome Jordan" or "Amen."

"Jordan," Tom said through his teeth, "stand up."

I rose and lifted my hand for a little wave. Everyone waved back and several people applauded as if I'd actually accomplished something. Am I a hater for cringing?

There were a few other guests there—a mother visiting from Fresno; a friend in from Albuquerque. Everyone waved and called out hello and it was no big deal. Really, what was the point of getting embarrassed? As Tom likes to say, It's just life.

"Before we start," said Pastor Walter, "does anyone have a praise they want to share?"

A slight woman in heavy denim jumped to her feet. "Yes, thanks." She wore a big, out-of-date phone clipped to her belt, a buckle that said, "Kick Ass!" and a pair of hearing aids. "As many of you know, Rusty had his operation this week and thanks to God everything went just fine. He was home the next day and I was able to take the drain out after only four days, even though the vet told me it would take a week." She went on a little longer about Rusty's condition and a lot of people said "Amen" and several people raised their arms as if invisible wires were pulling them from above.

A couple of other people shared their praises—a medical test that came back all right, the return of an estranged child, a new job: the usual stuff that is so common that you sometimes forget these events define our lives. It made me think of something I once read on a billboard: How we spend our days is, of course, how we spend our lives. Is that religion or just plain wisdom?

"Let us now each take a few moments to think about our blessings." That's when Tom put his arm around me. The pastor concluded the moment of silence by declaring, "I personally want to thank God for our new second bathroom! Brothers and Sisters, it's finally finished!" More applause and a lot of amens. "No more sharing a single toilet with a hundred people!"

If you haven't been to church in a while, you might forget how much chatter there is about day-to-day business—the newsletter, the board elections, the day care. I guess it makes sense. It's probably why a lot of people bother: the organization, the community, the belonging, the having something to do. A lot of the people here looked like they'd had a hard time fitting in—the blind dyke; the six-foot-four-inch tranny; the hairy bear ravaged by HIV; this kid, Lawrence. As if he were reading my mind, the pastor said, "Most of all, I want to thank God for our sanctuary where everyone is welcome, and where everyone is loved."

The pastor spoke with a curious accent I couldn't quite place, southern regal, something like that. He wore his longish hair oiled back so that it bunched up in little curls at the nape. He was about forty-five, elegantly handsome, and clearly had the admiration of his congregation.

There's no point in my recounting the service. Except for the lesbian couple passing the offering trays and the ushers in leather chaps and the shy tranny giving communion, it was more or less familiar. If it had a theological point of view, it was that Christ loves everyone and that Joseph Smith was right—the churches of the world had moved away from Christ's true message of universal love. Look at these people here—they were proof of it. "This is why I still believe," Tom whispered. "This is why I don't need their temples."

He pointed out a quotation in the bulletin:

The one who comes to me, I will certainly not cast out (John 6:37).

(Under that it said, "Please note: All communion stations use grape juice.")

Next the deacon stood up to give the sermon. "Today I want to talk about love," she said. Her name was Irene, and she was a sincere person with a limp, practical face. Soon her voice turned to noise in my ear because she was saying what you'd expect: love is the greatest gift, and God's greatest gift to man was Jesus, and that shows how much he loves us, blog, blog, blog.

"But instead of me telling you what I think love is, I decided to ask my students. So here's how a few first, second, and third graders define love." She flipped nervously through her notes.

"The first one's from Christie, who's only seven: 'Last year when my grandma fell and broke her hip she couldn't paint her toenails anymore. So my grandpa started doing it for her, even after he fell and broke his hip, too. For me, that's love.' " Everyone laughed and it was so sad and ridiculous I chuckled too.

"And Benjamin, who's just six, describes it like this: 'I know someone loves me from how they say my name. Like with my mom and dad, when they say "Benjamin" it's like my name is safe in their mouth.' " More laughter, and a couple of sentimental aaahs.

"And Catherine, age six, came up with this definition: 'For the people I love, I'll always give them the last bite of my ice cream without asking for the last bite of theirs.' "

"And Nancy, who's only seven but already a wise soul, says, 'I think the best way to learn how to love someone is to start with someone you hate.' "

And then Irene said the one that caused me—forgive me— to go to mush inside: "Melanie, who's just four years old, says, 'When my doggy licks my face, even after I've left her outside all day—I know that's love.' "

I couldn't take it anymore. Not because they were so corn-dog, which they were, but because they were true. Kids. They always call it as it is. I hated feeling this way. The combo of love and God was supposed to make me puke—so why were my eyes getting all misty?

Two things happened that morning in the Vegas LGBT-friendly ex–Mormon church two miles off the strip (try saying that real fast).

First, I got to sit through a sermon holding Tom's hand. Big fucking deal, I know, but where in the world do you get to do that? Not many places that call themselves houses of the Lord.

Tom leaned over. "Isn't this nice?"

The second thing was this: halfway through the sermon, the back door opened. Irene stopped and waved. "Come in, don't be shy." It was Johnny, his Raiders cap pulled low on his brow. He climbed over a woman to sit between Tom and me.

"You're such a player," I whispered.

"You know it, dude."

Then he listened as Irene read even more definitions of love.

"Oh, and I really like this one from Justine, who just turned eight: 'You should be careful about saying "I love you" too much. If you don't really mean it the words will lose their value. But if you do mean it, then you can go ahead and say it all the time.' "

"There," said Tom when we were back in the car. "That wasn't so bad."

"Do they always have doughnuts?" Johnny was laying out four apple fritters on the backseat, taking inventory the way a dog hoards his bones.

"They like people to stick around after. They're really into being a community. So what'd you think?"

"I don't know," I said.

"Is that a good 'I don't know' or a bad 'I don't know'?"

"It's an 'I don't know' I don't know. I mean, I'm still not sure it's for me."

"That's OK, as long as you understand that it's for me." He was pulling onto the freeway, maneuvering into the fast lane. For such a clean guy, he was a bit of a maniac driver. "Utah, here we come." He started fiddling with the radio, searching for NPR. "Boy, do I love Sundays. So what do you want to do when we get back? Go swimming? Or we could go for a hike when it cools down."

"I'm not really much of a hiker. I don't really like the desert."

"Around here," said Johnny, "that's like a fucking problem."

"Want to catch a movie?"

"I might have some things to do," I said.

"Jordan, is anything wrong?"

I don't know about you, but I hate the phrase *nicest guy in the world*. As in, *I just met the nicest guy in the world*. As if. But now it seemed true. So why was I being such an ass?

"I was just thinking about my mom," I said.

"When can you see her next?"

"Tuesday. That is, if I'm still around. I have a job that starts tomorrow in Pasadena."

Tom didn't say anything but a man doesn't have to speak to reveal his wound. After a while he pulled over at a parking area. He got out and walked several yards into the desert. Johnny ran after him and unzipped a few yards from Tom. He was talking over his shoulder, yapping about something or other, then a gust of wind came along, billowing the arc of his piss. Johnny laughed and kept on talking and shook off and hopped over to Tom's side for the walk back to the car. He was very small next to Tom, a pipsqueak of a kid looking way up into the eyes of a man. Tom rubbed Johnny's head. When he pulled his hand away, the spring of Johnny's cowlick popped back up.

Johnny fell asleep for the rest of the drive and Tom stayed quiet. Ten minutes before St. George, we cut through the Virgin River Gorge, and Tom said, "I want you to stay."

I didn't say anything. Not a word. When we pulled into the Malibu, Tom said, "I see."

He and Johnny went swimming. I stayed in Room 112 with the dogs and went online to check out that site 5 was talking about. It was a community/resource page for people dealing with polygamy one way or another. I clicked the tab that said, If You Need Help. Tom had left the History Channel on, and

377

while I read the website a navy crew was preparing to launch a missile from the deck of a battleship. When the missile was fired, a white yellow plume of fire shot out of its tail. That's when Tom came back to the room, dripping in his suit. The missile's fire flashed in his face. He watched it until the missile hit its target, blowing up a warehouse in the desert. "I was going to enlist," he said. "After college. Wanted to be an admiral."

"Really? Why?"

"I wanted to serve my country. But my country didn't want me." He changed into dry clothes, then lay down on the bed. "What're your plans?"

"I'm going back," I said.

"To California?"

"To Mesadale."

"All right."

"I mean now."

"I'll go with you."

"No, you stay with Johnny."

"We'll all go."

"I should go by myself."

"Should, or want to?"

"I don't know." You know what's the craziest part of living in a house with a hundred people? It trains you to be alone.

"You sure it's safe?"

"No."

"Let me go with you."

"No, you stay here."

"Jordan?"

"What?"

"What are you looking for?" I tried to answer, but the words didn't come. Lying on his side, his head resting on his elbow, he looked too pure to be a part of my messed-up world. "I know what you're thinking," he said. "You're thinking we hardly know each other. And that's true. But everybody has to start somewhere."

I got up and opened the curtains. They were gold and

backed by a heavy sheet of plastic. Johnny was lying on the concrete rim of the pool, his eyes closed, one foot tapping along to Tom's ipod.

"Jordan, don't overthink everything. You'll talk yourself out of a life."

"This isn't about you, Tom."

"I want you to make it about me."

Later, driving out of St. George, I called the number Alton gave me. "It's Jordan Scott."

There was a pause. Then, "Come to the house." He hung up. That was it. The Prophet and I had a date.

The sun was going down before I reached Mesadale, a livid ball plunging from the sky. The desert was burning, everything shot through with reds. In the last twenty miles I didn't see another car. That's what the desert's about: solitude. It's a test. A test to see if you can stand yourself.

I reached the turnoff. The last of the light was gone now, and the desert cried under the yellow moon. My headlights swept the hard dirt and behind the van the dust coughed up into the black. Up the road the big houses were lit up, gold and white lights in the windows and above the doors. How many did the feds knock on before they gave up? One more and would they have found their man? Taken the Prophet in? Booked him? Put him on secure visits like my mom? Why can't the FBI find this guy, while he's inviting me to his house?

Questions lead to questions. Answers aren't really answers. Mysteries don't get solved. Isn't that what it's all about? Knowing almost nothing. Accepting the unknowable as the end of the story? The end of life?

Maybe.

But if so, then why did I believe in the bottom of my heart I was this close to finding out who shot my dad and stuck the rap on my mom?

XV

THE PROPHET'S WIFE

THE 19TH WIFE

CHAPTER SIXTEEN
My Wedding Day

On April 6, 1868, I married Brigham Young in a secret ceremony in the Endowment House. The only witness was the old-timer Bishop who performed the rites. In a matter of minutes, I had become a Mrs. Brigham Young.

My first task as the Prophet's wife was to accompany him to a small community across the Valley that had found itself torn apart by tragedy. A few days before, two boys, brothers no less, had drowned in a swollen creek. The boys' mother had begged her local Bishop for an explanation, but the man had failed to console the woman in her time of grief. His inadequacy set off a public meeting of complaints about the Church, Brigham, and the unreliability of God. "What will you say to these people?" I asked Brigham as we drove to the meeting.

"I'll tell them what I know," he said. "And what I don't know, which is a lot. It's all I can do."

Our marriage was one hour old, and I found myself touched by Brigham's willingness to reveal his modesty to me. Brigham pushed his face out the carriage window to take in the breeze. The day was clear and cold, and the afternoon light colored the snow on the western mountains blue and on the eastern front the snow was pink and gold. Watching him, I must confess to a certain fondness, in the way one might feel toward an old, not especially close acquaintance who has maneuvered a place into the heart simply through the longevity of his presence.

As we approached our destination, the shadows off the mountains darkened great patches of the Valley and Brigham became somber. "I read the report," he said, staring at the empty space before him. "The two boys struggled for some time. The mother watched them cling to a branch. She wanted to jump in herself, but her sister wife held her down. Was she right to do so? Was there any chance of saving the boys? I can't blame them for wanting answers."

At the village nearly fifty agitated Saints awaited us. There was not a proper Meeting House, so Brigham stood before the community in the home of a local farmer. "If I could give you the answer that would heal your grief," he said, "and alleviate your sorrow—if I could explain the role of your boys' lives and deaths in the context of all things, then I would not be a man standing before you, then I would be our Heavenly Father Himself. But I am not He, nor is any man He, and therefore I cannot tell you what you so desperately want to know. But over time, with prayer and faith, you will come to understand, and your heart will know, even if your mind cannot, that these boys lived and died with purpose, and now await you in the Kingdom above."

When it was time to depart, the sorrowful mother kissed Brigham's fingers. As our carriage left the little hamlet, she ran behind as far as she could, crying, "God bless you, Brigham, God bless!" Her voice echoed across the blushing land.

For some time the carriage groaned along the rutted road, the wheels creaking, the leather snapping, the driver clicking and calling at his team. We were deep in the basin, surrounded by young scrub and new grass and the lonely cattle bent in search for early leaf. I interrupted our quiet by saying, "May I ask a question?"

"Of course, anything."

"What number am I?"

Brigham reached for my hand to warm it between his. "Number?"

"Which wife?"

384

"It's distasteful to me to put a number next to you, or any woman."

"I appreciate that. But I'd like to know."

"In that case, you are number nineteen."

"Nineteen? What about the others?"

"Others?"

"At the Lion House?"

"They're friends, but not wives."

"But I've heard—"

"Ann Eliza, you'll hear many things now that you're my wife."

"Nineteen, really? That's all?"

"Nineteen. Really. That's all."

As we drove on, dusk poured into the Valley and I fell asleep. When I woke it was dark. "You're a beautiful creature when you sleep," said Brigham, stroking my arm. The carriage curtains had been drawn, and I moved away from my husband to reopen them. The night was without a moon, and the Valley was black and empty. Other than the driver we were alone.

"You don't like me?" said Brigham.

"It's not that."

"Then what?" He shifted toward me, his great bulk tilting the carriage on its groaning springs. The horseman slowed his team, adjusting for the shifting cargo. I suspect he was used to this sort of situation. Lurching closer, Brigham attempted to kiss me. Soon he was on me, crying, "Tell me you've always wanted me as I've wanted you!" He pressed me into the corner of the carriage.

"Brigham, please—" But his animal had been set free from its cage. I turned my head, pressed my cheek to the curtain, and prayed.

Dear Reader!

I speak the truth when I tell you it was at this moment my bodice tore, exposing my sacred undergarments. According to Brigham himself, a woman must never reveal them to a man, even her husband. Eliza Snow had penned a letter to the women of Zion on the subject: "At the time of connubiality, the wife must open a slot in her sacred garments no bigger than necessary to permit the husband his entry. At no time should she preen before him in anything less than what she might wear on the street, nor reveal to neither his eyes nor hands what lay beneath."

Married half a day, I had already violated my husband's doctrines. "Turn the other way," I demanded. "Please don't look at me."

Brigham was stunned, apologizing, "I don't know what happened." He tried to fig-leaf my breast with the torn cloth.

"Turn around!"

"Yes, yes, of course."

His animal had retreated to its lair, and Brigham sat beside me, deflated. "I should drive you home," he said. He rang a bell, his signal, I would later learn, to the horseman to stop circling and head onward to his destination.

When we arrived at my mother's house Brigham said, "I'll send my man in, have your mother come out here, and you can ask her to bring you another garment." He leapt from the carriage. I could hear him speak to the driver, who then trotted to the front door. I could see my mother at her threshold, peering around the man to the carriage. They spoke briefly and she walked with some hesitation to the car.

"Ann Eliza? What is it?"

I explained my predicament. "I see," she said. She went into the house, returning with an old dress. When she entered the carriage she looked around at the velvet and the lamps and the mother-of-pearl inlay, appalled by the luxury. After helping me change, she said, "That should get you from the street to the door."

Brigham tapped the carriage with his walking stick. "Almost ready?"

Through the glass I said, "First I want a word with you." He climbed into the carriage. "Shut the door." He obeyed my command and settled into the seat with an obvious shame. "What has gotten into you?" I demanded.

"I'm sorry, I was overcome. I didn't mean to alarm you, but you can't know how beautiful you are."

"Thank you, but you're not fifteen."

I saw his anger rise, his color deepen, and the eruption begin. Yet he managed to check his passions and the color washed off his face. "I don't mean to offend you."

"It's too late."

"In that case, you'll have to forgive me. That's all I can ask." Brigham Young, the Great Man of the West, had the hurt look of a scolded boy. He stepped down from the carriage and crossed the street, waiting beneath a poplar. An old couple out for a night walk greeted him. They were astonished to see the Prophet in their path. Brigham spoke with them warmly, as if they were old friends, and the couple flattered him, babbling about the quality of his recent sermon.

My mother helped me out of the carriage, but I refused to go inside. I stood at her gate, waiting for my husband's return. "Come on," she said. "Let's go in." Slowly I realized my husband would not say good-bye to me on the street. He stayed with the couple until I was behind the closed door. From inside I watched him run back to the carriage, hopping on his fat tapered legs. The driver snapped his reins. The horses stamped and flicked and lunged. The carriage tore off before Brigham's foot was inside. His arm came out and closed the door behind him, and thus alone I spent my wedding night.

THE 19TH WIFE

CHAPTER SEVENTEEN
The Lonely Wife

I had not seen my husband for three weeks when he came around for a second drive. I tried engaging him in discourse, but he seemed preoccupied in thought. Gradually I came to understand he had not come to engage his new wife in conversation. Once the carriage drew beyond the city limits, Brigham sprang to life, listing across the seat. "Oh, my pet," he moaned, shrugging off his green cape and emitting an odor of the lemon drops he kept in a bowl on his secretary's desk.

Such was our marriage.

For three months our union remained a secret affair. Even my boys knew nothing of their mother's new status. I had wanted to tell them, but I could not bring myself to explain the peculiar circumstances. Often I thought of my mother, who had passed through her youth without shame. Yet in my case, whenever I left my husband after an assignation in the carriage, I carried the humiliation of a second-choice whore. Years later, during our divorce, Brigham would accuse me of demanding money at the end of our interludes, but there is no truth to this claim. I received nothing except a rumpled dress, a dented bonnet, and an urgent need to bathe.

During this time, what for most couples is known as the honeymoon, every Sunday I attended services pretending I had no more relation to Brigham than before. Sunday services in Deseret is a time for society to assert itself, and there is a great fuss put into where one sits and with whom. As a divorced woman, my status was lower than that of a widow or virgin. My secret wedding had changed none of this in the eyes of the community of Saints. I would sit with my mother and the boys on a bench at the back, while Brigham preached to his thousands of followers. Up in front, filling a dozen rows, was the brigade of his family—the wives, the daughters, the sons, their wives, and so on. To them, I was nothing more than one more eager disciple in a land filled with some fifty thousand. They paid me no mind.

Each Sunday, invariably, Brigham's sermon turned to the subject of Truth. Nothing winds Brigham up more than this, and he could spin out an hour's worth on the notion without so much as coming up for breath. As he did so each week, I would stew in a juice of shame and worry. If Truth was the key to Glory, as Brigham proclaimed, what did this mean for me? I took a great disliking to myself during this time, and in my thoughts referred to myself as simply No. 19. There were many times I could not look my boys in the face.

Finally, after months of ignominy, Brigham said he was ready to announce me as his 19th wife. "The first thing to do is establish you in a home suited to your position." He drove me to a sad little cottage of uncoated plank where he hoped I would reside happily, always waiting for his call. It was furnished with left-overs—I recognized the worn parlor rug from the Lion House, the black-stained lamp from the theater's dressing room, and the chipped crockery from Brigham's bakery. (An acquaintance I made in Washington after my divorce advised me not to dwell on such household matters when recounting my tale. "They're petty," he said. "And you sound petty when you do so." To this I told the esteemed gentleman, "You have, I'm quite certain, never attempted a compote in a leaky pan.")

Sensing my disappointment, my husband said, "You don't like it?" The truth was, I was not upset about the house, if that is the correct word for such a lean-to. Walking about the tiny

389

half-furnished parlor, hearing the echo of my step, I came to understand that I would lead a lonely existence here. True, I would have my boys, but I knew as the Prophet's wife my activities would be monitored and restricted. I could no longer expect to visit with friends as I once did, or stroll down the street alone, or do any of the daily activities that bring a basic kind of enjoyment to the day. I was now a married woman, and would be expected to behave as such, yet unlike most wives I did not have a husband in any sense of the word. I was neither maiden, widow, nor even divorcee. I was a plural wife, and this little house, with the cheap runner on the stairs, represented my conjugal purgatory in such fine relief that I felt a piercing to my heart.

To improve my spirits, Brigham moved my mother into the cottage with my boys. We tried to colonize it as best we could, but it had come with such few supplies that everything about our existence there would be best described as bare.

As one of Brigham's wives I was entitled to monthly rations to be collected at Brigham's Family Store. The store sits behind the Beehive House, and when my mother and I went for the first time there was a long line of women and children running out the door and down the street. Many had brought empty pushcarts and miner's sacks, and the children, proudly aware of their purpose, held hand-baskets with caution and care. A number of Indian women had also come to barter large lidded baskets and other weavings for soap and candles.

At the counter I gave my name to an efficient, wide-bosomed woman who ran her finger down a list. "There you are," she said, and disappeared into the storeroom. She was most likely one of my sister wives, yet our relationship was wholly transactional. She returned with a five-pound sack of beet sugar, ten pounds of smoked pork, a short pound of oily candles, a cake of lye soap, a spool of mending thread, and a small box of white-phosphorous matches.

"What I really need is some cambric," I said.

"So do I, Sister. Anything else?"

Now might be a good time to confess to my Dear Reader that which, at the time, I was unable to confess to myself. During the early stages of my marriage I had—I can see now—suppressed my skepticism. Despite the mounting evidence, I wanted to believe my marriage to Brigham Young, unorthodox as it was, had some measure of truth to it. I knew he did not love me as a young girl imagines a husband will love his wife. I knew I did not love him in any profound or cosmic way. Yet marriage has many purposes beyond the romantic, including the practical and the spiritual. I had hoped Brigham would be a surrogate father to my boys. I had hoped my mother's move to my cottage would free her from her rivals. Perhaps most important, I had hoped my proximity to the Church would blow fresh winds into the sagging sails of my faith. I was still a daughter of Mormondom, and at night, when I was alone, and the wind tapped the almond branch against my pane, I continued to pray.

After many months of marriage Brigham invited me to sup at the Lion House as his wife. "How will the others greet me?" I asked.

"Frankly, I gave up trying to predict my wives long ago."

On the day of my debut, Brigham asked me to meet him in the gardens behind his house. Brigham's gardens, it should be said, are like the estate of a king. Behind a nine-foot wall are acres and acres of flower beds and walking paths, as well as fruit and nut orchards, vegetable plots, racks of beehives, and a pigeon house. As I approached the garden at the time of my meeting with my husband, I saw ten paces before me Sister Amelia, whom I knew only by face—her youthful beauty cannot be denied—and reputation, which was so unpleasant, I willed myself not to think of it.

When first planning this memoir, I had no intention of dipping into the histories of my fellow wives. For one, such digression would divert my reader for too many pages. For another, each arrived at Brigham's bed in such a unique manner, through individual and sometimes mysterious circumstances, that I could not accurately represent all their paths. Yet in the case of Amelia Folsom, a diversion seems warranted. I hope my Reader will agree.

She had become the Prophet's 17th wife in 1863, taking, and holding quite firmly, the undisputed position of his favorite. He provided her a private carriage with her initials stenciled on the door in gold, although the other wives walked about the city in the dust. Amelia ordered her silk from France, while Brigham's silkworms spun tirelessly for the rest of us. And most frustrating to her rival wives (I exclude myself from this jealous lot), she visited her husband whenever she desired. She was known to arrive at his office and expel his present guests so that she could be alone with her mate. Most scandalously, I have been told she once demanded a diamond necklace before she would allow Brigham to return to her boudoir. Although this particular anecdote is second-hand, I trust its source, for were you to greet Amelia today you very well might find the diamonds gleaming at the base of her throat.

I also know that she intended to be Brigham's final wife. It was a condition of their marriage. We must give Brigham some credit. He kept his word for two years.

In 1865, not long before he began his campaign for me, Brigham broke his vow to Amelia to wed Mary Van Cott, a fair, strong-minded Saint from a devout family. Mary, who would become a friend, was always kind-hearted and selfless. She knew her presence would hurt Amelia and asked Brigham what she could do to assuage her. "Respect her," Brigham advised. Upon arrival in the Lion House, Mary sent a kitten named Honey to Amelia's room in a gesture of peace. Amelia set the poor creature loose in the city creek and returned the empty box to her rival's door. Honey was never seen again.

Mary was saddened by the cat's loss, yet she could not bring herself to blame Amelia. "I understand her devastation even more," she told Brigham, who later told me. (My detractors have often accused me of knowing things I could not possibly know. "She wasn't there!" they shout. Oh, but this shows their naiveté about plural marriage. In the Saints' troubled institution, a wife's confession to her husband hops from one pillow to the next with the determination of a bed bug.)

The standoff between Amelia and Mary continued until my arrival. They say nothing heals a wound better than time. In plural marriage, nothing dulls the pain of a new wife better than the next one after. There is a cruel logic in a polygamous household. A wife generally ignores the women who preceded her but loathes the first woman to follow. When that woman gets replaced herself, the previous wife takes an un-Christian pleasure in seeing her pained as she had been. This is not always the case. Many women are too noble in heart to nurture such feelings. But they are the exception. Amelia's rage was the rule.

Thus, my Reader, this is the household I entered that day.

As I went to enter Brigham's gardens, I found the gate purposely locked by Amelia. Leggett, Brigham's gardener, saw me fumbling to enter. "Be right there," he said, hobbling over. "There you are, ma'am. Sister Amelia's in quite a blow, isn't she?"

As much as I was tempted, I was not about to gossip about another wife.

"It's always a fine day around here, until she blows through," the man continued. "I should hire a militia to protect my flowers. Look at her." Indeed, Amelia was swiping a brush of cosmos with her parasol, destroying the blooms. But I would not take Leggett's line, and commented on the beauty of his lavender rose.

"I'm lucky to have it. Amelia took her shears to my butter rose the other day."

"Mr. Leggett," I said, "please remember her business is not mine."

"Of course," he said. "Until she makes it."

"I'm sorry she treats you so poorly."

"That's nothing. You should see how she cuts through Brigham. I'll tell you this much: it makes me love the man more. He stands up there on Sundays giving wisdom and all the such, and that's all right and fine, but I never trust a man until I've seen him weak. That's how I know he's honest. Everyone has his chinks!"

Later, at dinner, I made a point of sitting across from Amelia in an attempt to establish a rapport. She ignored me, spoke to no one, and never once touched her food. Each time another woman spoke to Brigham, Amelia pouted and fumed, and indulged in her unpleasant habit of picking at her face. I asked what was troubling her, but she chose not to answer. At the end of the meal, as the cake plate was passed, she shoved it under my nose. "You look like you enjoy your sweets," she said, the famous diamonds sparkling. I must admit the precious stones only enhanced her enviable complexion—while making the rest of Brigham's women, myself included, appear ordinary and plain. I took from the plate two slices of lemon cake, folded them into a cloth for my boys, and thanked Amelia for her kindness. Her lips twisted into a graceless smile. This would be the only time Amelia and I spoke in the five years we shared a husband. I once heard Brigham say that the most beautiful women are also angry, which must explain his unique devotion to Amelia.

I never became a regular wife at the Lion House, and after a few months I stopped dining there altogether. I remember one afternoon Brigham was visiting me in the cottage. He thought to ask, "When did you stop supping with us?"

"Months ago."

"Has it been that long? I miss seeing my wife."

"I'm not your wife," I said.

He rose from the bed and began to assemble himself, buttoning up and refastening his cuffs. He said nothing more, grunting incomprehensibly as he bent to pull on his boots.

He left my room without another word, as if wounded and retreating to his lair. Yet the space where he had stood did not empty. It was as if he had left the spirit of himself behind, a black ghost, large and shaped to his form. This apparition watched me as I dressed. It penetrated my thoughts as I worried if I had somehow destroyed my soul's redemption, and that of my boys. I do not believe in phantasmagorical events, but this presence was so formidable, and real, I must describe it as it seemed to me.

On the stairs I heard Brigham greet my mother. I heard the door open and the Prophet's heavy boots on the porch. I went to my window and watched him walk down the path. Outside the boys were throwing rocks at a lizard. "Lorenzo! James!" the Prophet called. "How would you like it if some great big thing was throwing stones at you?" Brigham lowered himself heavily to one knee and pried open the boys' hands. He took their armament of rocks and gently set them upon the ground. He whispered something to the boys, who listened carefully, then smiled and laughed, throwing their arms around him. At the same time, the apparition up in my room spoke. *Everything is for them*. The voice was Brigham's. *Everything you do now is for your boys.*

395

THE 19TH WIFE

CHAPTER EIGHTEEN
Faith in Marriage

On our first anniversary Brigham transferred me, along with my mother and my boys, to Forest Farm, his agricultural compound south of the city. "I know you don't care much for your little cottage," he said. "Many people say Forest Farm is one of the prettiest places in all of Utah. I think you'll find the land good for the boys. As for you—I spent twenty-five thousand dollars on the house. It has two stories, not including the cellar. If this doesn't suit, my goodness, I don't know what will." In this he was truthful: the house was a gabled, Gothic-style home laid out in the shape of a double cross. It sat upon a fine flat parcel of rich soil, with a black walnut orchard and open views to the mountains. It seemed as fine a place as any in Deseret to raise my boys.

What I did not know, nor did Brigham inform me until my arrival, was that most of the farm's operations were now my responsibility. Forest Farm served as Brigham's larder. Each day it delivered fresh milk, eggs, butter, vegetables, and meats to his scores of wives and children throughout Salt Lake. Every day in the black of morning I rose to begin my chores in the barn, finishing long after the sun had set. My mother did the same, looking after the house and cooking for the thirty farm hands who tended Brigham's field of beets and alfalfa, his cocoonery, and his thousand heads of registered cattle. When one chore was complete, five others waited. The end of each day simply brought the beginning of the next.

"I've never worked so hard in my life," I said to my mother.

"You don't know the meaning of the word." My mother had the common outlook of the Pioneer—that the ordeal of the early Saints would never be surpassed. In terms of toil and hardship, I am certain she is right. Even so, the farm work wore away at my spirits. "Do you ever wonder why we're doing all of this?" I asked my mother.

My mother buttoned up her expression in a manner that meant, *No point in asking about the will of God.* My mother is an intelligent, experienced woman. She has known many kinds of men. When people ask me now, why is it that I continued to believe in the teachings of the Mormon Church for so long, I speak of her. Dear Reader, let me tell you this: Love and trust are Siamese twins, as conjoined as Chang and Eng. I loved my mother and trusted her judgment, even more than I trusted my own. Every time doubt formed hard in my heart, my mother broke it apart with her love.

From time to time Brigham drove out to the farm to inspect his operation and visit with me. While engaged with my husband upstairs, I could hear the boys playing on the rope that hung from the locust tree. They played more loudly when Brigham was present, shouting in a way they never did when we were alone. As I lay with my husband, I imagined they were calling to me: *Mother! I have not forgotten you!* It was the thought I held to through Brigham's visits. This was how I put him out of my mind, even while he was there.

Each Sunday we rode into Salt Lake for services to renew our faith. Church lasted several hours, and with the afternoon meetings it took most of the day. For some it was also a social affair, with a few female Saints flaunting their garments as if they were sewn from the shrouds of Christ. Some men, though certainly not all, would boast of business transactions and successful crops and their latest wives. This kind of vanity is not exclusive to the Saints on Sunday, I know. Anywhere the devout gather to worship, there will always be a parade.

During this period I began to form new questions. I thought of the men around the country, indeed across the Globe—from the high-hatted Pope in Rome to the turbaned Caliph among the Turks—who stood before their people and proclaimed, each in his own language, a set of infallible truths, many similar to those Brigham offered. How can so many men claim the key to Divine Truth? At the time, I could not articulate this question or others, not in the manner I have just now on the page. Yet they were forming, in the manner of the pearl, I suppose, grinding into a truth. It was an all but imperceptible feeling, but on Sundays I sensed it, rubbing against me, deep within. It would be years before I would fully recognize this gem.

Above all, one sermon imprinted itself upon my mind. Many weeks had passed since I had received word from my husband. My daily life involved such a variety of tasks that many days would come and go without his name or image entering my mind. Over time Brigham became a distant figure, such as the men of Washington are distant to us. Certainly we know they exist, for we read of their declarations and pronouncements. Yet to many they do not feel alive, no more than a Roman statesman depicted in the History book feels alive to the student today. This was my benign opinion of my husband when one Sunday he opened up on the topic of his wives.

> Shall I tell you now the question most men and women concern themselves over? The truth most Brothers and Sisters seek? Shall I reveal to you the inquiry that most pre-occupies your minds? I know this because often I meet you on the street, or you call upon me at the Beehive House, or when I travel round the Territory, driving to the most remote Stakes to greet the Faithful—no matter where this is, it is always the same question brought to me. And so now I shall share it with you. Brother Brigham—the sincere man or the sincere Sister, and even sometimes the sincere child;

Brother Brigham, tell me how many Mrs. Youngs do you possess? How many women sleep at night in the Lion House? How many times have you been sealed? My goodness, is this your most profound question for me? You are at liberty to bring me all inquiries, any unsettling of the mind, and yet this is always the first off your tongues. How I wish you asked me something else. Brother Brigham—how do I know if I am living righteously? If I am serving the Kingdom? If I love my wife, if I love my husband, if I love my daughter or my son? Brother Brigham, what does our Heavenly Father want of me? How shall I know if I am His child? Brothers, Sisters, Saints everywhere—why not these questions, and many like them? Why not the enlightened questions about service and humility and devotion, and evil everywhere conquered by peace? Why no examinations of the Gospel? Of the Revelations? Why do I never hear the question—Brother Brigham, tell me how I can be a true Saint? Instead, always, tell me of your bed! Listen to your words—for in them are all truths of the spirit, and thus they shall be.

This sermon, long remembered by many, and reprinted before, had good effect in quieting Brigham's critics. It armed his defenders with rhetoric to respond to the many questions about polygamy. It caused many people, whose curiosity was natural, to feel profane for wondering about such things. It transferred the misdeed from Brigham to his opponents. By the end of the sermon, these powerful words had erased the question—*Brother Brigham, indeed, how many wives do you have?*—from the minds of thousands of Saints.

As for me, these fine words would have done much to buttress my eroding faith—were half of them true.

THE 19TH WIFE

CHAPTER NINETEEN
My Awakening

After more than three years at Forest Farm, an agent from the Church rode out one day to notify my mother and me our services were no longer needed and a wagon would come for our belongings in the morning. I did not know this man. He was one of the many polished, eager youths who worked for the Church administration. He told me I was being transferred to a new house in the city, while my mother was being sent home. "Home?" said my mother. "What home?"

The boy read through a letter but could not come up with an answer. "Your home, I presume."

"Don't presume anything, my boy."

The boy's face shone with the youthful dew that no one misses until it is gone. I did not know what he was thinking, what his ambitions were, how deep his faith, but I could imagine he hoped for wealth and a large enough house for many wives. Why should he not? Certainly many men in Deseret remained true and loyal to their first and only wife. The average man's family life was no different from that of the average man's in Babylon. But among the leaders of the Church and the leaders of the Territory, who were one and the same, among the men who controlled industry and land resources and deeds to water, who ranked in the militia and the police services, who managed the supply of goods and protected the routes between settlements, among

400

the men who administered the post and the judges who ruled from the bench—among these men, plural marriage was common and admired. Of course this boy, who was already serving Brigham in such intimate capacity, would want the same for himself. I told him I would be ready in the morning.

The next day the boys and I settled into a large, handsome, Gothic-style house of beige adobe located near the Temple. The house's most remarkable feature was a splendid stained-glass window depicting a golden beehive surrounded by sego lillies and opulent fruit. (Ever since my apostasy, the window has become a recognizable attraction to the curious visitors of Deseret, for many people hope to catch a glimpse of my former abode, and the unique window confirms that, indeed, I once lived within.) In fairness to Brigham, I must admit this new house was ample, clean, and in many ways appealing; and, most important, it was mine. I hesitate to complain about this fine dwelling except that two inadequacies burdened my days there. One, my mother was not permitted to live with me. Brigham claimed he could no longer afford supporting her, which had hardly amounted to anything at all.

The second inadequacy was a lack of a well, forcing me to draw water from my neighbors'. I tried to distribute my borrowings equally among them. I would take James and Lorenzo with me, so we could draw as much water at one time. I was always ashamed when I knocked on the doors, pail in hand, humiliated by every force that had brought me to this moment of begging before my boys.

When Brigham visited the cottage for the first time, he announced he was bearing bad news. "I'm afraid my revenues are no longer what they were," he said. "We're all scaling back. I'm going to have to cut your allowance."

"Cut it? By how much?"

"I'm afraid we're cutting your allowance entirely."

"You're giving me nothing?"

"Not nothing. You'll live in this house without rent and you can still collect your rations at the store."

Here I must honor the promise I made at the outset of this book. I swore that I would not withhold the details the Reader is most keenly interested in. In my experiences as lecturess, no matter the venue, no matter who sits in the audience before me, always the same questions arise. They are difficult questions to pose before your peers, but eventually a brave soul, typically a woman, ventures forth. Then there is great relief in the hall as everyone's mutual curiosity is satisfied. Never have I told my story without someone inquiring about the conjugal relations between Brigham and myself. I will sate your curiosity now by telling you those relations ceased between me and Brigham sometime in my third year at Forest Farm.

I now realized a great cost attached itself to this revised arrangement.

Once Brigham had removed me from the farm I was merely, like so many plural wives no longer on the schedule, a financial burden.

"How am I to feed my boys?" I asked.

"Start a garden. Hire out your needle. Take in some laundry."

"Take in some laundry! I have to walk up and down the street with bucket in hand begging for water. You don't know—no, you can't know—what it's like for me to have to ask for water. These people, these kind people, don't have the heart to turn me away. But they work hard too. The well is only so deep. Why should they have to share their water with me?"

"Because they are Saints and they would do well to remember who brought them here." His hideous anger spilled over. It squeezed out of him in perspiration and ire and a dire loathing of everything before him. The Prophet was reduced to a bilious, fat, old man. He blew out of the cottage. I could not know then he would never visit again.

* * *

To ease my financial duress, I decided to take in boarders. Ever since the completion of the railroad a few years earlier, Gentiles had been arriving in Deseret in numbers never seen before. There was an inadequate number of hotels to house them, and quickly there became a custom of Saints renting out rooms to these new visitors and residents. It was an odd evolution for our isolated Territory—Saints who had never known the outside world suddenly were sharing a home with Babylonian strangers. Of course, every Saint in Deseret had been raised on stories of depravity among the Gentiles: They worship falsely, they fornicate loosely, they eat their young! Although I did not believe every tale, they had left me with a general impression that I could never trust a Gentile. In the end, my empty purse overruled my superstitions and I placed an advertisement in the *Daily Tribune*.

The first person to reply was Major James Burton Pond, formerly of the Third Wisconsin Cavalry, ally of John Brown, and now a reporter for the *Tribune* itself. He arrived at my house in full uniform, with a silver-handled sword. "Is the room still free?"

"It's three dollars a week," I said. "Board included. Washing is extra. You must like children. I have two boys, James, who's nine, and Lorenzo, who's eight. They're good boys, but they are boys and can make noise. You're free to congregate here or on the porch, but not in the kitchen or the dining room. Visitors should be out by ten, and if you—"

I stopped talking, for Major Pond was regarding me queerly. "Is something wrong?"

"Are you really a Mrs. Young?"

I told him his information was correct.

"Why on earth are you letting out your rooms?"

"Because I have spare rooms and no income. I'd rather take in boarders than deprive my sons."

"What about your husband?"

"Would you like to see the room or not, Major Pond?"

Judge Albert Hagan, the old Confederate colonel, wise man of legal affairs, and mineral attorney, and Mrs. Hagan became my next boarders. Judge Hagan lived mostly in California, but his expertise in mining law brought him to Salt Lake for extended periods. He seemed to me, at least at first, a gentle, fluffy-haired soul, with a cautious mouth buried in a cottony beard. Mrs. Hagan was, in my estimation, the most suitable creature for her husband: She was ample in every sense, including a plentiful bosom atop an abundant heart. The nature of their relationship was a revelation. Judge Hagan never once failed to thank his wife, praise her intelligence, or appreciate her presence. Ten times a day he said, "I'm the luckiest man in the world," and lay his hand upon her soft behind.

Thus my house was transformed in less than a week. It was by coincidence and circumstances of the time, but in no part by design, that my three boarders were Gentiles.

In the evenings Judge Hagan and his wife, along with Major Pond, liked to gather on my porch for conversation. They invited friends and acquaintances, intelligent, lively men—lawyers, journalists, historians, and other reasoned Gentiles—who typically brought their equally bright and lively wives. These women, most of them wearing their hair in the loose (and prohibited) waterfall style, knew as much about any topic as their husbands. Almost every night outside my parlor window, a seminar of ideas and philosophy was conducted. "Have you any thoughts on the Modocs?" Judge Hagan would begin, initiating a long engagement of opinion, agreements, and disagreements. Everyone would participate, the women's estimation of all matters listened to with equivalent respect.

Each night I worked in the kitchen while listening in. I have always hated washing dishes, but never more so during these evenings when the water and the clinking cutlery obscured an important word in the dialogue. I took to propping the window with a block of wood so that the ideas could travel to the kitchen more clearly. I longed to join my boarders but knew I could not.

One night Judge Hagan said, "The more I learn of polygamy, the more I despise it. I admire Brigham a good deal, but he's got to be careful with this thing. Everyone knows it's the wild wick that burns down the house."

"More than anything," said Mrs. Hagan, "I think about the children."

"Has anyone," asked Judge Hagan, "ever met a partner in a polygamatic marriage, man or woman, who was happy? I mean truly happy?"

"What do you mean by happy?" said Major Pond.

"What does he mean by happy?" said Mrs. Hagan. "He means happy. Happy: cheerful, glad, fortunate, hopeful. Happy."

"I'm only asking, Mrs. Hagan. I'm not supporting. They of course believe this is their ticket to Heaven. Now if you believed that, I mean truly believed that, I mean believed it as much as you believed the sun will rise tomorrow and the sky will be blue, then wouldn't you be happy, even if a few extra wives caused some inconvenience or indignity in this present life?"

"I have an idea," said Mrs. Hagan. "Let's not speculate, not when we have Mrs. Young as an expert witness."

In a matter of seconds she was in the kitchen, begging me to join the conversation. I told her there were dishes and a late loaf in the oven, but Mrs. Hagan would not relent.

In addition to the Judge and his wife and Major Pond, that evening there was the Rev. Mr. Stratton, a Methodist. He was the first representative of a foreign religion I had ever known. All my life Brigham, the Apostles, the Bishops, the Elders—everyone in a position to know—had told me that I must mind my purse and person around Gentiles. "But a reverend, a preacher, a man of their cloth, he is the devil in our land," I had been warned since I was a child.

And now the Rev. Stratton was rising from his rocker to shake my hand. "Will you join us, Mrs. Young?" The group regarded me with gentle curiosity. I longed to open up, to tell them all I had seen. At the same time, I felt a lingering duty to defend my faith. "It's all rather complicated," I said. "There are many sides to the debate."

"Don't feel obliged," said Mrs. Hagan.

"It's quite rude of us," said Rev. Stratton. "Why, it's none of our business at all."

"I'm sorry," said Mrs. Hagan. "We didn't mean to make a specimen of you."

I accepted their apologies and left their company, although I longed to tell them all I knew.

The next day the Rev. Stratton sent his card and an invitation to call upon him and Mrs. Stratton any time. For two weeks I kept the card in my pocket, fingering it as I went about my work, rubbing the embossing so many times that it had begun to wear away by the time I decided to pay them a visit.

The Strattons lived several blocks away, in a new neighborhood where Gentiles clustered, a foreign land I had never visited before. I left the boys with Mrs. Hagan and walked to the Strattons, taking a circuitous route, careful to note anyone who might be spying on me. My relations with Brigham had deteriorated to such a state it was possible to imagine him trying to blackmail me with evidence of betrayal. A walk that should take no more than twenty minutes took nearly an hour, as I zigzagged through the neighborhood and finally arrived at the Strattons' gate.

Mrs. Stratton shared her husband's dual nature of seeming both youthful and wise. Her posture was so erect I never once saw her sit back in her chair. This was remarkable given that my visit, originally planned for twenty minutes, lasted almost four hours. I had not intended to unload all my grief to these strangers, but the Rev. Mr. Stratton broke away my reserve when he said, "Mrs. Young, you should know, my wife and I, we already consider ourselves your friends."

There was no reason for the Strattons to make such a declaration—Except, is this not how Man is meant to treat his fellow creature? I was too weary to be skeptical, too raw to protect myself further, and too depleted, in every sense, to lose anything more. "I don't know where to begin," I said. Rev. and Mrs. Stratton said nothing further. They were not going to pry, nor even, as some do, pretend they were satisfied with nothing said when in fact they craved every detail. "I hardly know what's happened."

"Everything in time," said Mrs. Stratton.

Thus I began to tell my story. It was the first time I had pieced it together even for myself. The afternoon slipped into evening. The plate of cookies turned into a platter of strips of ham and beef. It grew dark and I continued talking. Mrs. Stratton brought the astral lamp from the hall. A yellow radiance reached out just far enough to encircle us, and I carried on until the end of my tale.

THE 19TH WIFE

CHAPTER TWENTY
The Battle of the Stove

Emboldened by my new friends, sometime in June 1873 I went to see Brigham. I had to wait on line outside the Beehive House along with all the other curious visitors, the men conducting business with the Church, and the hundreds of pilgrims. I considered running up and down the line and telling the faithful the truth about my husband. What would the pilgrims think if they knew how Brigham's wives lived behind this very wall they leaned against now? Would they crave to rub the hem of his coat, or take home a sheet of paper from his wastebasket as a relic, if they understood the truth?

Yet I had a more practical matter to discuss with Brigham. I wanted a new stove.

"A new what?"

"A stove."

"What's wrong with the one you have?"

"It's fine for one or two people, but I'm now running a boarding house. I need to cook for twice as many as the kitchen's meant for, and I need a new stove. These people pay three dollars a week for room and board and what can I tell them when their supper isn't ready?"

"I don't care what you tell them, but I'll tell you, I can't afford a new stove. Do you have any idea how much they cost?"

"I do. I've picked one out. It can be delivered in four weeks."

Our argument continued for some time until Brigham said, "All right. I'll think about it."

"You won't think about it. You will give me a check now so I can place the order."

"Madame, you are not the treasurer of this household."

"Sir, I am your wife and you will provide for my most basic needs."

Brigham opened an accounting book and in a great show of irritation scratched out a check. "I always thought you of all people would understand what it meant to be my wife."

I left the Beehive House for the last time. Outside, one of Brigham's aides announced to the expectant pilgrims, "The President will meet no more visitors today." At least a hundred stood on the veranda and down the steps into the street. They cried about waiting for hours and needing the Prophet's advice. "Go home," said the aide. "Come back tomorrow, but go home." The man retreated into the Beehive and shut the door.

Even after the pilgrims were gone, I lingered outside my husband's house. A pair of Brigham's daughters, two of the Big Ten in fashionable mushroom hats, passed me on their way to the Lion House. I had shared several meals with these girls, and sat with them in the parlor on Sunday nights. Now they did not recognize me.

Dusk arrived, and still I remained at Brigham's gate. I do not know why I lingered, but I felt an urgent need to witness his household one final time. As dusk descended, one of Brigham's wives, I do not know who, moved through the Beehive House illuminating the lamps, the golden light filling one window and then the next. I saw Brigham pass from his office to his upstairs parlor, where Amelia was waiting with two of his sons. The parlor's large window allowed me to view a portion of their evening. Amelia leaned against the piano in a silver gown, the diamonds bright at the base of her throat. Brigham kissed her neck, then moved to look out the window as if to examine the night sky. For some time he stood motionless behind the glass. His eyes looked tired in their pouches of flesh. His beard was white and frayed. He looked, to me, like an old man worried about his fate. He gazed out, with an aurora of lamplight behind him, not at me but into his future, I believe. At one point he winced, a small shock of something running through him, his thick body flinching almost imperceptibly. It was a tiny jolt; no one in the parlor perceived it. Then it passed and Brigham returned to his family. Although I have no more evidence than this, I am certain that night I witnessed my husband looking into his heart and regretting what he found.

Shortly after my victory of the stove, I took to bed with a mysterious illness similar to the one that befell me all those years before. My boarders urged me to consult a doctor. When I refused, I know they believed I was doing so because of my faith. The truth was I could not afford the call. For two weeks, I was unable to look after them, and I feared they would rightly demand a refund on their rent. Instead they became my nurses and closest friends. They tended to me, not only Mrs. Hagan but her husband and the Major as well. They took over the house, cooking and cleaning and polishing the lovely stained-glass window, and looking after James and Lorenzo.

One day during my convalescence my boarders and the Rev. and Mrs. Stratton came to speak with me. "Mrs. Young, can we have an honest word?"

I was sure they were going to fairly complain that they were paying three dollars a week to serve me. "I know what you're going to say."

"It's none of our business," said Mrs. Hagan, "but it's impossible not to notice that your husband has abandoned you."

Judge Hagan continued, "If you were so inclined, you might consider bringing suit against him."

"Suit for what?"

"For divorce," advised the Judge.

I hesitated, then said, "You have no idea what that means."

"I think I do," said the Judge. "Let me be your guide. You have legal rights. Any court of law will see that your husband has abandoned you and you're entitled to be set free."

"It'll be a test case," Mrs. Hagan said. "For polygamous women everywhere."

I did not know how to perceive what they were saying. My new friends were emphasizing my legal rights while I remained concerned with my spiritual fate. "My whole life," I said, "everyone I have ever known, everyone has told me that this is the way to Salvation. How can I leave it all behind?" I turned to the Reverend Stratton, asking for his advice.

"I'm afraid," he said, "no one—not me, not Brigham, no one at all— can tell you what your heart has to say. You must learn to listen to yourself."

"If I may," said Mrs. Hagan, "with all due respect to the Reverend's wise words, I should like to ask you a simple question: Is this what you really believe? Even now?"

To you, reasoned Reader, the answer might appear obvious, yet doubt is not the same as knowledge. On my journeys I have met people who have forsworn any belief in God and Christ, and yet they are married in a church and plan to be buried beneath a stone cross. At the great moment of death, with the eternal future undecided, few are truly prepared to defy everything they have been told to be true.

"What about my boys?"

"They're the reason we've come to you like this," said Mrs. Hagan. "Do you really want them to see their mother so abused? Do you want them thinking this is how a man treats his wife?"

It was a terrible vision—ten or fifteen years into the future, my boys as young men, greedily acquiring women. There was no reason to think they would be any different from my father, brother, and husband. Unless something changed, their fate was sealed, as was mine.

411

* * *

After my health had improved, and I could take up again my duties in the house, two Ward Teachers paid me a visit. They were young men of twenty or twenty-one, one thick with fatty muscle while his companion wore a dense black beard. They sat in my parlor, perched at the edge of their chairs, their air an admixture of compassion and distaste. "Sister, we've been sent out to evaluate the quality of your faith," the bearded one began.

"We have a few questions," said the other.

"First," I said, "I have a question for you: What makes you capable of evaluating my faith?"

"Sister, don't you understand? We're teachers of the ward. We've received our ordinances."

"Yes, I know, but what makes you capable of knowing my heart better than myself?"

They smiled weakly. I could read the mind of the thicker one: He could not wait to leave my house and discuss with anyone he met my infidelity.

The bearded one cleared his throat. "If I may begin the evaluation. Now, first of all, do you remain faithful to the Revelations of Joseph and the Prophecy of Brigham Young?"

"No."

The men looked at each other. I doubt anyone had ever answered as such. The thicker man appeared astonished; his companion seemed pleased to meet a challenge. "I'm sure you don't know what you're saying," he said. "Brother Broadhead was asking if you hold the Prophets in your heart."

"I understand, and I do not."

The young men looked at each other once again. Their expressions changed from surprise to irritation.

"Listen, Sister," the fat one began. "What you're saying could get you in a lot of trouble, not just with God and in Heaven, but with Brigham and everyone else. You need to be

412

more careful. I'm going to have to report everything you say to the Bishop."

"Gentlemen, I'll do it myself, thank you." I told the men that their religion had betrayed me, their Prophet had abandoned me, their system of conjugality all but destroyed my family. "Tell me then, yes, please tell me, how am I supposed to love this religion? Perhaps it has brought you personally nothing but joy, and perhaps you, too, and your families and everyone you know. Perhaps you've profited under this system, found yourself nourished and enriched both physically and spiritually. In that case, I can understand your fervor and your desire to share it. But, Brothers, please try, for a moment *try* and see what it has done to me. If you do, you might understand why my faith is crumbling, even as we speak here now."

The heavy man's expression lifted, as if he had just arrived at a very good idea. "I know what you need. You need your faith restored. Here's what we'll do. We'll get you re-baptized. You'll go through the ceremony again and your heart will be cleansed and your disbelief will be washed away."

I argued for some time that I did not care for any more ceremonies, but the men would not relent. They warned me of my lonely fate and the chill of an eternity without the love of God. "On your deathbed, Sister, you will regret this day. On your deathbed, I guarantee it, you will hear my voice."

"I have no idea what will happen after I die," I said, "yet I know one thing for sure: Neither do you."

After this, I never again tried to believe in the Latter-day Saints. My faith had been emptied out like a can. When I told my mother, she said, "You don't know what you're saying."

"Mother, I do."

"You'll lose everything."

"I already have."

THE 19TH WIFE

CHAPTER TWENTY-ONE
The Apostate Wife

My escape from Mormondom began with six men and a moving van. They dismantled my house and hauled the load to auction. One man asked if he should pry the stained-glass window from its casement. I told him to leave it for the next wife, and the one after her. When the house was empty I sat on the porch with my boys to tell them about the great adventure we were embarking on.

"Like the Pioneers?" said James.

"Yes, something like that. And like all adventures, there will be difficult times. And now is going to be one of those. I need both of you to be brave and not cry even if you feel like crying." I was sending James, my eldest, to live with my father and his wives until I was settled. When I told him this, his eyes flickered with sorrow. He fought back his tears as best he could, but then the brave boy broke down.

"I promise we'll be together again very soon."

"Why does Lorenzo get to stay with you and I don't?"

The truth was I could not face my coming ordeal alone. I needed one of my boys with me, yet even one was probably more than I would be able to care for over the coming days. James begged me not to leave him. He wept on my breast until Judge and Mrs. Hagan drove him away.

I was so distressed by his departure that I considered canceling my scheme. Then little Lorenzo squeezed my hand. "Where are we going?" he asked. His warm fingers reminded

414

me why I had chosen this path to freedom, and why I could not turn back.

When it was dark Lorenzo and I set out for a walk through the neighborhood, pretending to be on a stroll, nodding at the neighbors. I carried nothing extraordinary with me, giving no one any reason to believe I was fleeing. While walking we met up with the Reverend and Mrs. Stratton. Lorenzo jumped up and down at the sight of them, for he loved them like a fond uncle and aunt. They fell in with us in a most natural way, and we moved about at a casual pace, noticing the summer vines on a trellis and the yellow pompoms in a bed of marigolds. With little effort, and no apparent intention, we meandered downtown, then wandered about until we were standing before the Walker House, the Gentile hotel. I told Lorenzo we would spend the night inside.

"Why can't we sleep in our house?"

"You saw the men take away the furniture."

"Why can't they bring it back?"

Sometimes with children it is impossible to catch up with their logic. Their questions are always sharp and full of perception, exposing the twisted thinking of the mature man's world. "They can't bring it back because I've sold it. We have left that house for good. One day we'll have a new house, but for now we'll live here."

Thus we entered the Gentile hotel.

On our first night in the Walker House I warned Lorenzo to remain silent. "No one is to know we're here."

"The bellman knows we're here."

"Yes, but he doesn't know our actual names. We are in hiding, do you understand what that means?"

He nodded. "It means you don't want Brigham to know where you are."

Since beginning my preparations to flee, I had been too preoccupied to ponder my fate. Now the fullness of it seemed to be pressing at the door of Suite No. 412. In abandoning my husband, I had given up almost everything I had ever known.

415

I was sleepless that night, alert to every sound in the hall. Several times I heard footsteps pass my door, my heart quickening until they retreated down the corridor. Once, around three in the morning, I heard the sound of a man moving carefully down the hall. Whoever he was, he walked deliberately as if he wanted to go undetected. They were big feet, I could tell, in clumsy country boots. Soon they were standing at my door.

I lay still, holding Lorenzo so firmly I still cannot believe he did not awaken in my arms. I heard the man breathing on the other side of our door. He stood there for some time. His breath was the sound of a man hesitating, or praying, before committing a dangerous act. I grew certain it was one of Brigham's Danites, come to assassinate me. I imagined the cold animal black in his eyes. I was too frightened to move. I awaited the rattle of the knob and the turn of the stolen key. Then at some point the man was gone.

I cannot tell you if I imagined an assassin at my door; or if in fact a killer had not been able to carry out his religious duty. I recalled Brigham's black ghost, the presence he left behind in a room. Was that what I had perceived? Had he come for me? Oh, sober-minded Reader! Never sneer at such fantasies. In the quiet of your mind, when the deep night is at its blackest, are you always so certain of what is real?

"Mrs. Young? . . . Mrs. Young? Are you in there?"

I sat up in bed. The mantel clock said it was a little past ten. Next to me Lorenzo stared up from the pillow. Two small, dark crescents of fatigue had appeared beneath his eyes.

"It's me, Mrs. Hagan."

When I admitted her, she had a hurried, anxious look, yet before stating the purpose of her visit she gave Lorenzo a steaming sweet bun. The boy took the treat to the corner and sat with it between his crossed legs. He pretended he was not listening, yet his ears, I know, were pricked.

"It's out," said Mrs. Hagan. "Your apostasy. Everyone knows."

416

Mrs. Hagan handed over the *Daily Tribune*, the Territory's leading Gentile paper, where Major Pond worked. Immediately I saw that its editors, all strangers, had become my friends. The lead editorial praised my fortitude and chastised Brigham for his indifference and hypocrisy. There were a number of items about my apostasy, including a satirical cartoon with the caption "Brother Brigham is forlorn—his last rib has deserted his bed and board."

"Did Brigham's papers learn of it?" I asked.

Mrs. Hagan hesitated, and I wrested the Mormon papers from her. I was not surprised to see my name denounced in his press, but I could not have anticipated the lies and false accusations. If you were to gather all your news exclusively from Brigham's papers, as most Saints do, you would believe I was woven of such dishonest fabric I might try to convince you to dig up your mother's coffin to hand over her wedding band.

To this day I do not know how my story got out, but the dissemination was so thorough and in such detail that Americans everywhere woke up to my tale. I would later learn I was on the front page of the papers in San Francisco, Saint Louis, and New York. The farther from Mormondom, the more lurid and scandal-loving was the reporting.

"Momma, look."

"Lorenzo, please. Get away from the window."

But the boy would not listen. He was peeling back the shade to look outside. I went to pull him away, but then I saw the crowd below. Some five hundred had gathered, jostling and shoving and trying to enter the hotel. The manager held his arms up, trying to bring order to the street.

"They're here for you," said Mrs. Hagan.

"Who are they?"

"Reporters, sympathizers, denouncers, everyone."

The truth comes both instantly and in a slow, steady seep. I was feeling it creep through me—a profound understanding of what I would be facing for some time to come. I could hardly move, and Mrs. Hagan had to help me dress.

Not a minute after I was clothed, and my hair prepared in a beaded net, did a knock come to the door. "Mrs. Young, it's me, Judge Hagan." At once the Judge's presence helped settle me. "Now that the cat's out of the bag," he reported, "I want you to know I'll be filing the divorce papers very soon."

"When can we leave Utah?"

"There's a mood out there," he said. "I'm not sure it's safe. You're best staying here for the time being. Here, I brought you this." The Judge handed me an envelope. I recognized the writing at once. There was no one I wanted to hear from more.

> My Dear Child:
> I would have come to deliver this message in person, but I dare not enter the Gentile Hotel which you now call home. I know you have suffered in your marriage, and that your husband has failed in many ways. It has pained me to witness this. I too know the hardships of our unique institution; often I have prayed for a relief to its strains; often I have contemplated quitting my own marital duties. Yet I am certain, as certain as I am of anything, that plural marriage will open the door to Heaven, and that my sufferings here on Earth are my path to Glory. My child, ponder your words and deeds, for they shall last far longer than your physical self. Be certain, my child, that I cannot know you in your present state.
>
> Your Mother,
> ELIZABETH C. WEBB

"Mother?" Lorenzo set his little hand on my knee, reviving me from the letter. "Mother, what's wrong?" He climbed into my arms, his breath warm from the sweet bun. I held him for some time, an hour, perhaps, pitying myself. I wish I could claim I faced my first day of apostasy with courage and certainty. Yet in truth, I had never felt more afraid.

MY MOTHER'S FLIGHT

From the Desk of
Lorenzo Dee, Eng.
Baden-Baden-by-the-Sea
Calif.

August 2, 1939
Professor Charles Green
Brigham Young University
Joseph Smith Building
Provo

Dear Professor Green,

How on earth did you find me? It has been a long time since I have had any contact with Utah, so my hat is off to you, Professor. Yet I am afraid I cannot answer your questions about my mother. I am not invoking my right to privacy, although I cherish it. No, I'm simply too poorly equipped to tell you what you would like to know. For example, when you ask, did Ann Eliza ever discuss her divorce with any of Brigham's other wives? My answer is: I have no idea. I understand why you ask—what a nugget such a conversation would be for your proposed narrative. But please remember, in 1873 I was eight years old. The events you are asking about took place when I was so young I do not trust my memory of them; or, at the very best, my memories are more like memories that time, skillful decorator that she is, has embroidered into something beautiful yet not wholly true. For your purposes, this simply will not do.

I should apologize for not writing sooner, but over the past few weeks a number of matters have kept me from my desk,

421

including the white-sided dolphins which have taken to appearing in the cove in the afternoons. It seems that every time I sit down to answer the mail I look out and see their pewter-tipped snouts in the surf. It's such a sight of uncomplicated joy, as you can imagine, that I hurry outside and down the path. Several years ago I built a viewing bench on the bluff. I conceived of it as a reading spot, but I can never get any reading done, what with the ocean and the sun and the dolphins in the waves. I go down there for twenty minutes and find I've lost the afternoon.

For some time I considered ignoring your letter. You are asking about so many events which have been recorded before. Newspaper accounts, the documents from the trial, the Church's repudiations, and of course my mother's book. The stories about her marriage to Brigham have been told and retold and disputed and dismissed by so many interested parties, I cannot imagine there's anything left to say. I am sorry to be so discouraging.

I must admit I was shocked when you pointed out that September next will be the 50th anniversary of President Woodruff's manifesto renouncing polygamy. It feels even longer ago—almost ancient in its distance from us today; and, at the same time, it feels like last night's dream. My mother, I know, took great pride in the Church's change of mind, perhaps too much. I'll leave it to you and the other historians to determine her role in bringing about its reversal. Certainly she played some. Certainly she cannot accept full credit. The truth lies somewhere in between, but isn't that always the case?

I will tell you—in the years leading up to the Church's about-face, what with the Edmunds Act in '82 and Edmunds-Tucker five years later and all the other drum-beating out of Washington, I was convinced the federal government and the Saints would have a showdown of biblical proportions, one that would leave the Mormons destroyed. Look at Brigham—he was willing to go to jail over the issue! (That reminds me, I do not recall any talk of a letter or a diary or what have you from his time in prison, but I really wouldn't know.) In the years leading up to 1890 I imagined a great battle of wills—the Saints fighting the U.S. Army to their deaths. But in the end, the Mormons relented. They gave up polygamy in a simple policy shift. In doing so, they chose the future. And look at them now! (I suppose I should say, look at you!) How many are you? How many millions more to come? If the Church had clung to plural marriage, it's safe to say it would have withered into a fringe.

Let me say, I appreciate your understanding the irony of all this. If your letter had failed to acknowledge it, I would have quickly filed it away. But, as you say, time changes our point of view. This notion has been on my mind lately. Frankly, it's been a trying summer. I lost my wife a year ago July. About nine months after her departure I managed to back my grief into its cage, but the anniversary opened the door and let the beast out again. There has been no solace. Her name was Rosemary. Her eyes were the blue of a winter ocean. We were married forty-three years. It's been difficult, more difficult than I could have known.

My goodness, I have just looked back at my opening paragraphs to you. I cannot believe how far from your questions I have already strayed. First let me acknowledge that your questions are fair and they show that you are an honest historian. You might know (or you might not) I was an engineer. I invented a small but useful device used to lay macadam accurately upon the roads. My point is, I like things orderly and as they are. And so I will say directly, in response to your questions, I cannot answer them for I was not there. I have no interpretation to add, no analysis to offer, no hearsay to pass along, no old family stories to share. If I did not witness it, I am not your source.

Except, you correctly state that I was with my mother during the period July–November 1873, while we lived in the Walker House. As you must know, she sketches this period in

The 19th Wife. Of course, some of what she writes can be dismissed as grandstanding. The same can be true of the stories Brigham published about her in his periodicals. They were engaged in battle. Manipulation of the truth has always been part of the warrior's arsenal. Neither Brigham nor my mother is more culpable, or less.

As I wrote that last sentence, the dolphins returned. I hurried down the path to my viewing bench. Can I describe the joy of a spouting blow hole? The white blaze of sea foam is, to me at least, one of the purest expressions of life itself. Will you forgive my lack of critical reasoning when I say I see God in that frothy column of water? I know nothing about you, Professor, but I trust you have seen the ocean. If you have, then you have witnessed the divine. How barren the ground is in comparison! If I could count the hours I have spent staring out at it! And yet those hours never feel lost. I cannot imagine how else I could refill them were I given a second chance.

As you know, on July 15, 1873, my mother and I moved into the Walker House. In Brigham's mind, and the minds of his followers, this was her act of apostasy, not the lawsuit she filed against him ten days later or the charges she laid out in the newspapers over the next many months. The Walker House was known throughout the Territory as a Gentile den. The rumors about it included orgiastic gatherings in the parlor, a Satanic altar in a linen closet, and murderous rituals practiced in the root cellar. It's laughable now, but such stories were told again and again in the Territory. No one questioned them. We believed every word.

I don't know if our lives were truly in danger that first night in the hotel. Indeed, my mother's statements in *The 19th Wife* have come to seem overwrought. I can tell you this, however: She was genuinely afraid. Imagine, if you will, departing the only world you have ever known— your family, your landscape, your customs, your neighbors, your faith, even if that faith has been shaken. Ponder it: saying goodbye without knowing where you are headed. It would be something like decamping for the moon.

I can tell you this as well about our first hours at the Walker House: I was frightened, too. At that age it is hard to know the root of one's fear, but I gather it was because I saw my mother in distress. There is nothing more alarming to a boy than seeing a mother, or a father, buckling. It says to him that all will not be well. The boy does not know this, but he senses it, as a dog senses his master's true state of mind.

I remember the hotel bed as quite high and laid out with bolsters and pillows faced in blue damask. Although it was summer I recall being cold and burying myself beneath the bedclothes in my mother's arms. We lay very still, never falling asleep. Whenever we heard a noise downstairs or in the corridor our bodies went rigid. At one point, I remember vividly, there was the sound of a man standing outside our door. I am sure it was a butler realizing he had gone to the wrong suite. But he stood there for what seemed eternity, breathing, waiting, hovering. We held each other, my mother and I. Yes, in fact I did fear for my life at that moment. I know she did, too. My mother had said nothing to me of the possibility of assassination by the Danites, but she didn't have to. You know how boys talk: in the schoolyard I had heard all about Brigham's secret police. The rumor was they cut the hearts out of anyone who abandoned their faith. There were stories of apostates driven into the desert and scalped to make it look as though the Indians had murdered them. I recall the tale of a man who one morning declared to his wife he no longer believed in Brigham's word. By afternoon he had simply disappeared. No trace, not a footprint in the sand, nor a glove fallen in the path. I don't know why, but that always frightened me the most—a person simply disappearing, poof! These of course were schoolyard tales, which tend to be among the tallest. There is no way to verify them, not now. Even so, think of the impression they would leave on an eight-year-old whose mother has checked

425

into a notorious Gentile refuge. And so, whether or not our lives were truly at risk, it seemed that way and our fear was as real as the white moon burning in the sky.

The next morning a number of visitors came to the room. One brought me a warm bun topped with walnuts and honey—a distraction, I realize. It was clear something significant had taken place. I did not know what, of course, but all day people continued to visit our suite—not just the Strattons and the Hagans and Major Pond, but others, men I did not know. During these visits my mother sat in a mahogany chair with a cluster of cherries carved into the frame. Her visitor sat opposite her, asking questions and writing things down. These interviewers reminded me of the Ward Teachers. I knew these men were not Ward Teachers, but I assumed they shared some sort of purpose. I did not connect these interviews with the newspaper stories about my mother that appeared the next day.

I am not going to recap for you how the feud between my mother and Brigham played out in the press. Suffice it to say Brigham's papers, especially the *Herald*, waged a robust campaign against her. I am sure you have read the accounts in the archives. He laid upon her every accusation short of murder.

All of this was to be expected. I recall Major Pond, whose uniform always impressed me, coming to the room and telling my mother and the others (who was it? Judge Hagan? I never cared for him, I will add) that Brigham had manipulated the Western Telegraph Office and the Associated Press's man in Utah. False stories about her were appearing outside Utah. Major Pond was red-faced, perspiration glistening in the branches of his mustache. "I'll fix that damn *Chronicle*!" he bellowed. I remember it distinctly—the way his brass buttons shook on his chest.

Of course, I was for the most part unaware of the daily items about my mother's apostasy. How could a little boy locked in a fourth-floor hotel room in Salt Lake know that editorial writers in San Francisco and New York took lurid interest in his mother? I knew that many people wanted to meet her. Often a crowd collected outside the Walker House, pointing up to our window. The hotel became another stop on the polygamy tour—the Beehive House, the infamous Lion House, and now the Walker House. Who on their way to California could resist viewing these sites? I remember I liked to peel back the shade to see them. It was clear they were not from Utah. I don't know how I knew this, but perhaps it was their impatience or their brightly colored clothes or the way they spoke casually of Joe Smith and Brig Young—the way you and I might refer to a character from a film or a novel. There was no reverence or awe or fear. Yes, that's what it was—that was their difference. They were indifferent to the profundity of belief. Faith was just one more hullabaloo on a long list. I remember one fellow in the lobby saying to his companion, "These people have lost their minds. Imbeciles, all of them, including Mrs. 19."

I'm sorry to say I don't have the letter from my grandmother. My mother's transcription of it in *The 19th Wife* will have to be accepted as true. It was the only time, I believe, my mother considered reversing her course of action. By then, of course, it was too late; and, no less important, she had surrounded herself by many whose interests lay in her pressing ahead in her defiance of the Church.

On the second day of our confinement, my uncle Gilbert came to visit. Until that point I had had little contact with the man. He spent much of his time at South Cottonwood with his two wives and eighteen children—my first cousins, but I could spend the rest of my days trying to remember their names. I remember Gilbert's first words when he entered the suite: "This is all my fault." I remember the tender woe in his voice. Gilbert always stood with an awkward, gloomy bend to his spine—a manifestation, I have since come to believe, of the regret he carried in his heart.

Of course, I did not know my uncle was on his way out of

427

the Church at this time. He promised my mother full support. I understand Gilbert helped my mother financially in this period. It could have been he who paid our hotel bill, yet I cannot tell you for certain. If it was, most likely his funds came from the payments Brigham gave him for his help in arranging his marriage to my mother. What do the Easterners call this? Karma? I suppose I'm asking the wrong man.

Before leaving the suite that day, Gilbert knelt down beside me. He set his thumb beneath my chin, tilting my head up so I was looking into his eye. "You'll look after your mother?" He fished two gold coins from his pocket and thumbed them, one after the next, into my palm. I will tell you, Professor Green, I have those coins today. They are mounted in a felt display atop the desk I write you from.

Before I continue, I feel I must say a few words about memory. It is full of holes. If you were to lay it out upon a table, it would resemble a scrap of lace. I am a lover of history, Professor Green. I can nibble my way through the sagas and biographies of the great men and the most tumultuous days. Napoleon, Jefferson, Elizabeth, Alexander! Herodotus, Thucydides, Gibbon, Carlyle! You should see my shelves. They sag under their tomes. I have the highest respect for your trade. The master historians have been my friends, never more so since Rosemary's departure. Even so, history has one flaw. It is a subjective art, no less so than poetry or music. The true historian has two sources: the written record and the witness's testimony. This is as it should be. Yet one is memory and the other is written, quite often, from memory. There is nothing to be done about this defect except acknowledge it for what it is. Yet this is your field's Achilles' heel. You say in your letter the historian writes the truth. Forgive me, I must disagree. The historian writes a truth. The memoirist writes a truth. The novelist writes a truth. And so on. My mother, we both know, wrote a truth in *The 19th Wife*—a truth that corresponded to her memory and desires. It is not *the* truth, certainly not. But *a* truth, yes. Your Church has exerted admirable effort in destroying her credibility. No one can deny she got many details wrong. But the elders and others responsible for dismissing her from the record have failed. Her book is a fact. It remains so, even if it is snowflaked with holes.

I am sorry. After that I had to take a walk. I meant to return to the typewriter in a few minutes, but I went down to my bench. The dolphins did not come today. Just as glorious as their arrival is the swiftness with which they disappear. The mystery of it! If I did not record my impressions of them in my letters and shamefully spotty diary, even I would wonder if they existed at all. They are creatures of the dream. There are times when I miss her terribly. My mother, I mean. She was a brave fool. I love her for that, and so much else.

I see no reason to recount for you the legal wrangling that took place between July and November of that year. It is all rather dull, isn't it: the back-and-forths, the petitions, the claims, the what-have-yous, the lawyers' verbiage as thick as sludge. When I discussed it with Rosemary I told her it was like any divorce case, only grimier by a magnitude of 1,000. One other difference, of course: although the case was about money (when are they not?), it was cloaked in the language of God. (Can I share a sacrilegious thought? When I think about such things—a husband declaring, in deposition, that his wife will be turned away from Heaven—I wish the dolphins were given the responsibility of turning our minds to God, not the clergy. Strike me down, but they have meant more to me than any man of cloth.)

Two things I recall from my child's vantage. Brigham sent, via an agent, an offer to my mother. This was a few days after we arrived at the Walker House. He must have realized she was determined to carry out as public a divorce as possible. He offered—I believe it was—$20,000, to, as they say, disappear. In *The 19th Wife* my mother insists she was indignant at the offer and dismissed it at once. That is not my recollection. Tempted by the large sum, she lingered over it,

429

consulting with her advisers. Both Judge Hagan and Major Pond told her it was not enough. "Twenty thousand dollars is enough to take care of my boys," my mother said. She looked to me as she said this. My memory of it is as clear as if it occurred this morning. Or right now.

Not long after this (it could have been the same afternoon), my mother and Judge Hagan had a disagreement. We were alone in the suite, and they behaved as if I were not present or did not understand them. As payment for his legal services, Judge Hagan wanted 50% of my mother's future settlement. My mother rightly objected. "You're robbing me," she said. "I need every penny for James and Lorenzo."

They settled on 20%, but I know thereafter my mother never fully trusted Judge Hagan again. As time passed, it became clear he was more interested in his own gain and notoriety than saving my mother from Brigham's wrath.

By the end of July, my mother had formally filed suit against the Prophet of the Latter-day Saints. To them—the Saints, I mean—it was no less an affront than serving papers to Christ. (I once read in the newspaper of a man from West Texas who, disappointed that his patch of dirt was not an oil field, filed suit against the Lord. Bureaucracy pondered the case for eleven days.)

On the subject of irony, Brigham responded with an unexpected legal maneuver. Via his lawyers he claimed my mother was not his legal wife for the simple reason that he was already married. At the time there was a dual justice system in Utah—Brigham's and the American code of law. They lay atop one another in a not always natural fit. Some matters were brought before the Church, others before the courts. Brigham chose to use the federal laws for his counterattack. The courts, of course, did not (and do not) recognize polygamy. Therefore my mother was not married to Brigham, never had been his wife, and hence had no valid claims to his property. (Do you ever consider, Professor Green, how the law can be both magnificent and idiotic?)

In essence, he made legal claim that he had never married my mother.

I don't know what my mother thought when she learned of Brigham's tactics. I know that would provide fresh detail for your book, but I'm afraid she never spoke to me directly about it. Was she "mad as Hades"? Professor Green, are you married? If you are, then you have learned the futility of guessing a woman's mind. And isn't that one of woman's 1,001 delights? She is not predictable. The moment you believe you can anticipate her, she will prove you wrong. Rosemary was like that. She used to say, "Don't tell me what's on my mind." If there is any constancy, it's that men are fools.

That's where I stopped yesterday. It was afternoon. No sign of the dolphins. Have they already moved south? They do not migrate as regularly as the whales. You cannot turn your calendar by them. Although they are gone, I will not be surprised if they return tomorrow or next week. Then again, if I were not to see them for many months, that too would not surprise me. Do you know what I miss most about Rosemary? Simply knowing she was there.

I'm afraid even your question about myself—was I ever excommunicated from the Church?—I am unable to answer. You probably have the resources to research that. In any event, whether or not through clerical error or grand scheme I am technically still a member of the Latter-day Saints matters none to me. I do not say that to offend you. I should think I would offend you more if I did not write in full honesty, especially on the subject of faith. In my adulthood I flirted with the Episcopals. Rosemary was a Catholic, although she disagreed with nearly everything they proclaimed. What do I consider myself now? A man attempting to be good. In this endeavor I have no use for church and steeple. If another man does, I only wish he finds what he needs.

I have just now reread your letter. Did Brigham really treat

431

my mother as she describes in *The 19th Wife*? Did she truly want to end polygamy or was she more interested in destroying Brigham? What was her final fate? I wish I could tell you where to turn to answer these questions, but I'm in the dark like you. On the last one—what happened to her?— I suppose in writing this letter, I am subconsciously encouraging you to dig around her story so that one day you may come to me and explain the mystery of her disappearance. How I wish I had even a clue to guide you in your search.

I think at this juncture it would be best if I jumped to November 1873. (I can hear Rosemary now, reminding me to get to the point!) My memories of the flight are clear and sure. I doubt I have given you any insight thus far, but concerning that long night I might be able to pull up a few fresh scraps. But first let me tell you how my mother's career as a public lecturer formed. During our confinement at the Walker House, while Judge Hagan and the others worked up my mother's legal strategy, Major Pond began to plot a different sort of path for her. At the time she was in a precarious financial position. Although future income seemed likely, at the present moment her purse was empty. Gilbert supplemented, but my mother had legitimate concern over how she would house and feed my brother and me. She never expressed this in my presence, but any child of an impoverished household can tell you when the coins are few. I offered her my two gold coins, but she told me to keep them, folding them up in my palm.

My mother's national notoriety was such that a number of promoters telegraphed with offers of representation. These men believed there was such interest in my mother's account that she would be a viable member on the lecture circuit. For the most part my mother ignored the appeals. She was truly interested in her legal situation and restoring her family, not in expanding her fortune. When Barnum wrote offering a substantial sum, her attention sat up for the first time. "Is it for real?" she asked Major Pond. "All this money?" (I never learned the sum, but I understand that a few years before he offered to send Brigham on the road for a fee of $100,000. One can assume Barnum's number for the 19th wife was in this range.)

In rapid response Major Pond, former Union soldier, irritable reporter, conferred upon himself a new profession: lecture agent. "I can get you more," he said. He realized my mother's story was gold. He instructed her to prepare some lectures concerning her experiences. In her writings and commentary she has shrilly denied she began to speak publicly of her ordeals for profit. She claims she solely took to the lecture podium as part of her crusade to demolish polygamy from the United States. On the subject of mammon, she said repeatedly she simply was trying to ensure a roof and food for her boys. As they say: True, but. I loved my mother, but God bless her—she loved her jewels.

I remember the days in early November when she worked at the writing table near the stove. Typically my mother was restless with energy, unable to sit for long. She was always moving about a room, rearranging her skirts and cuffs, turning her rings, patting down her hair. She spoke quickly, sometimes, I fear, without thinking over her words. She was not a born writer. For nearly a week she agonized at the writing table, drafting a sentence or two, standing up, moving to the window, pulling back the shade, sighing with exasperation, and returning to her chair. It was a melodramatic reenactment of what the writer endures to produce a page. (I should know: two days have passed since I began this letter, Professor Green!)

Eventually she wrote three lectures concerning her experiences married to the Prophet and an insider's view of Brigham's harem; the general conditions of polygamy; and the politics of the Mormon Church. Do I need to tell you which became her most popular?

In a trial run, the Major arranged a lecture in the parlors of the Walker House, inviting nearly every Gentile in the Territory. Hundreds, perhaps even 1,000, showed up. I was not allowed to attend the event, but from the suite's window I watched the river of people flow into the hotel. I waited alone in our rooms while my mother spoke downstairs. For more than an hour there wasn't a sound in the hotel other than my mother's clear soprano. I will confess I felt abandoned that night. I do not share this with you to wallow in an old hurt but simply to relay the feelings of a child. Eventually a great roar overtook the hotel. They were applauding my mother, cheering her name, pleading for more. Thereafter Major Pond began to plan my mother's triumph on America's stage.

He arranged her debut in Denver. But there was still the risk of traveling out of Utah. Judge Hagan worried Brigham might not let her depart the Territory; or worse, might send a pack of Danites after her carriage. I do not know on what basis this opinion was formed, but everyone believed it, and suddenly the mood in the suite had changed. (I'm sure you will recall that the investigation of the Mountain Meadows massacre had resumed at this time, and there was much speculation in Brigham's role in those terrible murders. I'm not telling you anything you don't already know when I say many people believed he ordered the killings, or at least condoned them. This speculation no doubt colored her perception of the dangers she faced.)

An air of busy planning overtook the suite. Allies came and went, secret methods of escape were proposed and dismissed. After a few days, a plan was settled on. My mother, Major Pond, Judge Hagan, and the Strattons swore themselves to secrecy. At the time I had no idea what the secret was, but soon it went into implementation. Whenever a guest came to visit, my mother sent him off with one or two items concealed in his coat: a pair of shoes, a hat, a notebook, her hair oil. Item by item, my mother decamped.

Once I realized my mother was planning to depart, I burst

into tears. "I don't want you to leave me," I told her. I expected her to say, "I'm taking you with me." She did not. She rubbed my back while saying, "I have to go."

Again I expected her to add, "I'll return for you." But she did not offer any assurances over our future. I cannot tell you why she behaved as she did at this moment. I like to think she was not so indifferent to my feelings. Yet I doubt there has been a moment in my life when I felt so uncertain of my place in the world as then. I lay awake at night with a sickened heart.

In the morning she said, "If I tell you a secret you have to promise to keep it. Tonight I will leave here for dinner with the Strattons. Later, your uncle Gilbert will come for you. You must do whatever he says. If he tells you to be quiet, you mustn't make a noise. If he tells you to hide in a box, you must fold yourself up like a cat."

In the evening she dressed for dinner as she might on any evening. Gilbert arrived, but he acted as if something were wrong. He gave me a peppermint stick, but became annoyed with my questions. "Lorenzo," said my mother, "remember what we discussed?"

When the Strattons called I began to cry. My mother had become preoccupied with her escape, and thus no longer had the capacity to comfort me. It was Gilbert who held me as she departed the suite. In *The 19th Wife* she writes there was no time for kisses and goodbyes. "I was already a fugitive, there wasn't a minute to spare!" No time for love? My goodness, I hope there's never such a time on my clock.

For about an hour my uncle and I looked at each other. He was never comfortable around children. He asked about my toy horse, but when I told him its name I sensed his interest was not real. Children can tell. I do not fault Gilbert for this. His life in plural marriage—two wives and eighteen children—had eaten away at the love in his soul. Gilbert was a good man; he tried to love his family. Whoever said love is a pie was correct, at least in the polygamous family; there is a finite number of slices to pass out. Eventually I lay down on a blanket and fell asleep.

I do not know what time he woke me, perhaps ten o'clock. The room was dark and I was very tired. Gilbert helped me into my coat and shoes and led me down the servants' stairs into the Walker House kitchen. A large woman in a wide apron was plunging her arms into a sink of hot soapy water. She barely looked up as we passed. At the door there was a tall round basket of the kind I once saw an Indian woman use to haul maize from a field. Gilbert told me to climb in. "I'm going to carry you out to the carriage. Once we're inside you can get out. It will be only a minute. But you can't be seen leaving."

I climbed into the basket, crouching with my knees to my chest. Gilbert set the lid on top. Light came through the basket and my vision was like that of a medieval knight peeping out through his mail. I could see the woman at the sink. She never once stopped washing the dishes. Gilbert heaved me up, and I felt a sway in the pit of my stomach. I wanted to cry out and beg to be released, but I told myself to stay still for the sake of my mother. The driver helped Gilbert set the basket on the carriage floor. When the door was closed, he lifted the lid.

We drove for several blocks, stopping in front of a large shrub that had turned skeletal with autumn. "You must be very still," Gilbert warned. We sat in the carriage for over an hour; the only sound was my heart in my ears. Then I heard footsteps. Gilbert pulled back the curtain. "It's them." He opened the door. My mother climbed in and the Strattons closed the door behind her. She took me into her arms. "I know, my child," she said. "I know. But we're not there yet."

The driver pulled away. With the curtains drawn it was difficult to know our destination. I dared not ask, for both my mother and uncle had looks of grave concern. When the road roughened I could tell we had left the city's limits.

The carriage rocked and creaked and the night was filled with the sound of the crying springs and the horse leather. Eventually my mother released my hand from her grasp, and I assumed we were safe.

I climbed over to the window and pulled back the curtain. From the mountains I could tell we were driving up the Valley, headed north. We drove through bare orchards silvered by the moon. The patches of alkali shone in the night. In the fens geese were calling to one another. Across a meadow a herd of cattle was standing in the dark.

We turned off the road into a canyon. I saw the canyon walls narrow around us. Because I had no idea where we were going, I did not think to alert my mother. Eventually we were driving alongside a frozen creek.

Everywhere neat mounds of early snow sat upon the ice. The moonlight, reflecting off the ice, illuminated the canyon. I pulled back the curtain farther to show my mother the ghostly effect.

She began to panic. "Where are we? What's happening?"

Gilbert banged on the carriage roof and leapt out to talk to the man. I heard the driver say he must have made the wrong turn. "I was certain this was the way to Uintah," he said.

"What if he's working for Brigham?" my mother said when Gilbert was back in the carriage. "What if we've been had by our own plan?"

As we drove out of the canyon, the walls retreated. Eventually the Valley opened before us and the cattle were standing where we left them across the meadow.

It was forty miles to Uintah. We arrived just before daybreak, pulling up to the tiny station. We were waiting for the eastward Union Pacific. As you probably know, Brigham owned the line between Salt Lake and Ogden. That's where you used to catch the U.P.—probably still do, I don't know. Anyhow, I'm sure you understand my mother's plan: anyone tracking my mother would have expected her in Ogden. By driving across the desert in the night, she bypassed their trap.

As the cold day took hold, and the sun revealed the tiny town encased in ice, we heard the air brakes from down the track. I could see the smoke puffing out of the engine. Shortly thereafter the train pulled into the depot, blowing snow all about.

Gilbert embraced my mother. To me he said, "Look after her."

My mother took my hand and we ran to the platform. A porter in white coat and gloves led us to our compartment in the Pullman, where our belongings waited. When the train lurched forward, leaving the station behind, my mother collapsed onto the bench.

"May I speak?" I asked.

She was looking out the window and did not respond. Her profile was very beautiful and still. The morning light had turned yellow and it poured forth upon her, giving her a golden quality. She looked like a woman in a painting in a foreign museum. She studied the landscape as it passed—the high meadows white and yellow in late fall, the sparkling wool of the frost-covered sheep, the mountaintops padded with ancient snow that will never melt. I climbed into her lap and together we watched the world go by.

Three hours later the air brakes screamed and the conductor called, "Wyoming! Evanston, Wyoming!"

Having crossed the Utah border, she said, "Now you can speak."

And there, Professor Green, in that little border town, my mother achieved her freedom. I could not understand the importance of the moment, of course. But I recall while we idled in the station how a cloud drifted before the sun, darkening my mother's face, and how seconds later it passed and her face seemed to burst open with the clearest of light.

Oh look! The dolphins have returned. Explain it! The coincidence, I mean. We can't. We simply have to take note of it and love it for its mystery. As you go about your

438

research about my mother, I ask you to forgive her errors and vainglory. Is she any more guilty than you or I? When you publish your research, will you send a copy? I should like to know what you have learned, most especially how she spent her last days. Sometimes I can hardly believe I don't know my own mother's fate. It seems like a dismal twist at the end of an epic tale. But so it is, and oh how the unknowable keeps me up. With Rosemary gone, the nights are lonely. I lie awake burdened by my mother's disappearance. I trust you'll share with me whatever you discover, even if the news is grim. It's the uncertainty I cannot bear. The not knowing. The endless speculation of where she was on her last day. A chill dashes up my spine when I think of it—there, just now, as if my mother's loving hand were stroking my nape. She's with me. She will always be with me. Remember this as you analyze her life and deeds.

I am, Most Sincerely Yours,

LORENZO DEE

XVII

WIFE #19:

THE GIRL IN SCL

A LITTLE SOMETHING SOMETHING

———

I drove into Mesadale and parked across the street from the Prophet's house. Officer Alton was sitting in his cruiser by the gate, one arm thrown across the seat back, looking down the road, waiting for me. "I'm glad you're here," he said.

"I want to get this over with."

"Go talk to Brother Luke." Alton pointed to a guard standing at the gatepost. "He'll let you in."

"I heard about the FBI. What's happening out here?"

"We don't know."

"How's Queenie?"

"Anxious, like everyone. But OK."

I looked over to the guard. He had his eye on me. I could tell he didn't like that I was here. "Am I going to be all right?"

"Jordan, you have to trust me. Now go inside."

I introduced myself to the guard. "I know," he said. He brought a two-way radio to his mouth: "He's here." The guard led me through a door in the gate and locked it behind us.

Few people get to see inside the Prophet's compound. My dad used to come here for meetings but he never talked about it. The house was by far the biggest in town, which makes sense because he had the most wives. Exactly how many was anyone's guess but definitely more than a hundred. Maybe 150. I don't know. I bet he doesn't either.

"We'll go through the kitchen," the guard said. He was in dark pants and a white dress shirt and a short red tie. If you ignored the Glock 17 in his belt holster, you'd think he was on his way to a sales job at a car dealer.

Three wives were baking in the kitchen. One was looking

443

up a recipe when she saw me. She froze with her finger on the page. The other two pressed themselves against the counter to step out of my way. "Evening, Sisters," the guard said. The women nodded and looked at their feet. We walked down a hall, past a large reception room with a white marble tile floor. Across the hall, a dining room with a U-shaped table for fifty. I saw a steel-plate door leading to, what—a vault? a safe room? an armory?

"Is he here?" I said.

The guard led me up three flights of stairs. Along the way we passed four more wives. They were young, younger than me. Here they were—the reason the boys get kicked out. The Prophet wanted the prettiest, youngest girls for himself. The pervy thing was, they all looked the same.

On the top floor, at the end of a hall, the guard knocked on a door. "Sister?" He knocked again. "Sister, he's here."

The door cracked, then opened wider, then wider still. It was the Prophet's first wife, Sister Drusilla. She waved us in with an old, blue hand. Her room was bare to the point of heartbreaking—a narrow bed shrouded by a dingy summer spread. A writing table with a goose-neck lamp. Two wood chairs. She poured a glass of water from a spiderwebbed pitcher and told me to sit on her bed.

"Is the Prophet here?" I said.

"What? You haven't heard?" she asked. "They came for him." Drusilla's soft mouth sank in on itself.

"I heard the feds couldn't find him."

"That's because he's gone," she said.

"Where is he?"

"I don't know." She looked up with watery eyes. "He could be dead."

"He isn't dead. I spoke to him a little while ago."

"I wish I could be sure."

The best way to describe Drusilla is something like a cross between the First Lady and the Virgin Mary. In the springtime there was a pageant in her honor. The girls in town would dress in yellow and dance to Pioneer hymns like "In Our House" while Sister Drusilla viewed the festivities from a platform. Other than that and Sunday services, we never saw her. Everyone loved her, but no one really knew a thing about her.

"I suppose you know I'm trying to find out what really happened to my dad."

"The Prophet told me."

"My mom's just not the murderer type."

"No one is until they are."

"How well do you know Sister Rita?"

"My whole life."

"I think she had something to do with this."

"Jordan, you don't know?" Drusilla's right, livered hand trembled in her lap. Was she frightened? Early Parkinson's? Or was she putting on a show to freak me out? "Rita's gone. Disappeared. I don't know when exactly. Sometime in the last twenty-four hours. I think they kidnapped her."

"What?" And then, "Maybe she ran away?"

Drusilla shook her head. "I know what's coming next. We've lived through this before."

"Through what?"

"The Siege."

The Siege. Every kid in Mesadale grows up learning about the Siege. We had to read about it, listen to the Prophet sermonize on it, in Sunday school reenact it, chirp songs exalting it, and the girls needlepointed scenes from it. Since breaking off from the Mormons in 1890, the Firsts managed to live in the desert for sixty years pretty much undisturbed. They started off as a cluster of renegades, led by Aaron Webb. Over time this minor outpost grew into a full-blown town, a polygamous theocracy tucked into the sands of the American Southwest. But by the early 1950s, the feds could no longer look the other way. Cut to July 26, 1953. Agents drove into town in unmarked cars, backed up by one hundred state troopers. Quickly they had Mesadale surrounded. You know this kind of scene: the troopers taking position behind car doors; the first-ins standing ready with rammer and shield; an agent in wingtips calling for surrender through a megaphone.

The Siege was about one man. The Prophet. Not the Prophet I've been telling you about, but his father. If he surrendered peacefully, the feds promised to withdraw. That's what the agent shouted through the megaphone: "If you come with us, this can all be over now."

At sunset the Siege began. The shoot-out lasted seven hours. By dawn seventeen Firsts were dead, including nine kids. Hoping to show the country the truth about American polygamy, the feds brought a news photographer. But one picture told the wrong story—that's all it took for the plan to blow up in the feds' clean, Barbasol faces. If you google it, you can find the picture: a little girl lying in a bean field, a neat bullet wound above her left eye. If you didn't know what you were looking at, you'd think it was a drop of jam. That picture ran in the evening papers. By the next morning the feds were caving. The Siege was over. The feds left town, trench coats between their legs.

But the feds got what they wanted. In the last hour a sniper nailed the Prophet. A shot through the neck. That's how the current Prophet came into power. He was seventeen at the time. The day after the Siege, the new Prophet did two things: he buried his father, and he married his dad's youngest wife, a pretty soft-chinned girl named Drusilla. A year later, on the first anniversary, the new Prophet renamed the town Mesadale. It used to be called Red Creek. He wanted America to forget all about the Firsts. And America obliged. Until now.

Sister Drusilla gathered up her skirts to sit beside me on the bed. "This time they want us all dead."

"I don't think so," I said.

"Your dad's dead. How do we know Rita isn't dead? And your mom—we all know what's going to happen to her. Maybe they'll say it's her punishment, but it doesn't matter, dead is dead. And now the Prophet. They want us all gone. But I'm not going anywhere."

"You don't have to."

"This isn't some story in the newspaper. This is my life. This is my family. This is what I believe."

"I know, but all I'm really trying to do is get my mom out of jail."

"They're afraid of us, Jordan."

"Afraid?"

"Afraid of the Prophet, because they know he's right." Her shaky hand balled up into a blue-white fist. "After the Siege, the Prophet always said they'd be back. He always said, Just you wait. And now here they are."

Seeing Drusilla sitting there, with her collar reaching high on her neck, I figured out one thing: some people don't want your help. No point in throwing them a line, they'll swim right by.

"The Prophet thinks you're looking in the wrong place."

"Wrong place? What's that supposed to mean?"

"We have so many enemies. In Washington, in Salt Lake City. Everyone wants us gone. Your father and the Prophet were very close. It makes sense they'd start with him. They want everyone to think we're falling apart from within when in truth, someone's standing outside and picking us off, one by one."

You know that feeling when you think you're almost at the end of a road, and you turn the corner and see only more road ahead?

"What do you think I should do?"

"Find that girl. Sister Kimberly's daughter, you know the one I'm talking about—Sarah 5? She's been working with organizations trying to stop us."

"She didn't kill him."

"How do you know?"

"She told me."

"And you believe her?"

447

"I do."

Sister Drusilla's worn face hardened into a mask. "Interesting." I asked her what she was talking about. When she told me, I couldn't believe it.

"Are you sure?"

"A hundred percent."

"Why didn't she tell me?"

"She's hiding something."

"I can't believe it."

"Believe it, it's true."

Turns out 5 was hiding a little something something: about twelve hours before he was killed, my dad took her as his latest bride.

SAN FRANCISCO EXAMINER

December 1, 1873

ANOTHER REVELATION
FROM GREAT SALT LAKE

Yesterday, in the Territory of Utah's Third District Court, the war between our friends, Brigham and Mrs. XIX, took a turn that even we could not have anticipated. At six o'clock in the evening, Brigham, via his imaginative lawyers, Mssrs. Hempstead and Kirkpatrick, filed a formal answer to his wife's bill of complaint against the Great Almighty Prophet of the West.

In a quick review of Brigham's legal papers we have determined his novel strategy for victory. His adamant reply contends that he and Ann Eliza were never married on April 6, 1868, as her suit originally claims. According to Brigham (whose sense of veracity and candor make him well-suited for our distinguished publication), Ann Eliza is not and has never been his legal wife. He makes this claim from a heartfelt and honorable position. Brigham touchingly claims his undying devotion to his first and only wife, the aptly named Mary Angell, who has been his rib since the tenth day of January, 1834, when they were happily betrothed in old Kirtland. Thus already married, Brigham could not enter into a second, let alone nineteenth union of the heart. That would be polygamy! So you see, Your Honor, this

449

woman's suit is without merit. She is—and here we must adopt the Prophet's unique words as our own—"merely a social harlot." What of Brigham's long-promoted custom of celestial marriage? Simply a hedonistic religious rite with no more legal standing than adultery, admitted the Prophet. Who are the women sleeping beneath the dormers of the infamous Lion House? Concubines, all of them, God bless them each—so sayeth the Prophet.

Next, Brigham confessed to a disloyal liaison with Madame 19. Thus he respectfully asked the court, in its wisdom, to dismiss the matter so that he may return in peace to his only wife, the previously mentioned Angell, to make the kind of restitution we are all too familiar with.

Meanwhile, Sister Ann Eliza, fresh from her escape from the penitentiary otherwise known as Utah, continues to blaze across America's mountainous hinterland, retelling her tale of conjugal woe to anyone who will listen (and pay up fifty cents). The Sister—retiring creature that she is, delicate as a sego lily, bashful as a desert morn—bravely musters her strength to go forth and tell the truth—her word, not ours—about polygamy. As Americans, each of us must do our part by celebrating her courage, and her message of liberty, while, of course, lining her pockets with gold. To anyone who doubts her sincerity, or her motives, we declare: Shame! Has a woman no right to translate her female subjugation into emeralds and pearls? Godspeed, Sister! Onward, Number 19! Take your pleas to Washington and the President! Thus, we shall predict the last stop on Ann Eliza Young's historic journey to freedom: The Bank!

THIS CAN'T GO ON

———

Tom was on the phone freaking out. "It's Johnny. He disappeared. I was doing some work at the front desk, I told him to stay with the dogs, and when I came back he was gone."

"When was this?"

"Almost two hours ago. I went driving around looking for him, but I didn't even know where to start. I just drove up and down St. George Ave. Jordan, where are you? I've been calling."

"There's no reception in Mesadale. Right now I'm in Kanab."

"I need you to come home, now. It's just that—" Tom stopped. "Johnny could be anywhere."

"Don't worry. He's like this."

"I'm going out of my mind here. What if something's happened?"

"Don't start thinking like that."

"I called the cops. They thought I was nuts. They said, 'Let me get this straight. You're reporting a runaway runaway?' They said they couldn't do anything for at least twenty-four hours. Jordan, I didn't even know his last name."

Part of me wanted to say: Tom, get a grip. The kid's a flake. He's gone and there's nothing you can do. Another part of me wanted to say: I know, I know, and turn this into a conversation between the sob sisters. But neither seemed right and all I could come up with was, "I'll be there as soon as I can."

When I got to the sandwich shop, 5 was closing up, her hair under a plastic beret. "Why didn't you tell me you married my dad?"

451

She went behind the counter for a cup of coffee. She took her time, pouring the cream and the sugar, stirring it, rinsing the spoon. Her eyes had a cold gleam, like chips of soda-machine ice. "Why would I want to tell you about the worst day of my life?"

"Because my mom's in jail for something she didn't do."

"That has nothing to do with me."

"You were his wife."

She sipped her coffee slowly, cautiously putting together her words. "If you think holding a knife to your stepdaughter's throat while you rape her is a wedding ceremony, then I guess I am his wife. Or his widow or whatever. But if you don't think like that—and for some reason I thought you of all people wouldn't—then you'd realize I'm no more his wife than you are, asshole." She started cleaning up the sandwich counter and throwing the prep trays into the sink, and they made a terrible clang, stainless steel on stainless steel. "You think your life sucks so much? Well, guess what? My life sucks worse."

"Jesus, I had no idea."

"Yeah, well, you have no idea about a lot of shit. Now go sit down."

I sat in a booth by the window, and she carried over two sodas and two wax-paper cups. "Don't say anything. Just let me tell you what's going on."

"OK, but first—"

"No, stop. When I'm done, then you can speak, all right? First of all, let me start by saying this whole thing sucks. Like big-time. OK, so let's begin. Like I said, I ran away a couple of months ago. I just split, caught a ride over here, and got this job. I knew it was crazy to stop here. I should've left Utah, but you know what, I love my mom. Or I used to, or I still do, I don't know. Anyway, like I told you, I couldn't leave her back there so I thought I'd go back and rescue her. Except, how the fuck was I going to do that? I didn't have a car or any money or anything. But I kept thinking it was possible. You know Sister Karen?"

"The postmistress?"

"She's been really helpful in all this. She got my letters to my mom without him seeing them. I kept writing her telling her I was OK and not far away and to hold tight, I was coming for her."

"And?"

"Jordan, let me finish. So that went on for a few months and I was kinda at a standstill. Then my mom writes me this letter saying she's sick, real sick, maybe even dying. Says she's had a heart attack or something, she was real vague about it, but she said the Prophet told her she didn't have much time. When I got the letter I totally flipped. I walked down to the end of town and caught a ride back to Mesadale. When I got to my mom's cabin, she was really happy to see me and started crying, but I was like, Mom, I thought you were sick? So she goes, Oh that? I'm all better now. The important thing is you're back. I know your stepfather will be real glad to see you. Then she walked over to the big house to get him. When they came back I was totally scared to see him, but he just said, I'm glad you're back. Please stay as long as you like.

"And that was it until the next day. I woke up and everything was really peaceful, you know how quiet the desert is in the morning before everyone gets up, and I was lying in bed just thinking about that when my mom came and sat down. Sarah, honey, there's something I want to talk about. That's when she sprang it on me. She wanted me to marry him, her own husband—I know, right? But she had it all planned out, or he did, or someone did. Obviously it was time for me to go, but when I opened the door there he was on the porch. He was in a bolo tie and his hair was greased back and he was wearing some sort of cologne, like old leather, and he wasn't alone."

"The Prophet?"

"You guessed it. He had this creepy smile, his lips curled up on his teeth, and it was so obvious what was coming next I

453

started screaming my head off, yelling, There's no fucking way! My mom, she took me into her room, told me to calm down, and when I didn't she slapped me, not hard, but just hard enough to show the Prophet whose side she was on. Then you aren't going to believe what she did, I mean no one's ever going to believe this, but it's true: she got out her wedding dress and said, real calm and everything, Now, honey, put this on.

"I was fighting her, kicking her, telling her to go fuck herself. Then there was a knock on the door. It was the Prophet. Sister Kimberly, let me have a word. When we were alone he came real close and squeezed the back of my neck the way you grab a dog. If you don't shut the fuck up, I'm going to kill your mother and then you. I swear to God that's exactly what he said, not that I believe in God, but you know what I mean. He goes, I'll kill you, you little slut. Not now. Not tomorrow. But I'll be coming for you and you'll be scared the rest of your life because you'll know one night I'll be at your door and when you open it you're going to find your mother's head in a fucking bag."

5 stopped. Her eyes looked like they'd seen the worst the world could offer.

Then she laughed.

"And so I married him. That night—the night he was killed—I took off from Mesadale. I heard all the screams in the house, I didn't know what was happening, but it was my chance to get out of there and so I ran down the road into the night."

"And here you are."

"Here I am. You know what the fucked-up part is? I still love my mom. Jordan, I'm only fifteen. I want her back. Am I insane or what?"

"You're not insane."

After that, 5 and I talked about the Prophet and Mesadale and all sorts of other shit too. If you drove by the sandwich shop that night, you would've seen the silver-green lights

454

burning through the plate glass and two kids at a booth in the window, eating corn chips and drinking soda and shredding their wax-paper cups on the table and talking for hours, just like two kids anywhere who'd rather stay out than go home to bed.

"Just one question," I said. "Why would Sister Karen help you like that?"

"You haven't figured that out by now?"

"Figured out what?"

"You really don't know, do you? Sister Karen's the conductor."

"The conductor?"

"Of our underground railroad. She's the one who helps the girls get out."

REDPATH'S LYCEUM

Under the Directorship of

JAMES REDPATH

PRESENTS

Mrs. Ann Eliza Young

The Notorious 19th Wife!
Apostate & Crusader!

LECTURING ON THE SUBJECTS OF:

MORMON POLYGAMY!

INSIDE BRIGHAM'S HAREM!

THE LIFE OF THE PLURAL WIFE!

&

OTHER TRUTHS ABOUT

MULTIPLE MARRIAGE!

THE TREMONT TEMPLE

BOSTON

• ONE NIGHT ONLY •

FEBRUARY 19, 1874

Admission — Only Fifty Cents!

Inside Room 112, I found Tom holding a bag of ice to Johnny's eye.

"What happened here?"

"Not much, dude. And you?"

"He's high," said Tom. "And he has a black eye. And I found this on him." He pointed to a cheap gold watch on the credenza.

"Where'd you get that?"

"This guy. It was weird, he just gave it to me. Isn't that weird?"

"Plus he's scaring the dogs." They were watching the scene from the bed. Elektra was agitated and shaking, and Joey was panting hard.

"Johnny, where were you?"

"With the ladies."

"There's no point in talking to him," said Tom. "He's totally looped. Thank goodness you're home."

Technically it wasn't my home, but it didn't seem like a good time to point that out. "What can I do?"

"Get him ready for bed. He should sleep in here tonight."

"Anyone got anything to eat?" said Johnny. "Krispy Kremes, maybe?"

"Bedtime, big guy." I pulled Johnny out of his jeans, dumped him on the bed, and threw a blanket over him. "Now go to sleep."

"I'd kill for a Whopper," he said. "Or some McNuggets." He was stumbling into sleep, his words slowing down. He smacked his lips, let out a soft moan, and pushed out a final thought for the night: "You think they got a Snickers in the vending machine?" Then he was out. He'd sleep till dawn.

Tom was on the edge of the other bed, stroking Joey's ear. He had to be pissed at me for bringing this mess into his life. "I was really worried," he said. "About both of you. What do you think got into him? Maybe he freaked out because you weren't around?"

"I'm afraid this wasn't a onetime event. Johnny's got a lot of issues."

Tom shrugged. "I don't care. He can stay as long as he wants." And then, "You too."

He went into the bathroom to get ready for bed. I opened his laptop and went online to that website, 19thwife.com. Under the If You Need Help tab, there was information about a place in Salt Lake called the Ann Eliza Young House. There was a picture of an old gabled house with a big stained-glass window. At the top of the page it said, We're always here.

Tom came out of the bathroom stripped to his sacred underwear. That's another thing I love about the Mormons: that crazy holy underwear is actually kinda sexy. Roland calls it God's lingerie. Which reminded me: I hadn't talked to him in days. He still thought I was coming back for the nursery job the next day. Isn't that how it works sometimes— the big decisions, I mean. You don't actually make them, you just roll into them once they've become inevitable. Sometime between meeting Tom in the lobby of the Malibu Inn and now, I had decided to stay in Utah to see this thing through.

"Question," I said.

"Shoot."

"Why do you still wear that?"

"What? You don't like it?"

"It's not that. I mean, don't you have to be a Mormon to wear that underwear?"

"Technically, but it's not about the church anymore. It's about me. Besides, it's actually pretty comfortable. You know what my mom used to say when I was a kid? She used to say, wearing these was like wearing a hug. I know that's cheesy but it's kinda true. The only problem now is you have to have a temple recommend to buy them. But I found this site online where I can get new ones." He sat on the bed. "What about you? Do you always sleep in your clothes?"

I hadn't even noticed that I had crawled into bed in my jeans. "I don't know, I guess. Does that bother you?"

"It makes me feel like you're ready to bolt."

"Don't think of it like that."

"Tomorrow I'm going to buy you some PJs."

"I wish you wouldn't."

We pulled up the blanket, and Elektra dug under and curled up between us. Joey found a spot at the foot of the bed. The room went quiet except for the sighs of the dogs. "Jordan?"

"Yeah?"

"Can I ask you a question about your mom?"

"OK."

"What was she like?"

"What do you mean?"

"What kind of mom was she?"

"I don't know, pretty average, I mean considering."

"Did you get to spend a lot of time with her?"

"Sure."

"What would you do?"

"I don't know, the usual stuff."

"Like what?"

"We'd hang out, I guess."

"Did she bake you cookies and things like that?"

"Not really."

"No?"

"It was kind of hard to do any baking. The kitchen had all these rules."

"What else would you do?"

"I'd hang out in her room sometimes."

"And talk?"

"Yeah."

"About what?"

"All sorts of stuff."

"Like what?"

"God and the church and things like that, but other things, too."

"Like what?"

"I don't know. Like the sun, and how different it was in the summer from the winter. And the mountains and how pretty they looked when there was snow. And Virginia."

"Who's that?"

"Our old dog."

"What happened to her?"

"She's still alive."

"You must miss her."

"Virginia? Yeah, sometimes."

"I meant your mom."

"Sure, I guess."

Tom dented his pillow and turned on his side. "Jordan?"

"Yeah."

"What do you think's going to happen?"

"She'll either get out or she won't."

"When are you going to see her again?"

"Soon, real soon."

In the morning I told Tom about the place in SLC. "I'm taking Johnny there."

"Maybe there's someplace closer." He was getting ready to go to the front desk, pinning his name tag to his shirt. He had a bright polished look, his cheeks shining with morning cheer.

"There's no place else," I said. "I don't want him to put you through another night like last night. I'll be back tomorrow."

"Wait till Saturday and I'll go with you."

"This can't wait. A lot can happen in a week."

460

"I'll miss you."

"C'mon, it's only been two days."

"Two days is enough." And then, "But I guess not for you."

I decided to leave Elektra with Joey in Tom's room. She didn't like that idea and ran out to the van and tried to jump through the window. I had to drag her back inside. As I pulled out of the lot her brown snout was in the window, leaving prints on the glass. Tom was in the lobby behind the front desk, keeping his eye on my van, watching me as I drove off. He waved as I pulled out but I don't think he saw me wave back.

Johnny slept most of the way on the futon, still hung over from last night. Every once in a while he woke up to announce he needed to piss, but other than that he was more or less passed out. It was nearly five hours to SLC, which gave me way too much time to think.

I first saw the temple from the freeway. I guess you'd say it's beautiful, what with all that white granite and the forest of spires and the gold angel playing his trumpet on top of that gold ball. I shook Johnny's foot and told him to wake up. "There it is," I said. "The mother ship."

Johnny stared out at the temple. "You ever been here before?" he said.

"Nope."

"Me neither. It's not really what I expected."

"What'd you expect?"

"I don't know, for some reason I thought it would look like heaven."

"Maybe it does."

"Where's this famous lake?"

"Out there somewhere."

"I don't see it."

"I'm sure it's there."

"So tell me, Mr. International Poster Boy for Gay Marriage, what brings us to Salt Lake?"

"What are you talking about now?"

461

"You and Tom, pretty serious, right, right?" He started whistling *here comes the bride*. "No, seriously, why'd we drive all the way up here?"

"I've got an appointment."

"Is it one of our chat session ladies? I've been dying to meet the others."

"I never heard back from them. This is someone else."

We were off the freeway now, driving toward Temple Square along an eight-lane road pumping traffic into the city. Except there wasn't much traffic and no one was walking around. I stopped at a red light for a tram to cross. I was the only car waiting and there wasn't anyone on the tram.

"I'm going to drop you somewhere and I'll go have my meeting and then come back for you. I'll probably be gone a little more than an hour."

"Whoa whoa whoa, wait a minute, you want me to do what?"

"Just hang out somewhere."

"Why are you giving me the heave-ho all of a sudden?"

"Because you look like shit and smell like pot. I can't take you to a meeting."

"No way, dude, you don't haul my ass to SLC and then leave me in the van."

"I won't leave you in the van. We'll find a park somewhere."

"I'm not sitting in a boiling ass park where all the repressed Mormon fags can chase me."

"Johnny. You know how I feel about that word."

He mimicked me: *"You know how I feel about that word."*

"Here. Right here." I pulled over, cutting off the guy behind me. "Here's a mall right here. You go in there and hang out. Give me two hours. Here's ten dollars. Buy yourself a hot dog and go fuck yourself."

"Someone didn't get laid last night and is now taking it out on me."

"Why are you always so nasty?"

462

"Because I'm from Mesadale, you mother."

"That excuse is getting old."

"Look in the mirror, buddy."

"And none of your running-off shit, either. If you aren't here in exactly two hours, I'm driving back to St. George and you can have a really nice life."

"You're a total motherfucker, you know that?" Johnny popped the door and ran off, the black soles of his sneakers flashing until he was gone.

The Ann Eliza Young House was located on East South Temple Street, a block from the LDS Temple, the Tabernacle, the Family History Library, and all the rest. It looked like a lot of the old houses around there except I recognized it by the golden beehive in a pane of stained glass. I rang the bell and a girl a few years older than me opened up. I told her I'd seen the website and wanted to know if it was true.

"If what's true?"

"If you're really here to help."

She laughed like I'd made a joke or something, and then she saw I was totally serious and led me inside to a back office. There were a couple of pictures of the girl on her desk, shots of her with her arms around other blond girls. One picture showed the girl in her missionary outfit, with the black-and-white name tag and the long dark skirt, standing in front of the lights of Times Square.

"Have a seat. Our director's out for about an hour, but you're welcome to wait right here."

"I only need a little information."

"I'm happy to tell you about our program, get you oriented and everything, but only the director can formally admit you. If you want, I can show you the boys' room and you can take a shower and put on some—"

She stopped. "What's wrong? Are you hungry? We have some veggie lasagne left over."

I told the girl I wasn't hungry. I told the girl I wasn't there for me. "I've got a kid. I mean, he's not mine, he just started hanging out with me down in St. George." I told her the whole story. Well, not the whole story, just the part about Johnny latching on to me.

"I am so sorry," the girl said. "I thought—"

"I know."

"You look so young."

"I wanted to check this place out. But I don't want to leave Johnny just anywhere."

"Of course not. You want to leave him someplace where he's going to have a chance."

She was an attractive girl, pert, maybe twenty-four, her banged hair well conditioned and full of shine. Her features were small and precise, almost a little hard and cold, and she gave off a fresh, antibacterial soap odor. "The Ann Eliza Young House is a really special place," she said, her voice a little formal and practiced. "There's nothing like it in Utah, or the country, for that matter. With all this debate about polygamy and the Firsts, sometimes we lose sight of the fact that there are kids out there who need a place to sleep. Tonight. That's why we're here, for those kids who don't have anywhere to go and can't wait for the policy debates and law suits to get sorted out. You want a quick tour?"

She led me down a hall, saying, "I don't know how much you know about what's going on with polygamy these days."

"A little."

"Then you know how much help these kids need. What we do is give them a place to live and begin the process of letting them be kids again. What was happening before was they'd go from a house with eight or ten wives and thirty or forty kids—"

"Sometimes more."

"Yes, sometimes more, and then they'd get dropped into a foster family and the kids would be sent off to school, and everyone would say, OK, they're fine. Well, they weren't fine.

464

These kids have some unique issues, and we're here to help them adjust. By the way, what's your name?"

I told her. "And yours?"

"Kelly. Kelly Dee."

She showed me around upstairs, the boys' bunk room, the community bathroom, a lounge with a box of DVDs and a rack of worn-out paperbacks. She was leading me down the staircase when she stopped on the landing to point out the stained-glass window. The sun was hitting it, illuminating the beehive, and the pieces of glass were thick and smooth and gold and white. "Isn't that beautiful?" she said. "That's original to the house, from the 1870s. Stained glass was very rare at the time around here. That window's sort of famous. Do you know who Ann Eliza Young was?"

"No idea."

"She was one of Brigham's wives. She lived here for a while, before she divorced him. She always said he put in this window so his spies could find her house, but there's no proof that's true, but that's what makes it pretty well-known today. Anyway, she went on to become a crusader in the fight to end polygamy."

"I guess she failed."

"No, not at all. She played a big part in forcing the church to give it up."

The tour was over and we were back in her office, sitting around waiting for the director to show up. "How long have you worked here?"

"Actually, I'm just a volunteer. I'm here full-time in the summer, and two days a week during school. I'm getting my master's at BYU. In history. Women's studies." She said it with a touch of pride, or rebellion. "It's how I got involved with this place. I'm writing my thesis on Ann Eliza Young. That's how I first heard about what was going on with polygamy today. I had no idea—I mean, I heard the stories about places like Mesadale and everything, but I never really thought it was as bad as everyone said. At the time I was really immersed

465

in my research. Because I'm writing about the nineteenth century, it's all old documents and texts, you know—rummaging around the archives. I was learning a lot, but one thing I was having a hard time understanding was her rage—Ann Eliza's, I mean. She was really mad at Brigham and the LDS Church over polygamy. Not mad like pissed off, but mad like she was waging spiritual battle. Over the years a lot of Saints, they've just kind of dismissed her as this angry ex-wife, but this was more than that. This was a woman on a mission, so to speak. It had become her faith, which was a really interesting idea to me, you know, to give up one faith for another, one that's so opposite to what you used to believe.

"Then I thought—you know, the best way to understand what Ann Eliza was feeling, to actually understand why she was so outraged, was maybe to truly comprehend what polygamy was like for her. At first I just couldn't wrap my head around it—I mean, I'm just your average LDS girl with a mother and a father and an older brother and a younger sister and a dog named Lily. Sure I saw the world when I was on my mission—here, that's me in New York, which I totally loved. Maybe it was my time on mission that helped me realize that the only way to understand people is to listen to them. So anyway, I decided I had to meet someone who had come from that world, someone who could help me get what she'd gone through. Eventually I found the website 19thwife.com and arranged an interview with a plural wife."

"You should've called me."

"What?"

"Nothing. It's a joke. Not funny. You were saying—"

"I met this woman in a coffee shop not far from here. I took my tape recorder, my notepad, and I felt, you know, almost like a detective. It was very exciting because usually historians, we only meet people through documents, never in person. Then this woman walks in and she was very thin and very frightened, and very young, younger than me by a couple

466

of years. Her eyes were red—I'll never forget how red they were—but she wasn't crying. That's when it hit me: this isn't a research project, these are people's lives, people's lives ruined by this doctrine that is a by-product of *my* church. Of course I knew that before, but it's one thing to know something intellectually, it's another to meet it face-to-face. This woman, she sat opposite me in the booth and her back was very rigid and she just began to tell me about her husband and her twelve sister wives, very quietly, very methodically, as if she had practiced it over and over. Eventually she ran away, eventually she decided that if this life was what God wanted for her, then she didn't want God, but what was killing her, the reason she wanted to talk to me in the first place, was she had to leave her kids behind, a boy and a girl. You should've seen her—she just kind of crumpled as she said she decided the only way to save her kids was to leave them and come back for them later, but you could just tell it was one of those terrible decisions a mother shouldn't have to make, but she made it, and there she was. Now she wanted to get them out, but she really didn't have any way of doing that. I mean, they talk about the disenfranchised, but this woman had nothing, not even her faith. Eventually she took my hand and said, 'Can you help me?' I'll never forget how cold her hand was, like a claw of ice.

"It was then I knew I had to do something. I couldn't just sit in my library carrel and read through all my texts and take my seminars and write a master's thesis that was full of ideas but empty on people. Of course, that's what the department wanted me to do, but I couldn't, and fortunately my adviser, Professor Sprague, she totally understood what I was talking about and sort of sponsored me. So I got an internship here and that was two years ago. And now I just try to help out women like that, and the kids. This whole experience has changed my life."

Kelly looked at the clock. "The director should be back soon."

"So this lady you were talking about?"

"The lady I interviewed?"

"No, the lady this place is named after. What'd you say she did?"

"She really helped bring an end to polygamy. She went around giving lectures, telling everyone what it was really like. People all over the country went to see her, and for a while there she was as famous as, I don't know, a rock star or someone on tv, but this was in the 1870s. Eventually she went to Congress and described polygamy and met President Grant and told him all about it. After her visit to Washington the government finally started putting some teeth into the antipolygamy laws. She got the ball rolling, and eventually the church had to give it up. She called us on it, and she won."

"How do you know so much about her?"

"I've spent the last two years of my life reading everything I can about Ann Eliza Young. There's a lot out there, she wrote this really famous book called *The 19th Wife*, and there are diaries and letters and all these records by people who knew her and the more I read, the more I want to know. You know what's funny, even today a lot of members don't like her. She fought Brigham pretty hard in their divorce, and she said lots of nasty things about the church in her book, some of which were misleading and completely biased, but she also made us see the truth about something very important. She saved the church, in her own way, you know, by forcing us to give up polygamy. There's no way I could believe in a church that supported that, especially now that I've seen it for myself. I feel like I owe her so much—my faith, it's the most important thing I have, along with my family, of course, but I love my church as much as I can love anything. I'm just really glad she put us through that, and flushed it out of our system.

"To some she was a real hero. But a lot of Saints, even today, they're angry at her. Some people, like some of Brigham's descendants, won't even say her name. A few years ago they put out a book of remembrances about Brigham, you know, collecting old letters and other papers by Brigham's children and grandchildren describing Brigham at home, what kind of father he was, and in the back there's a list of his wives. They completely left her off. Edited out of history! Thankfully not everyone's like that. This house, it was started by a group of LDS members who felt the need to do something about polygamy today. It wasn't very hard to raise the money to buy it and fix it up. A lot of people wanted to help. They see it as I do, as our duty, you know, because in some ways it's part of our legacy."

"I know I need to talk to the director," I said, "but can you tell me how this whole thing is going to work for Johnny?"

"Sure, first she has to meet him and make sure he'll fit in. This is a community, and we can't have someone destructive or violent or what have you."

"He's not like that." Which wasn't exactly true.

"Of course there are rules, which we're real strict about. Among the many things these kids need is discipline. No drinking and drugs, no stealing, no weapons of any kind— any signs of those and you're immediately out. It's a no-tolerance zone. Before he's admitted Johnny will have to sign a statement saying he won't break the rules. It's an important step, making a commitment and keeping it. Last but definitely not least, there's a lot of paperwork, filing with the various agencies, but that can happen after he checks in. We try to spare the kids from the bureaucracy. How do you think he'll feel about all that?"

"He's a bit, I don't know, unpredictable."

"Usually the longer they've been on their own, the less they want to stay. They're scared they're going to be kicked out again. It's perfectly natural. Whenever I think about what these kids have gone through"— Kelly looked up and her face darkened, as if it had been slapped—"it makes me really mad. You see, I finally understand what Ann Eliza was so outraged about. It's the kids. These men, in their search for an unlimited supply of women, they end up destroying a lot of kids."

"Tell me about it."

"You know what makes me the angriest? That someone has put them through this in the name of God. That's the saddest part, these kids come out and they've been robbed of everything. Their childhoods, their families, but, worst of all, they've been robbed of God. And most of them never find him again."

"That's not the worst part," I said. "The worst part is you come out of there and it's pretty much impossible to ever love anyone again."

"You're right," she said. "But I think we're talking about the same thing."

I told Kelly it was fine if she had something to do, she didn't have to wait with me, but she said she didn't have anything else to do. "So this lady," I said, "Ann Eliza Young? She was like wife number what?"

"It depends."

"On?"

"Who's counting."

"I'm asking you."

"Then I don't know. She was commonly known as his nineteenth wife, but everyone agrees that she was at least his twenty-seventh. But there's a lot of evidence that suggests Brigham married more women than that. With all the secret weddings, the numbers get pretty screwy."

"They always are."

"That's one of the things I'm researching. Not what number she was, because to tell the truth I don't think we'll ever know for sure. I'm more interested in what it meant to a woman to not even know her position in her family. It's one of those things that gets brushed over and a lot of scholars say, Well, what difference does it make? But I think it must've had a huge psychological impact on these women to not know their number."

"My mom. She's a nineteenth wife."

"Come again?"

And so I told her. Everything. It just came out, and it took a long time, but I told her like I've just told you.

At the end of it Kelly said, "I wish there was something I could do."

"You can help Johnny. He won't make it if he stays with me."

We stopped talking. There was so much to think about. I can't tell you what Kelly was thinking, but I was thinking, Look at this girl. LDS through and through. BYU rah rah rah. *Rise, all loyal Cougars and hurl your challenge to the foe.* No coffee, no tea, no Diet Coke, never a drink or a smoke or a hit, temple garments as white as Wasatch snow, Relief Society chick, missionary missy—where was it she went in New York? Times Square? Blond, banged, sharp-nosed Kelly Dee bringing the word of the Restoration to New York City, bringing the news of the Prophet to 42nd Street? Two years with her companion, Sister Kimmie probably, or Sister Connie or Sister Meg or someone, the two of them always together, never apart, smiling, talking, chatting, helping, maybe handing out a book, maybe not, Sister Kelly never tiring, never giving up, never getting angry or disappointed or dispirited when someone on the street said Joseph Smith can suck my dick, just continuing firm in her belief, never once thinking, I'm better than this, never once thinking, I'm better than *you.* Here she was, Kelly Dee, of hearty Pioneer stock, always well loved, always loving, three years from marriage, four from motherhood, Sister Kelly, who probably plans for weeks in advance when it's her turn to stand up in church and bear witness, Sister Kelly, who probably keeps a to-do list clipped to her fridge, who probably spends Sunday nights shampooing those waves of blond hair, so clean, so hardworking, a human honeybee, she of the chosen people, of the desert kingdom, of the Saints. Yes, here she was, sitting in a crappy office chair helping kids like me. And not just

471

helping, because there are people who are like, *Oh, you poor thing*, and cluck their tongues, and maybe give you a dollar, but they don't understand and don't want to understand. And then there are people who are like, *Oh, you poor thing, now come and meet my God, He is the only way*. But not Kelly—she wasn't just helping, assisting, offering a hand. No, she was researching, reading, learning, talking, understanding. Working hard to understand, wanting to understand, telling herself that's the most important thing she can do. And it meant more to me than anything else. She got it. I could see it in her blue-as-a-Deseret-morn eyes. She got me. She knew I had been completely totally royally screwed. She knew religion had fucked me, like that nasty john who paid me fifty bucks to shove his arm up my ass. And she also understood there's a point when you have no choice but to get up and move on. And, oh boy, there I went, more of those goddamn tears, I couldn't believe I was cracking up in the Ann Eliza Young House. "I'm sorry," I sobbed. "I didn't come here for this."

Kelly handed me a tissue. "It's all right," she said. "I understand. I completely understand."

XVIII

RESTORATION
OF ALL THINGS

THE 19TH WIFE

CHAPTER TWENTY-SIX
The Stones of Nauvoo

After a brief stop at the border between Utah and Wyoming, Lorenzo and I rode on to Laramie. It was my first time in a Gentile city, and I expected the highest form of civilization. Surely any metropolis ruled by law and reason, rather than superstition and tyranny, would have organized itself into a Great City. Yet in Laramie, this proved not to be the case. We exited the station to find a frozen town of dirt, cows, and pigs. The wind whipped from all ends and the livestock used much of downtown as its huddling shed. The ranchers and cowhands walked around in the caliper-legged manner of the man molded on horseback. The women, it seemed, were as rough as the men. I asked one the direction to my hotel. She was corseted up in red and black, with a velvet ribbon about her throat. She eyed me warily. "Why? You working there too?"

I must confess my disappointment. Brigham's city outranked this town in every way but one. Walking down the street, dodging the hogs and the sheep, I counted six steeples, spires, and bell towers. At one crossroads, Baptist and Methodist Churches faced one another in seeming harmony. Despite the rustic quality of my environs, I was grateful to be free of Orthodoxy.

Lorenzo and I had sequestered ourselves in a hotel room for two days when Major Pond arrived from Salt Lake, carrying the newspapers. The *Tribune* had run an article on my escape entitled, "Godspeed, Mrs. Young!" He was very excited and worn from his journey, and I urged him to rest before we got on to business. But he would not hear of it. "Everyone wants to hear from you," he said. "Look at this telegram, they want you to speak here in Laramie." I told him I wanted to rest for a few days and spend time with Lorenzo, who had suffered much during our flight.

"I understand, but you'll need to be in your finest form in Denver," the Major advised. "We'll need money for the trip, the hotels, a new dress for you." With my consent, he wanted to rent a lecture hall at the Wyoming Institute. "We'll charge a dollar fifty a head, and the hall can hold four hundred."

Reader, I was not practicing false modesty when I said, "Surely there can't be four hundred people in all of Wyoming who want to hear from me."

But there were! My first night of lecturing in a free land was a success. Every seat was sold, and Major Pond regretfully turned many dozen away. I have been advised by my wise editor, to whom I owe a certain amount, that a personal story such as mine will inevitably lose the reader's attention if I go on too long about triumphs and success. ("The reader wants challenges, obstacles, and despair!" he has suggested, and perhaps once too often.) Although I do not wholly agree with this fine man's opinion, on this and other matters, I will spare my Reader any further description of my lecturing triumphs in Laramie, and move onward with my tale.*

After my evening at the Wyoming Institute, more invitations arrived. Major Pond convinced me that en route to Denver we should stop in Cheyenne and Fort Russell. I tried to decline, worried that I had already spoken to everyone in the Teton Range who might take interest in my tale. Major Pond assured me many more would be found. Again I will

---

* The authoress wishes to point the more serious reader to the archives of the *Laramie Union* should he care to read their substantial review of my appearance. The same is true of the local newspapers of all the cities I appeared in as I journeyed to Washington (with, of course, the exception of New York).

spare you the details of those events, but I can assure you (and the newspapers will attest) that my success at the lectern continued in Cheyenne and Fort Russell. Interest in the harem, it seems, runs deep.

In Denver, a newspaper out of Central City greeted me with my first blast of skepticism: "We can only hope Mrs. Young does not expect the citizenry of Denver to be as easily astonished as she has become accustomed to. Our ladies and gentlemen have listened to the greatest speakers of our day, company by no means which we include her in."

"Ignore them," advised the Major. "You will be loved."

As I took the lectern of Denver's New Baptist Church, a heavy anxiety overtook me, burdening me with the sensation of walking through deep sand. Looking out into the mass of faces and the clamshell lights upon me, I recalled my days on Brigham's stage. How easy that job was in comparison— simply spilling out someone else's words! That evening I gave my well-practiced lecture, "My Life in Bondage." I began nervously, I know, for many minutes I stirred no response in my audience. There is no greater silence than that of an auditorium waiting anxiously for something to happen. In the front row two young girls, each no older than ten, stared up at me. One was dark in the brow, with wide-set wondrous eyes. Her sister wore her red hair down in ringlets. They regarded me sincerely. If I had any doubt about my purpose, their lovely gaze blew it away. By the time I began recounting my mother's conversion, I lost myself in my tale. The feeling was such that I was no longer lecturing, but reliving my ordeal. The Reformation, the hand-cart fiasco, Mr. Dee! Were someone to tap me on the shoulder and ask, Do you have the date and time? I would have regarded him blankly, unaware of where I was. My story possessed me, as that black ghost of Brigham had once possessed me. It controlled the words forming on my tongue. I have gone on to meet many great writers in my time. It was Mrs. Stowe who described the act of composition similar to this. "I become, quite simply, the vessel for the muse," she said to me. For those of you who wonder how Joseph could put his face in a hat and dictate his Book: I offer this alternative explanation. Imagination can take command of the person. Ask the artist, the actress, the poet feverishly producing line after line of his Epic! Is it God speaking, or the mysterious mind?

Now it seemed my life's adventure was in possession of my audience, too. Anyone who has stood before a gathering knows when he has captivated his audience, or when he has failed to do so. There is a spirit in the hall for each scenario, and they are as opposite in nature as the bright angel and the dark demon. Tonight the angel visited Denver, shining his light upon me. As I concluded my story, describing my escape through the night, my audience exploded with applause. When I left the lectern at least a hundred rushed the stage to meet me.

The lecture was such a success, even the skeptics out of Central City commended me: "There is no doubt her story, if true, holds a certain amount of interest for many." Major Pond showed me a telegram from James Redpath, whose Lyceum Agency in Boston represented the talents of Susan B. Anthony and Frederick Douglass, personas whose names I recognized but whose reputations, at the time, I little understood. He proposed a contract of fifty lectures for $10,000. Major Pond dismissed the offer: "We can get more."

Major Pond concocted a plan for us to travel to Boston, where Mr. Redpath could listen to me in person. "I'm convinced once he has sat at your feet, and heard your tale, he'll sign you on as his biggest attraction for whatever fee we demand."

"As long as we get to Washington."

"We will," the Major promised. "Washington is our last stop. But tonight you're the toast of the Rockies, the Queen of the Eastern Slopes."

Despite my local triumphs, I felt little pleasure. My mission was not to entertain, nor to haul in high-grossing receipts, nor

478

to serve as top-billing for Mr. Redpath, as much as Major Pond admired his roster. I took little reward from the thunder of twelve hundred hands beating in applause, or as many feet tramping upon the floorboards. The columns of newsprint praising my bravery and my orating skills, my sense of timing, and my gentle comic touch—these could not embolden me. None of this mattered except as a weapon in my larger Crusade. I had left Utah with a single purpose, and I would not rest, or find comfort, or sense joy, or measure pride, until at last I had presented my story to the men of Congress, and President Grant, too, forcing upon them, and our nation, the Truth of so many women like myself, and the plight of our children. I had but one hope—to witness the rewriting of our laws.

From Denver we toured the middle of the country—Topeka, Lawrence, Leavenworth, St. Louis, Peoria, Quincy, Chicago. In some cities the halls were full, in others only partially so, but each night I achieved my objective of informing those gathered of this relic of Barbarism. Wherever I went many good men and women greeted me with sympathy, the newspapers reported on me understandingly, and the editorials acknowledged my purpose. Even the more prurient columns, as undignified as they were, supported my cause, for there was hardly a soul in the vast middle of our great land who was not shocked by Mormondom's peculiar institution. "How can this go on in America?" asked many. No one denounced, contradicted, or maligned me. I should have taken comfort in this general warm reception. Instead, my enemies' silence concerned me.

"Nonsense," said Major Pond. "In Utah, you might have enemies, but the rest of America loves you!" If ever there was a man meant for promotion and salesmanship, it was Major Pond. In a futile effort to console, he showed me Brigham's Salt Lake papers. Only occasionally did they report on my crusade. By now, they mostly ignored me.

In the frozen days after the New Year of 1874, I visited Burlington, Iowa, a red-brick metropolis approximately thirty miles up the Mississippi from my birthplace of Nauvoo. It was here that I encountered my first rival on the lecture circuit. On the same night I was to speak, by coincidence a second, somewhat smaller venue had booked Mrs. Victoria Woodhull, the suffragist, spiritualist, labor reformer, newspaper editoress, Wall Street broker, and unsuccessful candidate for President. Of course I did not know Mrs. Woodhull in person, but her character had long before made my acquaintance— for Brigham often invoked her as an example of Gentile depravity. Among her many beliefs, for which she was paid handsomely to discuss, Mrs. Woodhull held a deep conviction in the open sensuality of women and the female's "right" to amorous satisfaction. Her other accomplishments included the exposure of Reverend Beecher's compromising interlude with the wife of his dear friend, thus destroying his repute; and, I am told, a sojourn in the squalid Ludlow Street Jail. To call Mrs. Woodhull's reputation notorious is to label the lion timid or the buffalo delicate on the foot.

Having become familiar with the public's interest in the lurid, I worried that she would draw away my natural audience. Major Pond assured me not to concern myself, and set out from our hotel, with its fine view of the icy river, to gather information on my competitor's numbers.

I was in the room reading to Lorenzo when a clerk announced Mrs. Woodhull was downstairs, calling to pay her respects.

"Tell her I'm not in," I said.

"But, Mrs. Young, you are in." The boy was young, with waves of corn-colored hair, and hobbled by a limited under-standing of the ways of women. I told him I was busy with my son, this was my only time to spend with him, and that he should inform Mrs. Woodhull that I was not present. The boy persisted. "She knows you're here. She said she saw you return an hour ago."

"Then tell her I cannot see her but I'll accept her card." I closed the door, dropping the woman's card into the stove. From the window I saw Mrs. Woodhull move down the street, her sturdy comportment making way, the plum ribbon of her hat fluttering with the snow flurries. Suddenly she stopped and turned around. Her eyes quickly found me in the window, and I shall always remember how they acknowledged me and dismissed me in one succinct glare.

That evening, at my lecture, I expected some sort of return of favor from Mrs. Woodhull, but none came. At the end of the night my audience embraced me for sharing with them my story. The lecture was a success, but I went to bed needled by concern.

In the morning, we crossed the Mississippi and drove by sleigh down to Nauvoo. We approached from the North, our hired team stamping happily in the crisp snow. It was a clear day, the sun high and cold, the sky a thin, brittle blue. Lorenzo kept peering from beneath the blanket, anxious to see the city he had heard so much about from his grandmother. Major Pond was in a fouler mood. "It's another fifty miles to Quincy," he said repeatedly. "We don't have much time."

My memories of Nauvoo were both distinct and limited, the miniature portraits of the young child's mind. They came to me with a warm bathing sensation, as memories of early childhood often do. I recalled the orderly streets where we had lived, our tidy brick house facing its opposite across the way. Thinking of my father's wainwright shop churned up other memories I had not conjured for years. I recalled the bitter smell of the thick smoke in the blacksmith's chimney, the glowing red of iron in the flame, and the sparks spraying from Gilbert's shodding hammer. From there, I thought of the fetid, almost animal smell of the river in summer, the way the stench rolled up the bank slowly; and the dry, lifeless scent of winter's wind running down the Temple's hill. I recalled my mother as a young woman, her pure devotion, her simple manner. And my father, quick and hardworking, his complexion yet to toughen and brown. Brigham's younger self came to mind, sturdy but not yet fat, with his boyish grin. How I remember him walking down the streets of Nauvoo, touching his followers, inviting them in, feeding them, helping them, praying with them, lending them a hand in building a house, a barn, or planting a field. He had a sense of humor in those days, for I recalled the day he visited our barn and named our buckling, with his unusual high-hat of white hair, Mr. Pope.

Above all, I remembered the Temple on the hill. When I was little, no matter where I was in town, I would look for its tower topped by the golden statue of Moroni. The sun on the gold was as comforting as my mother's hand upon my head. I thought of the limestone blocks, like enormous cubes of ice, and how my father and brothers, along with all the men and boys of Nauvoo, worked to put them in place with rope, pulley, and mule. And how the sun cut through the panes in the elliptical windows; and how the bronze bell rang. Perhaps most vividly, I recalled the Temple high above the Mississippi, standing firmly as we retreated across the river in our journey to Zion. For many miles I watched it as it became smaller and smaller, throwing back the sunlight, gleaming on the horizon, until it fell from sight.

"Are you sure this is the right way?" I asked our driver.

"Nauvoo. Straight ahead."

I said there must be something wrong, I could not see the tower.

"What tower?"

As we entered town, and mounted the hill, the driver said, "You mean that?" He was pointing at a set of ruins, broken stones lying haphazardly atop one another. All that remained of the famous Temple was an end wall with two supporting columns, its edge jagged as if the rest of the building had been torn from it. The decay was similar to what you might encounter, I understand, in Rome or Greece.

Opposite us were a pair of pilgrims, an old couple, looking

482

out over the destruction. They were small creatures, bent with age, their complexion an everlasting gray. They surveyed their lost sanctuary with dying eyes. They stood separate from us, yet the winter day was so clear I could peer across the distance to see the tears frozen to their cheeks.

There is a great shock to seeing a building you've known since childhood destroyed. There are certain structures in our lives—our first home, our first school, our first house of worship—which we naïvely believe will stand forever. To see these toppled bluntly delivers life's coldest lesson: Time will take all.

We drove down the hill to the Flats. Where houses once stood, I found nothing but an empty lot or a pile of bricks. At the corner of Parley and Kimball Streets, I saw the outline of a foundation in the snow. The snow lay upon it higher than the rest of the ground. Other than that, there was nothing but a lonely fence post leaning in a drift. I told Lorenzo I once lived here.

"But there's nothing here."

"There used to be." With that, I told the driver to head on. On our way out of Nauvoo we passed the site I knew to be Joseph Smith's grave. There was no marker, only a neat mound of blue snow.

As much as I now opposed the Latter-day Saints, I took no joy in seeing such total destruction. I do not believe the mythologies of the Ancients, with their bickering gods and thunderbolts, yet even so I feel a loss when I see etchings of their ruins. Who cannot pity the lonely Doric column standing in a field of rubble? Or the severed marble torso of a precious youth? Seeing Nauvoo destroyed was like learning an acquaintance from long ago has been dead for years. Such news comes with an awkward guilt—how is it I did not know? As we drove on to Quincy, a difficult question formed in my mind—was my mission not to destroy the Saints in similar fashion? How would I feel if one day I found Great Salt Lake ruined to a pile of stone?

THE 19TH WIFE

CHAPTER TWENTY-SEVEN
Distant Enemies

In Boston the lion roared. After a successful tour of the country's middle parts, including a diversion into Wisconsin's warm embrace, Major Pond, Lorenzo, and I traveled East. The journey was, above all, unpleasant to the nose. The railway car smelled of nothing but decay—the sloshing spittoon, the stale sandwiches, the unbathed travelers, and the sour latrine. As much as we could Lorenzo and I sat beside the window, preferring the cold blast to the stench. We spent hours looking out, surveying the winter flatlands of Indiana, then Ohio and beyond. The fields banked with snow, the brown cornstalks standing valiantly in the drifts, the farmhouses huddled against the gales—the train sped by these, and then they appeared again, on a different farm, all but the same. In the distance the land stretched flatly, nothing rising from it but a stand of chestnuts, skeletal in the winter light, or a silo, as solitary as a minaret. No mountains, no ravines, no vast valleys—already I missed the majesty of the West!

On February 18 at last we arrived in our nation's cultural capital. Outside the station, while orienting ourselves to this busy metropolis, I found my name shrieking out from an advertising bill. Under sponsorship of Redpath's Lyceum came an announcement of my lecture the following evening in Tremont Temple. I was grateful for such promotion, yet I felt uneasy. I assigned the feeling to fatigue and the anxiety over meeting Mr. Redpath for the first time. My lecture in Boston would determine whether I would join his roster, or if he would send me on my way. Under his sponsorship I could travel on to New York and Washington. Without it, it was doubtful we could arrange any more engagements in the world-weary East.

We met Mr. Redpath in his Lyceum Bureau on Bromfield Street.

"Here she is," he said, "Brigham's headache!" This little man, who weighed no more than 150 pounds, hustled about his office waving letters and telegrams concerning me. He had followed my progress across the country, sending for the local news accounts and gauging my appeal through a string of contacts. "You might be the most popular woman in America," he said. Excited, he told us about the advance ticket sales and the general anticipation for my appearance. He had arranged a series of interviews with the Boston newspapers in the afternoon, with a precise plan for the stories to run in the morning. "Once they hit, we'll be sold out. Now let me give you one piece of advice: Keep telling the truth."

I assured him I had no other weapon in my arsenal.

"And another thing: Don't shy away from the more—how should I put it?—difficult aspects of your ordeal. People are fascinated. Absolutely fascinated. You can't tell them too much." I came to see how such a small man, with his wispy side whiskers and rather high, feminine voice, had overwhelmed the nation with his speakers. He had made his name promoting John Brown, which was the connection to Major Pond, and had earned a specialty of putting talented women such as Anna E. Dickinson and Mrs. Stanton on the boards. I told him ultimately I had one goal: to speak to the highest levels of Government. "If everything goes according to my plan," he said, "that will happen." The meeting concluded with this little lively man calling me his future star and giving Lorenzo a yellow and green cup and ball.

We hurried to our rooms at the Parker House to begin the newspaper interviews. Major Pond organized the men outside the room, while I sat with each individually by the fire. Lorenzo played with the cup and ball all afternoon, challenging himself to catch the ball in the cup one hundred times consecutively. As I answered the reporters' questions, which were of such a standard variety I had answered them a hundred times before, I kept a fond eye on my son at the bench by the window as he tossed the yellow ball and caught it in its green cup. He counted in his soft, careful voice, nine, ten, eleven . . . When he missed, he said to himself, "Shooty shoot."

Long after dusk Major Pond admitted the final reporter, a Miss Christine Lee representing the *Sun* of New York. "I hear you're on your way to New York," she began.

"If all goes well here."

"I have to say, Utah feels very far away to most New Yorkers. Tell me why we should care about the Brighamites?"

I explained my purpose was to speak more about polygamy than the Saints themselves, but of course to do so I needed to provide some information on the religion and territory that introduced the practice to the United States. "As I see it," I said, "it's a relic of Barbarism, and I believe most Americans, especially New Yorkers, should be interested in banishing Barbarism from the land."

"I see," said Miss Lee, writing something down. She was not yet twenty-five, wore her yellow hair loose about her polished face, and had a small jagged smile. I had no doubt there was a dangerous quality to her beauty.

The interview began routinely. She asked the general questions about my experiences, and I answered them as I have always done. For thirty minutes we spoke in a straightforward manner and I sensed she was responding to my biography. When I described my early months of marriage and the indignities of my cottage, she clicked her tongue and said, "It must've been terrible." When I depicted Brigham's

486

mistreatment of my mother, her reply was, "Such cruelty." When I described my flight, and my son's fear, she said, "Unbelievable."

I concluded by describing my lectures and the general response.

"Let me ask you this," said Miss Lee. "I still don't understand why you married him."

"I had no choice."

"Yes, you said that, but what I don't understand is why you went through with it. You disliked him already, or at least you said you did. You did not trust him. You had seen with your own eyes how his wives lived. If you knew all that, why on earth would you agree to marry such a man?"

I had encountered this skepticism before and clipped at it without concern. "You must remember, I was born into this system. It was all I knew. I did not know a Gentile until I was an adult woman. I had been told the world beyond Deseret was Babylon and Sodom combined. I had been raised to believe Brigham delivered messages from God. And above all, I was told this was my spiritual duty, and that if I wanted to enter Heaven—and who among us, Miss Lee, does not?— then I would need to submit to Brigham's command and become a plural wife."

"Yes, you've said that, but I still don't understand."

"What don't you understand?"

"You despised this man, yet you married him. Is it possible, Mrs. Young, you didn't despise him as much as you say? Is it possible, even a little, that you were enticed into his arms by thoughts of becoming the Queen of Utah?"

"Not at all."

"I must tell you, Mrs. Young, before I came here, I spent some time following certain aspects of your story. Did you know I've been to Utah? I was in California. On my way home I stopped by. I happened to be at the Walker House the night you departed, and I read about your exit in the *Tribune*. It caught my eye. So I stayed a few extra days, then a week, to look around. I had the opportunity to visit the Lion House, in fact."

"Good. Then you saw it for yourself."

"Yes indeed. And it is as you described it."

"I'm glad that's not in dispute."

"Except in one manner."

"What's that?"

"I didn't see the misery."

I would be dishonest if I withheld from my Reader my true feeling at this moment: I wanted to swat this woman with my handbag.

"Miss Lee," I said, "sometimes, in my experience, misery is not always apparent to the casual visitor."

"Very true, but I had a chance to speak to a number of his wives, and no one gave me a report that was at all similar to yours."

"I cannot tell you about anyone else's experience but my own."

"Of course, but it makes me wonder if yours is perhaps exaggerated?"

"It isn't."

"Or if not exaggerated, then perhaps unique to you? That you and President Young were simply not compatible and so you fought, as all incompatible couples do, and it's this reason you have stories to tell from an unhappy marriage?"

"I wish that were true. I wish my experience was wholly alien to the women of Utah. If that were the case, I could go home to my other son today and settle into a house somewhere with my boys, and live out the rest of my life in privacy. My mission would be done. But this is not the case. And until it is the case, I intend to speak about what I know."

"Do you know what people say about you?"

"I've heard many things."

"You know the expression 'The lady doth protest too much'?"

"I can't say I do."

488

"What? How can't you know that? It's Shakespeare. *Hamlet.* Surely you're familiar with *Hamlet*, being a former actress."

"In fact, no, I'm not. Do you know why I'm not familiar with *Hamlet*? Because Brigham banned Shakespeare from the stages of Deseret, unless the scripts were revised to suit his theology. So in my days on the stage I never encountered *Hamlet*, nor in my schooling, nor upon the shelves of my parents, or in the homes of friends, because, Miss Lee, anything or anyone who contradicts Brigham's doctrine is edited, banished, or destroyed."

"May I read a quote to you? This is one of President Young's wives answering some of your charges. 'She is a liar of considerable skill. She uses her dramatic training to bring her inventions to life. If half the things she speaks of were true, this Church, and family, would have been devoured already by its own rotten soul. I'm here to tell you this is a happy household, with sister wives loving one another and our children, and nothing brings us greater joy than knowing we have set out on the path to Heaven.' Do you have a reply to that, Mrs. Young?"

"Miss Lee, do you plan to marry?"

"Yes, in fact I'm engaged. How did you know?"

"I had a sense. That's wonderful for you. Tell me: Who's your groom?"

"I'd rather not say."

"All right. But tell me one thing about him, so I might begin to form an image of him in my mind."

"One thing? He's a printer."

"Very nice. A man of your trade. Then imagine this man, this printer, with his inky fingers, and, I'll venture to say, handsome appearance, and a way with words—for knowing you now a little, Miss Lee, any man you've settled on must have a way with words. So think of the day your printer first told you he loved you, that he hoped to marry you, to spend his life with you, to begin a family with you. Think of that

489

day. Yes, it's a fond memory, is it not, Miss Lee? Of course it is, as it should be. A man, an attractive printer, he must be strong—for those plates are heavy, aren't they? This printer wants to be with you all his life. It is the definition of love, of Christian love, I will add. It's a wonderful thought, even the hardest cynic would have to agree. Where is this printer now? While you're on your journeys?"

"He's in New York. He prints seven days a week."

"Of course. He's industrious, isn't he? Like yourself. But he can't work day and night. What does he do when he puts the press to bed? He has a meal, he talks with his friends, they drink whiskey? He talks about you, perhaps? And why not? Now imagine he spent his free time, what little of it there is, not with his friends from the print-shop, but with eighteen other women. So that when he's not at his letter press, not slaving over those boxes of letters and all those tiny dingbats, he is slicing his time and affection and money and everything else into nineteenths. You will get your share, and your future children will get their share. One-nineteenth. What is rightfully yours will be yours, but no more and no less. Now, Miss Lee, will such a situation bring you happiness or misery? And if someone were to tell you it brought her happiness, could it possibly be true? Isn't it possible she's been told to lie? Or, isn't it also possible she's deceived herself into believing she's happy when in fact she's anything but? And why shouldn't she lie? Either way, she's been told her marital suffering will be rewarded in the Afterlife. She's been told she must defend the system to death. She's been told that Gentiles will be left on Earth at the time of the Resurrection. Now if you've never known anything else, anything other than these statements which sound so impossibly untrue to your keen New York ears, isn't it perfectly possible you would claim to a reporter from the East that you were happy? Even if you were not? Miss Lee, do not present me with your cold, skeptical questions. Not when I'm describing a world founded on fear, intimidation, and anti-reason."

The woman sat back, all courage and puffery eliminated from her soul. "I have one final question."

"Please."

"If polygamy is a religious practice, if it's part of the Mormons' eternal beliefs, why should you, or anyone, stop them from pursuing their faith? Don't the Mormons have the right to practice their religion as they please under the Constitution?"

"And if someone were to say, I believe in slavery because it appears in the Bible, would you say, Go then, and be free to practice it. I believe this country has answered that question rather firmly. Anything else, Miss Lee?"

Soon thereafter Miss Lee departed, leaving me to worry over the story that would await me in New York City.

Later that night I sat restlessly by the window. It was very late and Lorenzo was snoring lightly in the bed. Outside it was sleeting, the street lamps burning a thick ugly yellow upon the fog. Although I had won my spar with Miss Lee, the encounter had left me uncertain of my path. I returned to the image of the ruined Temple in Nauvoo—the piles of stone, the column holding up nothing, the chipped piece of the baptismal font. Did any sect or creed, any group of men, deserve such a fate? I believed in everything I said at the lectern, I knew it was true. Surely Brigham, when he stands before his people, would say the same. He believes everything he says, and he knows it is true. How to reconcile our competing truths? By obliterating one? Is it the only way? I turned the question this way and that, doing my best to look at it from each end, pressing upon its points, and I began to feel anxious. Perhaps the Temple ruins were not a symbol of the Mormons' fate, but my own. If one side must be right, and the other wrong, how could I be so certain of everything I knew? Inevitably we were both right, and both wrong, or was this not true? It was a circular question, like an iron hoop, and I could trace my finger along it, around and around, and never reach its end. I fumbled with this idea for a long time, losing my grasp on my beliefs, until the early sun came through the fog, and the streets illuminated with the goodness of day.

It was time to dress, and just as I went to wake Lorenzo, Major Pond knocked on my door. "Mrs. Young? . . . Mrs. Young?"

"What is it?"

"I'm sorry to disturb you so early, but there's something you must see."

The situation was written out in the Major's eyes. He handed me a newspaper. The story came from the *Chicago Times*. The author was identified simply as Special Correspondent. It began with a benign description of my lectures through Illinois and Iowa and a general appreciation of my appearance. Yet soon enough the secretive writer began his assault:

> Now I shall turn to the portion of this report that will no doubt most interest the reader. Mrs. 19, like other lecturesses, employs an agent who arranges her schedule and travels along her side. In most cases these are wise old gentlemen, blunt in manner but also efficient, capable of settling whatever matter that might arise on the road. Mrs. 19, however, has chosen as her business partner a debonair and suave military gentleman by the name of Major Pond. Pond's reputation begins with his features—his good square jaw, a fine nose, and teeth as white as china. He speaks elegantly, with all the powers of persuasion, and there are rumors of his physicality, which can be previewed through his snug uniform, that have caused more than one woman to swoon—as far as this Correspondent knows. While the pair visited Bloomington, Iowa, residing in its most luxurious hotel, several guests and maids noted an unusual closeness between Mrs. 19 and the Major, an intimacy that needs no further explanation to be understood.

I did not need to read any more. I was as aware as anyone that the people who came to my lectures, those who rewarded me with their applause and approval, the newspaper editors who spent ink on my cause, did so because they sensed I was a modest woman. Were they to think I was an adulteress just as my husband was an adulterer, my message would be lost in the haze of scandal.

How to describe the day? Even now, after writing so many pages, I feel incapable of depicting those first lonely hours after this attack. I forced myself to dress and traveled to Mr. Redpath's office. Had my new sponsor seen the news? Of course, as had most of Boston, by his estimation. A few inquiries supported my larger fear: the telegraphs had carried the story to news outlets across the country. Anyone interested in my tale, or the plight of Utah's women, knew of it by noon. I imagined Brigham in his office at the Beehive House, cloistered by his account books and maps, settling into his armchair and reviewing the reports. His assistants would come and go, bringing him accounts from the East and the West, each more devastating to me than the previous. The effect was like a shovelful of dirt into a grave— slowly the hole fills in and the body is buried. I imagined the thin smirk upon Brigham's lips, imperceptible even to the clerks. I was certain one word was running through his mind—Success.

I asked Mr. Redpath if I should cancel my appearance.

"I'll tell you in an hour." He set about gauging the effect of the scandal on my repute, sending half a dozen nimble assistants and clerks about the city to listen in on the morning talk. He would trot over to the Tremont Temple himself. Were tickets being returned? Were people gathering to denounce me? "I'll find out," he said, and out he went, like a red fox.

He returned an hour later with good news. "We've sold out. It seems there was a stampede for tickets when the box office opened."

The afternoon brought more hostile news. A second report, also from our nameless friend at the Chicago Times, had run across the telegraph lines. Now Mrs. Woodhull was claiming she too had encountered evidence of my indiscretions while in Burlington. Yet this great lady, friend to the female race, wanted Americans everywhere to know she was not denouncing me. In fact, she fully supported my "right" to amorous liberty. "Now she is truly free," the woman said of me.

"What time's the next train?" I said. "I don't care where it's headed, but I need to leave right away."

"Mrs. Young," said Mr. Redpath, "you need to steady yourself."

But I could not—I hurried about his office, gathering my hat and bag, my gloves, and the purple coat that had brought me so much luck since Denver. I called for Lorenzo. The boy, at one corner of Mr. Redpath's desk, was preoccupied with a drawing he was making. When I told him it was time to go, he held up his artwork. "It's you." And it was—a kind, loving portrait on the very newspaper that maligned me. The black ink of his art had all but covered over the lies.

It was the betrayal of strangers that most alarmed me. Who was the Special Correspondent so intent on destroying me? And Mrs. Woodhull— had she punished me for ignoring her call? For some time that afternoon I could not speak. I sat anxiously in Mr. Redpath's office, looking about at the framed telegrams from Presidents and Generals, and the memorabilia from the stage, the engraved swords, the autographed playbills, and a dusty ostrich plume. I felt something slip out from beneath me. The Temple ruins returned to mind—the piles of rubble, the winter sun bright on the worn white stones.

Since the news that morning, a feeling had been taking shape in my heart. At first I could not identify it, but now it was there, as solid as a stone. "It's Brigham," I said.

"What's that, Mrs. Young?"

"Brigham did this. He bought that story in the press."

Historians speak of the unintended consequences of planned events. The consequence of this attack on my character was a mob on the steps of Tremont Temple. Nearly one thousand people had to be turned away. Behind the curtain, waiting to take the stage, I heard the commotion, the shouts and calls, the irate voices claiming they had been promised a seat. "I could fill this place twice over," said Redpath. "Ninety-five percent of them are on your side."

My lecture in Boston was standard, but its reception was not. I was received with the greatest wave of enthusiasm I had yet to encounter. I concluded the discussion with a rebuttal of the charges and a challenge: "I do not know how, or by what means, but I know in my heart, just as surely as I know the faces of my sons, that Brigham's Church was involved in this assault on my character. In time I will prove it, and if anyone here tonight remains skeptical of my ordeal, of the truthfulness of my life, you shall see, with this lie exposed, the extent to which Brigham Young can deceive."

The triumph in Boston was followed by failure in New York, for Miss Lee's pointed story preceded me. The editors of her newspaper buttressed her opinion by a handful of essays questioning the veracity of my life. The reports out of Boston failed to impress the doubting Thomases of New York. More than half the seats of Association Hall stared back at me empty. My declaration of innocence was met with a phlegmatic yawn.

I asked Mr. Redpath if the scandal had wounded my appeal.

He stroked his whiskers. "New York is an odd place. I suspect the scandal hasn't hurt you as much as your response to it. This town loves a sinner more than a saint."

While in New York, I met with editors from the publishing houses to discuss my memoirs. Mr. E—— of Easton & Co. impressed me the most. He is a lean, subtle, Prussian-looking man, with a full nose like a small turnip. He spoke intelligently, if nervously, about my plight, his brittle, alabaster fingers fluttering about. "The important thing," he said, "is to show everyone what it's like for the women of Utah. You'll need to make it clear how bad polygamy is, how it's not only disagreeable, but how it destroys the soul. You need to show it's not only a conjugal issue, but a moral one. That's how to draw readers to your side. It's a travesty, and it seems to me Brigham's making a mockery of the rest of us and the very foundations of this country." For a man who has never taken a wife, and of whom I suspect deep theological skepticism, he showed unusual sympathy for my topic. I agreed to pen a summary of my life for this young, feline editor. A contract was produced, a date agreed upon, and we signed on our respective lines.

(Since then many critics have wrongly accused me of walking out of the offices of Easton & Co. with bags of money. One newspaper even ran an illustration of me dragging a large sack of gold with Brigham's head on the side. This is another distortion. I received nothing for my efforts, not until Easton's salesmen began to canvass the nation, selling subscriptions to the volume you are now reading. Mr. E—— sent a telegram announcing advance orders comparable to Mrs. Stowe's and, only then, my first remuneration. Is it wrong for an authoress to earn a penny for her toil? For the record, Mr. E—— urged me not to include this paragraph. The parentheses are a concession to his concern.)

We continued on to Rochester, Buffalo, and Baltimore. During this time, Major Pond and I spent many hours, and much money, investigating Brigham's libel. With Mr. Redpath's help, we collected a list of every newspaper in the country that had reprinted the falsehoods. I personally wrote a letter to the editor of each. Major Pond did the same. My story was widely known, but his was not. He was a widower when he arrived in Salt Lake, having lost his wife only recently. There was not a day in our relationship when he did not speak of her, and how he longed for the peal of her laugh.

We hired a detective out of Chicago to investigate the story's origins. The man's fees totaled nearly half of what I had earned at the lectern, but I was happy to turn over every cent when he delivered his findings. After two weeks of sleuthing, he unearthed a check in the amount of $20,000 made out to the editor of the *Chicago Times*. The signature on the check was a man named George Reef. I knew nothing of Mr. Reef. It took the detective another week to locate him in Provo. Rich from mining, devout to Brigham, married to two dozen women, perhaps more, Mr. Reef was prepared, he later confessed, to wage war for his right to an infinity of wives. Upon the exposure of his bribery, it is reported he said, "I should have paid more."

Brigham denied any relationship with Mr. Reef. A statement bellowed out of the Beehive House: "This man, whoever he may be, has acted without my authority or consent, and his actions should be punished, as the law sees fit." Our detective never could produce the evidence to make the connection between Brigham and Mr. Reef. It seems only fair, then, to give him the last word on the matter. But first I must make a point— even if Brigham did not coordinate this attack, is there not something foul in his Church that would inspire a believer to launch such an assault? Is the leader responsible in any way? To you, Friend, I leave this question to ponder.

Within two weeks of the scandal's debut, reports began to appear declaring my innocence. Editorials cleared my name and restored my relationship with Major Pond to propriety. More followed, and soon nearly every paper that had printed the rumor was forced to correct its error. Yet when the fire burns itself out, ash and the stench of smoke remain. When we are told a woman is an adulteress, and then this description is revised, the untruth will continue to linger in the mind. It is a ghost-thought— an idea proven unreal yet present even so. Such is the subtle shaping of reputation and

497

legacy; and such was the perception I had to contend with. Wherever I went I recognized the look in the eyes of men with profane imaginations. They assessed me as they might a whore. In Rochester, on the street, a young man outside a foundry called out, "I live around the corner, Mrs. Young!" In Baltimore, a man as old as my father hollered, "Go get another one of those wives and meet me upstairs!" When this happened, I held Lorenzo close to me, continued on, and sealed my eyes to fight away the tears. He understood my pain, for every time I was assaulted with insults, the boy squeezed my hand within the tiny mitt of his.

Out of this interlude of slander, libel, and the clearing of my name, I found my purpose even more defined. I had learned something I had heretofore failed to see—in fact, I was not Mormondom's destroying angel, as so many claimed me to be, intent on reducing the creed to a pile of lonely, winterblown stones. In truth, it was plural marriage itself, with all its inherent corruptions, that would destroy the religion, razing its temples and tabernacles, and poisoning its way of life. This cruel practice would end the Saints' legitimate right to their faith. The day would come when the religion would collapse upon itself—a future implosion now so very clear to me, I was surprised that I had not perceived it before. I came to understand that were I to succeed in my mission, and eradicate celestial marriage from Deseret, I would also be saving the Latter-day Saints from themselves.

With this awareness came another. A few days later, after the libelous episode had seemed to blow clear from the fields, our detective in Chicago wrote with news of his investigation's final clue.

Dear Mrs. Young—

Although I have failed to find any connection between Mr. Reef and Brigham Young, and now do not expect to do so, there is one link of another sort that has recently come to light. I do not know the meaning of it, yet it stands out among the many clues and therefore I bring it to you. Mr. Reef is an associate of your brother, Aaron Webb. The two share a title to a small, not especially productive copper mine in Southwestern Utah, near a settlement called Red Creek. Your brother's first wife, Connie (my records show he has taken an even dozen in total)—she is the sister to Mr. Reef's seventh wife. I have yet to turn up evidence connecting your brother to Mr. Reef's actions pertaining to you, but the coincidence of association is noteworthy. Before I investigate any further, is there any reason to suspect your brother might have had a hand in this libelous plot?

I await your instructions.

Yours sincerely,
CARL CUMMINGS, INVEST., CHICAGO

Although no betrayal is as painful as that inflicted by a family member, Mr. Cummings's revelation, distressing as it was, did not come wholly as a surprise. Ever since his involvement in the Reformation, Aaron had become a blind defender of polygamy. He reveled in his right to acquire women, blithely bringing a fresh bride into his bed whenever he desired conjugal variety. He embodied the hypocrisy of the Mormon polygamist so well that even before my apostasy I had done my best to limit my boys' interaction with their uncle. For his part, I am sure Aaron recognized my skepticism even before I did; although brother and sister, it was obvious we were enemies.

At this point, after having endured so much, I chose to ignore Mr. Cummings's ominous but circumstantial evidence. What good would come from it? I looked to my conscience for counsel and never responded to Mr. Cummings's letter. The truth would have to lie privately in Aaron's heart and mine, where God would judge it.

Sadder still was the silence from others. My dear father, so regretful over his own multiple marriages, never found the courage to speak out on my behalf. My half-sister Diantha, whom I loved, went missing from the debate. And most painfully, my mother's farewell letter always burned in my pocket, where I protected it, hoping another would come to revise its contents, to change her view of me. On the eve of my arrival in Washington, where I would meet my most important audience, a letter from my beloved brother Gilbert was delivered to my door.

Sister—

I know the news about you is untrue. Anyone who knows you will say the same. Anyone who believes in your crusade knows it too. Don't worry about your friends. We remain steadfast and true. Yet you have enemies. They repeat these tales, adding to them and puffing them up. I hear them in town, at the mill, in church. Whenever I can I tell the speaker to shut his mouth but there are too many mouths in Deseret for me to finish the job.

Since your departure I've been planning my own. By the time you read this, I should be half way to Albuquerque or El Paso. I'll have to leave my wives behind, and my children too—an abandonment I know I'll feel painful about for the rest of my days. But I have no choice. I no longer believe anything this Church has to say. When I see Brigham, it's like looking at the face of a criminal. I know he feels the same about me. If I were to stay, I'd be dead soon enough, so either way my family will be left without husband and father. If I make any money, I'll send it to my wives. But I won't promise anything I don't know for sure I'll have. When I settle, I'll write with my news. Until then, you should know I believe you, and only you.

Before closing, I want to tell you our Ma's sick. Not of body but in heart. She's twisted up about how Brigham's been talking about you. She can't stand it, I know, because she knows he's telling lies. If I were a wagerer, I'd put a dollar

500

down on her apostasy too. It's a pitiful sight— watching someone so devout lose her faith. If you can, you might write her. Right now, only words from you might soothe. I can't tell the future, but I suspect one day soon you and she will reunite. I know she wants to bring James to you. She's in South Cottonwood, but how long she'll last I can't say.

Your Brother—
GILBERT WEBB

Immediately I wrote my mother, posting the letter in Baltimore.

My Dear Mother—
On this journey of mine, of which I know you are aware, each night, kneeling before the stiff hotel bed, I pray twice. Once for a swift return to James. And once for a reunion with you. If these prayers are not answered, I will live out my days burdened with doubt about the value of my Crusade. If I succeed in my mission, and eradicate polygamy from our land, and yet remain separated from you or my son, then I will ask myself, At what cost? Indeed, at what cost has all this been? These are my most private thoughts, shared with only you and my God.

—Your Daughter

THE 19TH WIFE

CHAPTER TWENTY-EIGHT
Defeating Polygamy

In Washington we drove up a muddy street, past a row of one-story private houses, narrow, crowding structures displaying squalor in their windows. Here and there were patches of springtime grass, ready to be trampled by the pigs who seemed to outnumber the Capital's citizens. The street led to a wide avenue, grandly laid out, yet its buildings were no more elegant, or noble, in design than the huts we had previously passed. Had the Capitol's dome not beckoned us, flashing in the April sun, I would have been sure we were on a highway to nowhere. On that drive it was impossible not to compare Washington to Great Salt Lake. The former had a fifty-year advantage on the latter, and yet any fair observer would crown the capital of Zion the more colonized metropolis.

We were a party of four—Lorenzo, Major Pond, Mr. Redpath, and myself—who entered the Capitol building, through a dim hall known as the Crypt. A clerk in epaulette informed us we were standing directly beneath the famous dome. The room was held up by forty brown columns, the veins in the stone coursing with force, as if revealing their strain as they worked to hold aloft the building above.

The clerk, a birdy fellow with clipped, flapping arms, led us to the House chamber. I was shown to the Ladies Waiting Area, a cordoned section of chairs, while the Major and Mr. Redpath were invited to sit with the gentlemen. The clerk

502

wanted to seat Lorenzo with them, but I insisted he remain with me.

Mr. James Blaine, the House Speaker, is a quick-minded, flinty man, trained and fortified in the cold blasts of Maine. He has the inscrutable eyes of a newspaper editor, which he once was in Portland. When I arrived he was orating from his chair of authority, the famous gavel in his grasp, filling the chamber with, by chance, a lecture on the subject of the separation of Church and State. The clerk delivered to him my card and letter of introduction.

To my surprise, the Speaker set down his gavel, left his chair, and invited me into the elegant Speaker's Room. By the warmth of a fire, and beneath the gentle glow of a French chandelier, Mr. Blaine invited me to tell my story. I began, and not far into it, he sent the clerk back to the chamber with the instruction of having another member replace him in the Speaker's chair. I continued with my story, and some twenty minutes later, the person responsible for filling in for the Speaker gave up that position to come listen to me as well. For two hours I spoke; every few minutes another member of the great Chamber quit the floor to join me in the Speaker's Room. Before I had finished the room was full and more members stood on toes in the hall.

I told them everything I have disclosed here, Dear Reader, from the early glories of Joseph Smith to the story of my parents' conversion. I described my first meetings with Brigham, my unhappy marriage to Dee, and Brigham's friendship at the time of my divorce. I discussed my mother's sorrow as one wife, then the next entered her house, and my sense that I had lost my father to polygamy, so demanding upon his moral soul was it. I portrayed for these Gentlemen the workings of the Lion House, and the authority of the Beehive House next door. I recounted Brigham's courtship, and my brother's legal troubles, and my eventual submission. I offered every honest detail of what it has been like for me to be the 19th wife—the few morsels of affection and support it afforded me. All of this I portrayed for the Gentlemen of Congress, those responsible for the laws of our miraculous land. I could perceive the effects of my tale in their wincing eyes, in their agitated lips, twitching behind mustaches and beards.

I urged them to pass the necessary laws to ban this relic of the barbarian. "What kind of country are we that we let this pass? That today, beside this warm fire, sitting in this fine furniture, under the roof of this great building, we should be here while thousands of women and even more children suffer under this system. The Mormons will appeal to you in the name of religious freedom. They will tell you—indeed have already told you—that to subject them to the laws of the land is to persecute them for their faith. If you are inclined to believe this, if you are hesitant to trample on the rights of the religious, then I beg you to consider the question this way: Let a man be with a woman and another and another after her if he so chooses, and if they so choose. Let this happen for the sake of freedom, which we all hold so dear. But as soon as there is a child, as soon as one boy or one girl enters the house, you can no longer look away or protect the situation for the sake of religious freedom. Doesn't every child deserve something better than neglect? Don't you, and we, and all of us, have the obligation to protect that child? And what of this child's rights—his right to be protected, her right to grow up to choose his or her own faith?

"Good Gentlemen, Sirs, I implore you, do not let doctrine ensnare you. Don't hesitate over questions of God and the Lord. You are lawmakers, and your laws have been circumvented. Make it a crime to neglect a wife. Make it a crime to neglect a child. Make it a crime to force one woman to accept another into her home. Make it a crime, for that is what it is. It is not a religious practice, it is not a declaration of faith, it is not a testament of freedom, it is a crime of cruelty and abandonment. And it is permitted today, in your borders, with your consent. Brigham has sanctioned adultery in the name of God, and you, in doing nothing, have condoned it.

Your silence has allowed Brigham to claim it to be true. I, of course, cherish my freedom, but I shall never want my freedom to restrict the freedom of another. In that case then I am not truly free, and none of us is truly free.

"Gentlemen, here, let me introduce you to my son Lorenzo. He has traveled with me all this way. I selfishly took him with me, for I could not imagine the journey without him. I should have left him in school with his brother. But I could not, for he, ultimately, is the reason I wage this fight. I look at him and am reminded of my purpose. If my story has not impressed you, consider it from his eyes. Imagine what he has seen, and how it has affected him. If you owe me no protection, I at least ask you to give it to him."

When I concluded my speech, the Gentlemen of Congress rushed to meet me, offering their cards and promising their support. For some time a circle of men ten-deep surrounded me and there was a general noise of congratulation, like at a party, with a hundred voices collecting to form a roar. At some point, something I could not see was taking place at the rim of this crowd, for many men fell silent, and urged others to do so too, and the men began to step aside. The quiet was sudden and complete and had an ominous quality to it. The men were making way for someone to pass through, I could tell, and at first I could not imagine who. Then, slowly, it became clear that somehow Brigham had followed me to the Capitol. He was here, but I did not know why. The Gentlemen continued to step aside, and I waited for my husband to appear from behind the shoulders and heads. I saw a presence, a form moving to me. I held on to Lorenzo, my fingers digging into his shoulders, and I loathed myself for not pushing him out of harm's way, but I could not let go of my child. As the crowd continued to part, the man stepping forward began to take shape, and when at last the final ring of men moved aside, letting the visitor pass—just at this moment I saw before me, as close as my hand is to my face when I hold it out, President Grant. Mrs. Grant was at his side, her eyes crossed with fury. "Our nation will stew in shame," the President said, "if this Congress does not heed your call."

I thanked the President for his support. Next I introduced my son, and the great General knelt to discuss matters with my boy, including the quality of fishing in the Potomac. At the end of our interview, President Grant pledged his full support.

But the final word came from Mrs. Grant. "I want to assure you," she said, "I won't let him sleep until he gets this done."

A few weeks after my visit, Congress passed the anti-polygamy Poland Bill. I can claim only a fraction of the credit for it, for many others have taken part in this Crusade. Time will tell of the bill's effects, and its ability to dismantle what Brigham has so vigorously fought for, but my mission, as I saw it, was complete. I had brought to the nation's attention the suffering of Utah's women and children and forced the country to respond. How Brigham and the Church would react to this new onslaught would be up to them. Would they accept it, give up polygamy, and finally enter through our nation's gates? Or defy it, and invite a battle that would lead to Deseret's humiliation and defeat, along with the surrender of its leaders, like that of the South a decade before? I could not predict the next chapter in the Church's life, nor the future of Brigham's reign, or the prospect of his household, nor the final outcome of this tale of faith. At this point I was certain of only one thing—I had played my part and was ready to reunite my boys and find a home, wherever that may be.

THE END

506

PRISON DIARY
OF
BRIGHAM YOUNG

CLOSED ARCHIVE

BY ORDER OF

WILFORD WOODRUFF
Prophet & President
October 5, 1890
SEALED

———

**Access Shall Be Limited to
The Prophet & Leader of the Latter-day Saints,
Whoever He Shall Be.**

Night has come. Outside my window, the snow clouds have cleared, allowing the moon, my old friend, to burn through. The snow atop the Penitentiary walls reflects the moonlight in a glowing ring. Beyond the walls the valley basin lays dark and mysterious. I can see nothing, although I know someone is out there, waiting for me.

I could look out this window all night if I did not have this other task before me. They have given me the Warden's office. It is a bare room with a bare floor, and a simple, rectangular writing table where the Warden drafts the papers for the incoming and outgoing prisoners. Earlier Warden Paddock drafted my papers here. Out of deference to my age, I gather, he has decided to house me here with a guard outside the door. Upstairs the Warden's wife is looking after her children, including a newborn, a singing babe with a yellow forelock named Esther. Earlier Mrs. Paddock brought a plate of bread, spiced peaches, and a strip of apricot leather. She asked if I needed anything else. I requested a longer candle, an ink pot, and these pages. I will not sleep tonight.

The Warden's house stands outside the Penitentiary's adobe walls, adjoining them at the gate. From the window, I can see into the prison yard, an acre of snowy mud, and the Penitentiary itself, a block-house better suited to corral sheep than to house men. I see the barred windows, the gate studded with iron buttons, and the chimney coughing white smoke. At least the men have a fire. The Warden has fourteen prisoners tonight, myself included, and two guards, not including himself. If there is a rebel among us, a riot could break out easily. I have not met the other prisoners, although

I saw them an hour before dusk running in a circle around the prison yard. The men wear black-and-white striped pajamas, the stripes running horizontally, and simple Chinese-style caps. They are mostly young men, imprisoned, the Warden tells me, for crimes as mundane as stealing flour and as heinous as ravishment and murder. Looking down at them, all thirteen, running about the yard, kicking their feet high to clear the mounds of snow, I, nor anyone, could tell who has committed the worst crime. Which man has stolen the sack of flour off the mill's wagon? Who ravished the maiden down by the creek? Which man among the thirteen slit his neighbor's throat with a deer knife, as the Warden tells it, from ear to ear? Each man appears the same; he is hungry, cold, and anxious to be free.

I too wear a prison uniform, although my stripes run vertically. I asked the Warden about this, but he did not have an explanation. I believe he is too thoughtful to attribute it to my girth, which has expanded in proportion to my years. My younger wives tease me about this. Mary calls me her water buffalo. Amelia, she likes to poke me in the middle until I laugh like a child. During the brief time we were fond of one another, Ann Eliza would fall off to sleep with her head on my belly. She was a good wife. I am only sorry it has come to this.

The events that led me to this writing table—with its short fourth leg and the rapidly burning candle—began with her apostasy. I knew our relations had soured; I am too familiar with the ways of marriage to expect them all to last. What surprised me, and continues to surprise me, is her tenacity. In truth, I expected her to quit my household, perhaps accept a small sum, and be gone. In all this noise about my 19th Wife, people have ignored the fact that Ann Eliza is not the first woman I have separated from. Mary Woodward, Mary Ann Clark Powers, Mary Ann Turley, Mary Jane Bigelow, Eliza Babcock, Elizabeth Fairchild—all fine Sisters who requested a release from our engagements. They were young, a few not yet

511

twenty if I recall, and our time together was sweet but shallow, not unlike a pie. A pie on the table is always a marvelous sight, but soon it shall be gone, its tin nicked by fork and knife. In each case they requested a disunion and I agreed. In the case of Mary Jane I paid her five hundred dollars and wished her joy and peace. Once outside my household, these good women proceeded with their lives. A few might have married again, I am not certain. Yet I know none ever spoke of our time as man and wife. My first mistake was assuming Ann Eliza would be the same.

Four weeks ago the subject of my sermon was "How Have I Come Here?" Before some two thousand Saints, I spoke of our chosen paths, and the meaning of these. I invoked the Pioneers pushing across the plains in '47 and '48, and the thousands of emigrants since, sailing, riding, walking to Zion. Each man, woman, and child present has come to God, I said, and yet the course of each has been different, and so it must always be. I asked my followers to go forth and consider this question in their prayers. How have I come here? Indeed, ever since, when I have met Saints on the street, many have told me they have spent much time pondering the question for themselves.

And so I must do so as well.

After Ann Eliza's apostasy in the summer of '73, a long legal battle has ensued. Yet throughout it has seemed to me Ann Eliza, in her public statements, wants both sides of a coin. She has claimed that in my bountiful household, with so many wives and children, she was never truly a wife. If this is so, let the woman complain. Yet she also says I owe her a vast sum of alimony. If this is so, let the woman complain. Yet according to her own logic, it cannot be both. Either she was my wife and I owe her a claim, or she was not my wife, and I owe her nothing. My lawyers, good men, perhaps too eager to please, have advised that under federal law she was never my wife. The civil courts, which so despise our marital customs, would never honor her request for alimony. Thus our

512

legal strategy was set: Ann Eliza Young was never my wife. My mistress and my confidant, yes—but not my wife. My lawyers were the first to publicly call her a social harlot—an unfortunate outburst of hostility yet benign compared to the charges she has hurled against me.

For many months the lawyers argued. The man she hired, Judge Hagan, never truly had her interests in mind. In truth, I did not pay close attention to the case, for so many other matters engaged me. I admit bewilderment then, when on February 25th of this year Judge McKean ordered me to pay Ann Eliza alimony in the sum of five hundred dollars a month by March 10th or be held in contempt of court. When I read the court order I remember thinking, It is a bluff. The United States government has ordered me to pay alimony to a 19th wife? It would mean they believed my wives to be legal in every sense. It would mean an acceptance of plural marriage. I knew this had not come to pass, and I shredded the court order, throwing the bits into the fire.

It was after nine o'clock this morning when the Deputy United States Marshal, A. K. Smith, a modest, dutiful man whose brass buttons shone like the sun, arrived at the Beehive with a warrant for my arrest. My loyal men—Brother Adam at the guardpost, Brother Caleb at the door, Brother Orson and Brother Herman in my office—each attempted to stop the Marshal from arresting me. The man had come armed with certified papers, and I told my men that we must always respect the force of law, and its majesty. "A piece of paper written with legal will is a weapon more powerful than a rifle," I advised. "And so it shall be."

The morning was cold, blustery, the winds throwing fresh, fine-grained snow against the window panes. At the time of the Marshal's arrival I had been planning an emergency rescue for the citizens of Big Cottonwood. Yesterday's snows, and those from the day before, had caused snow slides from Canyon Flat to Porcupine Cabin, burying the canyon in near fifty feet of snow, blocking the creek and the road for one mile. We did not know how many pitiable souls lay under the snow, whether dead, frozen blue into the frost, or alive and awaiting rescue. Together my men and I were organizing the teams to be sent when the Marshal entered my office.

The Marshal said we were due in court but allowed me the time necessary to sign my morning letters and documents. His orders had been to bring me at once, but he is a good man and understands that every man, whether crook or king, has business to finish before he can leave his house. I dressed in my cape and hat, hung my watch from my shirtwaist, and said goodbye to my men. I told them to continue with the rescue, and worry none for me. In the hall, as I was leaving the Beehive, I met Sister Mary Ann. She is nearly as old as I, fortified in her routine, suspicious of all Gentiles, Babylonians she names them, refusing to greet any outside our faith, even President Grant, she often says, were he to call. When she saw the Marshal, she looked as if she was about to reach for her pistol and bucket and chase him from the house in the fearless manner she drives the rats from the orchard. I told my good wife to be still and pray.

At ten o'clock we entered the Third District Court Room and the Marshal seated me in a chair on the east side. So many had gathered for the spectacle, supporters and enemies alike, that mine was the last vacant seat, with the exception of the chair awaiting Judge McKean. My supporters included many of my sons and sons-in-law, who sat in a row headed by Hiram Clawson; members of the Nauvoo Legion, some of them now older than I, their shoulders bent under fond memories of the olden days; a variety of Bishops, Elders, and other well-wishers; and Captain Hooper from the co-op's hat department, who, just before the proceedings began, called out, "All of Zion rise up for our Prophet, Brigham Young!"

Judge McKean silenced the court room with his angry gavel. With each bang of the mallet's head he looked at me with obvious disdain. From whence his adversity to our Faith comes I know not. True, the recent publication of Ann Eliza's memoir has soiled my character in many parts of the nation. I am told it has sold more than 100,000 copies, sending the publisher back to the printing press three or four times. Are there 100,000 men and women interested in the Saints? If only they had read our Book, not hers. Now, for many, knowledge of our Church, and of me, comes mostly from her pen. I have not read *The 19th Wife*, but I have it here with me, should I need the company. I hope it does not come to that.

My attorneys, Brother Hempstead and Brother Kirkpatrick, had prepared themselves with an armory of books and briefs. Their adversary, Judge Hagan, stood nearby, solid with confidence. In dealing with him, he is the kind of lawyer who grants you the sensation of victory, while in truth you have lost everything.

Hagan began by declaring I had shown disdain for the court's mandate by refusing to pay Ann Eliza's fee in the stated time. Judge McKean asked my attorneys if this was true. Kirkpatrick attempted first, claiming it was not. Hempstead fortified Kirkpatrick's position, saying, "While it's true Brother Brigham has not paid the fees, he has not shown disdain for the court or its mandate." Both men continued adequately for more than an hour, incorporating legal thinking derived from American and English courts, all in my support. While competent in legal history, they possess ordinary imaginations and therefore they could not create, as an artist would, a means for my escape. At 12:35, Judge McKean called an hour recess. When the court returned, I was found in contempt and ordered to the Penitentiary.

The cheers and whoops of hurrah drowned out the weeping of my supporters. The Marshal shackled me at the wrist, apologizing for having to do so. As he led me from the court room a voice cried out, "Remember Carthage!" A second echoed the first, "We'll always remember Carthage!"

I, too, was thinking of Carthage, of the stone jailhouse where the mob assassinated my dear Joseph and his brother, Hyrum, nearly thirty-one years before. Joseph had submitted to the rule of law, giving himself up to the Gentile authorities, yet in the end the law could not protect him from the mob. I was away on mission that terrible day. I did not speak to him in his last hours. What were his thoughts? Those who witnessed him said he was pensive and in peace. Yet there is no greater mystery to me, at least among matters from here on Earth, than what occupied Joseph's mind on his last day. We have his letter to Emma, but how often I have wished he had kept a deeper record of his final hours. I know he was not afraid, yet there is much more I wish I could know.

If this candle burns out before dawn, I will have to write by the light of the moon. Perhaps the guard outside my door will ask Mrs. Paddock for a second, yet he must do so now, before she falls asleep. To do this he will have to leave his post and he will only do so if he can trust me. The guard, a Catholic boy named Christopher, he reminds me of my son Willard. They share the same supple smile and wave of chestnut hair. They could be the same age—I shall ask when I request the second candle. I think of Willard often, of how bravely he withstood the slander when he arrived at West Point a few years ago. Many called for his removal from campus, writing Senators and Congressmen letters of disapproval, disparaging him as the son of whores. When I read this in the newspapers, I telegraphed Willard, inviting him to return home. His reply was swift and short: "Father, will stay." Now he's preparing to graduate from the Military Academy with a commission in the national Corps of Engineers. He is the kind of brave son I have always hoped to rear.

There, I have now spoken with the guard. His name is Officer O'Conner, he is twenty-three—Willard's age by a month. He will fetch a second candle from Mrs. Paddock's cupboard. While waiting for him, I have been standing at the window for some time. The immense valley lay in blackness, yet the moon on the snow casts a revealing silver-blue light. While gazing out, I have come to sense a movement out there. I cannot perceive it with any precision. That is what it is to my eye—a movement in the dark. I do not know if it is a trick of the light, or a wolf pack crouching through the snow, or men gathering. Or perhaps there is no movement, perhaps all is still, and it is time for me to sleep.

When Officer O'Conner returned I asked if he worried I might try to escape. "No, Sir," he said. "You gave me your word." He handed me a long tapered candle barely burned at the top.

Now, with ample candle-power, I should have the friend of light to guide me through the night. When I think of all there is to do, I become anxious and walk in circles around this small room. I am not restless for lack of freedom. During my house arrest in the winter of '72, I could stay at my desk day and night, hacking away at my tasks at a pace even I had never before known. There is always much to do, matters to consider, works to accomplish. Next month I would like to return to St. George to review the progress of the Temple. The roof will rise soon—how I hope to witness that. When it is up, and the building stands secure, we can begin our many important rites, starting with the baptism of the dead. Then I must tend to the United Order, which has yet to take root. Later this summer I should like to reintroduce the New Alphabet. How much easier it will be on our emigrants when they arrive in Deseret, unfamiliar with English as they are. The last attempt failed, I know, because I did not lead the Saints to it. This time they will know its importance to me. And always so much more—the letters I owe my sons, including Willard, to whom I must describe the guard. The upcoming conference of the councils of the Priesthood. The audit of the statements of the Z.C.M.I. The meeting with the Board of Directors of the Deseret Bank, and of the Street Railroad Co., too, and that of the Deseret Telegraph Co., all of which shall be held very soon, and a review of the Utah Southern Railroad's future tracks, and the annual meeting of the Gas Co., &c. &c.— these are the matters, and many others, preoccupying my mind of late. The misperception among those who do not know me, or care not to know me, is that my spoiled marriage to Ann

Eliza has consumed my days. Ann Eliza does not hold such a commanding position in my thoughts. She is perhaps 87th on a list of tasks and items requiring my attention. This no doubt has fueled her rage. I should have been more mindful of this. My rage for her, however, has never matched hers for me. I admire her, and always will. I remember the night she was born. There are no words to depict the joy she brought her mother, herself a true Saint. As a baby Ann Eliza was dark in the face, with two slits for eyes. How those eyes opened as she grew, blossoming into a beauty that, even tonight, can catch upon my old heart.

After Judge McKean declared me in contempt of court, the Marshal led me from the courthouse to a carriage. Hundreds of Saints waited along the cordoned path, all somber and withdrawn, many weeping softly, a few Sisters wailing with grief. I walked as proudly as a man can with his hands manacled behind his back. "Pray for the wisdom of our Father," I called to them. "Pray for the mercy and justice of our Lord." But my words could not travel far, for pressing against the Saints were nearly a thousand enemies, their fists in the air and calling for their own interpretation of justice. How I longed for the days when we were alone in Deseret! I always knew we would rue the railroad.

Marshal Smith ushered me into the carriage. His orders were to deliver me directly to the Warden of the Penitentiary. Again, at my request, he disobeyed them, driving first to the Beehive. I sent my guardsman to bring me Mrs. Young. Sister Mary Ann approached the carriage, torn apart by tears. I explained to my wife the task I needed her to perform. She understood, pushing a small cloth at her damp nose, and ran inside. She returned with a pair of caramel leather boots. These were the boots Joseph had worn when he rode to Carthage to submit to the jailhouse. In the carriage I changed my shoes, donning Joseph's boots for the first time. Although our feet were not the same size, the boots fit as if they had been cobbled for me. I wear them now.

518

Admirers and enemies had gathered along the route to the Penitentiary. Several times a rifle was shot into the sky, sending fear and paranoia through the crowd. I cannot know the total number of people in the streets, yet I shall estimate it to be ten thousand. Most were my followers, yet the relative few who were there to oppose me controlled the argument. What astonished me, even more than the noise and the rancor, and the vicious shouts of slander—*American Sultan!* and *No More Harems!* and *Isn't 19 enough!*—was the piety my Saints maintained, for they understood what they were witnessing. Their Prophet, shackled, being led to punishment. At a crossroads near the city's limit, where the crowd was smaller and the shouting less, a small girl ran into the road, pelting my carriage with blue crocus. "Like Jesus before him," she cried, running back to her mother, who kissed her head.

By the time we reached the Penitentiary gate, four miles from the city, twenty carriages were following us. I realized my men, friends all, filled them, and they had come to protect me. Warden Paddock met us at the gate, while his guards, Officer O'Conner and his partner, held back the men in the carriages. As the Marshal led me from the carriage, my men cried out for my release. Many held rifles in the air, while others raised up axes, scythes, and other blades.

Warden Paddock welcomed me, leading me up the stairs to his office, where I now sit. He instructed the Marshal to release me from the cuffs. The papers were drafted and signed, and officially the Marshal transferred me into the custody of the Warden. I thanked the good man for his attendance and said good-bye. From the window I watched him return to his carriage. The pair of Penitentiary officers escorted him through the throng of my supporters onto the road.

The Warden looked out the window with concern, for no doubt the crowd appeared ready to boil over into a mob. I assured him they would not attack the Penitentiary as long as they deemed I was safe. I asked to speak to them. The Warden considered this unusual request from his newest prisoner. I had never before met this man, yet surely he knew of me. I wondered with which portion of my public character he was familiar. I realize, more than anyone else, that for all the Saints who understand me as their Prophet, and trust me as their spiritual guide on Earth, and into the Afterlife, many more people believe me to be a scoundrel. I can accept this misperception if it means being constant in my faith.

"You have five minutes, Sir." The Warden led me down to the gate. With the two guards stationed beside me, I spoke to my followers. "Do not worry for me tonight, for these are good men here, who understand the rule of law. I am safe, and now you must disperse."

The men, however, did not want to disperse. Many called out, "Carthage!"

"Please, Brethren, you must withdraw."

Still the men stayed in place. "Carthage!" the men cried again. "Carthage!"

I tried a third time. "My dear friends, you must listen to me and disperse now. You wonder why you should do so and I shall tell you. For we are a people of law, and rule, and Christian kindness. We do not attack because we fear being attacked. Even if you worry for my safety, you must now push back, go out, and disperse. Do so now, for that is what I want of you. I know you want to protect me, but understand, God protects me, as He protects you. His will, whatever that may be, shall be borne out tonight, whether your rifle is drawn or not. Do not defy me, for in doing so you shall defy our Heavenly Father. You cry, Think of Carthage! Brethren, one day has not passed since June 27, 1844, when I have not thought of Carthage. I think of Carthage on days of joy and rest, on days of fear and toil, always I think of Carthage. At night, before sleep, I call Joseph's name, knowing he awaits me, as he awaits you, all of you! Joseph came to tell us the Latter-day Saints are the inheritors of Christ, and Christ has shown us that we do not take an eye for an eye. Friends, go now, leave the Warden in peace, and his guards in peace, and this Penitentiary in peace! Even if it is now my home, and I know not my future, you must leave in peace, for that is what we believe."

Silently the crowd broke, drifting out in all directions, to the factory and to the mill, and down the road to Salt Lake. Would an enemy mob replace them? Here at my window I have been anticipating it ever since.

It is late now. Half the night is gone. What will the darkness bring before the dawn? The prisoners are asleep. The Warden's family has retired. Outside my door I hear Officer O'Conner pacing to keep himself awake. When I look out into the dark, into the land beyond the Penitentiary, I see the movement again. Now they are black shapes shifting against other black shapes. I cannot tell what they are. Wagons? Buffalo? Men on horseback? A forming brigade? For a long time now I have stood at the window, with my new candle burning itself down, staring into the night, trying to perceive what moves out there. It occurs to me I should snuff out the candle, so that I may stand in the darkened window, but then I will have no light until daybreak. The longer I look out, the more certain I am that there are men out there. Friend or enemy? I look for a signal, but see none. The snow has muffled the sounds of the Earth. An attack could come as a surprise. If it does, and they are assassins, I pray they spare Mrs. Paddock and her children. And Officer O'Conner—I should note he even speaks like Willard, slowly, with his tongue soft against the roof of his mouth. The similarity is perplexing. If it is a sign, I cannot interpret it. So I continue to stand alert at my window, considering so much.

Yesterday a reporter from the *San Francisco Examiner* came to see me. This man writes a daily unsigned column that has made him famous and, I am quite sure, rich. I would hold a grudge against him, for he has spared no venom in dissecting me and my divorce. But I cannot hold a grudge for he loathes everyone equally, and with good aim. Against the opinion of my advisers, I invited him to the Beehive. During our meeting he asked a question I am still pondering tonight.

"What mistakes have you made?" I assured him there were many, but he pressed me for details.

First, I was wrong about Ann Eliza. Quite simply, I judged her incorrectly. I sensed she understood, or would come to understand, the arrangements of my household, and know that while I could not tend to her in every manner, I would always care for her. She is a selfish woman, by which I do not mean to condemn her, for most men and women are selfish, in that most often they think of themselves first. It is man's most natural instinct, an impulse that connects us with the animals. Yet some women are extraordinary in this regard, they can submerge their natural impulses for the sake of their belief. These are the women best suited to plural marriage. Ann Eliza, I have learned, is not this kind of woman. So be it. I only wish we could have settled our matters more kindly. For now, with our case on the public stage, all the world it seems has become curious about my wives. Every day the mail brings a hundred letters wanting to know how many I have. Yesterday, the man from the *Examiner* pressed me on that question. "Surely, you must know how many wives you keep?" he asked not once, but eight or ten times.

Each time I replied, "I do."

"Then why won't you tell me how many Mrs. Youngs there are? Why is it a secret?" He is an intelligent man, but not so intelligent to realize he is most likely the thousandth person to inquire on the matter. Why this neverending speculation over how many wives? Why do visitors to Great Salt Lake stand outside the Lion House, and the Beehive House, too, counting windows and doors, attempting to estimate the number of spouses therein. Surely they must know it is a futile exercise—one cannot know how many sleep inside a house by counting the dormers! Yet they do, I see them outside the wall every day. One, two, three, four, five, their moving lips say. Next they wonder if I keep two wives in one bed. Or perhaps three, a rude man suggests to his friend. They share a debased laugh, a putrid guffaw, one that degrades the very idea of woman and her dignity. Next they wonder how I can manage my conjugal duties with so many wives waiting her turn. Their interest in the number of wives is always prurient. If, on the other hand, it were spiritual and came as a true inquiry into the will of God, I would explain my household to them, count up the wives to show the abundance of our faith. Yet I see no point when it will only feed the imagination of the profane.

The good Saints know why I do not announce the number of wives. Wife is an inadequate term, for each woman plays a different role in my life, just as each person plays a different role in all our lives. For lack of a more precise term, we label them all wives, but they are not all wives. Indeed some are my mates and mothers of my children. Yet others are more like affectionate aunts. Others are intellectual friends, with whom I can debate and discuss all matters. Others still are, indeed, the keepers of the house, the kitchen, the children. Others remind me, in their distance, of neighbors to whom one might wave across a wall. Others still are very old and retired in their rocking chairs. They find comfort in knowing I shall provide them with a bed and meals for the rest of their days. Only a few are like a wife in the common sense, none more so than Amelia. She is all of this, and more, but imagine the uproar—among my women and the public at large—were I to so publicly dissect the ranks within my household. I shall not subject these good women to that, and therefore I do not answer the question how many wives. I must admit to the smallest pleasure it gives me—how this numerical mystery irritates the world!

Sometimes, also, I permit the hypocrisy to bemuse me. In the evening, when I am with Amelia, or my sons, or other friends, and the business of the day is done, and we can sit by a fire, and loosen the laces in our shoes, I allow myself to chuckle, like when I have been told a fine irony. These indignant Gentiles, lamenting the nature of my household, having never known it in person, tolerate in their midst a broader range of crimes—drunkenness, infanticide, neglect of the elderly, prostitution—crimes that are all but unknown in Deseret. Let's ponder the latter. I have seen the whore at work—the painted lips, the exposed bosom, the voice darkened by whiskey and tobacco. She is an unnatural sight, in defiance of God's grace and the beauty of man given to us by Adam. Yet visit any Gentile city at dusk, or thereafter, and stroll the streets. You shall find one lady after the next vying for her spot on the corner. Or enter a tavern, where drink is deified, and you will find a woman prepared to spill her breasts onto the counter for a dollar, or less. In my younger days, when I saw Gentile whores on the street, I thought back in time. I imagined them as little girls in their Sunday dresses, with white collars an straw bonnets. I envisioned their mothers brushing their flaxen hair, kissing their smooth brows, and praying to our Father to protect them. Then I saw them now, before me, in the dim corners of the Gentile city—the whore with her nest of false curls permitting any man with a coin to paw her parts, to reach beneath her skirts in search of the desecrated hollow raked over by a thousand men. Where is the outrage among the Gentile crusaders? Why do they not demand an end to her whoredom? Only hypocrisy can explain it, and withered reasoning.

Each time my enemies attack me as America's foremost adulterer, they fail to admit an important matter to the debate. Their society is rife with adultery, yet among the Saints, this sin remains mostly unknown. To my mind, adultery is worst among the sins, with the exception of murder, for the one act corrodes many souls. The practice of plural marriage has eliminated adultery from our society, freeing us of its ill effects. I look to King David with many sacred wives. He was a good and devout man, but when he stole Uriah's wife, snatching her from the heart of her husband, he became an adulterer, and in God's eyes he had committed sin. Worse still, his selfish act—prompted by the other sins of greed, vanity, and lust—forced her to become an adulteress. Thus the sinner created a second sinner. This is not right.

I wonder if Ann Eliza has illuminated this truth to her reader. Opening her book at random, I find this declaration: "Brigham leads the Church, and all of Utah, as a tyrant rules from his throne. He will not tolerate dissent or open opinion, for in his claim to be Prophet of God he believes there is no truth except that which he has spoken." My goodness, am I really such? I laugh over her depiction, for I've heard it before, and will do so again.

I must say, Ann Eliza always proved insightful. Behind her denunciation, she has illuminated one of the most troublesome aspects of my leadership. There is, and, to my mind, always will be, the problem of balancing the Truth, as I know it, with the rights of man, in which I believe. How to reconcile this problem? I know my faith to be the true faith of God, and Joseph His first Prophet since Christ, and myself after him, yet I cannot force belief upon others—or can I? Is this not my task, my mission? How to solve this quandary of religious duty? If we are right, and our faith is the true expression of God's will, to what extent should I enforce that will? This is not merely a practical question of conversion and missionary work, but a theological question concerning divine duty. I have pondered it for many years, without full resolution. In my heart I know we are right, and Joseph has brought us the Truth, and now I am to carry it forth. In my heart I know I am to bring it to all the lands with the force of God, and His wrath, too, for Truth can never respect falsehoods and lies. But it is not always feasible to do so. Is it a failing when I tell my Brethren to respect the Methodist, the Episcopal, the Jew? Am I failing God? I cannot know. I must accept it as one of our Heavenly Father's many mysteries, its answer unknowable until our last day.

Just now I have returned from the window. I am certain men have gathered out there, for they are closer, maybe a hundred yards from the Warden's house. I can see the flash in their horses' eyes. I hear the hoofs stomping on the snow. I can see the orange embers of burning tobacco which tells me, then, these are not my men. When the mob attacked the jailhouse in Carthage, two hundred men had painted their faces black to mask their identities. The men out there—they are using the black of night as a mask. I respect them less, and fear them less—for a camouflaged enemy is a cowardly enemy. Stand in the daylight and fight for what you believe! I will grant Ann Eliza this—she has taken her shot at me from a stage where I can see her.

Often I think back to my old friend and enemy E. L. T. Harrison and his well-argued words against me in *The Utah Magazine*. Among men's mental powers, I have always had a special fondness for logic. I remember Harrison's words of dissent as if they were on a page before me now. "I believe in the right to discuss freely, provided I do it respectfully and moderately, any measure or principle that may be presented. I do not believe I have the right to be rabid in regard to my use of vindictive language, but provided I am temperate— provided I accord to others the same privilege I do myself, I believe that men should be guided entirely by their own light and intelligence. I do not believe in the principle of implicit obedience, unconditional obedience without the judgment being convinced. If it is apostasy to differ with Brigham on some points, I am an apostate because I honestly differ with him. I do protest that I differ in a spirit of love and due regard for him." How to reconcile his views and mine, when I know mine to be the wisdom of our Father, and his to be the sincere but misguided inclinations of a good man? Liberty, I know, rests nowhere but in Truth. Freedom—always in Truth! Must I, then, for the sake of Liberty, respect Harrison's thoughtful but defiant judgments? Ignore them? Condemn them? How can I guide others in the principles of Truth if I do not condemn these opinions? Oh! were He to tell me with all certainty my course. Yet I have come to know that wrestling with this question shall be my fate while on Earth. I only pray that when I kneel before Him in the Heavenly Kingdom He shall tell me I have acted wisely.

I have faced such opposition since the Gladdenites, for there is no more ferocious enemy than he who comes from within. Apostasy is inevitable to holding firm to one's belief. That a few believers will fall away is the by-product of unbending faith. If this were not the case, if I never lost a follower, I would wonder if I had bent, unbeknownst to myself, to popular opinion. My duty, I know, is to lead. I cannot offer an array of options. I must offer a long but narrow path to Salvation, and guide the Saints down it. Were that path wide and varied, it would lead nowhere; and I will then have failed both God and man. I cannot go forth into the next life, with the knowledge I will meet Joseph there, without knowing I have made every effort to promote and preserve his wisdom on all matters, including plural marriage. How have I come here? It is by this.

Outside, beyond the adobe walls, the men are moving in. I see them— the last of the moonlight burns on their muzzles, it illuminates the hatred in their eyes. I see them, crouching, sneaking forward, preparing their siege. And so it has come to this. Is this now my hour? Did Joseph see his enemies in the Illinois brush before they stormed the stone jailhouse? Did he see the blue-white of their seething eyes? How have I come here indeed! If they are to take me, they are to take me while preoccupied with the work of God.

This, then, has been my second mistake, and its effects are more dangerous than my first. I was wrong to let my attorneys persuade me to claim I have only one wife. They convinced me that in declaring Ann Eliza and all my other wives social harlots, the matter would fall away. Their tactics are legal, with no concern for the theological or moral. I am to blame for accepting their counsel. This, I know, has been my gravest error, for in following their advice, I renounced my faith. I know the force of my leadership has come from always standing firm before friend and foe. What did the Saints everywhere think when they heard me, via the legal brief, dismiss our most sacred institution? Calling the good sisters of the Lion

House social harlots? I am ashamed to think of the turmoil I have unleashed in their hearts. And what of God? He who has given me wisdom for many years? I turned to lawyers for answers, not Him! Consider it! The loss of faith! Oh, Joseph! Joseph! How great is your capacity to forgive?

Now I must speak to the guard. "Officer O'Conner!" I call, rapping on the door. "Officer O'Conner!" My ear tells me the young man is asleep. The men outside the walls have anticipated this. Ambush relies on the element of surprise. The young guard, Willard's unknown twin, will awaken to a rifle in his face. He will unlock my door while the assassin presses his gun to his temple. The poor boy—he knew nothing of what it meant to protect me. "Officer O'Conner!" How he sleeps! His mind must be free of worry. For me, I have no resource but prayer.

I do not know how long I have been on my knees now. These words here I write from the floor, putting down the pen between prayers. The candle burns low, the soft wax folding over the candlestick. Just now I have looked out the window. I see the men. The siege is about to begin. In Carthage, Joseph had a six-shooter smuggled in by a friend to defend himself. He fired all his shots before succumbing to the assassin's ball. I have nothing but my pen and my prayers. With these, I will hold out as long as I can.

But, look—on the horizon! A sliver of light! Not yet pink. Silver and blue. A minute ago all was dark, now a crevice of light, and with each breath of man it expands. In the time it has taken to write those words, the light has grown. Now beyond the black mountains I see a wash of blue. With it I can see the horses and the men. There must be two hundred— no, three hundred out there on the roads. They have blockaded the road to the mill, and the other to the factory. When will they attack? Do they wish to see my face in the clear light of dawn? If so, they are not cowards. They are fearless—the most dangerous enemy. Come! I say. Attack! I shall stand before you and never relent!

I have returned now to my knees to ask our Dear Heavenly Father for forgiveness, for I have turned away from Your wisdom. I am not afraid for my life, but I fear dying by the assassin's ball while having renounced You. Grant me another day on Earth to return to Your path. Bring me the wisdom to know the course I must take. I believe, as I have always believed, in the doctrine of plural marriage as You revealed it to Joseph, as You have confirmed it to me. Your word is the word of God, and always shall be. I will go forth and affirm its Truth, if only You will grant me another day.

Thus I prayed. I have been on my knees for so long they are sore from the boards. Outside, dawn's arrival is now irreversible. The colors fill the sky. The mountains are lit, the valley is lit, the river runs in its canyon, carrying chips of morning ice. If the assault is to come, it is to come now. Why do the men wait? What is their hesitation? I will check the window. I will show them my face. I will give them their target. I will let them know I am here.

Dear Heavenly Father! The men on the roads! They are packing up! I can see them rolling blankets, saddling horses, storing guns. I can see them turning the carriages around. Who are they? Why did they not attack? How often does life prove itself unknowable? How many mysteries can the heart bear? I only know this is the mercy of the Lord! I know it, I recognize it, I feel the warmth on my skin. The men are leaving! They are leaving! My enemies have quit.

"Officer O'Conner! Officer O'Conner! Wake up! Tell the Warden I want to return to court! Call the Marshal! Call Judge McKean! I admit to my error!" I shall inform Judge McKean I accept his orders. I will pay Ann Eliza's fees. I will grant her a rightful divorce. Her demands are just. She has been my wife. For five years she was my wife. How true she is, she has been my wife! The women of the Lion House—God has granted each to me as a full wife!

I will go forth now and declare to the Saints everywhere, and to the world, too, that these are my wives! And that by accepting all my women as my wives, and declaring my conjugal duties to them, as so prescribed by the court of law, I am declaring, and you, Dear Gentiles, are accepting, our right to celestial marriage. My admission of husbandly duty to Ann Eliza, and my monthly check of alimony, will be an early declaration of responsibility to her, and to all my women, as you have demanded it. Americans everywhere, make no mistake: this is our right! Your laws, which are our laws, have declared this so.

Yet I do not expect you to accept the plural wife now, even though your laws have forced me to publicly accept her. I do not expect your leaders in Washington to readily accept my right, and the rights of the Saints, to our beliefs. I do not expect to come to agreement today, or tomorrow, or any time soon, on this matter that is of nuisance to you, but of eternal importance to us. No! This shall be our last battle, for you have made it clear that we can never agree, and I shall make it clear that the Saints of Deseret shall never relent. We will defy the authorities, the army, even the great General, President Grant! If we must, we will take up arms to fight in the name of God. I can only hope my new resolve will inspire the Saints to fight for this principle until the end of time. He who abandons it is not a Saint, as I now understand, for God has spoken. His words are clear.

The desert sun now pours through the window, warm on the writing desk. How I long to be home among my women! The sacred practice of celestial marriage is not my will, or Joseph's will, but the will of God. And so the Truth has come to pass. It is as clear as the morning outside. Through Revelation, God has spoken, and we must obey. Saints of Zion—be not afraid! We know the wisdom of the Lord! Now go forth and defend it until our Last Day!

XX

WIFE #19:

THE CONVICTION
OF JORDAN SCOTT

ENDING IT ALL

———

I checked the food court, the gadget store, the men's room. I spent more than an hour looking for Johnny in the mall. The last place to search was the LDS bookstore. I asked a clerk unloading a carton of books if he'd seen a kid hanging around. The guy didn't recognize Johnny from my description but said he'd keep an eye out.

"Wait a minute," I said. "What's that?"

"What, this?" The clerk looked at the book in his hand. There was a modelly gay-looking guy on the jacket. Its title: *Overcoming Same-Gender Attraction*. The clerk had already unloaded a dozen copies onto a table and there were another dozen in the box.

"Yeah, that. What is it?"

"It's, uh, I don't know." The guy flipped the book over and started reading the copy. "I guess it's something for parents who think their kid's gay or something."

"I know what it is."

The clerk looked at me like, Huh?

"You sell a lot of these?"

"Excuse me?" We were probably the same age, could've been born on the same day, two young men from opposite ends of the state, opposite ends of the world, really.

"Do you sell a lot of these?"

"That's not really, I mean, I can't really—" But he pulled his wits together, as if he'd been trained to deal with nut jobs. "Sir, is there something I can help you with?"

I started looking at the book myself. It was written by a couple whose son had noosed up his missionary necktie and let it all hang out because he was gay. And right there on the first page they wrote, "Although bereft, after Josh's death we were overcome by a certain peace because his anguish had come to an end."

Don't. Make. Me. Scream.

"You realize you're selling total and complete bullshit."

"Sir?"

"This book. It's a total lie."

"Sir, if there's nothing here you want, maybe you should leave."

"What? I'm not allowed to browse?"

"I really don't want to have to call security."

"Be my guest." I was bluffing. We both knew it. I threw the book on the table, turned around, and bumped right into Johnny.

"Dude, *what* has crawled up your ass today?" He grabbed my t-shirt and led me out of the store.

Out on the street I said, "You've got to stop disappearing like that."

"You're the one who dumped me on the curb."

"I told you I'd be back."

"That's what they all say." He punched me in the shoulder, as if to say he couldn't hold a grudge. "C'mon, I'm starving. There's this cool place across the street."

He led me over to an old gabled house with a stone lion above the door. "Wait a minute. You want to eat here?" I said. I couldn't believe it. We were standing in front of the Lion House. It was now a museum and catering hall.

"There's this major buffet down in the basement. All you can eat for four ninety-nine."

I told him no way. I wasn't going to eat in Brigham's harem.

"Why not?"

"Why not? You know what this place represents?"

"Get over yourself. It's only fucking lunch."

There was nothing special about the place. A cafeteria in the basement, heaps of carby food in enamel pans. We filled our plates with limp turkey and macaroni with fake cheese and sugary dinner rolls.

"So what was that all about in the bookstore?" said Johnny.

"I don't know. That book just struck a chord." I described the book and I didn't want to, but I let a tirade get the best of me. Off I went, lamenting all the gay Mormon kids who are lied to, the *Ensign* articles warning them to deny who they are, eighteen-year-old Josh hanging from a necktie in his Ogden closet, those parents finding peace—*peace!*—after his death. And then writing a book about it. I went on and on, flailing my hands, banging the table in the corner of the Lion House basement, preaching to a kid who listened with a give-me-a-break face while picking his nose.

When I was done Johnny pushed a slab of turkey into his mouth and went back to the buffet for seconds. He returned to the table, saying, "Isn't this place awesome? All you can eat for five bucks. You gotta love the Mormons."

"Johnny, did you hear anything I just said?"

The kid was busy chewing, flashing gray-blue bits of turkey on his tongue. "I heard."

"Well?"

"When are you going to realize you're not the only person in the world who's been fucked? I mean, crap, welcome to the club."

An hour later we parked in front of the Ann Eliza Young House. The sun was hitting the stained-glass window and the house looked special, like Martha Stewart might live there. "Let's go in."

Johnny looked at the house, then me. "Where are we?"

"It's a home for kids."

"What kind of home?"

"There's someone I want you to meet."

His mouth bit into a hard line. "Are you fucking with me?"

"C'mon, let's go."

"Because if you are, at least have the guts to admit it to my face, you lying piece of shit."

535

I thought he might take off, run down the sidewalk, and disappear. I could imagine it—his little black-soled sneakers slapping the concrete, taking him around a corner, down an alley, through a lobby, anywhere. I'd go looking for him, but this time he wouldn't turn up. It seemed like the most obvious outcome to all this. There'd be the days of searching, the panicked calls to Tom, the sorry explanation to Kelly, the police report, the false hope, the dead ends, the giving up. It was as if it had already happened, like I'd already seen this movie and knew the ending line by line.

But Johnny didn't run. He walked up the path with me to the door, silent and furious, picking a daisy along the way, shredding its petals, and hurling them at me. They hit the back of my head with the impact of a moth. "Who the fuck is Ann Eliza Young, anyway?"

"Some Mormon lady, it doesn't matter."

"Now I get it, it's all coming clear. Earth to Johnny: once again you're the last one to realize you've been screwed."

Kelly met us at the door. She looked very pretty and very calm. When she talked to Johnny she talked to him like a person, not like a messed-up booted-out kid. "Can I get you something to eat? Maybe an apple or a banana?"

"Next." His livid eyes were saying, *I'm going to kill you for this.*

"The director's here, she's looking forward to meeting you."

"And I'm looking forward to telling her she can suck my—"

"Johnny."

"Kidding!" The dimples ran up his cheeks like when you hold your finger on the))))))))))) key. He turned to Kelly. "All right, sweetheart. I suppose every outlaw has to eventually come in." He took her hand and they walked down the hall. The amber light from the old brass sconce silhouetted them, two figures retreating into a celestial glow, like lovers strolling into the sunset on a corndog greeting card. And that was it. Johnny was gone from my life.

Or, almost.

"Johnny, wait!"

He turned around.

"Your knife!"

"What about it?"

"I'll keep it for you." I walked to him with my hand out. He hesitated, then pulled it out of his pants. We looked at it, at his mom's name taped to the handle.

"I'll be wanting that back," he said.

"One day," I said.

"I mean it, it's all I got from her." The kid shoved my shoulder and lurched forward for an awkward hug. "Now get out of here before we both start breaking up like a couple of girls."

SAN FRANCISCO EXAMINER

March 16, 1875

PROMETHEUS UNBOUND

Even we do not know what to say. On Friday last, the Lord's Lion, fresh from a good night's sleep in the United States Penitentiary, emerged with a changed heart. He marched into Judge McKean's courtroom to declare, Sir, you are right! Brigham paid the fees, in doing so admitting Ann Eliza had been his wife and she was due a proper alimony.

Now, in any other part of the world, this would be an unremarkable event. Yet this is Deseret, and oh, how we enjoy its many ironies! In accepting Brigham's gold, and releasing him from custody, Judge McKean acknowledged Ann Eliza, and all the rest, numbers one through nineteen, and beyond— all of them to be lawful wives. Thus, for our slower readers, a federal judge, appointed by the President himself, had given legal claim to polygamy.

Oh, what we would have paid to be present when the news reached old Grant wheezing in his bed. How his mustaches must have fluttered from his bellows! The General fumed, orders were given, and in swift time Judge McKean has been removed from the court, replaced by a jurist with a finer under-standing of the case's subtleties. Summarily, Judge McKean's original decisions were reversed. Brigham Young was found to owe Ann Eliza nothing, for she never was, and never will be, his wife. The case was dismissed, the parties thrown out, and by God, the General screamed at poor Mrs. Grant, these Mormons are going to be the end of me!

This, as far as we can tell, is the end of the tale of the 19th Wife. To all, Godspeed!

WE MET ONLINE

——

It was past midnight when I pulled into the Malibu. Tom's alarm clock washed the room in digital green. He was asleep, a dog on each side. The dogs were snoring lightly, their snout lips fluttering, their breath filling the room with the castoff of sleep. Watching Tom and the dogs, I felt something I didn't quite recognize, something so tender I worried it would pop and disappear if I asked for its meaning. I unlaced my sneakers and dropped my jeans and pulled back the blanket.

Elektra stirred first, lifting her head. Then Joey, and at last Tom. Each looked momentarily confused. Elektra was the first to recognize me, her tail thumping. Tom said, "Oh, hi," and Joey budged himself over for a lick.

"I think everything's going to be OK," I said.

"You mean you left him there?"

I kissed him—Tom, I mean.

"What are you going to do now?"

"Shhh," I said. "Go back to sleep. We'll figure it out tomorrow." I reached for Tom. His sacred underwear was so thin and diaphanous it was like touching his chest through an ethereal gauze. On the undershirt's belly there's a short line of stitching called a navel marker; it's there to remind you of God's nourishment, or something like that. It's just a little dash of thread, and as Tom and I fell toward sleep I rubbed it over and over, the way a finger returns impulsively to a scar.

In the morning I went to Heber's office. "I was just about to call you,"

Maureen said. "Mr. Heber wants to see you."

"Actually, I came to see you. I want to apologize for that stuff I said."

Her eyebrows locked in a line of contemplation. She was thinking about whether or not she believed me. Then she reached her conclusion. "I know you didn't mean it. Now come on, let's go see the old man."

She led me down the hall. More than a week had passed since we'd first met, and she was fresh out of the beauty parlor again, her hair curled under at the nape. "It's going to be a real scorcher out there," she said. "I hope Elektra's someplace cool."

When we entered his office, Mr. Heber said, "Where's the dog?" I told him, but I still couldn't tell if he really cared. "The Malibu Inn? Sounds like a good place to be on a day like today. So listen, I've got news, that's why I wanted you to come in. It's hit the radar."

"What has?"

"Everything. Mesadale, the Prophet, and most important your mom. A tv crew from New York is on its way. They land in Vegas in an hour, they should be in Mesadale by midafternoon."

"What for?"

"To report. And just as I thought, this is going to change everything. I spoke to the producer. They're real sympathetic to women like your mom, they want to tell the story from her side, they want to get this right. And so here's the thing: they want to talk to you."

"What for?"

"You're the guy who can tell America what it's really like out there."

"I don't think I can do that."

"Of course you can. They're setting up in the conference room tomorrow at two."

I know how tv works. They make you explain things that can't be explained. Some questions don't have answers. There's a mystery to all this—I mean, the reason why we do

541

what we do. After a week it was the only Eureka! I'd had.

Mr. Heber gave me more details about the tv crew. The reporter was that cute guy with the silver hair you see all the time. "You might want to wear something other than a t-shirt," Mr. Heber advised. "Dress it up a bit, all right? And we'll need to work on what you're going to say. I want to write out some talking points."

Heber still didn't get it, or I guess what I really mean was Heber still didn't get me. I don't dress it up a bit. I don't have an interview outfit. I don't do talking points.

"I went back to Mesadale Sunday night," I said.

Heber looked up. "You need to be careful, Jordan."

"I heard something pretty interesting. About Sister Rita."

"What's that?"

"She's disappeared." I told him what Sister Drusilla had said. Heber was interested; the flesh on his face didn't move.

"Does this mean what I think it means?" I said.

He hesitated, as if he needed a moment to put it all together. "Yes, I think so."

"We're getting closer."

"But there's still that IM from your dad. He told us it was your mom."

"I know," I said. "That's the problem with the internet. Nothing ever disappears."

I decided not to tell Tom about the tv stuff. I still didn't believe they'd fly in from New York, spend all that money to help my mom. They'd probably flash that picture of her ducking into the cruiser, then air a story about a holy roller who dumped her son and shot her husband. Not only would it be wrong, I was pretty sure it would mess things up even more. Heber said we could trust them, but he didn't give me a good reason why.

Tom was busy anyway. There was a problem with Room 208; the guests had trashed the place with lighters, burning brown skid marks into the furniture. "I sensed something was

542

wrong the moment they got here," he kept telling the cop writing up the report. "I mean, I don't like to judge people, but I just had a feeling." What feeling was that? "Like they'd steal my dog."

I took this lull in my day to go online. An email from kadee@byu.edu looked ominous. Something must've gone wrong with Johnny.

> Hey Jordan—
> Just wanted to let you know Johnny's doing fine and I think everything's going to be all right. Call me if you have any questions or anything. He's lucky he found you.
> —Kelly

When I closed her email I found a new message in my box. The subject line—"Might Be Important"—looked spammy, but I opened it anyway.

> i'm not sure if you got my last email or what so i thought i'd try again. i remember chatting with your dad, that wasn't the first time, we sort of had this online poker/flirting thing going on, it didn't mean anything never in a million years would i have ever met him or anything, it was just one of those internet things and I don't know if i know anything that might be useful but i might. maybe we should talk. by the way my name's not really desertmissy (obvi), it's albert but he didn't know that.

I wrote DesertMissy, asking what he knew, and he replied right away.

> first of all i'm sorry about your dad i read about him in the register and stuff i've been following the case and what's been going on out in mesadale and somehow i knew he was manofthehouse2004. we'd been chatting for several months and we talked about a lot of things not just poker and sex but all sorts of things like life and he told me all about his wives

543

and kids and was really honest about it all about how hard it was on a lot of them and he felt bad about that. he said sometimes it broke him up having to see so many of his kids wanting him to be a normal dad and he couldn't be that kind of dad because there were too many of them. but he always said it was worth it because this is how god wanted it. i'm not too sure about that myself i've never been much of a god person but i admire a man who knows what he believes and sticks to it. all great men are like that and who am i to say what he believes is any crazier than the rest of the shit everyone else out there believes, including me. i was at that point of actually liking your dad a lot and i could tell he liked me but there was this problem you know of how do i tell him the truth, i mean about me, and i wasn't sure how to bring it up then our chat session just stopped that night and he never responded and i read about a plural wife killing her husband out in mesadale and i knew it was him, i just knew, you know how sometimes you just know? that's why i wasn't surprised when i got your email last week.

I asked Albert where he lived, if we could meet. We needed to talk.

no that won't be possible this is the internet i don't meet people over the internet.

What about a phone call?

no i'll talk to anyone online but i always want to remain anon but i'll tell you this much i'm not like other people online i always tell people the truth for me it's a place i can really tell people what i think and feel. it's so hard to do that in real life for me it's the only place i can truly be myself. except the desertmissy thing (obvi) but that's just a name.

I begged Albert for his help.

i'll tell you what i can but i can't tell you who i am.

"Hey, how's it going?"

I jumped. "Oh, Tom, shit. You scared me."

"Who you writing?"

"Just some lead on my dad. I don't know. How'd it go with the cops?"

"They'll trace the license plate and stuff, but I've been through this kind of thing before. The paperwork's crushing."

"Anything I can do?" "Maybe check on the dogs. I've still got a lot of checkouts." In Room 112, the dogs were sleeping butt to butt on the bed. I refilled their water bowl and went back to the lobby. I was thinking about Albert. Could he possibly know anything? And even if he did, would it count— info from an anonymous online source? Can they subpoena a man named DesertMissy?

I sent Albert another email, asking if my dad ever talked about any of his wives.

all the time he really seemed to love them. i know he thought of some of them more like aunts or grandmas than wives, like sister what's her name the first wife i guess she's real old he always said she's a good woman. he loved the newer ones like sister kimberly to be perfectly honest we sometimes got a little graphic when we talked about them he was definitely still in love with kimberly she gave amazing head or at least that's what he said, sorry that's probably more than you want to know. he had just married a new girl Sarah and he was talking pretty macho about her and what he'd done to her after they were sealed. i know i should be outraged but you know what he was my friend she wasn't so i always saw it from his point of view. but in general he loved all the wives in his own way, i know that much for sure

From this stranger, a binary voice flashing in from somewhere—was he nearby or around the globe?—I was learning more about my father than I had ever known.

damn it just occurred to me she might be your mom you never told me who your mom is. i hope i haven't insulted you.

So I told him who my mom was.

holy crap that's crazy. that was your mom? maybe i shouldn't say anything more i mean i really don't want to get involved.

Albert, I wrote. You are involved. If you know which wives my dad liked to fuck, you're very much involved.

i guess you're right. besides i have nothing to hide.

I asked him if he knew anything else about the wives, was there anything else going on? I told him about the fuck chart, but it still didn't mean anything to me.

i don't know about that but you know i guess there was shit going on in the wife department he was pretty excited about that. i don't know if you know but that night he talked to your mom about their relationship i guess i'm not really sure but he said that it'd been a long time since they you know had been together and there was no point in trying to pretend they were really man and wife. i don't know but that's what he said which is why when i read that she had killed him i was shocked but not really surprised.

"Hey, Jordan?" said Tom. "Isn't it time you got going?" I looked at the clock on the computer. Shit. I was late for my visit to see my mom.

An Open Letter to President Woodruff
And Latter-day Saints Everywhere
October 23, 1890

———

I, the undersigned, stand in opposition to the recent manifesto of September 26, and approved October 6, regarding the doctrine of plural marriage. Section 132, as revealed to the Prophet Joseph Smith by our Heavenly Father, states plainly that anyone who shall not believe in this doctrine, and pursue it to his fullest extent, shall never attain Eternal Glory. I accept the truth of the Doctrine & Covenants, including Section 132, and refuse to edit God on this, or any, matter. As Brigham Young preached for more than thirty years, "To ignore it is to ignore His will." So said he until the last day of his life thirteen years ago.

I, the undersigned, challenge you to reverse this decision. Written in the spirit of political compromise and capitulation, rather than in the spirit of Truth and Glory, this manifesto shall send a fissure through the heart of our beloved Church, forcing Saints everywhere to choose between political expediency and Divine will.

I, the undersigned, demand a retraction of the manifesto, and all its meaning, or face a splintering of faith never before seen among Christians in the two thousand years since the days our Lord, Jesus Christ, walked the Earth, in the company of men.

I, the undersigned, declare openly that until the manifesto has been rescinded, and our natural rights restored, I, and all

Saints everywhere, shall pursue our faith fully, as we have known it since the days of Joseph and Brigham, as we shall always know it, in these last days.

I, the undersigned, declare myself, and all those who share my convictions stated herein, the First and True Latter-day Saints, for that is what we are.

ELDER AARON WEBB
& Wives

Red Creek
Territory of Utah

"Officer Cunningham," I said, "I'm really sorry I'm late."

"You know the rules."

"I know, ten minutes' grace time, then that's it, appointment canceled. But I have a really good excuse."

"I'm listening."

"It's just that . . ." But where to start? And where to end? I stood in front of the metal detector, unable to come up with an explanation for any of this.

"Oh, what the heck. I don't know why I like you, but I do." She winked, and for a flash I could imagine her out of uniform, her gun and shield locked up, walking through her front door, receiving a hug from her husband and kids. I thanked her. I thanked her for everything.

"Quit the mush, all right? OK, you know the drill: last cubicle in the row. Officer Kane'll bring her out."

It was just like before: the women, the babies, the glass screen. I waited on the stool, staring into the space that my mom would soon fill, looking at the yellow receiver, thinking about how lifeless it was and how in a few minutes it would crackle with her voice.

"Jordan," she said. "It feels like forever."

"Same for me." I told her everything that had happened, and it took a long time, and by the time I was done the wall clock said we had only a few minutes left.

"I'm not surprised to hear about Sister Rita," she said.

"Why's that?"

She hesitated but she knew this wasn't the time to bite her tongue. "I'm not sure if you know that I replaced her.

After I married your father, he stopped—how should I put this?—seeing her."

"Do you mean what I think you mean?"

Her cheeks flushed with shame. "He had his list," she said. "His list of wives. The wives he still—you know, visited. From the day I entered that house Rita treated me like I'd stolen something from her. She wanted to turn him against me, she was always trying to catch me doing something like ignoring my housework or forgetting my prayers or sneaking you more food than your share. When you were a baby she was really hard on me. You used to cry in church, and you know how the Prophet never liked that. She used to tell your father it was because of me—that I was holding you too tight or not changing you or whatever nonsense she could think of. You know your father, he never knew much about babies, so he didn't know what to believe. Over time I tried to be friends with her, I really tried. But all she'd do was lie to him about me."

"She was a total bitch."

Her lip crumpled. "I'm afraid you're right."

"Mom, I've seen the chart, but I can't really figure it out. What does it all mean?"

"It was his way of managing the wives, of keeping up."

"That, and Viagra."

"Don't be crude, Jordan. Not with me. I know everyone thinks we've lost our minds. The gals in here, they never use my name, they call me Nineteen. They make all sorts of cracks about orgies and whatnot. They have no idea who we are, they don't understand—they don't want to. I know the whole world thinks we're crazy or delusional or what have you. I'm sure a lot of people think I should be locked up. But I don't care. I don't care what anyone thinks about me. Except you. I don't know how I'll hold up if you start saying I'm crazy, too." The tip of her nose darkened and she turned to ask Officer Kane for a tissue.

"I didn't mean to make fun of you," I said.

She nodded. "I know." And then, sniffing, "Jordan?"

"Yeah."

"Do you think I'll get out of here?"

I thought about it for a minute. "You might."

"If I do, it's all because of you."

"Maybe."

"No, it's because you believed me."

"There's more to it than that."

"No," she said. "That's the reason. It all boils down to that."

"Let's not get ahead of ourselves. There's still a lot we don't understand."

"I know, but we'll figure it out."

Was she right? To have so much faith? In me?

"Mom, let me ask you a question: did Dad ever talk about his list?"

She took her time before answering, wiping up her face. "Only a little. I know there was a point for some of the wives when he decided he no longer wanted to be married to them, in that way, I mean, and he would tell them, just so it was clear, you know, expectations and all. From then on he always treated those wives a little different from the rest. We always knew when one wife was taken off the list—it was usually right before he married a new one—and when that happened we would look around and figure out who he was, well, not visiting as much."

"I had no idea it was so methodical."

"We never talked about it with the kids. It would break their hearts."

"Mom, what about you? Were you still on the list?"

She looked to the ceiling, the tears pooling in her eyes. "I never thought I'd have to talk to my own son about this."

"You don't have to. I understand."

"He no longer wanted to see me."

"It's OK," I said.

"I wish that were true. But now I'm worried about what's going to happen to me."

551

"I know, but I'm working on that."

"No, not in here, or in court, but after I'm gone. Oh, Jordan—I'm so afraid of going to heaven without him. I'm afraid he won't be waiting for me there."

My mom, on the other side of the glass—she didn't have an ally in the world.

"That night," she said. "He told me that night. That's why I was down in the basement. He asked to see me. He asked me to come very late, so there wouldn't be any talk among the sister wives. But Rita saw me leave the basement. He was about to get married. He said the Prophet had granted him a new bride and he was going to marry her the next day. And so he told me that I could live the rest of my life in the house, but I was no longer his wife in that way."

"I thought he had married someone that morning."

"This was someone else. Someone the Prophet wanted him to take."

"Who?"

"I don't know."

"And so he kicked you out of his bed."

She nodded slowly, as if she were just comprehending it now.

"Why didn't you tell Mr. Heber any of this?"

"I'm not a fool, I know how this looks. Everyone's going to think that was my reason for killing him. Except I didn't kill him. And no one believes me. Except you."

Then I saw it, everything, the numbers falling into place like lotto balls. "How many wives did he have?"

"Total? Between twenty and twenty-five, but I can't be sure. He never said. The Prophet told them never to say because when the battle came, our enemies would use the numbers against us. We each had our number, and we had a rough idea of where we fell on the list, but if you tried to add them up, it never made sense. There were gaps, and sometimes a wife would come and stay a year and then leave, and sometimes you'd get this feeling you were

552

no longer the number you thought you were. It went like that, but the Prophet always said when we got to heaven we'd know."

She stopped. Her face cleared and her eyes dried out. She saw it, too. "That must be it."

It was all clear. Clear as the inch and a half slab of glass between us.

"You were no longer his nineteenth wife."

I called Tom. "He was about to marry some girl."

"I'm not following you."

"According to polygamy's wacky math, my mom wasn't his nineteenth wife anymore. Someone else was about to become number nineteen."

"What'd you say?"

"She didn't count anymore!" The connection was bad and getting worse. "If he wasn't screwing them, he didn't count them."

"He didn't what them?"

"The girl he was about to marry—that's who killed him!" I knew I had only a few more seconds before we lost the signal. "I'm almost there!"

"Where?"

"I feel like I'm five feet away from the answer."

The signal became good again and I could hear Tom breathing. "Maybe you should back off now. Let the cops take over."

"Not when I'm this close."

"At least go to Mr. Heber."

"He'll only slow things down."

"Jordan, I don't like this anymore. You're about to bump into a killer."

"Please don't worry about me."

"Too late."

"You know who knows the answer?"

553

"Who?" His voice was getting smaller.

"The Prophet."

"Jordan, I want you to come home."

"I'll call you as soon as I can."

"If something happens to you, I'm not sure I'll be able to forgive you."

"Oh, c'mon. Don't put that shit on me. It's not like we're—"

The call broke. A lost signal or did he hang up? I drove on to Mesadale, wondering if I'd ever know.

At the turnoff a guard in a pickup motioned for me to stop. "What brings you out here?"

"I need to go to the post office."

"Why here?"

"I need to pay my electric bill," I lied. "It needs to be postmarked today."

The guy was an elder, silver hair buzzed down, red shiny lips. He fidgeted with his ammo vest, poking his finger in and out of an empty cartridge slot. "You tell Sister Karen hello."

I drove up the dirt road. Along the way I passed a couple of trucks parked in the dirt. Inside each a man was waiting, his left leg dangling out the open door. The trucks' gun racks were empty, which meant those guns were out somewhere being cradled. I expected one of the trucks to pull out in front of me, blocking the road, and then a team rushing from the brush. A little paranoid, I know, but something was happening even if I couldn't tell you what it was.

It was late afternoon, the sun burning the face of Mt. Jerusalem. Everywhere the red rocks were glowing and the mesas out in the direction of Arizona looked like they might combust. The Prophet used to talk a lot about the Apocalypse. "Any day now," he'd say. "Any day." I always imagined it would come at this time of day at this time of year, when the sun floods the desert and the thermometer keeps going up and you forget what it's like to be cold.

554

When I reached town there were Firsts everywhere. Men walking up the street, and some women, and a few couples, I mean real couples, one man, one wife, maybe with a kid. Except for the prairie dresses, it looked like a busy afternoon in Anytown, USA, women shopping, kids playing, men bitching at the fence.

Sister Karen was at the counter, closing up her station. "I heard you need a stamp. I've got to close up in seven minutes"—she pointed to the wall clock—"so we don't have much time. What can I get you?"

"Actually, I don't really need—"

She tipped her chin to the security camera in the corner. "I've got some new stamps in. Here, you might like the superheroes and action figures." She showed me a sheet: Plastic Man contorting himself, Flash in a skimpy bodysuit, Superman ripping off his clothes. "If you want five, that would be . . . let me total that up real quick for you." On a scrap of paper she wrote *if you whisper the camera can't pick up your voice*.

"I need to see the Prophet."

"He isn't here."

"I know, but I need to see him."

"I have no idea where he is." And then in a regular voice: "Or do you want to see the American flags?" Sister Karen sorted through her stamp sheets. "Mind telling me why you need to see him?" she said under her breath. I began the whole story, but she interrupted. "You need to be out of here in less than four minutes, so make it short."

I told her my theory and she said, "You need to be very careful, Jordan. You don't know what you're dealing with here."

The door opened. "Sister Karen, you closing up?" It was the old fucker who'd been guarding the road.

"Right about now, Brother." She punched up my bill, her face straight. After I left the post office, she pulled a folding metal wall across the lobby, locking it into place. The brother stood on the slab of white concrete outside the post office, kicking the dirt from his heel, eyeing me and the road. Someone was driving into town; you could see the cloud rolling up our way.

"You expecting someone?" I said.

"This is not the day to mess around."

"Have a good one."

I sat in the back of the van for a while, thinking it all out. One of Johnny's t-shirts was wadded up on the futon. It smelled like feet. I kicked it into a garbage bag but then took it back out. I'd wash it at the laundromat and send it up to him. With a note. First I'd need to figure out what to say.

There was a knock on the side of the van. Then again. The van is such a tin can it sounded like a wooden spoon gonging a baking pan. I was sure it was the old brother, and I was sure it was a good idea to ignore him until I knew what I was going to say.

"Jordan?" But it wasn't the old guy's voice. "You in there?" A dog barked.

"Elektra?"

"Jordan?"

Elektra started scratching at the side of the van. Then Joey joined in, a gentle howl.

"Tom?"

"Jordan?"

"Elektra!"

"Tom!"

He stuck his head through the driver's window. "You all right?" The dogs shoved past him, leaping into the back, attacking with kisses from both sides. "We're here to help," said Tom. "And don't even try to say you don't need it."

"Who's taking care of the Malibu?"

"The assistant manager. It's no big deal."

But it was a big deal. I was about to solve a murder, and now here were Tom and the dogs. I had a crazy image of the three of them bound and gagged in a warehouse somewhere, and I'd have to rescue them. Unlikely, I know, but I kept thinking about it and it was so clear in my mind it was as if it had already happened. "We need to be careful," I said.

"What we really need is for this whole thing to be over."

"Come on," I said. "Let's go."

Alton's patrol car was in front of Queenie's house, the sun glinting on the lightbar. "Is that good or bad?" said Tom.

"Good. I think."

We leashed up the dogs and headed to Queenie's front door. God, look at us: the gay couple out with their dogs. Except we were in the polygamy capital of America with a murderer on the loose, a Prophet on the run, and a bunch of wives freaking out. If it weren't so serious, it would be a joke, or a skit on *Saturday Night Live*. I know some gay people think polygamy and gay marriage are part of the same stay-out-of-my-bedroom political argument, and I'm generally a live-and-let-live kind of guy, but it's all different when there are kids, and sure, anyone should have the right to sleep with whoever, and marry whoever—this is America, after all—but you can't do whatever you want when you've got kids. You can't do whatever you want to kids. Have I said that before? I'm sorry. Political loudmouths are such a drag.

Queenie opened the door. Somehow she knew I was looking for her husband. "He isn't here," she said.

"His car's out front."

"He's down at the church. With the tv cameras, they all went down there."

"Mind if we wait?"

She looked at Tom, Joey, Elektra. "Sure, but not in the house. She's allergic to dogs," and she led us out to the garage.

"The new wife?"

"Who else?"

557

"How's it going with her?"

"Oh, just great. Nothing like listening to your husband screw another woman in the room next door."

"Queenie, what's wrong?"

"Everything."

"Is there something I can do?"

She laughed, and in laughing she softened up. "I'm sorry, Jordan. I didn't mean to be such a c-word. I'll be fine."

I asked if I could use the phone. She brought me the portable, but then she thought to ask, "Who do you need to call?"

"Just someone."

I dialed, and on the fifth ring I worried maybe I'd forgotten the number, but then he answered. "Yeah, Alton?"

"No, it's me, Jordan Scott."

A pause. "What is this?"

"I need to see you."

"Jordan, what are you doing there?"

"It doesn't matter. I need to see you. Where can I meet you?"

"Jordan, it's too late."

"No, it's not too late."

"Please don't call me anymore."

"You were the one—"

Click.

"Was that the Prophet?" said Queenie.

"Yes."

"Shit, you guys should go. You're going to get me in a lot of trouble."

I told her to calm down, everything would be OK. "I know this is going to sound weird, but the Prophet and I, well, we're sort of working together."

"That didn't sound like working together."

"He's just freaking out because of the media and stuff."

She looked at me the way you look at someone you know has turned against you. There was a terrible silence in the

558

garage, and leave it to Tom to fill it up. "So how many months are you?"

"It's still early, only two."

"Is that your little girl?" Tom pointed at the picture of Angela taped above the workbench. A little blond girl petting a cow. "So adorable," said Tom. "What about the next, boy or girl?"

"I'm hoping for a boy."

"A brother for Angela! How sweet." Tom had a starry look to him, like his daydreams were carrying him to a world where everyone was more or less good. He was too honest for this. Too kind. He deserved a tidy, reliable life. He wasn't equipped for the messier world of me. Look, there he was goo-gooing over baby pictures with Queenie and talking about boy names, and he was totally clueless she was lying. Last time I was here she was three months preggers. Something was wrong.

"I've always wanted kids," Tom sighed, then looked at me. Why was he looking at me? It was so time to go.

In the van I said, "She's lying. She must be hiding something. I don't know what, but she was definitely lying."

"You're being paranoid."

"No, Tom, I'm not. I'm seeing things for what they are." I drove to the end of the block, turned the corner, and parked. "Alton was in there."

"How do you know?"

"I just do. He didn't want to see me. You stay here, I'm walking back."

"No way, I'm coming with you."

"You need to stay with the dogs."

"Speaking of which, it's their dinnertime."

"Fine, you feed them while I go back to the house. There's some kibble under the seat."

"Joey can't eat any old kibble. He needs his high-protein food. Let's go back to my car and I'll make their dinners and then we'll figure out what to do next."

559

"Tom, it doesn't work like that. I need to go in there now before he leaves."

"Goldens have sensitive stomachs."

"We don't have time for this."

"Look at Elektra, she's practically begging for her dinner."

"You've got to be shitting me." But let's face it, I was going to lose this argument. I drove down to the post office thinking, Tom shouldn't be here. I kept telling myself that. When we get to his car I'm going to tell him to leave.

But before I could he got busy preparing the dogs' dinner. His trunk was like a pantry: tupperwares of organic dry food, water, bowls, squeaky toys, paw wipes, paper towels, and Febreze. He set everything out on the hood and measured out the food down to the last kibble. I'm so not a smoker, but if I were, right about now I would've lit a cigarette and gone for a walk. I needed to step away from this. I strolled around to the other side of the post office. A thunderstorm rolled in the western sky, the clouds gray and blue and green. I leaned against the post office wall and shut my eyes.

That's when I heard something. Something like a box falling. And softly through the wall: "Oh, crud."

I stepped back to look at the post office. At the top of the wall, there was a long window running the length of the roofline. It was too high to see into, but the lights were on. I walked back to Tom. "Sister Karen's in there."

"In the post office?" Tom was cleaning up the dog bowls and putting everything away.

"We'll leave the dogs with her."

"I don't like that idea."

Too late. I was banging on the lobby's glass door. Eventually Karen rolled back the folding metal wall. "Can you take the dogs?"

"What?" she said through the glass door.

"I need someone to watch the dogs for twenty minutes, a half hour, max."

"Not today, it's a bad idea."

But I begged. And kept begging. Sensing an adventure, the dogs ran over to press their snouts to the glass. It took some more begging, but I knew she'd give in. She unlocked the door and led us into the back room. "I'm doing some organizing. They can stay with me. But please don't be long."

Tom's arms were full of supplies—bowls, water, a dog bed. "Jesus, Tom, they're only going to be here a little while."

"Just in case." He arranged the bed in a corner and filled the water bowls. He moved with such precision and purpose, it was as if in the giant cosmic scheme of things he had been put on earth to tend to the needs of these two dogs.

That's when I saw them. And I kept looking at them in a way Sister Karen wouldn't notice. A shopping bag filled with little-girl clothes. And a duffel bag stuffed with pants and shirts.

Tom was giving Sister Karen a litany of instructions. "They shouldn't have to poop, but if Joey walks in a circle three times, that means he has to go. Here are some baggies." He had a whole list of doggy do's and don'ts.

The duffel was open and I kicked it open some more. My foot gently moved aside the white dress shirt on top. Beneath it was a dark blue shirt. The shoulder braiding confirmed it was a police uniform. I kicked the bag again, and now I could see half of a brass nameplate: Alt.

"You know what?" I said. "It's too much of an inconvenience."

"It's fine," said Sister Karen. "Just don't take all night."

"No, they're so fussy. I don't want to stick you with all their issues."

"Jordan," said Tom, "I just walked her through everything, they'll be fine."

Elektra chose this moment to decide she was tired. She yawned, walked over to the dog bed, and plopped down with an extended sigh. Joey followed suit, falling over on his side. His moist panting fogged up the linoleum tiles.

"Tom, please," I said. "It's too much to ask."

Tom turned to Sister Karen. "You tell us. Is this all right?"

"Look at them. They're going to be fine."

"Sister Karen, you really don't have to—" But she scooted us out the door.

In the van I said, "Why didn't you listen to me? Something wasn't right."

"What? Sister Karen's on our side."

"I don't know if this has sides anymore." But Tom drove on, down the dark streets of Mesadale. He parked about a block from Queenie's.

"Maybe this isn't such a good idea," I said.

"No, it's a good idea. Until you figure this all out you're never going to get on with your life."

We walked up the road. It's hard to move silently on gravel, but we tried. Across from Queenie's house we stopped. The bedroom light was on, a gold outline around the drawn blinds. Everything else was dark. The storm clouds blotted out the moon and the yard was black, the patrol car a large dark shape. "What's the plan?" said Tom.

"I want to see if he's in there. Now be quiet. And follow me."

I crouched down, ran up the side of the yard to the house, pushing myself flat against the garage. Tom was right behind me. I mouthed, *Let's go round back*. We stayed close to the wall, bent at the waist. We continued along the wall until we were behind the house near a window. We crouched to our knees. I could hear Tom's heart in his chest. He whispered, "Are you OK?"

I brought my index finger to my lips. I wanted to listen. At first I couldn't hear anything. Then sounds of someone moving about, a door closing, a piece of furniture being dragged. I heard footsteps, then a second pair. Someone said, "Have everything?"

I waved to Tom, *Let's go*. We crouched back along the wall until we were beside the garage. "He's in there," I said.

"What do you want to do?"

"Ring the doorbell. Act casual. We don't want to startle them." We made our way along the front of the house until we were on the concrete porch. I rang the doorbell. No answer. I rang again. Eventually, "Yes?"

"Officer Alton?"

He opened the door. "Jordan. Hi. Queenie said you stopped by. I didn't realize you were coming back."

"Do you have a second?"

Alton was blocking the door, his hand tight on the frame as if prepared to fight off an assault. "This really isn't a good time."

"That's the thing. This can't wait. I mean, you said to call if anything came up. And something's come up."

His lips twisted. "All right." He led us into the living room, turning on a floor lamp and pointing to the sofa. "So what's up?"

"You're about to leave town and I want to know why."

Tom looked at me like I was crazy. But Alton stayed cool. "Jordan, what's gotten into you?"

"Why are you sneaking off?"

He laughed once. He was sitting in a recliner with his legs open, relaxed but engaged, like he was watching a ball game on tv.

"I know what I know," I said.

"Look, I don't know what to tell you." He slapped his hands together. "I'm not going anywhere. And even if I were, what would that have to do with you?"

"I don't know, but I know it does."

"You're free to think whatever you want." He stood, moved to the door. Nothing threatening, more like a party host who has grown weary of his guests.

"You told me to call if I needed you. Well, I need you. Actually, I need the Prophet. I need to see him. And something makes me think you're about to skip town with him."

Alton froze, then cocked his head. "Is that what you think?"

"Yes."

Tom stepped forward. "He's just trying to help his mom."

"I see," said Alton. "OK, why don't you sit down and tell me what's going on. You're right: I was going to see the Prophet tonight. I'll tell him anything you want."

So I told him my theory about my dad's latest wife, why I needed to find out who he was about to marry. When I finished I sat back on the couch. Alton looked bewildered. "You're quite the sleuth," he said. "That's some deduction work. Well, I'll tell you, I'll find out what you want to know. I'll go call him now."

Alton went into the garage. Tom shrugged. "That went all right."

A minute later Alton said, "Guys? Come on in here with me, OK?"

He stood in the door, his finger on the trigger of a semi-automatic. It was such a shocking sight—an off-duty police officer with a dumb-dude smile and a thick, muscled body one or two years away from fat standing in his socks aiming the muzzle of a gun. At me. It wasn't happening. That's all I said: "This isn't happening."

"What's going on?" said Tom.

"Don't say anything. Just come in here." We were too dumbfounded to get up from the couch. "I'm not joking. Get up. Now . . . That's right. And don't try anything. Stay apart, just come on in here. Move slow and keep your hands up, that's right, just like that."

"Officer Alton," I said.

"Nope. Don't say a word."

Tom gave it a try. "Please, we really don't want—"

"Shut up. Right now. No more talking."

"Does Queenie know what you're doing?"

"I said shut up."

When we were in the garage, he pointed the muzzle at Tom. "You, Boyfriend. You see that?" He waved the gun at a loop of laundry line. "Take it down and tie him up."

"What?"

"You heard me. Tie him up."

"I don't know how."

"Start with his wrists."

"I can't."

Alton pushed the gun into my mouth and told me to kneel. "I think you can."

Tom took the rope and began measuring off a section.

"Now, Jordan," said Alton. "Put your arms together, wrists facing, and stick out your hands . . . That's right, just like that. Now you, tie them up. Make it tight."

Tom looped the line around my wrists. "Jordan, I'm sorry," he said.

I tried to say it was OK but the gun barrel was heavy on my tongue.

"Guys, no talking." When the line was tight around my wrists, Alton said, "Now tie up his ankles."

"Why are you doing this?" said Tom.

"Just do what I say."

He stood up. "First I need to know what's going on." Alton pointed the gun at Tom.

"Tom, do what he says."

"Why should I?"

Alton pressed the gun to my chest. "Because you and I both don't want to see his heart splattered across your nice pair of khakis."

"You're bluffing."

"Are you really willing to risk finding that out?"

"Tom, please, do it."

Tom stood in place, his eyes burning. Then his jaw slackened and the light in his eyes went out. "All right."

"You, Jordan, lie down on your side so he can tie up your ankles."

In five minutes I was looped together with forty feet of laundry line.

"You're next," said Alton. He yelled back into the house: "Queenie! I need you."

565

When she saw me she gasped. "Jordan, my God!"

"Honey, tie him up." He pointed to a yellow nylon rope, then to Tom.

"Is he all right?"

"He's fine."

"Queenie," I said.

"Don't talk to him," said Alton.

She tried to ignore me, turning her head in the opposite direction, but our eyes met. She was scared, I could see that. Otherwise I had no idea what was going on. She got busy with Tom's wrists, then ankles. Soon we were both lying on our backs. "Now tie them together," said Alton. "At the ankle and wrist." We had to turn to face each other, then she tied up our hands. She was out of rope so she used a bungee cord to loop our ankles together. By the time she was done we were so close together I could feel his breath on my face. "Romantic," I said.

"Now gag them."

"Please, don't do this," Tom tried.

"Gag them." He handed her two rags, strips from an old flannel shirt. Tom resisted, shaking his head and sealing his lips. Alton laid his fingers around my throat. "I wouldn't do that if I were you."

Queenie gagged me next. There was no way she could do it without looking at me. Before she could get the rag in my mouth, I managed to say, "Why?"

"Honey, don't talk to him. Pretend it's someone else."

When she was finished Alton checked the knots. "Good job, everyone." He left the room.

The line pressed hard into my skin, and the gag made it difficult to breathe. But more than that was the fear. I suppose for everyone there's a moment when you realize you're about to die. For some people, the moment is extended over the course of a long illness. For others, it's just a few seconds before a flash. For my dad, it must've come once he saw the gun. Even people who die instantly, they must have a tiny,

566

immeasurable moment of awareness. I like to think that. It seems only fair. And now here was mine. I didn't know how much time I had left, but I understood very clearly I would not survive the night. Tom had been very still until now. He saw me crying and his eyes filled too.

"I'm really very sorry about all this," said Queenie.

I looked at her. "Queenie!" called Officer Alton from the living room. "Let's go."

"I'm coming." She touched my cheek. "I never thought it would be like this." She kissed my forehead and her lips were warm. "You too," she said to Tom, stroking his ear. "You take care of him, all right? Give him what he deserves."

Tom yelled, the gag muffling his words.

"Don't yell," she said. "We can't leave if you're yelling."

"Queenie!"

"I'm coming." At the door she waited another moment, looking at us, her face flat with pity. "Good luck." She turned out the lights and shut the door.

I heard the front door close, then car doors slam, an engine turn. Tires on gravel. In my mind I could see the patrol car backing out of the drive, headlights sweeping the yard. I could see it as if I had seen it in a movie; everything about the scene was that clear. When Alton's cruiser was gone, the only sounds were Tom and me trying to breathe. It was too dark to see his expression, but his eyes were glowing. One of his fingers found one of mine. They clasped together, locked at the knuckle. I'm sorry, that's such a bunch of corn, but that's how it went—lying there on the concrete floor, bound and gagged, we reached out, our fingers found each other, and they linked. We were alone like that for a long time.

After some time we heard a car out front and a door slam. Then footsteps in the house. This is it, I kept thinking. This is it. Here we go.

The door to the living room opened and a head peered around. A pair of silver eyes. A fish-faced look of surprise. It was the Prophet. And he was shocked to see me like this.

Really shocked, not fake shocked. This wasn't part of his plan. My face—well, I have no idea, but I bet I looked just as surprised. There we were. Two faces shaped by the same set of emotions at the same moment in time. We went on looking at each other for a while, saying nothing because there was nothing to say. That's how it goes, right? Eyes meeting up like that. Through a slab of glass. In the cineplex dark. At the Malibu Inn. Eyes saying goodbye in a garage.

Who's to say what will come next? Who can say they know what it all means? You got to live with it. The not knowing. The wondering. The unanswered questions. The murk of life. You got to accept it—the why.

"Jordan," the Prophet said.

I said, They set up my mom. Except because of the gag my words were lost in my throat.

"What's this all about?"

I said, My mom. It's about my mom. Except I sounded like someone shouting into a towel.

I don't know how long we stared at each other like that. Tom's back was to the door. He was trying to maneuver himself to see who was there. He said something, but what?

The way the Prophet was peering around the door, I could see only his head and a hand. A dried spotted hand, knuckles yellow and white. And that sunken, tired face. An old man. Almost any old man.

The Prophet left, the door closing. The ghost of his face remained, hanging in the space where he'd been, an afterimage, or maybe even a dream. Then it too was gone and Tom and I were alone on the cold concrete floor.

June 12, 2006

President and Prophet Gordon Hinckley
The Church of Jesus Christ of Latter-day Saints
50 East North Temple
Salt Lake City, UT 84111

Dear President Hinckley,

I want to thank you for making the Church Archives available
to me. My research into the complicated legacy of Ann Eliza
Young and the end of LDS polygamy has been invaluably
aided by the wealth of documents I was able to study thanks
to your intervention. I hope you agree that your decision to
open previously sealed records has been beneficial to our understanding of our history. I know some people think these
matters should be left alone, but I have always found inspira-
tion in the title of your book, *Truth Restored*.

With your help, I have completed my archival research and
will soon begin writing my thesis. I look forward to sending
you a copy when I submit it for graduation next April. My
conclusions may not be what you expect, but I can assure you
they have been reached through careful study of the record.

I also want you to know how helpful Deb Savidhoffer of
the Archives has been. She is a friend to scholars, and to our
beloved Church. I owe her much indeed.

Most Gratefully Yours,
KELLY DEE
Candidate for Master's Degree
Brigham Young University

I HAD NO IDEA

I know I need to explain what happened. It's pretty simple. You probably figured it out on your own. After two hours in the garage, Sister Karen found us. She knew something was wrong when we didn't come for the dogs. When she saw us like that—tied up on the concrete floor—she cried out in terror. That's how I know she didn't have anything to do with it. It's hard to fake fear.

Once she got over the shock, she started working to free us. First the gags. The old flannel pulled from my mouth. We told her what happened as she tried picking the knots loose. The knots wouldn't give. "In my pocket," I said, "I have a little knife."

She pulled out Johnny's knife and started cutting Tom free, then me. As she worked she told us what she knew. "You don't know what's going on, do you? I helped them escape tonight, Hiram and Queenie. The Prophet was coming down hard on them because Brother Hiram hadn't taken another wife."

"He just married someone."

"No, the Prophet was pressuring him to marry a girl, but he wouldn't, he loved Queenie too much. They knew they had to leave. It nearly killed them, but they had to go."

That didn't explain everything. "I guess it doesn't make much sense," Sister Karen said. "Unless . . ."

"Unless what?"

"I don't know."

On our way out we found the note on the living room sofa. I could've walked by it, but something told me to look over and there it was.

Jordan,

I never wanted to do anything like this to you but by the time you find this we'll be on our way and everything will be better that way. I'm sorry for doing this to you. And Tom. He seems like the nicest guy in the world.

I love you,
Q

The second note arrived three days later at the Lincoln County Sheriff's Office, postmarked Denver. It's all we needed for this to end.

Sheriff,

In regards to the death and murder of Brother Scott, husband of Sisters Rita, BeckyLyn, and etc., I'm the one you want. He was about to marry my wife. The Prophet didn't like me not having more wives. As punishment he was taking Queenie away from me and giving her to Brother Scott. She went to see him that night to talk him out of it. I followed her and was real pissed. I didn't plan on anything, but outside his door I heard him saying all sorts of things you don't say to another man's wife, and I lost my head. I picked up his Big Boy and shot him. I don't know why he had that suppressor on the gun but he did. It took as long to kill him as it took me to write this sentence. He was gone. I didn't intend any of this. We slipped out the well window. No one saw us come and no one saw us go. I was always surprised they didn't notice the open latch. Queenie had nothing to do with it. We never wanted Sister BeckyLyn to take the heat. We figured they'd never know who did it, so many had their reasons that they'd never arrest anyone over it. I was really upset when they arrested Sister BL. That's not how we meant it. The only reason we tied up Jordan and his friend was because they were stopping us. We were planning on leaving tonight anyway and sending this note so the truth could be known and Sister BL could go free. That's how it happened, I swear by my love of God. How can you be sure? I was careful to leave prints all over this note. They'll match those others you have on the Big Boy and all over the basement. I know you'll try to find Queenie and me but I'll tell you now, you never will. Feel free to start in Denver. Be my guest.

HIRAM ALTON
Formerly of the Firsts

EPILOGUES

THE 19TH WIFE

PREFACE TO THE REVISED EDITION

Since the publication of *The 19th Wife* some thirty-three years ago, the Mormon Church has been forced to denounce its belief in plural marriage. Before his death in 1877, Brigham ordered his followers to fight until the Day of Judgment for the right to pursue their faith in full glory. This included the doctrine of plural marriage. He anticipated a future day when many pressures, from both outside and within, would persuade some Saints to abandon the doctrine for the sake of political and cultural expediency. He warned them never to succumb: "For the doctrine, as far as I know it, and as far as Joseph knew it, is and always will be the Word of God. Let no man tell you otherwise."

When Brigham passed on that hot August afternoon, felled by cholera morbus, his final word of life was a quiet call to his friend and Prophet. "Joseph," Brigham cried out. Then he was gone. He left behind a household of an unknowable number of wives and children—many of them estranged friends of mine—and an estate worth tens of millions of dollars. His unusual will categorized his wives into an inheritance pyramid, with Amelia, his favorite, placed proudly at the peak. Beneath her, the few favored wives. Beneath them, those he visited from time to time. And so on. The many wives he had abandoned in every sense but name received nothing more than lifetime room and board at the Lion House. That would have been me.

Brigham's legacy includes a vast colonization of the

American West. In thirty years he erected an efficient, far-reaching civilization whose institutions stand as solidly as those in countries with five hundred years of history before them. He organized the immigration of more than seventy-five thousand men, women, and children to his desert kingdom, many of them penniless foreigners who had no hope in their original lands. Often Brigham waged peace with the American Indian, at a time when other national leaders preferred execution to accommodation, and thus set an example for our nation's future relations with our Native friends. Most important to him, I am sure, he provided spiritual comfort and moral direction to thousands of needy souls. These are few among his many achievements. They must be noted by all.

Yet upon quitting life on Earth, Brigham left another legacy, one of a darker, more ominous variety—a fervid population of Saints determined more than ever to defend polygamy.

Not surprisingly, Brigham's death heartened those fighting for the abolition of marital bondage, whether they lived inside Utah or out. The next decade brought about unprecedented changes in federal law, each a deeper nail in polygamy's coffin. By 1890, only thirteen years after Brigham's passing, President Wilford Woodruff, the fourth leader of the Latter-day Saints, recognized his Church was on the wrong end of a national moral battle. A savvy politician, he also understood Utah would never achieve statehood as long as the Mormons practiced polygamy. In his famous Manifesto of September 1890, he denounced polygamy forever, declaring it no longer the will of God. When I first read of this change, I was elated, believing the institution was at last dead. How wrong was I!

As they say, once a polygamist always a polygamist. A number of distraught and confused Saints denounced President Woodruff for abandoning the doctrine they held most dear. These dissenters included my brother Aaron, whose harem sweet Connie still ruled, and my half-sister, Diantha, whose husband had married in total six cheerful, youthful women, Diantha being the exception. After unsuccessfully petitioning the Church to reverse its position, Aaron and his followers broke from the Latter-day Saints, establishing themselves as the First Latter-day Saints, with their capital in the remote outpost of Red Creek, in the southern portion of Utah, just across the Arizona border. Here they remain today, practicing a faith they claim to be the true religion of Joseph Smith and Brigham Young. Polygamy stands at the center of everything they believe. The enmity between the Firsts and the leaders of the Mormon Church in Salt Lake will remind many of the animosity between the Reformation's Protestants and the Bishops denouncing them from the palace balconies of Rome. The full story of this new religious splintering has yet to be told. Many years must pass before we understand the outcome of this divide.

In recent years, it has come to light that many Latter-day Saints, including members of the leadership, have continued to marry plural wives in secret. In public they decried it, in private they swooped up wives numbers one, two, and three. Under pressure from Congress and elsewhere, in 1904 President Joseph F. Smith, the Mormon Church's sixth leader and nephew of the Prophet Joseph Smith, had to issue a Second Manifesto, reinforcing the Church's stance against polygamy. In this Manifesto, the Church warned its members that any man or woman caught in a plural marriage would face excommunication—the one fate all Saints feared. (I should know.) And yet, even today, stories of the man with a dozen wives upstairs continue to pour forth from Deseret. Although these abundant households are no longer sanctioned by the Church, they continue to exist. How can this be? Some leaders of the Mormon Church today are secret polygamists themselves, and thus they willfully look the other way.

Now, with the debate over polygamy revived, and commanding much of our nation's attention once again, I offer here a revised edition of my life, taking into account my full journey from daughter of polygamy to emancipator. I humbly offer these memories and political ideas to my Dear Readers everywhere, hoping they will sustain the women of Utah, now hidden from view, who continue to live in conjugal chains.

—Ann Eliza Young, 1908

From the Desk of
Lorenzo Dee, Eng.
Baden-Baden-by-the-Sea
Calif.
October 15, 1940

Professor Charles Green
Brigham Young University
Joseph Smith Building
Provo

Dear Professor Green,

Thank you for sending me a copy of your book about my
mother. I took it down to my viewing bench at once to read.
It was a still day, the sunshine on the flat ocean, but no
sight of my old friends. A good few hours passed before the
sunset, and by nightfall, back in my study, with the steady
crash of the ocean always in my ear, I finished your volume.
First, let me offer my admiration and praise. You are a fine
scholar—no, a courageous one—for it seems to me you have
bravely unraveled the role of polygamy in your Church's
history. I am only sorry to see, if I am to read your
somewhat cryptic notes correctly, that the Church leadership
denied you access to many important documents. It would
be laughable if it weren't such a serious matter. There will
be a time, I am sure, when they will open themselves up
fully to an honest scholar. I am only sorry that this honest
scholar has not been you. You are right, fifty years is a
long time. But you are also wrong—fifty years is no time at
all. Perhaps another fifty need to pass before the Church
leaders, whoever they may be, can say to the world, Here

are the facts, this is our history, we have nothing to hide.

I myself would be less than open if I failed to confess the disappointment, and sorrow, that overcame me after I closed your book. Since your first letter last year I have been carrying around an uncomfortable hope that you would take up the mystery of my mother's fate. It was difficult to discover that she plays no role in your narrative after the 1890 Manifesto. True, she gave up her crusade once she believed polygamy had been eradicated. But also true is she returned to the lecture stage in the first years of our century, once she saw that polygamy in fact lived on, whether secretly among the Mormons or defiantly among the Firsts. Granted, her role thereafter was of lesser importance. I am not criticizing your scholarship. No, I'm merely registering a son's regret about his mother. I must admit that since we began our correspondence my greatest fear has been that after your many efforts and investigations you would know no more about her fate than I already do, which is to say almost nothing. And so, upon closing your book, I realized this was the case. I am not faulting you, I am only acknowledging my grief. I am a son who has lost his mother, in every sense.

I have refrained from telling you any of this, for I did not want my pessimism nor my personal curiosities to color your investigation. Furthermore, I should have revealed something to you, Professor Green, in my first letter to you. Something about the relationship between my mother and myself. If I had done so, you would have been better equipped to spot my biases, which I humor myself into believing I do not nurse, but of course I do, for everyone does, and I am as guilty as the next man, perhaps more. I kept some important information from you and I was selfish to do so, probably just as selfish as those Church archivists, bent and gray with caution, were in denying you the right to read the dusty documents that could only illuminate the truth.

By the time I settled in California my mother and I had

become estranged. It was over the subject of my wife, Rosemary. Her religion, to be precise. My mother, with her many blind spots, dismissed all Catholics as superstitious. I can understand the root of her suspicions, but what most angered me was her inability to pull beautiful Rosemary out of the lot. By that I mean my mother's inclination to cast judgment on an entire faith, an entire population, rather than come to know Rosemary for who she was. Rosemary, I must add, did not help the cause. Although she was a rebellious Catholic, she recognized at once my mother's hypocrisy and leapt at the chance to dismantle it. Rosemary, always mischievous, stood up to defend her faith as if she were Joan of Arc. After one unpleasant spat, I said to her—to Rosemary, that is—"You don't even believe half the things you said." She acknowledged I was correct, that she had a hundred bones to pick with the Pope. Even so, she was not going to let my mother's attacks fly without a response. You can see the position I was in. I am not the first to stand in the treacherous no-man's-land between mother and wife. There is no safe position. And so we decamped for California, as so many others have. This was in 1890, or was it 1891? I'd have to look it up to be sure. My, how the mind's cold fogs are beginning to roll in.

There was no formal estrangement between my mother and me, no final exchange or argument. This is often the case. We left and the communication dropped off to less than occasional. In 1908, when my mother published the revised, unsuccessful edition of *The 19th Wife*, I realized nearly ten years had passed since we had corresponded. I wrote her at her last address in Denver. The letter was forwarded to an address in El Paso, then returned. I meant to write her via her publisher, but time deceived me—I believed I had all of it in the world. When I finally contacted her, nearly a year later, I failed, for her publisher had gone out of business. It seems her editor, I don't know his name, it began with an E, had run off to South America with a street youth and the company's funds, what there were left of them. I was told the revised edition of *The 19th Wife* had failed to such an extent that it nearly bankrupted the little firm. The editor's thievery pushed the house over the brink. Quite simply, there were no files to search.

Again time played its trick on me. I pushed off the task of contacting my mother for a few more years. Then, sometime just before the war, I started asking around; I made a trip east. I hired a detective, a sincere man named Scotty Rivers; he was a gentle soul, some terrible abuse had shaped him early in life, I am sure. After two months Detective Rivers handed me an empty file and returned his fee. "The trail ends in 1908. She was leasing a cottage in Arizona, the rent paid through the year. At the turn of 1909, the landlord went for his rent but found the cottage cleared out. No one could say when she left or where she went. After that I found nothing, no insurance papers, no medical records, no police reports, nothing from an estate. One old woman, a neighbor, says she remembers your mother talk of traveling east to promote the revised edition of her memoirs, but her mind is faulty, I discovered, and her word can't be accepted as fact. Other than that I'm afraid I don't have anything for you," the man said. "I won't take your money."

I said to Rosemary, "How can someone vanish without a trace?"

But so she did. We never heard from my mother again.

I have to assume she's dead now, but where she rests I have no idea. This outcome, no doubt, colors my perception of my mother. To what degree, in what shade, I should say, I cannot say. If Rosemary were here, I would leave it to her to assess the effects of my grief. I should have told you all this sooner. I did not want you to think I am a man who thinks under the influence of sentiment. But I suppose I do, for not a day passes without my wishing to speak to my mother one last time. When I think of her now, I feel like that little boy locked up in the Walker House, waiting for her return.

My mind tells me to end my letter here, yet my heart compels me to continue. I would like to share with you my speculative thoughts about my mother's fate. You must put no more weight into them than you would do so with the theories of a conspiracist.

First, I must lay out the three possible outcomes.

One, she died naturally somewhere, a once famous woman forgotten, penniless, laid to peace in a potter's field. With the failure of the second edition of *The 19th Wife*, and her career as a lecturer over, I cannot imagine how my mother sustained herself. No one wanted to hear her tale. Her Cassandra-like voice could not arouse the nation a second time. Rage is a candle, it will always burn out. And we must acknowledge that this was now the twentieth century, not the nineteenth. So much had already come to pass. And so a disease came upon my destitute mother, a quick and vicious illness, or a slow one, or a tumble down the stairs, or a reckless automobile ran her down on a sparkling afternoon—I cannot know the details. But something felled her and a quiet neighbor gave her a grave.

Two, an enemy murdered her, scattering her remains to the buzzards, or some other such thorough manner of disposal. This scenario, of course, leaves us with the very large question, Who? Your enemies, the antagonists of the Mormon Church, I mean, would say it was someone affiliated with the Saints. I cannot imagine it, for what cause? The old attacks on Brigham Young? Unlikely. More probable, it would seem to me—if this bleak scenario were true, which I have no evidence that it is—the break-away Saints, the Firsts they call themselves, I believe, those men and women splintered off in Red Creek and elsewhere, polygamous and paranoid, upon seeing my mother reemerge on the national stage with the second edition of *The 19th Wife* wrongly anticipated she would bring the law's wrath upon them to end their polyamorous ways, just as she had done with the Mormons of Salt Lake. Any reader of mysteries will tell you the key to

583

solving a crime is understanding the motive. So here is one, concocted by the imagination and a scarcity of facts.

Three, she is alive today, on the verge of her ninety-sixth birthday, rocking in a chair somewhere very far away. In this scenario she looks out upon a still landscape, the red desert, no doubt, pondering all that she has achieved. Her day will come soon, she knows, and she awaits it with a devotion that is tinted with anticipatory glee.

Change the details, and one of these three outcomes is more or less true. Which one, however, I cannot know with any kind of empirical certainty. Although I will never know the truth, it does not mean I have stopped pondering the puzzle of her last days. I am like the devoted but less than brilliant mathematician who knows he will never unlock a certain equation, yet still he keeps probing it diligently, trying again and again until his own final hour.

Since reasoning and logic have not helped me solve the mystery of my mother's disappearance, and I expect they never will, I will allow myself to tell you what my heart says, although I know I should not. Yet here I go. The first scenario and the last strike me as unlikely. The second, therefore, must be true. The Firsts of Red Creek silenced her. They had every reason. My uncle Aaron was their first Prophet. He never liked Ann Eliza, anyone will tell you that, their antagonism goes back to their youth. And so he removed her, or sent out his followers to remove her. I think of her fear, the terror of her final moment—the blade shining in the dark, the club falling through the air, the gun's muzzle taking aim of her, and the white flash when the trigger was pulled. I like to believe she understood what was happening to her. At the moment of her death, knowing the meaning of her fate was her only comfort. She saw the face of her enemy. In her last second on earth, she could hope her death would have significance. Then she was gone. Dead but not silenced, for *The 19th Wife* will always live on. Although I cannot prove this scenario, I know it—and isn't that the ultimate definition of faith? Knowing what we can't know. Seeing what isn't there.

And so there you have it, my friend—the end of Ann Eliza Young. All speculation and imagination, yet so true, I know, so true.

Yours most fondly,

LORENZO DEE, SON

Women's Research Institute
Brigham Young University
Thesis for Master's Degree
Adviser, Professor Mary P. Sprague
April 13, 2007

WIFE #19:

Introduction

My research into the life of Ann Eliza Young (1844–unknown) began more than two years ago. After studying her mother, Elizabeth Churchill Webb, and her father, Chauncey Webb, I turned to Ann Eliza herself and her complicated legacy in Church history. Fortunately for my scholarship many people, especially those closest to her, left written memories of her in the form of letters, diaries, depositions, testimonies, and news accounts.[1] In reading these, I have been able to construct what I hope is a complex view of the woman known as the notorious 19th Wife. My research has led me to form five conclusions about Ann Eliza and the role of polygamy in Church history.

One, her reports on the moral and spiritual debasement of the nineteenth-century plural wife are more accurate than generally recognized. For many of us this is an uncomfortable truth, for it has been more convenient to dismiss her so-called exposé as an exaggerated depiction of how the plural wife lived. In truth, polygamy generally compromised the moral and spiritual development of its women and, equally important, its children. Ann Eliza Young's memoir, for the most part, tells it as it was.

---

[1] Transcripts of the documents I have studied have been placed in the WRI's archives.

Certainly her depiction of Brigham Young is limited mostly to his role as polygamous husband and thus omits his many achievements as spiritual leader to thousands as well as those related to his colonization of the West. This partial portrait, by its very nature, is skewed. Yet her account of Brigham, in relation to her, her family, and her beloved sons, I regret to confirm is factually correct. As a husband and father, he failed many, including his so-called 19th wife.[2]

Two, by studying her father, Chauncey, and her half-brother Gilbert, I have come to realize that plural marriage could compromise the husband's soul as much as, if not more than, that of the plural wife. The false promise of sexual freedom, cloaked as it was in religious righteousness, led some men into an abundance of marriages they were not prepared to sustain financially, emotionally, or spiritually. This too is an awkward revelation, for it suggests our beloved leaders Joseph and Brigham, each of whom had at least half a hundred wives, were morally compromised by their conjugal indulgences. It brings me much pain to type this conclusion.

I often wonder how Brigham, who saved his people from mass extermination, who risked everything to deliver tens of thousands to the glory of Zion, could go on to nearly destroy his followers. Was it blind faith? A raging libido? I have an idea about it. I believe most men, even the greatest, can offer salvation only once in their lifetime; for if he succeeds (and most do not), he will overestimate his powers and thereafter will behave recklessly. Brigham achieved so much for us, assured us our survival and place on earth, yet he risked all in the name of polygamy. As Saints, we must consider this difficult truth. Its meaning resonates today.

---

[2] A final note on numbers: My research shows Ann Eliza was most likely Brigham's 52nd of 55 wives. As far as I can tell, she was called the 19th because removed from the total tally were the wives who had died, who were barren, or whom Brigham no longer had sexual relations with. This discrepancy in marital accounting speaks volumes about Brigham's complicated relations with his spouses and polygamy's moral corrosion. If anyone still wonders why Ann Eliza was so ticked off, they need only consider this footnote.

Three, in bringing the issue of polygamy into the national debate, Ann Eliza Young indirectly saved the LDS Church from itself. She was not alone in this; many others played significant parts, yet her leadership in the campaign to end polygamy, and the impact of the first edition of *The 19th Wife*, cannot be denied. This is an awkward fact, for it means one of Brigham's fiercest enemies set the course for the Church's future—a future that we thrive in today. In this irony, however, I believe we can find many Christian truths.

Four, with the 1890 Manifesto, and the more forceful second Manifesto, issued in 1904, the LDS Church made its position on polygamy clear—any Saint participating in a plural marriage would face excommunication. Yet in abandoning polygamy, the Latter-day Saints were now burdened with an untenable theological problem. The doctrine Joseph and Brigham had preached as the Word of God was now being revised. If polygamy was no longer a divine doctrine, many in and out of the Church asked, what about the Doctrine & Covenants as a whole? And what about the Book of Mormon itself? Could it too be edited, revised, trimmed, amended, and otherwise altered by Church leaders in Salt Lake?

Furthermore, the revised Doctrine left many polygamists, including President Woodruff himself, who had five or six wives, in a legal and theological purgatory. If polygamy was no longer a religious doctrine, and no longer the path to salvation, what should a man with a dozen wives do? Abandon the last eleven? Live on as a historical curiosity? And how should a plural wife feel about herself now? To use Brigham's own uncharacteristically cruel words, was she now merely a social harlot? The Church was woefully inept in guiding the Saints through these confusing days. This spiritual ambiguity pushed many Saints, under the leadership of Aaron Webb, to break away from the LDS Church, forming the so-called Firsts in and around Red Creek, Utah, which later became known as Mesadale.

Through my work at the Ann Eliza House I have come to know many women and children whose lives have been defined by polygamy today. I formally interviewed twenty-two of these, recording their experiences.[3] These conversations were first done for background purposes—to gain insight into the life of a child of polygamy and the life of a plural wife. Yet the more women and children I spoke to, the more pressing their stories became. At some point, I saw the connection between Ann Eliza Young, nineteenth-century Mormon polygamy, and the polygamists of today. Polygamists like the Firsts in Mesadale are not Mormons; we are not of the same Church. This is not in dispute. Yet they are the unintended consequences of Joseph and Brigham's polygamous policies. To deny this is to deny the cold facts of history. To ignore their stories is to abandon Christian principles. And so I could not look away.

Five, to my profound disappointment, I was unable to determine the fate of Ann Eliza Young. We know that after the publication of *The 19th Wife* in 1875 she reconciled with her mother, who apostatized after Brigham sought to destroy her daughter's reputation. Elizabeth Churchill Webb died in 1884, presumably while living with Ann Eliza. In 1890, after seeing the Church renounce polygamy, Ann Eliza retired from the lecture circuit. She married a wealthy Michigan industrialist, but the marriage soured after a few years and they divorced. We know that by the late 1890s she was living in Arizona, most probably on limited means. There is a large gap in her biography until 1908, when she reemerged with the second edition of *The 19th Wife* from a vanity press. It seems she spent most or all of her assets on the book's reissue, which failed to sell one thousand copies. Thereafter there are no reliable sources documenting her whereabouts. There are two reports of sightings: A son of James Dee, her first

[3] Transcripts of these interviews are in the WRI's archives.

husband, claims to have seen her in Phoenix in 1915. One of Brigham's sons, John Willard Young, wrote that he passed her by near his apartment on Broadway in New York City the year before his death in 1923. Although intriguing, neither claim can be confirmed. Both strike me as unlikely.

Lorenzo Leonard Dee, Ann Eliza's second son (and my great-great-grand-uncle), believed that his mother was murdered by a member or members of the Firsts community. Certainly Aaron, or his followers, would have the most reason to silence polygamy's most effective opponent. Yet as tantalizing as this theory is, there is no evidence to support it, other than the distinct voice of a grieving son.

Then what happened to Ann Eliza Young? My searches through archives in Utah, California, New York, and Washington have turned up nothing regarding her last days. None of the local or national papers ever ran an obituary. As far as I know, there are no police reports, insurance records, estate papers, or any other clues concerning her fate. I have come to the conclusion, alas, that the mystery of her final outcome cannot be solved. Indeed, there are some mysteries that must exist without answer. In the end we must accept them for what they are: complex and many-sided, ornamented with clues and theories, yet ultimately unknowable— like life itself.

Thus, with these five conclusions formed, I submit what can only be described as an unorthodox thesis. After more than two years of research, I realized that a historical paper would not suffice. With this in mind, I have worked closely with a young man named Jordan Scott for several months. I interviewed him for nearly sixty hours about his life among the Firsts and, especially, his extraordinary relationship with his mother. At first, I tried to retell his story in an analytically detached way. Always, the results were cold and uninspired. Although his story offers much illumination on Ann Eliza and her legacy, my scholarly approach sucked the life out of his life. After many attempts I abandoned my voice for his. I edited the transcripts of our interviews into an early draft, then went back to him for more interviews. Together we edited the draft into a final narrative, *Wife #19: A Desert Mystery*.

Whether or not this will meet the thesis requirements is up to the Department. Yet I ask you to consider the questions *Wife #19* asks of the reader, and of itself. In my opinion these inquiries are serious and urgent and worthy of a scholar's attention. Although the words are Jordan's, it is shaped by my years of scholarship and thought, and a lifetime of open faith.

WIFE #19:

EPILOGUE

Focus on the Family

A week later Maureen and I went shopping. We were in a discount women's store, pushing a shopping cart down the aisle. Maureen had a firm sense of what we needed. "At least three pairs of shoes, one for dressier situations, one for every day, and one for walking and other activities. Any idea what color she likes?"

"Red," I said. "Mostly red."

"I'm afraid red can only go so far." Maureen inspected permanent press slacks, braided belts, t-shirts with piped sleeves, nylon socks, and other basics. "Now let's go get her some bath things."

"I have some soap."

"A woman needs more than a bar of soap." She examined a jar of face cream. "I've gone ahead and made her an appointment at my beauty parlor. She'll need to figure out what to do with her hair."

An hour later we unpacked our purchases in Room 111. Maureen hummed about, snipping off tags and folding the shirts and slacks into a drawer she had lined with tissue. When she was done she clapped her hands. "All done. Now, if you need anything else . . ."

"I'm all set."

"I know, but if you ever need anything else, you let me know." She hugged me, her handbag clobbering me in the back.

"I couldn't've done this without you," I said.

"Of course you could've."

"No, actually, I couldn't."

"I'll just go say good-bye to Tom and the dogs." Then she was gone, a blur of blue.

The next morning at a quarter to eight, Tom and I waited at the security entrance of the jail. Officer Cunningham was manning the desk. "Big day," she said. "It'll only be another minute." We talked some about our dogs; she was taking her corgis to a show in Colorado next weekend and had their grooming on her mind.

At five to eight a photographer showed up, three cameras hanging around her neck. She gave her card to Officer Cunningham, who told her she could set up in the corner. The photographer opened a camera bag and changed her lenses, wiping them with a small tissue, readying everything so that when the moonfaced clock said it was exactly eight, she'd be all set to capture that picture everyone loves—a wrongly accused prisoner being freed.

I saw her face first through the chicken-wire glass in the door. Really, all I could see were her eyes. "There she is," said Tom. Officer Cunningham buzzed the door open, then an eternity—as if time stopped and whoever runs the universe went out for a smoke—and finally the door swung open.

"BeckyLyn, over here!"

My mom looked at the photographer. A flash, a click, another flash, more clicks.

"*St. George Register*," the photographer said. "Can you hold right there?" She wore the dusty pink prairie dress she'd been arrested in, the heavy stockings, the handmade shoes. Her steps were tentative, like she was learning to walk.

"Mom," I said, "this is Tom."

He couldn't help himself: he lunged to hug her. "I've heard so much about you!"

"BeckyLyn," the photographer called, "is that the son who

593

saved you?" She took a picture with one camera, then the same picture with the next, and again the same shot with the third.

"Let's go," I said.

"How about a family reunion shot?"

"Time to go."

I led my mom out to the van. The photographer walked around us, crouching and stepping backward, click click click, saying *how do you feel?* and *happy to be free?* and *this is great, just great.* When we were in the van, the photographer stopped taking pictures. "Good luck, BeckyLyn! Our readers love you!"

Tom was driving. He asked if she wanted the windows up or down or if she needed water. "Or if you're hungry, we can stop now, but Jordan and I thought we'd take you back to the Malibu first."

"I'm fine," she said. "Really." She was looking out the window at the red sandstone cliffs, her face ghosted in the glass.

"Mom, how does it feel to be free?"

"I'm figuring that out right now."

"And *this*," said Tom, pushing the key card into the slot, "this is your room. You've got a tv, cable, movie channels, a/c, the ice machine's down the hall. And *this*"—he pointed to an interior door—"this door connects to our room."

Behind the door Elektra started barking, then Joey. Tom opened the door and the second behind it. The dogs ran into Room 111, snouts pointed right at my mom. Elektra jumped on her, pushing her back onto the bed. After a lot of petting and licking, Elektra relented and my mom stood up and straightened out her dress. She was laughing and saying, "Ah, what fun," and then her voice went serious and she sat on the edge of the bed. "This is so nice of you, but I'm not sure I'll be needing any of this."

"Mom. Tom and I, we want you to stay."

"As long as you like," said Tom. "I talked to the owner and we've worked it all out."

"I appreciate it," she said. "I really do." And then, "But it's probably time for me to go."

"Go? Go where?"

"Back to Mesadale."

"I'm not taking you back there."

My phone rang. Roland. I don't know why I answered. "Honey, I just read about you on the *Register*'s home page. You're like a little Angela Lansbury out there. Now if only you could solve the mystery of my expanding waistline."

"Roland, I can't talk now."

"All right, but I want to hear all about it, especially that cute thing you picked up, Miss Utah. Leave it to you to solve a crime *and* find a hubby-hub."

"Not now, Roland."

"Anyway, when are you coming home?"

"Later."

"Oh no, don't tell me you're going all O Pioneer on me."

I hung up. "Mom, sorry, an old friend. Like I was saying, I didn't go through all this to take you back to Mesadale."

The sunshine through the plate glass made her face look very round and very clean. It was a pure morning light, the kind that reveals everything for what it is. "God was right," she said. "He said you'd come, and he was right." She looked around. "This is such a nice place. And these clothes—I can't believe you bought them for me, they're so pretty. But I can't take them."

"Mom, you can."

"No, Jordan, I can't."

Right then, before she walked out the door, I felt like I had one last chance to save her. I opened the dresser, showing her the new slacks and blouses, the shoes lined up at the door, the face cream and beauty soap laid out on the vanity. I showed her the tv remote and promised to teach her how to use the internet in the lobby. "Mom, please, I want you to stay. Here. With me." I was trying to tell her we could pick up our lives in Rooms 111 and 112, get the second chance you almost never get. I was frantic to prove the Malibu Inn would make a nice home.

"And there's a pool! We didn't show you the pool! Right here, through the patio door." I opened the glass slider.

Then I stopped. "Mom, please. I don't want you to go. You can stay here and do what you want. We won't get in your way."

"Jordan, I'm sorry."

"Mom, please."

"Jordan, I know you understand."

The thing was: I finally did.

"What if I need to call you?"

"You won't."

"What if it's an emergency?"

"Then you'll know what to do."

"Will we ever see each other again?"

"I believe we will."

My mom and I drove over to Denny's for the breakfast special. We pushed around our eggs and searched for things to say. The truth was, we'd already said it, and twenty minutes later we were on the road to Mesadale in my van. My mom rolled down her window and the wind blew about the shrub of her hair. We passed the shot-up marker and the wasteland of scrub. I saw the stand of cottonwoods and pulled over to turn onto the road.

"I'll get out here," she said.

"I'm not going to leave you on the highway."

"I want to walk the rest of the way home."

I turned off the engine and helped her down from the van. The sunlight was warm on my face and cast her skin in gold. The wind kicked up the sand and the dust and I could feel my throat drying out. "So I guess this is it," I said. "Mom, are you sure?"

596

She nodded. "I love you. I know you know that. That's why I can say good-bye."

We held each other for a while and at some point it was time to let go. She headed up the road, the dust collecting around her ankles, and the sun burned down, and we both knew it would burn hot and high on the desert until all our last days.

When I got back to Room 112, I couldn't believe it—Johnny was asleep on the bed. The dogs were curled up around him, and Tom was sitting on the other bed, reading. "Shhhh," he said. "They're sleeping."

"I can see that. What's he doing here?" Johnny's legs were scratched up, bug bites and a couple of bruises, but otherwise he looked all right.

"He ran away," he whispered. "I guess he missed you."

"What are we going to do with him?"

"Shhh, you'll wake him," he said. "We'll figure something out." And then,"Jordan—"

"Tom—"

"He can stay with us if he wants."

"Let's just see, all right? We have a lot going on."

"I know, but wouldn't it be nice if he stayed?"

"God, what a family we'd make."

"Sounds perfect," said Tom. "Now be quiet."

"He might not want to stay."

"He'll want to."

"I don't know."

"Jordan—"

"Tom—"

"What are you thinking?"

"Stuff."

"What kind of stuff?"

"You know what they say?"

"What's that?"

597

"Endings are beginnings."

"Is that what they say?"

"Oh, for Christ's sake," said Johnny, opening one eye. "Will you two please shut the fuck up." He cracked his smart-ass smile. Elektra moaned and reasserted her position on the bed. Joey swatted his plumed tail. And Tom put his arm around me. The sun was in the western sky and the room filled with its light. I began to imagine my mom walking back into town—the dust in her hair, the hope in her eyes. The road, the post office, the mountain shadow. The excitement as someone recognized her, then someone else, then someone else again. Where would she go? Would she return to her old room? I became anxious and felt a shiver on my spine. Would I wonder about her fate for the rest of my life? Could I handle the not knowing? Would I accept an ending without end? Then I saw four wives greet her, kiss her, take her inside the house. I saw three small children circling her skirt. I saw her old apron hanging on its peg. I saw her swing open the door to her room. I saw her move to the windowsill and stroke the leaf of her aloe plant. I saw my mother on her knees. And I saw myself in her prayers.

THE END

AUTHOR'S NOTE AND ACKNOWLEDGMENTS

This is a work of fiction. It is not meant to be read as a stand-in for a biography of Ann Eliza Young, Brigham Young, or any of the other historical figures who appear in it. Even so, it's human nature to wonder if a historical novel is inspired by real people and real events, and if so to what degree; and thus I feel an obligation to the reader to begin to answer that question.

Anyone attempting to write about the history of the Church of Jesus Christ of Latter-day Saints, even a sliver of it, will immediately encounter the difficult task of accuracy. That is because on nearly every issue in the Church's past, and in regard to every person who has played a part in the Church's often remarkable life, there are at least two, and typically more, combative opinions on what each side sincerely calls "the truth." In the preface to his 1925 biography of Brigham Young, M. R. Werner states the case plainly: "Mormon and anti-Mormon literature is frequently unreliable."

Ever since her apostasy from the Church of Jesus Christ of Latter-day Saints in 1873, Ann Eliza Young has been a figure of controversy among Mormons and non-Mormons alike. I don't expect to settle that controversy with this book. One reason the controversy has lingered is that she left a substantial record of her experiences as a plural wife in her two memoirs and many public lectures. Her enemies and allies have used her own words to denounce or support her, and thus in order to write about Ann Eliza Young I inevitably began with her lectures and passionate memoirs,

Wife No. 19 (1875) and *Life in Mormon Bondage* (1908). The books have their flaws. In them, Ann Eliza can come off as simultaneously hypercritical and hypersensitive. She is selective in her presentation of her story and Mormon history, carrying out an agenda with little subtlety or nuance. Too often her tone becomes strident and vengeful. Her portrait of Brigham Young lacks the complexity for which he was known. And she can get basic information wrong. Yet despite these limitations, her memoirs, as well as her public lectures upon which the memoirs are based, remain the best sources for the plot of her life and, just as important, for appreciating her point of view. If she had not spoken up there would be much about her life, and especially her marriage to Brigham, that we could never know. It is one reason her story is so remarkable—she dared to reveal what thousands of other plural wives bore in silence. Therefore I gratefully acknowledge her original efforts in autobiography. Without them, *The 19th Wife* would have been a far lesser, far more opaque book. Ann Eliza wrote her books to affect public opinion and change policy, but also to shape her legacy; inspired by this, I wrote chapters of an alternative memoir as part of this novel. My long process of thinking about Ann Eliza and her family, and the context of her life, began with her books, and so it seemed only natural to begin my novel where she does, and then veer away.

The 19th Wife follows Ann Eliza's basic biographical arc as she describes it, although often I fill in where she skips and I skip where she digresses. I continue past her conclusion and reinterpret where her point of view limits an understanding of her life and times. I also spend time on members of her family, about whom she has little meaningful to say. It is with them—Chauncey, Elizabeth, Gilbert, and Lorenzo Leonard— that I take the most liberties because their biographies are less known and because of the novelist's need to weave the disparate into something unified. As for Brigham Young, my portrait of him is mostly consistent with that presented by people who knew him, some historians, as well as the sermons, declarations, letters, and diaries he left. Often when he speaks in my narrative, especially at the pulpit, his words are inspired by a sermon we know, through the historical record, he made. I am sure his admirers will argue I linger too long on his egomaniacal tendencies as well as his appetites; and that by quoting him directly on the subject of blood atonement on pages 215–16. I am overemphasizing his calls for violence. Brigham's detractors, on the other hand, will probably say I let him off the hook. Thankfully the historical record is vast and accessible; the curious reader can visit the library or go online to form his or her own conclusions.

Which leads me to the documents (or "documents") that run throughout the novel—the newspaper articles, the letters, the Introduction by Harriet Beecher Stowe, the Wikipedia entry. Although I am the author of these, they are fictional representations of what it's like to spend time in the archives and online researching Ann Eliza Young, Brigham, and early LDS history. Many are inspired by an actual text or a kind of text. For example, my Howard Greenly interview with Joseph purposely evokes Horace Greeley's well-known interview with Brigham in 1859; the devotional poem "In Our House" is my limp attempt at the sincere hymns many Pioneers wrote to reflect their experiences; and the Wikipedia entry is (obviously) written in a style very much like a Wikipedia entry.

The mighty lens of history has enabled me to see Ann Eliza's life as she could not, and I have used this perspective to tell her story in a way that perhaps broadens it and connects it to our day. All of this is a longwinded answer to the original question, is *The 19th Wife* based on real people and real events? Yes. Have I invented much of it? Yes, for that is what novelists do.

Inevitably I relied on a variety of sources to write this book, each important to my task and worth acknowledging. Many times I turned to Irving Wallace's thorough biography,

The Twenty-Seventh Wife (1961), itself indebted to Ann Eliza's original memoirs. I recommend it, along with *Wife No. 19*, for anyone who wants to know more about her life. In addition, the Irving Wallace Archive at the Honnold Library at the Claremont Colleges holds a fine collection on Ann Eliza Young; I'm grateful to Mr. Wallace for making his original research available to the public and to Carrie Marsh and the other archivists who maintain it today. Just as important were the archives of the *Salt Lake Daily Tribune,* one of Ann Eliza's most vocal allies. This paper published almost daily reports on her battle with Brigham, devoting dozens of news columns to her story and many editorials to support her cause, and reprinted most of the legal filings in their divorce case. Throughout the 1870s and '80s the *Tribune* featured a number of articles about the general conditions of polygamy in Utah and serialized sensational personal narratives, such as "Tied to the Stake; or Martyrs of Latter Days" by Mrs. A. G. Paddock, many of which supported Ann Eliza's claims. This thorough repository— today housed on microfiche at the magnificent Salt Lake City Public Library—helped me with crucial details about Ann Eliza's life, as well as to better understand its historical context. On the other hand, the *Deseret News,* Ann Eliza's inevitable opponent, reported on her story from Brigham's perspective. While other local and national papers covered Ann Eliza's story in great (and often tabloid) detail, these two publications documented her life story and her apostasy from the Mormon Church as well as any periodical during her day. (The *Anti-Polygamy Standard,* which published out of Salt Lake City in the 1880s, is a useful source for stories of plural marriage a few years after Ann Eliza's apostasy.)

Some people argue bibliographies have no place in fiction, but several books and documents have helped me with so many matters large and small that I want to give them the thanks they are due. I haven't included this list to show off the extent of my reading (or lack thereof) but to acknowledge a set of authors whose work I learned from: "Ann Eliza Young" by the American Literary Bureau; *Brigham Young: American Moses* by Leonard J. Arrington; *Twenty Years of Congress* by James G. Blaine; *No Man Knows My History* by Fawn M. Brodie; *Emma Lee* by Juanita Brooks; *The City of the Saints* by Sir Richard F. Burton; *The Pioneer Cookbook* by Kate Carter; *In Sacred Loneliness* by Todd Compton; "Forest Farm House and Forest Dale" by Edith Olsen Cowen; "Brigham Young, His Family and His Wives" compiled by the Daughters of the Utah Pioneers; "Unique Story—President Brigham Young" compiled by the Daughters of the Utah Pioneers; "Autobiography of Moses Deming" by Moses Deming; *The Women of Mormonism* edited by Jennie A. Froiseth; *Nauvoo Factbook* by George and Sylvia Givens; *By the Hand of Mormon* by Terry L. Givens; *The Mormon Question* by Sarah Barringer Gordon; "Letters" by Irene Haskell; *Solemn Covenant* by B. Carmon Hardy; "Eliza Jane Churchill Webb, Pioneer of 1848" by Olivette Webb Goe Henry; "Chauncey Griswold Webb, Pioneer of 1848" by Olivette Webb Goe Henry and Nina Beth E. Goe Cunningham; *Old Mormon Kirtland* by Richard Neitzel Holzapfel and T. Jeffrey Cottle; *Old Mormon Nauvoo* by Richard Neitzel Holzapfel and T. Jeffrey Cottle; *Life of James Redpath* by Charles F. Horner; *111 Days to Zion* by Hal Knight and Dr. Stanley B. Kimball; *Under the Banner of Heaven* by Jon Krakauer; *The Story of the Mormons from the Date of Their Origin to the Year 1901* by William Alexander Linn, especially Chapter IV, "The Hand-Cart Tragedy"; "Utah's Forty Years of Historical Amnesia" by Theron Luke; *Historic Dress in America* by Elizabeth McClellan; *Redburn* by Herman Melville, especially Chapter 38 for its vivid depiction of Liverpool's slums; *Sounding Brass* by Hugh Nibley; *The Fate of Madame La Tour* by Mrs. A. G. Paddock; *Eccentricities of Genius* by Major J. B. Pond; "August Announcement of 1875" by the Redpath Lyceum; "Brigham Young Divorce Case" by Brigham Henry Roberts; "Ann Eliza—Mrs. Young's Lecture Last Night—The Story of Her Life" by the St. Louis Republican, December 30,

1873; *The Book of Mormon*, translated by Joseph Smith, Jr.; *The Pearl of Great Price* by Joseph Smith, Jr.; *God Has Made Us a Kingdom* by Vickie Cleverley Speek; *Brigham Young at Home* by Clarissa Young Spencer and Mabel Harmer; *Mormon Country* by Wallace Stegner; *Expose of Polygamy in Utah* by Mrs. T. B. H. Stenhouse; *Tell It All* by Mrs. T. B. H. Stenhouse (it's worth noting that Stenhouse's books inspired Ann Eliza's memoirs in many ways); *Roughing It* by Mark Twain; *Mormon Polygamy* by Richard S. Van Wagoner; "Interview with Joe Place, April 23, 1960" by Irving Wallace; *Brigham Young* by M. R. Werner; *The Bold Women* by Helen Beal Woodward; *The Journal of Discourses*, Volumes 3 and 4, by Brigham Young; *Diary of Brigham Young, 1857*, edited by Everett L. Cooley; *My Dear Sons: Letters of Brigham Young to His Sons*, edited by Dean C. Jessee; *The Complete Sermons of Brigham Young*; and *Isn't One Wife Enough?* by Kimball Young.

I owe a great deal to the following institutions and their staffs for making their collections readily available through open stacks and policies of access. Each contains a variety of useful, idiosyncratic materials that I gladly co-opted for my use: the Salt Lake City Public Library; Brigham Young University's Harold B. Lee Library; the University of Utah's J. Willard Marriott Library; the Provo Public Library; the Washington County Library in St. George; the Daughters of the Utah Pioneers Museum; and the Nauvoo Family History Center.

The Church of Jesus Christ of Latter-day Saints has devoted countless resources to creating and staffing dozens of historical museums, many of them free and open to the public. I visited these institutions several times, lingering to take notes and talk to the missionaries serving as docents and guides. Without the church's careful and abundant preservation of the past throughout Utah, as well as in Nauvoo, I could not have conjured up Ann Eliza's world.

I want to thank the Metropolitan Community Church of Las Vegas for warmly welcoming me into their sanctuary.

Although the sermon on pages 376–78 is inspired by one I heard there on December 18, 2005, the scene itself is fictitious and does not depict this actual church or anyone in its loving congregation.

A number of people generously shared their stories with me. Without them I could not have written this novel as it is: Flora Jessop, Carmen Thompson, Steve Tripp, Mickey Unger, Beverly White, Kevin, Jimmy, Peter, and Susan. Thank you all.

Kari Main of the Pioneer Memorial Museum read the book in manuscript, correcting a number of errors. Her sharp, knowing eye fixed the book in many ways. She was an ideal reader and these few words are not enough thanks for her efforts.

The supremely talented Catherine Hamilton drew the illustration on page 263; it is based on an original 1876 etching by Stanley Fox.

I'd like to thank the Danish Arts Council for their support while I was revising the novel; Peter and Gitte Rannes for their warm hospitality at the Danish Centre for Writers and Translators in Hald; and Nathaniel Rich and Martin Glaz Serup for a productive retreat.

Alexis Richland provided much needed editorial guidance on an early draft. Her thoughtful response helped solve some problems that had lingered in my mind for years. Mark Nelson read several drafts, each time raising important questions in need of resolution. His fierce intelligence improved the novel in every sense. I'm grateful for the many hours he devoted to this book, and for his unyielding friendship and support. Daryl Mattson, who has never tired of listening to me gab about almost anything, served as a sounding board for a number of ideas in this book, even when he wasn't aware of it. The name of the internet café in St. George, A Woman Sconed, comes from him.

For ten years Elaine Koster has been a formidable agent, insightful editor, and loyal friend. Her unflagging encouragement helped bring this book from an early idea to the pages you now hold. I owe her much.

Lots of thanks are due to Marianne Velmans and her colleagues at Transworld. They are the kind of publisher every writer hopes to have.

The thanks I want to offer Random House are vast. So many people there have helped me over so many years that any list of names is bound to forget someone crucial. So I'll make a blanket but sincere expression of gratitude to everyone at 1745. I know how books are published, and I know that each of you played a part. I hope you'll forgive me for not printing the company roster. But I must thank my editor, Kate Medina. She is a brilliant reader, and her wise pencil made this book better in many, many ways. Frankie Jones and Jennifer Smith shouldered the burdens of turning a manuscript into a book; each did so with grace and generosity. Jynne Martin, publicity-goddess: it's an honor to be on your roster. And to my publisher, Gina Centrello, thank you for your support, which has shown itself in so many ways.

 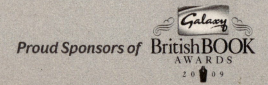